Death Among Brothers, Book Three

The New Shogun

Death Among Brothers

Book 3

The New Shogun

a novel

Marc Charles

The Ross House Press

Published by The Ross House Press,
an imprint of Canopic Publishing

Canopic Publishing
601 Indigo Lane
Woodstock, IL 60098
www.canopicpublishing.com

Designed and edited by Phil Rice

ISBN-13: 978-0-9997182-3-0

For Sako; all my love always

Dedication

This, the last of the *Death Among Brothers* trilogy, is dedicated to four people. One is from the martial arts world, two help me with the writing and one was my oldest friend from the Marine Corps. They are Sensei Richard Gonzalez, Michelle Charles, Tom Tyner and Sam Free.

Sensei Gonzalez ran a small dojo on Camp Geiger, Camp Lejeune, North Carolina in 1976. He was not my first martial arts instructor but later when I would start my own dojos, it was he who I patterned myself after. He was knowledgeable, approachable and interested in the growth of each of his students. Why did I use him as a him as a template? His knowledge was tempered with humility! He was the opposite of most martial art school leaders. He was focused on kata and teaching what each student needed to launch them on a path for the future. I would not let my wife Sako come close to any of the other dojos I trained in. They were too rough and full of machismo. I felt comfortable enough with Sensei Gonzalez to ask if I could bring Sako to learn. Sensei Gonzalez granted her entrance and both of our careers in a true Okinawan karate and kobudo system commenced. We found a home with Okinawa Kenpo Karate and Kobudo. Sako loved it and to this day both of us consider Richard Gonzalez as our sensei. This was my first experience with karate that was not totally focused on fighting. Instead we learned empty hand kata passed down from generations and weapons such as the bo, sai, tonfa, kama and even iai-do. This ryuha had history and tradition. We still dusted each other up as only young Marines can if that was the path you were on, but Sensei Gonzalez taught as his Master Seikichi Odo taught him. Choosing your path was part of the art.

Secondly, I'd like to dedicate this book to Michelle Charles. She is my sister-in-law who is my alpha and beta reader for my books. She is also the lady that introduced compassion and caring to the Charles family. I met Mother Theresa in Calcutta. She and Michelle have a lot in common. Both could be as tough as whang leather when need be. But both wrap every action in love. She cares for my brother Dr. Raleigh Glenn Charles who requires occasional feeding and much guidance. Michelle splits time between her home cleaning business, a nearby aging mother and three wonderful adult children who seek her advice almost daily. Then there are her two grandchildren, Camden and Brodie, who clamor for her attention when time and Delta Airlines routes are favorable. I believe the grandchildren's demands trump all others. Somehow she fits everyone in. I take advantage of her because I know her to be a voracious reader who will shoot me straight on criticisms. I don't feel guilty because I know she would just donate her time to some other less worthy (from my perspective) cause. I feel almost worthy of her attention most of the time.

Tom Tyner is a professor at Middle Tennessee State University and an old family friend. He is the one who introduced me to my publisher, Phil Rice. Tom has been instrumental in turning my musings into prose for this entire series of books. He doesn't carry a wand but his ability to spot errors is nothing short of something you'd expect from Harry Potter. In the first two novels he bled over every page with red ink correcting my peccadillos. Despite my instruction to be a beta reader on this one, I am sure he will not be able to help himself and will make me feel the fool once again. I am greatly indebted to him for his time and talent once again.

The last person I want to dedicate this book to is an old friend of mine Sam Free. I first met Sam when we were Private First Class Marines at Camp Pendleton, California in early 1969. He was senior to me in many ways but took a liking to me and showed me the ropes of surviving at the bottom of the totem pole. His escapades are too numerous to mention here and I'm not sure if the statute of limitations has run out on all of them, so I will just say that he took me home to Louisiana and introduced me to a world I'd never imagined and people with big hearts. We stayed in touch over the years. He became a civilian as soon as he could and raced to "the house" as quickly as possible. He would work on oil rigs and survey and eventually start his own appraisal business. What you saw was what you got with Sam. He was politically astute and loved his Democrats. But he was a good friend and I forgave him for his short sightedness. Sam died unexpectedly in January. Semper Fi, Sam. May you have calm seas and following winds.

Contents

Principal Characters

Listed Alphabetically

Abe: Lieutenant in the Ronin Army.

Aika: Second in command of all the Wako Pirates; Wako pirates are historical.

Bishop Inshin: Inshin Suden, bishop of Daito-Kuji Temple in Kyoto; supporter of Tadanaga.

Chiyo: Young wife of Yoshi; Dewa ninja.

Fugi: Grandmother to Umi; poor farmer eking out a subsistence living.

Hanaa: Wet nurse to Yuki and nanny to Yoshinobu.

Haru: Owner of Yamakaya clothing store; wealthy purveyor to the Imperial Court.

Hideki: Second grandson of Jii; younger brother to Nagamasa.

Hidetada: Historical character; second shogun in the Tokugawa dynasty; son of Ieyasu and father of Iemitsu and Tadanaga.

Honzo: Historical character; nicknamed the Ninja Killer; leader of the Iga ninja guarding Iemitsu.

Iemitsu: Historical character; oldest son to Hidetada, second Tokugawa Shogun.

Ito Itosai: Head of Ito-ryu fencing style; hired as chief strategist for Tadanaga.

Jii: head of Yoshinobu clan, grandfather to Nagamasa and Hideki.

Matoumoto Rei: Ronin seeking employment; master of the wakazashi.

Matsu: Mother-in-law to Yoshi; poison expert; Dewa ninja.

Midori: Second in command of the Five Families of ninja; lover to Jubei.

Mist: Koga ninja; second in command behind Ugai; supports Tadanaga.

Mondo: Captain of the Ronin Army.

Munenori Yagyū: Father to Jubei; chamberlain to the first three Tokugawa shoguns.

Murata Shingen: In charge of Kukuchinama castle in Kyoto; last resort safe-haven for Tadanaga.

Myo: Current head of Five Families ninja; lover to Hideki.

Nagamasa: Older brother of Hideki Yoshinobu.

O'Fuku: Historical character; real name Tsubone; stepmother to Iemitsu.

Oyeo: Mother to Iemitsu and Tadanaga.

Saemon: Scar faced member of Team Wang Zhi.

Tadanaga: Historical character; younger brother of Iemitsu; wants to be shogun.

Taka: Member of Team Wang Zhi.

Token: Monk at Daito-kuji temple; expert with the naginata.

Ugai: Current leader of the Koga ninja.

Ume: Old nanny to Haru.

Umi: Seven-year old farm girl.

Wang Zhi: Wako pirate; ship captain; leader of Team Wang Zhi in the Ronin Army.

Watanabe: Lieutenant in the Ronin Army.

Yagyū Jubei: Historical character; eldest son on Munenori; former fencing instructor to Tokugawa.

Yagyū Munenori: Historical character; chamberlain to two Tokugawa shoguns; patriarch to Yagyū clan.

Yamada Arinaga: Satsuma Clan representative to Tadanaga in Kyoto.

Yokan: Merchant of Kyoto attempting to get Wako Pirates to ship his cargo.

Yoshi: Dewa ninja now serving Yoshinobu as chief strategist; friend to Hideki.

Yoshitsune: Baby to Nagamasa and Yuki Yoshinobu; heir to the Yoshinobu; nephew to Hideki.

Yuki: Wife of Nagamasa Yoshinobu; mother to Yoshitsune; sister-in-law to Hideki.

Death Among Brothers, Book Three

The New Shogun

I

Doubts

Ugai gathered his trusted followers to him. There were only four. It was dark outside and in. Ninja did their best work at night. They had been steeped in the old refrain, "I was born in the dark; I will die in the dark." It was a multilayered saying with different interpretations for different situations, but they all knew the universal essence. They were not part of the public at large. If they went into the world beyond their clan, they did so in disguise and there was a purpose behind their foray into the light.

They were meeting in a gardener's shed on the grounds of the hereditary Tokugawa castle in Edo. Two ninja clans served the Tokugawa, the reigning Shogunate of Japan. The Iga were the oldest, having saved the founder of the dynasty in his early years attempting to flee an opposing warlord after a defeat. The Koga was the second clan working for the Tokugawa and had been added recently by the now dead Shogun Hidetada.

Things were chaotic. Hidetada had just died, leaving two possible successors. The eldest son was Iemitsu. He was the rightful heir. But he was despised by most lords. He was a stutterer with a birth mark on his face and he liked to bed boys. The younger brother Tadanaga was handsome, liked girls, and was the better martial artist. Everyone liked him. Even the boys' mother, Oyeo, supported the second son. That was not surprising. She hated her eldest. But the younger son liked to kill people. He had an uncontrollable temper and placed no value on human life except his own.

The now dead shogun had brought the Koga clan ninja under his control because he didn't want to be reliant on just one clan. Hittori Honzo oversaw security for the Tokugawa and directed both ninja clans. He was samurai trained by the Iga ninja. Arrival of the Koga had been anything but harmonious. Hittori Honzo had finally settled the minor bickering and occasional bloodletting by assigning the Koga to grounds security inside the castle walls. The Iga remained responsible for the castle. The Koga bristled at the insult but bit their tongues. On the official ledgers of the financial branch of the castle the Iga were carried as servants and paid accordingly. The Koga were carried as gardeners and paid less.

"Are you sure she asked for me by name?" Ugai asked.

Ugai's cousin cocked his head to the side as if to say his question was ridiculous. "Yes Ugai," he said instead. "She wanted to meet with you in person and alone. The meeting is at midnight tonight in one of her little used apartments on the far side of the castle."

Ugai's mind whirled at the possibilities. "Do any of you have any recommendations?"

"Do not go," one volunteered. "She is treacherous."

Another pulled his black face scarf down from its position tucked into his head wrap. "If you go, do not go alone. She is a devil," he said.

Ugai's cousin raised his hand to halt the discussion. "Ugai knows all this but when O'Fuku (the rightful heirs' stepmother) summons him to a clandestine meeting it is time to think. Ugai already knows she is a villainess. He is looking for suggestions on how to mitigate the danger. Do we tell our clan leader about this invitation? Do we ignore it all? These are the things he is asking."

"Does she know you by sight?" one asked.

"I do not think so," Ugai said.

"Then send your cousin," the man said.

"That will not work," the cousin said. "We are dealing with a masterful manipulator. You saw how she had the Fox Gang safely roaming around the country killing off all Iemitsu's competition about two years ago when his father announced a false retirement."

"We remember," one offered. "She had those arrogant Iga ninja quaking in their socks."

"Yes, she would have made Iemitsu shogun then over Oyeo's objection if the Yoshinobu had not spoiled her plans," another said.

"That is right," the original chimed in. "Too bad the younger Yoshinobu just broke her elbow. He should've killed her."

Ugai took their conversation under advisement but he was not listening anymore. The discussion had lent little to his thinking. He already knew what he was going to do. He would meet her. To not do so was almost as dangerous as being in her presence. She no longer had her rogue ninja clan calling themselves the Fox Gang from the little island of Shikoku to do her bidding. But she had Iemitsu's ear. Iemitsu was going to be the next Shogun.

This despite the younger brother Tadanaga's pipedreams of succeeding his father and Oyeo's attempts to discard her oldest child. Iemitsu being born with a birthmark on his face, a slight stutter when excited and a desire to bed young boys and not women meant little. Samurai morals tended to favor the powerful. O'Fuku had already tried to assassinate the younger Tadanaga twice. These death threats from her were the real reason Tadanaga and Oyeo had fled to the Imperial capital of Kyoto despite O'Fuku's campaign to discredit Tadanaga by saying he had been expelled.

O'Fuku wanted to meet Ugai at midnight clandestinely. She had not wanted to notify the leader of his Koga ninja clan. This was disturbing as he was only third in the chain of command. The Mist was number two and the right hand of the old master. So, whatever she was planning it must be subversive and fraught with danger for others and himself.

He would not talk to the old master. Part of him was flattered that the woman who wielded so much power in the samurai city of Edo wanted to talk to him alone. He would talk with her, but he would be on his guard. He just needed to devise a plan to ensure she was not trying to assassinate him. He must also carefully think through whatever proposition she was proffering.

"Okay," Ugai said. "I will meet her."

"Cousin, are you sure?"

"Yes," Ugai said. "She is too powerful to deny. But I only trust you four here. Mention my decision to no one. Be especially careful around The Mist. She is the old master's favorite. If she gets wind of this meeting we will all die."

"We will remain quiet cousin. What would you have us do?"

"I want you three to scout the meeting rooms. I need access and egress routes. I want to know what is on the other side of those apartment walls. I want to know where the access to the rafters are," Ugai said. "I also want to know if any Iga ninja patrol that part of the castle. We have very little time." Then, turning to his cousin, "inform your chambermaid friend that brought you the meeting offer to tell the lady that I accept. The rest of you get to work. We only have a few hours."

II

Secrets and Assassins

The room was well appointed with the finest silk and porcelain from China. There was a Western dining table and chairs imported through Nagasaki. A traditional Japanese would find the decoration almost garish. There was just too much on display. Color was everywhere. The room did not give off the impression the lady wanted. Instead of opulence the room bordered on cheapness. But no one dared tell the lady that.

When O'Fuku entered she had two female attendants in trail.

"Prepare my bath and get my futon ready," O'Fuku commanded imperiously. "I am expecting a caller later."

Both attendants went about their tasks. One moved to the next room and set up the bathing area with soap and towels and perfumes. The attendant made sure there was a bucket of hot water and large sponges available. She then moved to the large wooden tub to check the water temperature. After taking every minor detail into account she moved to the sliding main door and sat on her shins.

The other attendant moved to the sleeping room and checked the work of the evening maids. The large futon (bottom mattress) and kake buton (top down filled quilt) were laid out on the tatami floor. The padded wooden pillow to protect the woman's hair was in place at the head of the futon. She checked on the two paper lanterns to ensure the candles inside would not extinguish too early in the evening. Then she moved to the dining table where she placed warm sake and several cups. The woman had mentioned a guest but never specified how many. It was not common for powerful women such as the lady to have male visitors, but the attendant assumed nothing.

When the second attendant was satisfied she joined the first attendant at the main sliding door to the apartment and sat on her shins beside the first attendant. Then they waited.

To serve a powerful lady in the castle was an honor. But to serve this lady was a dual edged sword. This lady was volatile. You could get in trouble for following orders or get into trouble for not following orders. One never knew. Rumor had it that attendants that fell out of favor were sent to the government run brothels in the Yoshiwara.

The lady that entered was older. But she moved with a grace of one much younger. O'Fuku didn't acknowledge the presence of her attendants. She strode past them and inspected every inch of the apartment. She then dismissed them with the wave of her hand. O'Fuku waited until she heard the footsteps of the two attendants disappear down the polished wooden floors.

The lady swished back to the room with the Western table.

"Are you there?" she asked.

"I am here," a male voice said.

"Come sit with me and have some sake," O'Fuku said.

"Men who you invite into your chambers often turn up dead," the male voice said.

The lady laughed. "Are you afraid of me?"

"Only a fool would not be afraid of you," the male voice said.

O'Fuku could not pinpoint where the voice emanated. That worried her. She had been the leader of Shikoku Ninja until the Yoshinobu had crushed her followers and her elbow.

"Do you not get tired?" O'Fuku asked.

"I am in my prime. I do not get tired," the man said, moving silently along the opposite side of one of her walls. The use of a small megaphone pressed against his side of the wall defused his voice, making it hard to pinpoint his position and impossible to identify who was speaking.

"Yes, you are in your prime. But who notices you? You should be the leader of the Koga," she said.

"We have a leader," the man said. "Something you know full well," he thought.

"Yes, but he is very old. He may die soon. Then who would be the leader?" she asked, wondering if the man was in the rafters.

"I do not know. It would be either me or The Mist. The clan votes on a new leader when the old one dies or retires," the man said.

"Is The Mist a more capable leader than you?" she asked, stepping on one of the Western chairs to get closer to the ceiling trying to pinpoint his location.

"I am the best leader," the man said. "No one in the clan can stand up to me."

"That was my assumption as well," she said. "If you were the leader where would you take the clan?" she asked stepping down from the chair.

"Where would I take them? We have nowhere to go," the man said. He had heard her step down. Next she would move to the walls in her attempt to locate him. He used the ceiling tiles and rafters to move quickly and silently to the far side to another wall of her apartment. Then he dropped down.

"That is correct. Your clan are mere gardeners. That is how you are paid … mere gardeners. There is no one in the history of your profession as great as Koga. But you are relegated to being mere gardeners," she said, placing her ear to the wall.

"That is because we are kept down," he complained. "Hittori Honzo does not trust us."

"Yes, I can see how he plays favorites," she said. "What if I could change all that?"

"Why would you get involved on our behalf?" he asked, moving his ear to the megaphone listening for her footsteps.

"I am just tired of seeing good raw talent being misused," she said, her ear to the wall hearing vibrations in the wall but too faint for him to be on the other side.

"Yes, we are not the favorites of Hittori Honzo," he agreed.

"If the old man died let's talk about how you would rise to power," she said moving to a second wall and placing her ear to it.

Ugai heard her steps coming toward his wall. He moved into the rafters through the ceiling tile and retraced his steps to the original wall. "I am not sure most of the clan would vote for me. The Mist is the favorite of our current leader. I am sure he has influenced enough people to ensure her rise to power," he said, silently shifting again to another wall.

"Is she as strong as you?" she asked.

"You must be kidding," he said. "She is as weak as a kitten compared to me."

"Is she as intelligent as you?" she asked.

"I am the smartest in the clan," he bragged. "Smart enough not to be caught by you," he thought.

"Does she have more vision than you?" she asked.

"No way does she have more vision," he said. "She has no more ambition than to do what the leader tells her."

"That sounds to me like you would be the logical choice for the new leader," she said, finally giving up on her search for him by taking her ear off the wall and sitting down.

"You were not listening. I told you the current leader has influenced the clan in her direction," he said, relieved when he heard her sit.

"On the contrary, I am always listening," she said. "You just need a mentor to help with a larger vision."

"You have my interest piqued," he said. "What do you have in mind?"

"Your current leader is old. He is favoring someone else over you. But she is weaker than you. She is less intelligent than you. She has little ambition," she said. "I would think your course of action is obvious."

"It is not so obvious to me," he said. "I need to hear you speak it," he thought.

"What do you do when you are on a mission and you come against an obstacle?" she asked trying to gage this man's intellect.

"If I can, I go around it," he said.

"What if you cannot get around it?" she asked.

"Then I either destroy it or I go over it," he said.

"Well that is what you are facing now," she said. "Your obstacle is your current leader. Not only is he an obstacle, he is creating another obstacle by throwing his support to The Mist. He is telling you that you are not good enough to be his successor."

"You are correct," he said, wondering if she was ever going to get to the point.

"After all the years of service you have given him that must sting," she said.

"It hurts a lot. I am stronger and more dangerous than anyone in the clan," he said. "But a woman of all people will be given my position."

"Yes, I could see how that would bruise your confidence," she said. "You must take action on your own to seize the position. You cannot let it be given away by an old weak man."

"If Hittori Honzo finds out he would have me killed. He is known as the Ninja Killer," he said.

"Are you afraid of death?" she asked. "I would have thought not in your profession."

"All men are afraid to die," he said. "But we are more afraid to die in a stupid undertaking."

"Then you must seize this opportunity. If you are the leader you can protect your clan and ensure you are not sent on a stupid assignment," she said. "Besides, after this is over you would oversee castle security. Your rivals, the Iga, would then be gardeners. The Koga Ninja would surpass the arrogant Iga Ninja."

"I had not thought of that," he said. "I would be protecting the clan and elevating our status." But what is the catch, he wondered. You are not known for your benevolence.

"Not only that but you would have the protection of the new shogun," she promised.

"If I do become the new clan leader, what would you have us do?" he asked.

"I would assign you tasks that would bring greatness to the clan," she said.

"Who is going to be the new shogun?" he asked. "I know there are factions supporting Tadanaga, the younger brother. But you are on the side of the elder Iemitsu, are you not?"

"Yes, Tadanaga and Oyeo, that conniving mother of his, are trying to usurp the shogunate from the rightful heir Iemitsu," she said.

"How successful is he likely to be?" he asked.

"It is unknown at this time as to how successful Tadanaga will be. He is dashing and charming and good-looking. The problem is he is a murderer. He kills indiscriminately."

"We are killers also," he said, smiling to himself.

"Yes, you kill but there is purpose to your killing. You do not fly into rages and kill your friends do you?" she asked.

"No, I do not do that," he said.

"Where do you think the country would go if we had a shogun who likes killing people?" she asked.

"You are saying Tadanaga kills for the fun of it?" he asked, already knowing the truth.

"Why do you think his father had him moved out of Edo and into Kyoto?" she asked.

"I thought it was because he is the second son and should not confuse the lords who are always trying to influence the shogun," he said, playing along but offering just enough interrogative to keep her guessing.

"That is a very astute observation on your part," she said. "However, Tadanaga is in Kyoto to keep him away from the powerbase in Edo. He has killed several retainers, more servants, and is likely to repeat his acts at any time."

"So Tadanaga is in exile?" he asked knowing the answer but wanting to see how long she would keep up this story.

"Yes," she said. "But now he is in Kyoto to curry favor with the accursed Satsuma clan from the south. They are very powerful. If Tadanaga can convince the Satsuma to support him for shogun the country will go to civil war. You do grasp how important it is to keep that from happening do you not?"

"Yes, I understand," he said through the megaphone. What I don't understand, he thought to himself, is why you are trying to prevent a war. A year ago, you were killing people by the hundreds with your Fox Gang.

"Then the first thing you must do is seize power," she said. "You must control the clan. Then I will use you to help rid our country of threats. You will support who I tell you. You will help me destroy the usurper. You will be the most important clan and you will be the most important man next to the new shogun."

"I can do that. But how can I trust you to continue to support us? I do not want to be labeled as a betrayer," he said.

"You are correct to be mistrustful," she said. "But I will be right beside you. If you are labeled as a betrayer so will I be. We are doing this for the betterment of our country."

"I will want something in writing. That way if I am exposed then so are you," he said, hoping she would agree.

"I knew you were smart," she said.

"Yes, I am very smart," he said. "Smart enough to stay out of your trap," he said to himself.

"Okay, we can draft up such a document. The question will be who is to have possession of it?" she asked.

"Oh no, you cannot keep it," he said. "That is no different than me trusting you verbally."

"Yes, that is true," she said. "But you cannot keep it in your possession either. So, who do you know that we both trust?"

"I do not have anyone that I trust," he said.

"Yes, I feel the same way," she said. "You know anyone that we could both agree on?"

"No, I already told you, I do not trust anyone," he said. "I especially do not trust you," he mouthed silently.

"Would a priest satisfy your suspicion?" she asked.

"I do not want him to be your priest," he said.

"No, that would be unfair. Let's pick one far away," she said, wondering if he was stupid enough to fall for her ploy.

"How far away are you thinking?" he asked.

"Let's pick one far enough away that it would be difficult to retrieve the scroll we put in his care. But not far away enough that it would be impossible to get at it if we need to," she said. "I will let you pick the city."

"Very well, I picked Kyoto," he said.

"Yes" she thought. "Do you know of a priest in Kyoto?" she asked.

"I do not," he said.

"Do you know of a temple?" she asked.

"I know of one," he said. "I know of Daito kuji temple." His father had taken him there once as part of his education. They were dressed as farmers that day and his father had let him ring the bells to wake up the kami.

"And how do you know of that temple?" she asked with just enough distrust in her question.

"It is famous," he said. "It is in the capital city and it is one of the oldest surviving temples from ancient times."

"Now that we have agreed on a place how do we decide on a priest?" she asked hoping, he would take the last step into the trap.

"Let us give it to whoever oversees Daito kuji. We give it to him in a sealed box with instructions not to open it until we both appear before him," he said. That should keep you in check, he thought.

"That seems fair to me. You are a very intelligent man," she said.

"Yes, I know, I am very smart," he said.

"To seal our agreement and to fatten your pockets without having to go through the captain, I have a target I would like eliminated," she said.

"Who is the target?"

"Does it matter?"

"It matters greatly," he said. "I have to know who it is, so I know how to set up his demise. I also must figure what the cost should be based on the risk involved. I told you I am very smart."

"Yes, you did, and I will not forget it again," she said. "He is a ronin. And he has been a pain in my side for several years."

"What is his name?"

"You do not need his name," she said. "He is arriving tomorrow night by packet ship from Nagasaki."

"Does he travel with anyone?"

"He does not travel with anyone of consequence," she

said. "Including himself there may be four people."

"Will he be met by anyone?"

"No, I have taken care of that," she said. "I have also made sure that the police will not be in attendance."

"To go to all that trouble, you must really want this person dead," he said.

"That is none of your business," she said.

"It is because it affects the price," he said. "The more you need it accomplished, the more money I need."

The woman reached into her kimono and pulled out a small leather bag. She bounced it in her hand several times so he could hear metal clinking.

"There are twenty gold coins in here for you and whoever executes this mission. It is a down payment," she said. "You will get the same amount when the mission is complete."

"Something is not right here," he said. "That is too much money for a simple killing."

"Is it beyond your capabilities? I thought you will be the new leader of your clan?" she challenged.

"No, it is not beyond my capabilities. I just feel you are not truthful," he said. "But I will take your tasking and take your money."

"Then that concludes our business for now. It was a pleasure talking to you Ugai, although I never got to see you. I look forward to seeing your clan elevated and you leading it," she said.

"You do not need to see me. Leave the money outside the door," he said, and his voice came no more.

The woman did as the voice instructed. She dropped off the pouch and continued down the long corridor. She waited until she was back in the most secure apartment on the main side of the castle.

"How did it go?" a young man asked.

"He thinks he is very smart," O'Fuku said.

"Did he tell you that?" he asked trying to remember if he had ever met the Koga ninja.

"Oh yes," she said. "He boasted of it several times. He is very arrogant for one so stupid."

"He is arrogant," the man said. "I guess that comes

with ignorance and overconfidence."

"Yes, they go hand in hand. He wanted a document to chronicle our deal," O'Fuku said.

The man's eyebrows rose. "That might prove dangerous," he said.

"You have not heard the best part. I let him pick a temple to secure it in," O'Fuku said.

"This could get very dangerous. Which temple did he pick?" he asked concern in his voice.

"Daito-kuji in Kyoto," she said.

"Really?" he laughed. "Is there no end to your deviousness?"

"No there is no end to deviousness when it comes to your future," she said. "But the best part was when he picked Bishop Inshin to hold the document."

"Well one thing is for sure," he said relaxing now.

"What is that?" she asked.

"He is not as smart as you," he said. "But then, very few are. If he makes good on his seizure of power, you will have your own ninja force again. Do you think the Yoshinobu will call you Bird Woman again?"

"Do not joke about those bastards," she said. "If my plan falls into place, I'll eliminate several of your enemies at once, and those damn Yoshinobu will disappear."

"I think the Yoshinobu may surprise you," the man said.

"Why?" the woman asked.

"Because they do not appear to be motivated by the same goals as most," the man said. "They are my cousins, yet they do not strive for the shogun position. They lead quiet lives unless called upon. Like your appointing the eldest son to the South Magistrate's position, that really did not turn out as you had planned."

"Yes, I'll admit they surprised me," the woman said. "Instead of me getting rid of a minor irritant the Yoshinobu turned it into an opportunity to plague me."

"Actually, I think they turned it into an opportunity to clean up Edo," the man said. "The citizens walk the streets safely now."

"No, they turned it into an opportunity for the citizens to

sing the praises of the Yoshinobu. You are wrong," she said. "They are just more devious than I expected. You will come to see their lust for power one day. That is if I don't stop them first."

"You may be right," the man said. "It was just a thought."

III

The Reminiscing Man

It was another dark and dank bar. There were hundreds of them in Edo. They served the disenfranchised. He sat on a wooden bench matched to a rectangular table of rough wood. He fingered one of the many initials carved in the surface attesting to previous generations of hopeless drinkers. Lighting, if you could call it that, was supplied by several whale oil lamps hanging from hooks along the walls. The soot from the lamps had turned the wooden beams of the roof black. It hadn't improved the looks or the disposition of the bartender any. He looked as sooty as his ceiling wrapped in heavy clothing to keep out the chill. With no door but a canvas flap and walls so uneven you could throw a cat through the cracks, everyone in the place shivered.

He stared into his empty cup and remembered. He remembered when its contents were sake and not the cheaper and stronger shochu. He remembered when his companions were clean-cut and forthright samurai. He remembered when his kimono was the best silk and his hair trimmed, oiled and tied back. He smiled to himself as he looked at his current five colleagues sitting around the rough wood table in the dirt floor bar that acted as their gathering place tonight. "They are the garbage of the nation," he thought. So was he.

He remembered, but it did no good. His past was far behind him. Now he would take the woman's money. He wondered how much she would pay this time. She had been generous in the past.

He wondered who the target would be. He wondered if

the target had any idea how little time he had left. Probably not, most dying men realized their mortality too late, at least that was his experience and he had seen a lot of death.

There was another thing he remembered. Most assassinations were contracted by unsavory types or self-important merchants needing a troublesome competitor eliminated. She was different. He was not sure who or what she was. She was young. Based on the clothes she wore, she struck him as high born. But she brokered murder. Whatever her past, it could not be as sordid as his. He was samurai once. But like most samurai who have had their clan disbanded by the Tokugawa, he had fallen far. But he had to eat. He held onto some vestiges of bushido he told himself. He would not kill women or children. The woman in black knew that. They had worked together before.

"Is the bitch coming?" The old man on his right asked.

"You know how careful she is," the reminiscing man said. "She is probably outside watching this bar as we speak."

"You and your yari lead us," the old man said. "Can you get us decent work? Why do we have to work for a woman?"

The reminiscing man looked into the old man's face. "All those scars and you have learned nothing. We take the jobs we can find. We are not samurai anymore. We are not even ronin. We kill people for a living. The only difference between us and the bandits on the roads is we get paid better. I do not care if a woman or a crippled old man has the contract. I take the contract, we get paid, somebody dies, and we get to eat and live another day. That is all there is to it."

"I just do not like sitting around doing nothing, being belittled when she does show, then being paid a pittance for our work," the old man said.

"You can always try the open road," the reminiscing man said.

"I tried it once. There is less chance of being caught out there. But I do not like sleeping rough," the old man said. "My old bones ache too easily."

"Then sip your alcohol and remember better days. It almost works for me," reminiscing man said.

When she entered all eyes moved to her. "She is feminine and mysterious, and she knows it," the reminiscing man said under his breath.

She was wearing an expensive black kimono that clung to her lines. The black material was not dull. It shimmered in the lantern light and the red piping meant she had money. Her feet were covered in black tabi socks and expensive getas. Her hair was jet black and hung down her back. Her face was white like porcelain, the part he could see. A black scarf wrapped around her head, passed around the lower part of her face and tucked back up. Only her forehead and eyes were visible. Given the parts he could see, he guessed she must be beautiful.

"Sometimes when I see you, I forget how thoroughly dangerous you must be," the reminiscing man said.

"I think that was a compliment. Thank you," the woman said.

"We have been waiting a long time," the old man said.

The woman ignored him. That incited the old man more.

"I say we take that scarf off and pass her around," the old man said, getting nods from some of the rest.

"That makes real good sense. You are going to rape the lady who pays us. Are you crazy?" the reminiscing man asked.

"She always comes in here and treats us like dirt," the old man said.

"If you want respect learn to read," the woman said.

"By the Buddha, I will kill you for that," the old man said reaching for his sword.

The reminiscing man pushed him back. "The lady pays my wages. If you attack her, I will have to kill you—if she does not do it herself," the reminiscing man said.

"You are kidding, right?" the old man asked.

"I am not kidding at all. She could probably kill over half of us before we got to her. She is either a murder broker or represents a ninja clan. Either way I do not plan to be in the half that gets killed. So, sit down, shut up and let me do the talking."

"Very good," the woman said.

The old man sat down and sipped his shochu. The woman

chuckled and sat at the end of the bench away from the others. The reminiscing man joined her. They spoke in hushed tones.

"You should replace him," she said.

"We have been through too much," he said.

She nodded. "It is your call," she said. "Family and friends can be a burden."

"Who is it this time?" he asked.

"Have you become particular?"

"The shogun is dead," he said.

"Yes, I know," she replied. "The information is all over the marketplace. Every housewife is aware."

"Getting caught up in someone's kyodai goroshi is not my idea of preparing for the future," he said.

"Kyodai goroshi, brother killing brother … you are afraid we are trying to kill one of the competitors for shogun?"

"The thought had occurred to me," he said.

She laughed a little and covered her mouth, forgetting he could not see her teeth with the scarf.

"You will meet the target tonight on the well-lighted corner where Canal Street crosses Merchant. If he is either Iemitsu or Tadanaga, then feel free to walk away," she said.

"Why is he so accommodating?" he asked.

"He has only two ways to go. If he travels the Canal Road, he is your victim. If he goes by water on the canals, he is not your problem," she said.

"Do we get paid either way?" she asked.

"You get half," she said. "If he goes by water you get to keep the down payment I give you tonight. I do not want to have any hard feelings between us. I may have need of your unique services later."

"You have well-placed sources," he said.

He thought she smiled by the way her eyes rose in the corners.

"You have no idea," she said.

"It is immaterial anyway. I need this job to survive. If he is not a direct descendant of the shogun or a woman or child, I will take the assignment," he said.

The woman looked into the reminiscing man's eyes. He

met her stare. Then she looked at the other five. All the others broke eye contact before she did. "This is why I use him," she thought to herself. "He is a murderer, but he is honest in his own way. He would not kill women or children and he had enough self-respect to look me in the eye."

"He is a ronin," she said.

The reminiscing man's head came up. "He is a ronin? Why did not you say so earlier? No one will miss a ronin," he said.

"That is the spirit," she said. "Prey on the down trodden."

She reached into the folds of her kimono and extracted a wallet. She counted out six small gold coins.

"Agreed?" she asked.

"Agreed," he said and picked up one coin. He motioned and one by one the other five stood and moved to the end of the table and picked up one each. Then the five returned to their drinks at the other end of the table.

"He should be easy to identify. He is young and left-handed," she said.

"Does he travel with any companions?" he asked.

"He is traveling with no more than three others," she said.

"Are they ronin as well?" he asked.

"That is unknown. One is suspected to be. One is a merchant and the fourth is a young woman," she said.

"You know I do not kill women," he said.

"I do not care what you do with his companions, I am paying to have the left-handed young man killed," she said.

"When?" he asked.

"About an hour from now at the place I mentioned. It is a wide area and well lighted by whale oil lamps conveniently placed by the city."

The man smiled. "That intersection is right outside," he said.

"Convenient isn't it?" she asked.

"We have met many times. I do not know your name," the man said.

"Names are such an inconvenience in our business, do you not agree?" she asked. "I do not know your name and I do not care to. You are not going to get all romantic on me are you?

But if you must have a name, I am called The Mist."

"Fitting," the man said. "You come and go like the mist."

"Yes," she said. "I guess I do."

The reminiscing man grasped his yari and pulled the protective leather sheath off the bladed tip and tucked it into his jacket. He smacked the non-bladed end into the dirt floor and pushed himself up.

"Let's go boys. It is time to view the ambush site," he said.

They nodded and filed past the lady in black. Each one eyed her. She ignored them all.

The reminiscing man walked into the intersection and explained their task to his subordinates.

"You know the rules," he said. "No women and no children. If one is injured even by accident you will deal with me."

"Yeah, yeah," the old man said. "We get the same talk with each job."

"Who is the target?" one asked.

"He is a ronin. He will be walking into this intersection soon," the reminiscing man said.

"How will we know him?" the old man asked.

"He is left-handed and young," the reminiscing man said.

"Is anyone with him," another asked.

"He is believed to be traveling with another ronin and a woman and the fourth is a merchant," the reminiscing man said. "So be careful of the woman."

"That is a very strange combination of travelers," the old man said.

"That could be said about us as well," the reminiscing man said.

"How are we going to set up?" the old man asked.

"Two behind them and four head on," the reminiscing man said.

"That should work," the old man said. "Who is in the rear?"

"You pick them," the reminiscing man said. "I want you up front with me."

The old man picked two of the six and directed them to

take up position several buildings toward the docks. Before they departed he told them, "No pipes and you've had enough drinks to get your courage up already. Stay awake. Attack once we have entered the fray."

Both gave little nods that could not be construed as bows and took up positions one on each side of the road and in the shadows.

The reminiscing man, the old man and the remaining two gathered.

"We will meet them head on. We will attack two up. I will be in the front line. The old man will be in the second line. You two split up and join each of us. The second row bring up the rear in case these ronin are handy with the sword. When the two hit from the rear this should be an easy kill," the reminiscing man said.

"If only there was such a thing," the old man said.

IV

Return to Edo

Hideki came up on deck and stretched. The cold air hit him. He wrapped the happa coat more tightly around his shoulders. The frantic flapping of wings startled him as it always did. The below deck quarters where everyone slept had a covered hatch that opened amidships on the government packet ship. The captain had explained he seldom got out of sight of land. They pulled into a port almost every night. This was the one exception. They had been at sea for two nights and today would pull into Edo Bay.

"By the Buddha, are you still playing with those filthy hato?" Hideki asked.

"These filthy birds may save your life," Yoshi responded.

"So, you keep saying. How did you know we would go back home on this ship?" Hideki asked. "There must be ten packet ships moving back and forth between Nagasaki and Edo."

"What was my mission?" Yoshi asked.

"From what you have said it was to get me back to Edo."

"Exactly, except you left out the as soon as possible part," Yoshi said. "So, what is the fastest way between Nagasaki and Edo?"

"Ship, I guess," Hideki said.

"Exactly," Yoshi confirmed.

"Are you telling me that you put those birds on all the ships moving between Nagasaki and Edo?" Hideki asked.

Yoshi just stared at him.

"Of course, you did," Hideki said. "You always try to see all contingencies."

"So should you," Yoshi said. "You will not always have me to think for you."

"Do not leave anytime soon Yoshi. Things are going to get interesting," Hideki said.

"Ergo the birds, young Prince of the Yoshinobu," Yoshi said.

"Okay, okay … I give up," Hideki said. "Where are Jubei and Midori? They were not below."

"They are forward, talking," Yoshi said.

"Jubei is talking?" Hideki asked. "I traveled with him all year and he barely spoke a sentence."

Yoshi grabbed the pigeon with his left hand and put a note into the small capsule on its foot. Then he sent the bird skyward into the cloudy sky. Yoshi nodded in agreement. "I do not understand it either," Yoshi said. "But you are not a female and you do have to admit; they have a lot in common."

Hideki stepped around the cluster of coops and looked forward. "Are you talking about both of them being stone cold killers?" Hideki asked.

"No, you idiot, they are both trained shinobi no mono," Yoshi said. "And by the way, you can count yourself in that category."

"I can count myself a ninja?" Hideki asked.

"I was referring to the stone-cold killer part of your description," Yoshi said. "You have certainly killed your share."

"You are correct again, Yoshi," Hideki said and then turned toward the prow again. "I just hope they find happiness."

"I do not know about happiness," Yoshi said. "But they may well find release."

On the government packet ship, it was the hour of the rooster when Hideki and friends docked. The sun was just setting.

"Feels strange does it not?" Hideki asked.

"You mean it isn't moving?" Jubei offered.

"Exactly," Hideki said.

They had just walked off the gangway and onto a government pier in Edo.

"I think the voyage would have been more pleasurable without those stinking birds of yours Monkey," Jubei said.

"Those stinking birds may save your life sword master," Yoshi replied.

"If you say so. I'll be glad to get their stench out of my nose," Jubei opined.

"What now?" They all turned toward Midori. It had been her question.

"I'm going to the Yoshinobu mansion. Anyone who wishes to join me will be welcome for as long as they like," Hideki said.

"I must report to my father," Jubei said. "We have a lot of politics to catch up on."

"I must report to the Five Families," Midori said.

"I guess that leaves you and me, Yoshi," Hideki said.

"I understand everyone's desire to return to their family and friends," Yoshi said. "It was a long journey from Nagasaki. But my filthy, stinking, noisy birds last told me there is treachery afoot in Edo. Everyone is choosing sides."

"Choosing sides? What sides?" Midori asked.

"Hidetada Shogun has died. Do you not remember what happened last time that position was to be vacant?" Yoshi asked.

"Everyone with a Tokugawa connection was called back to Edo for a selection process," Hideki said. "If it had not been for Musashi sensei and Yoshi my family would not have made it to Edo alive."

"I remember our leader telling us how our Five Families came to work exclusively for the Yoshinobu," Midori said.

"That was Yoshi's doing and one of the best decisions we Yoshinobu have made since I've been alive," Hideki said.

"Whenever these successions come up, you can expect a period of kyodai goroshi," Jubei said.

"What is kyodai goroshi?" Midori asked.

"It is brother killing brother," Jubei said. "Shogun is the

most powerful position in the land. Powerful men have been known to kill others to keep their man in consideration for that position. Brothers have been known to kill brother for the power."

"A good deal of the time, the kyodai goroshi stems from those that surround the old shogun. Those in the upper houses of the government, the Roju and Tairo have the most to lose if a shogun unfavorable to them is chosen," Hideki said.

"Yes, that is how the Five Families got into trouble," Midori said. Then turning to Yoshi, "And you got us out."

"But all the kyodai goroshi is set aside this time and everyone is choosing sides between the dead shoguns two sons, the oldest Iemitsu and the younger Tadanaga," Yoshi said.

"That is much more dangerous than kyodai goroshi. This could lead to civil war," Hideki said. "Then we'd be back in the Warring States period where everyone suffered."

"Now even the lowliest samurai has a stake in the outcome," Jubei said. "Everyone with a sword will be choosing sides."

"Who are the two choices again?" Midori asked.

"The choices are the same as last time. Iemitsu is the oldest son but is a lover of men, a stutterer, and has an ugly birthmark on his face," Yoshi said.

"Wow, what is the younger son like?" Midori asked.

"Tadanaga flies into rages and kills those around him," Yoshi said.

"Two bad choices," Midori said. "Who are the Yoshinobu supporting?"

"I do not know," Hideki said. "I have been in Nagasaki with you."

"We will know when we get to the Yoshinobu mansion," Yoshi said. "I recommend we stay together. There is strength in numbers."

"Good advice Monkey. I am forgetting the smell of those birds already," Jubei said.

"Okay," Yoshi said. "The next decision is do we return to the mansion via the canals or streets?"

"I have had enough water for a while. Let us go by streets," Hideki said.

The four friends moved down the docks and into darkness.

The old woman wore a torn, dirty and threadbare kimono that might have once been blue. Her face was creased with long wrinkles and her hair was short and stringy. The years, the sun and the grime had turned the kimono a rancid gray. She wore a vest-like garment that looked as if it had seen as many winters as the rest of her attire. She was bent almost in half as she meandered down the Edo Street. Her conical straw hat and long walking staff dwarfed her petite size. She talked to herself and swayed from one side to the other as she walked due to obvious hip problems.

"Alms, alms for the poor," she chanted when she came within earshot of another citizen. She was not very successful at begging. It was the hour of transition. The sun had just set. All the workers and shoppers of the daytime were in their cozy homes eating supper with their families going over the highlights of the day. The night dwellers had not yet emerged. They would. The Yoshiwara with its brothels, the little sake shops that catered to those without families and the mobile noodle vendors with their candle lighted handcarts would soon emerge and take their spots in the fastest growing city in Japan.

The old grandmother was making her rounds a little early. She looked like many of the downtrodden citizens of Edo, interested in her next meal and a bed for the night. Sleep was important when you are old. The footsteps of several people approaching made her stop and tip up the brim of her straw hat so she could see who she would be addressing.

They were samurai. Beggars had to be wary of samurai. Chances were good they would curse or beat you. Old beggars had to be especially wary; it took too long to heal. But beggars had to eat. There were two commoners with the two samurai. A beggar should approach them first. And this was an odd grouping of people. The commoners were not walking behind the samurai with their head down. Instead they were walking four abreast and conversing like friends. It was very strange to most Edo observers. This was the right group.

The old woman stopped to look around as the four approached. Here was a convergence of the road from the canal and Merchant Street. The canal itself cut into the heart of the city while the street with the same name clung to the canal for several blocks then got lost in the maze of other streets festooning throughout the city. It was a wide area at this intersection. She was about to open her mouth when she noticed others.

They came from the opposite direction. There were four that she could see. These men looked even stranger than the original four. Three looked like ronin. At least they wore two swords. One had a spear and a short sword. Maybe he was ronin as well. The old woman knew trouble when she saw it. When they moved to intercept the four walking abreast she knew something was about to happen. The beggar stopped.

"Not the kind of welcome I had imagined," Jubei said. "Did those nasty birds of yours announce our arrival Yoshi?"

"They did sword master," Yoshi said. "I am as surprised as you."

"I wonder where the police are. I have not seen a patrol since we landed," Hideki noted.

"I do not think the police will help us now. I think these may wish to do us harm," Yoshi said.

Hideki moved closer to the old beggar woman with the straw hat and long walking stick. "Better move inside grandmother. There will be trouble."

"Domo, domo," the old woman said as she bowed even lower. "Who is giving me this good advice?" she asked in a high-pitched creaky voice.

Hideki stopped. "I am Yoshinobu Hideki grandmother. Please go inside so you will not be harmed."

"Praise the Buddha and thank you young man. But do you have any alms for the poor?"

Hideki could not believe what he was hearing. He had only meant to protect the old woman from harm and now she was begging for alms. He reached into his kimono and extracted a leather pouch. He pulled out a gold coin and placed it in the old woman's outstretched hand.

"Take this and get inside grandmother, please," he said.

The woman took the gold coin and stared at it. "Is this real?" she asked in her creaky voice.

"Yes, now go. The bad men are close." Hideki pleaded.

They were getting closer. Hideki could see four of them. He did not know how many would be behind them.

The old woman bit into the coin. "Praise Buddha this is real," she exclaimed. "I can both eat and sleep well tonight."

"Yes grandmother, if you will not go inside please stay here under this awning. It will be dangerous in the street very soon."

"Bless you, bless you young man. You have made an old woman's heart sing," the woman said as she pushed the gold coin into some crevice deep inside her dirty kimono. Then she moved her straw hat upward so she could watch the confrontation.

"How is your haragai Yoshi?" Jubei asked.

"Strangely silent," Yoshi said.

"I make four in front," Hideki said. "But there must be some behind."

"That is correct," Midori answered.

"I don't see any long-range weapon except one spear," Hideki said.

"Correct again," Midori said.

"Then let us see what the gentlemen have in mind. Yoshi, you and Midori disappear," Hideki said.

"What? And save ourselves?" Yoshi asked.

"Of course not, stupid," Jubei answered. "He wants to see if they let you go or if you are targets of the assassination plot as well."

"Oh," Yoshi said smiling as if he was just understanding.

Yoshi and Midori hiked up their kimonos and fled down a side alley way. The attackers let them go.

"Now we know," Hideki said.

"Now we know," Jubei confirmed. "Do you want to talk to them first?"

"Would it do any good?" Hideki asked.

"Probably not, there are so many of them. We will have to kill a few," Jubei said.

The ronin drew their swords. The spear man advanced first.

Jubei drew his katana. Hideki drew both his katana and wakazashi. His katana was in his left hand and a short sword in his right.

"Do you want the spear man?" Hideki asked.

"Absolutely," Jubei said.

Before Jubei could engage, a shuriken struck the spearman in the left eye. He screamed and dropped the spear, his hands needed to remove the starred weapon embedded in his eye.

The second rank raised their swords and started forward. They stopped when they heard screams coming from behind Hideki and Jubei. The screams gave way to loud moans.

"Welcome back Midori and Yoshi," Jubei said. Then he clashed with one of the swordsmen before him. The attack had been a thrust. Jubei slapped it to the left with his katana and tried to slice the enemy's arm by bringing the sword back to the right. The ronin was too fast and leapt to his right to make Jubei miss. Unfortunately for him that placed him within Hideki's reach.

Hideki sliced at the ronin's throat with his long sword. When the ronin brought up his katana to block, Hideki stabbed him in the stomach with a short sword. The ronin fell to his knees trying to hold in the blood escaping through his fingers.

Two more ronin advanced on Hideki. One was old. Hideki felt sorry for him for a moment, and then banished the thought. This was combat. "Either he will take my life, or I will take his," Hideki reminded himself.

The other was a middle-aged ronin. Both were holding their swords as if they were skilled. They advanced in unison. Hideki was pressured. He could see no opening. This was dangerous. He had almost decided to throw his short sword at the old man and attack the middle aged ronin when the little grandmother with the conical hat and long staff flew from her bent position into a lunge at the ronin closest to her. Her long walking staff struck the middle-aged ronin in the throat. No scream emanated from him. He dropped his sword and fell to his knees with both hands grasping his throat trying to suck air into his collapsed windpipe.

The surprise of the attack startled the old ronin in front of Hideki. It gave Hideki the opening he needed. Hideki launched an overhead attack with his long sword in his left hand. The old ronin deflected it easily and brought his sword down toward Hideki's head. Hideki caught the sword with his short sword in his right hand and brought his long sword up under the man's elbow slicing through into his ribs.

The old man screamed and dropped to his knees surprised. He still held onto his sword. The old grandmother moved like a young girl and brought the hardwood staff down on the old man's head. He toppled over unconscious and bleeding.

It was over.

Midori and Yoshi appeared magically.

"Is everyone okay? Is anyone hurt? Hideki asked.

"Only my pride is hurt. Where did that shuriken come from?" Jubei asked.

Hideki turned to the old woman. She had straightened up and removed the hat. The stringy hair was attached to the hat. Underneath the hat she wore a headscarf that protected her long black hair.

Hideki moved closer. He saw the lines on her face were drawn with charcoal.

"Who are you?" Hideki asked.

The woman rubbed the black off her teeth with a cloth dipped into a water bucket and removed most of the charcoal lines as well.

"Welcome home," she said in a voice he knew well.

"Myo?" Hideki asked.

"Hello lover," Myo said.

V

Sleep or Something Akin

Hideki had bathed, eaten with Jii, Naga and Yuki and gotten to hold his nephew baby Yoshitsune for the first time. It had been a memorable return to the Yoshinobu mansion if you discounted the assassination attempt on the canal road earlier. Jubei had returned to his father's mansion and Yoshi had departed to find his wife and mother-in-law in another part of the estate. Myo and Midori had last been seen leaving the Yoshinobu mansion headed toward Edo. They had to return to the Five Families ninja headquarters. Hideki had waved at her departure and willed that she come back to him later. It had been so long since he'd slept with her and his heart ached for her touch. But she had excused herself claiming important clan business.

"By the way, Naga," Hideki stated. "Your police were not in attendance during my little ambush earlier."

"It is the north magistrate's tour this week, Hideki," Yuki volunteered. As his brother's wife and mother of the heir of the Yoshinobu she sat beside her husband Naga, the South Magistrate for the city of Edo.

"Makes you wonder doesn't it?" Hideki said.

"Are you accusing the north magistrate of collusion with your assassins?" Naga asked.

"Not yet," Hideki admitted. "But the pier is usually heavily patrolled."

"The Bird Woman may be trying to settle old scores," Jii said. "They do not know where we stand yet."

"True," Hideki said. "I knew she was going to be a problem I just did not expect it so soon."

"Did you question any of the survivors?" Naga asked.

"Not me, Midori did. She learned they were hired by a female. She called herself The Mist. She dressed in a black kimono with red piping," Hideki said. "They were paid one gold coin each."

"Anyone know this Mist?" Jii asked.

"Yoshi has not heard of her," Hideki said. "But he did mention a troubling rumor."

"What rumor?" Naga asked.

"That the Koga clan is no longer in the employ of the Tokugawa," Hideki said.

"What?" Jii asked. "I am a member of the lower house of the government, the Roju. Why have I not been told?"

"Probably because Lady Oyeo, the mother of both of the Tokugawa princes, has just convinced them to switch sides," Naga said.

"Do you think she has that kind of influence?" Hideki asked.

"Who else could it be?" Naga said defensively.

"I do not know. It is something to ponder," Hideki replied.

"If this is true, my father's life just became very complex," Yuki said.

"I should assume so my dear," Jii said.

"Why so, grandfather?" Hideki asked.

"Yuki's father is the third Hittori Honzo," Naga said. "The original saved the Tokugawa founder from being wiped out by warlord Nobunaga Oda."

"As a reward for their help, the Shogun put Hittori Honzo and his Iga clan ninja in charge of security for the Tokugawa castle," Yuki said.

"Is that why the north gate of the castle is called Honzo gate?" Hideki asked.

"Yes," Naga said. "The position of head of security is hereditary. Yuki's father, grandfather and great-grandfather were all Hittori Honzo and all in charge of protecting the Tokugawa."

"What does that have to do with the Koga?" Hideki asked.

"Several years ago, our recently departed Shogun Hidetada asked Yuki's father to bring in another ninja clan," Jii said.

"Why?" Hideki asked.

"The way the Roju tell it, the responsibilities got too great for just one family to handle," Jii said.

"However, my father said there were politics involved. Hidetada did not want to be totally dependent upon one family," Yuki said.

"So, the dilemma facing your father is if the Koga have changed sides ..." Hideki started.

"How long can Hittori Honzo be trusted?" Yuki finished.

"Everyone's loyalties will be tested before this is over," Jii said.

"Do you still plan on holding a gathering of all the retainers tomorrow?" Naga asked.

"Yes," Jii said. "I want to look everyone in the eye and hear them swear allegiance."

"Beside the samurai retainers, who else will be present?" Hideki asked.

"Everyone who works for or with us will be there," Jii said.

Hideki reached over to take Yoshitsune away from his mother. The baby squealed in delight.

"I was afraid I would not live to see you nephew. Now we must be extra careful to make sure we can watch you grow," Hideki said, passing the baby back to Yuki.

"I will retire with your permission Jii," Hideki said. "These assassination attempts wear me out."

"Do not leave this compound Hideki," Jii warned.

"He is telling you not to go searching for your true love brother," Naga teased.

"I will not. I am too tired tonight," Hideki said, turning more than a little red.

"Of course, there is nothing keeping her from visiting you," Naga said.

"True," Yuki said. "She is ninja and can travel where she will."

"Enough you two," Jii said. "Let the man alone."

Hideki bowed to the room, turned, slid the door open and exited. He padded down the hardwood floors to his room where his futon and kake buton were already waiting. One candle on a tall stand illuminated the large room. Hideki placed his two swords in the rack just above his pillow, blew out the candle, pulled back the kake buton and got into his futon. It took a while for him to warm up.

"I hope she does come," he said to himself. He was disappointed when fatigue overcame him. He fell asleep.

Something awoke him. He listened intently. Nothing … yet he felt a presence in the room. In one swift move Hideki was up with a sword in each hand.

"Be at ease Prince of the Yoshinobu. I come to talk," the feminine voice said.

Hideki did not recognize the voice.

"If that is the case, step out of the shadows," Hideki said.

"I will if you will replace the swords," the voice said.

"I do not know you. You have breached our security, so you must be a skilled ninja. I believe I will keep my swords," Hideki said.

Hideki waited. Out of the darkest corner stepped a ninja clothed in black. Although wearing the traditional black gi top and dark hakama tucked into black leg cloth wrappings above black tabi shoes, she was obviously female. Only her eyes and forehead was were not covered in black. She was carrying a short straight ninja sword in one hand.

"You would be The Mist," Hideki ventured.

"I am The Mist and you are the Tengu killer, Yoshinobu Hideki," she said.

"You tried to kill me earlier tonight," Hideki accused.

"Not at all," The Mist said. "We merely wanted to test you."

"That was no little test. I am still alive. I guess I passed," Hideki said.

"Yes, you are skilled. We wanted to know how skilled. But the people you surround yourself with interest us a great deal," she said.

"Oh, you do not have enough friends of your own?" Hideki asked.

"I am ninja. I have no friend," she said. "You travel with a master swordsman and a funny little man he calls Monkey."

"I'm sorry, was that a question?" Hideki asked.

Hideki was sure she smiled behind the mask, but he had no way of telling.

"I see you are skilled in some of our ways," The Mist said.

"Just a very few," Hideki said.

"No matter; Yagyū Jubei's reputation speaks for itself. You have your own reputation," she said.

"I have a reputation?" Hideki stalled while giving his eyes time to focus in the darkness. He kept looking around the edges of the woman instead of straight at her giving his night vision time to adjust.

"Oh yes, you killed a Tengu. It is believed you also had something to do with the change of leadership in Nagasaki," she accused

"So, you have come to settle the score for the Tengu?" Hideki asked.

The Mist laughed into her mask. "Hardly, I came to tell you something you already know. The country is about to be split."

"Go on," Hideki suggested.

"The Yoshinobu are not only a respected family, they are liked by the people. You could sway the country to support one of the brothers for shogun," The Mist said.

"And you have come to tell me who to support? Let me guess. You are Koga and you have thrown your support to Tadanaga," Hideki said.

"You are well informed Prince. He is the best choice and he can bring your family great wealth," she said.

"Next will come the threats," Hideki said. "If we do not support Tadanaga then we will all die."

The Mist moved toward Hideki. "I got in here easily. Your ninjas are no match for me. I could kill you in your sleep," she said.

Hideki stepped off the futon toward The Mist. Both sword tips were pointed down in front of him. "I recognize your skillfulness and I think you are probably correct about being able to sneak in here again. But I have one question for you."

"What is the question?" The Mist asked.

"How will you get out of here alive?" Hideki asked.

"I was hoping you would let me go," The Mist said.

"Why should I do that? You are skilled and you are a threat to me and mine. Why not take care of the problem now?" Hideki asked.

Hideki could see her clearly now. He thought he noticed panic in her eyes.

"You should let me go because I just put your ninja to sleep. I did not kill anyone," The Mist said.

Hideki relaxed and moved his swords up to rest on his shoulders. "That is a good argument. I hope it is true."

"It is true, no one has been hurt permanently by my visit," she said.

"Because you have spent the time to visit me and not hurt my ninja, I will tell you the truth. I do not know who the Yoshinobu will support. It will be decided tomorrow. I'm sure my opinion will be asked, but I do not speak for this family. Why did you not drop in on my grandfather instead?"

"He is part of the current government. He will most likely support Iemitsu and that awful woman," The Mist said.

Hideki chuckled. "We can agree on one thing," Hideki said, moving back toward his futon. "She is an awful woman. She tried to burn me alive once."

"So that is how your hand was injured," The Mist said. "I believe the head of the Five Families herself saved you. That is how O'Fuku lost her Fox Gang."

"You are well informed Mist," Hideki said.

Hideki replaced his swords in their scabbards at the head of the bed and sat on his futon facing The Mist.

"Please light the candle Prince. I came to talk and still have a little time before the drug wears off your ninja in the rafters," The Mist said.

Hideki moved to the candle and picked up the small flint and steel at the base. He struck the two together close to the wick creating a spark that became a flame. He placed the flat rectangular flint and the steel in the holder on the candle stand.

"What would you like to talk about Mist?" Hideki asked.

The Mist returned her sword to the scabbard on her back.

Then she moved closer to Hideki and sat cross legged in the center of the room.

"I am interested in why and how you took a ninja lover," The Mist said.

"You came here to deliver a serious message about the future of the country, but you are really curious about my ninja lover?" Hideki asked. "Human nature never fails to surprise me."

"Make fun of me if you wish, but I am still curious about your lover. You are a cousin to the Shogun. You are from a renowned family. Your brother is the South magistrate of Edo. Yet you take a lowly ninja for a lover," The Mist said. "Who would not be curious?"

"Her name is Myo. She is the leader of the Five Families. I met her by accident while her family was targeting me for assassination. She did not know me as a samurai. She knew me as a ronin because I used to go into Edo in simple clothes to learn from various dojos. I met her in a noodle shop. We flirted but I was not used to women. I did not know what to say to her. Some bullies came into the shop and started harassing the owner's daughter. I stepped in and stopped the harassment," Hideki said.

"Oh, so she fell in love with the dashing hero?" The Mist asked.

"No, not quite," Hideki said. "She did become interested however and when we met again, we became lovers. It was not until much later that she learned my identity."

"I bet she was quite angry," The Mist said. "I know I would be."

"Yes, I think she was angry with me because I had lied, and her father was terribly opposed to a samurai-ninja union. He was almost as angry as my grandfather," Hideki said.

"But you overcame the negativity somehow," The Mist said. "Your relationship is the talk of every ninja clan."

"She is a remarkable woman. She is my first love. I cannot see life without her," Hideki said.

"You are refreshingly honest. Are you this open with everyone?"

"No, I am not usually this talkative. However, you are a

young ninja woman yourself. I am telling you this so that you understand love can overcome most things," Hideki said.

"You cannot marry her because you are not of the same class. So why do you continue?"

"We continue because we do not know what else to do," Hideki said. "We both have other duties that keep us apart, but when we meet, we want to spend as much time as possible with each other."

"But a famous samurai like yourself must have other lovers," The Mist said.

"I have no other lovers," Hideki said.

"Truly?" The Mist asked.

"Truly," Hideki said. "Do you require anything else of me Miss Mist?" Hideki asked.

"No Prince; anyone who can kill a Tengu, overthrow a city government, keep a ninja leader as a lover and still remain humble is a man that interests me. He is not one I want to kill," The Mist said.

Hideki returned to the candle and blew it out. He then lay down and brought his kake buton up to cover himself. "But you will attempt to kill me if we do not support Tadanaga?" he asked.

"I will most assuredly try Prince of the Yoshinobu," The Mist said. "And I will reluctantly succeed."

Hideki lay his head on the pillow. "You will try," he said. But he knew no one was there to hear.

Hideki shut his eyes and drifted off to sleep. He awoke and remembered the visit.

"Interesting woman," he said to himself. "Not the ninja I had expected."

"You are expecting a ninja? A female voice from the corner asked.

Hideki sat straight up. "Myo?" he asked.

Myo moved to Hideki's futon. "I am she, in the flesh so to speak."

"Did you see her?" he asked.

"Did I see who?" Myo asked.

"The Mist, she is a female Koga ninja. She came to warn

the family to support Tadanaga," Hideki said. "She is the one that set up the ambush earlier tonight."

Myo moved back to the darkest corner of the room and disappeared. Hideki got out of the futon and struck the flint again to light the candle. He moved to the corner of the room and could see a ceiling tile slightly ajar. He went back to the futon and lay down. A moment later Myo was beside him.

"She was here all right," Myo said. "My people appear to have been drugged with a blow dart."

"Are they okay?" Hideki asked.

"Yes," Myo said, "but we will have to make some changes with security around here."

"Like what?" Hideki asked.

"Like put out that candle and move over," she said.

VI

Street Killers

It was night in the capital city of Kyoto. Two samurai trudged down the dirt roads. They were headed south. There was much activity in the Emperor's city. It was still early and as they moved down along the river toward the Gion district, music and laughter became more prominent.

"Are we there yet?" the younger samurai asked.

"Patience, Uesama," the older samurai said.

"Do not call me that you idiot," the younger said.

"Sorry lord, a slip of the tongue," the older said. "We have arrived."

"That was too far to walk. We should have come by kago." The younger man complained.

"A kago would raise suspicion where we are going," the older said.

"I see kagos all up and down the street," younger said.

"That is because the Kamo (Duck) River is the eastern boundary for the Gion district here in Kyoto. Here on the east you'll find Ochaya houses with oiran and geishas," the older said.

"Prostitutes?" the younger asked.

"Yes and no," the older said.

"I do not need a strategist who is not clear. Which is it, yes or no?"

"Oiran and geishas are entertainers. They sing, dance and play instruments. They are a well-respected part of Kyoto nightlife. If they are the most popular, they are given the title of Taiyu," the older said. "Their time can be bought for the night if they like the man and they may become concubines or even wives of rich merchants. Many retire to open their own tea houses. But they are not the type of prostitute you are thinking about."

"You seem to know a lot about them," the younger said.

"Any man of wealth and power knows this," the older said. "Well anyone who gets out into the city's night life."

"Why are we still walking?" the younger asked.

"Because Bishop lnshin has asked for our help in a specific case," the older said.

"Anything that old bastard wants probably involves young girls, much sake or killing someone," the younger said.

"I believe our prey tonight are merchants. I think he wants them killed to take over their business along with the young widow, all under the guise of helping your coffers of course," the older said.

"What is my part in all this?" The young man asked.

"It is up to you lord. You may play as little or as much a part as you want," the older said, stopping. "We can rest here for a moment. This is the teahouse."

"If we go in, will we not be recognized?" The young man asked.

"We are not going in. But even if we did, we would not be recognized with these masked hoods," the older said. "Witnesses can only see your eyes and nose and we removed any family insignia from our clothing. Neither of us is wearing mon that identify our families."

"How do we go about this?" the younger asked.

"I have been told they are concluding a deal with some cloth wholesalers. They should leave soon. Of course, that assumes Bishop lnshin's information is good," the older said.

"lnshin again, he has really thought this through has he not?" the young man asked.

"I think you will find that Bishop lnshin thinks everything through thoroughly," the older said.

"Yes, I think I will call for a review of his finances as soon I can," the young man said.

"That would be prudent," the older said. "The two we seek must travel up the Kamo River walk which is the way we came down. We will go back a few paces and pick a secluded spot for our little ambush."

"This is exciting." the young man said.

"I thought you might like it." the older said. "Remember not to talk and to have your blade loose in the scabbard. I want to see the one-cut technique I taught you."

Moments later the younger one moved the blade in his katana forward in the scabbard with his left thumb. A sudden reduction in friction let him know the blade would slide effortlessly.

Two men in merchant garb, one old and one middle-aged stopped their walk when a samurai in a hood stepped out of the darkness beside a long-closed candle shop. "I am sorry gentlemen," the older one said. "Are you perhaps the owners of Yamakaya?"

The two merchants started to move back the way they had come when another samurai appeared and blocked their retreat. The second samurai also wore a hood. The first samurai repeated his question. The older merchant bowed. "Yes samurai-sama, we are on our way back to Yamakaya now."

"As I thought," the first samurai said as he stepped forward, making a low draw with his sword at amazing speed and slashed the old merchant open from right hip to left shoulder. The old man gave a sudden intake of breath, collapsed to his knees with both hands clasped to his belly trying to hold his blood and intestines inside. He was dead before his face hit the packed dirt road.

The second merchant holding the long-stemmed lantern started to scream but the sound was lost as the second samurai's sword separated his head from his shoulders.

Both samurais took paper from inside their outer garments, wiped their blades free of blood, dropped the now red paper to the ground and returned their katanas to their scabbards.

"Let us depart," the older samurai said. "We have one more stop to make."

"Excellent, really excellent," the younger samurai said.

"Won't someone report them?"

"Someone will but we will be long gone by then. Besides, they were only merchants."

"Where are we going next?" The younger asked as they made their way on the river walk.

"We will cut west at the next street and head to the Shimabara," the older man said.

"That is the government approved prostitute area is it not?" the younger asked.

"Yes, and there is no better place to practice your one draw one-cut technique. Everyone is a prostitute, a whore monger or one of the thugs that is supposed to protect the girls but instead live off their earnings. They are all parasites," the older man said.

"Let us hurry up then," younger man said. "I am ready for some more action."

The two samurai moved past the gates of the Shimabara into the dingy bar and unauthorized brothels to the west. Here the pleas for clients for the night got much more strident. On these fringes worked the desperate.

Down one dark alley they found three thugs taking turns slapping a girl. Her pleas for mercy unheeded.

"They are probably members of some gang. They call themselves gumi. The gumis run prostitution and gambling and other nefarious activities in Shimabara and outside," the older samurai said. "This will be a poor demonstration."

"Proceed," the younger samurai said.

The older samurai stepped up to the tallest thug and kicked him in the rear. The thug went flying across and into the woman, interrupting her beating. His two partners reached for their single sword, the favored weapon of the gumi.

"Matte," the older samurai said raising his hands ordering the two to stop.

"Who in Buddha's name do you think you are?" the thug on the right asked. "This isn't your affair. We run the day to day operations in and around Shimabara."

"Yes, I know," the older samurai said. "But I have my young protégé with me this evening and I want to impress him with my sword skills. So please wait to draw on me until you companion has righted himself."

"You want the odds to be three to one against you?" the thug on the left asked.

"Exactly, you two would be no threat. Even three will not stretch my capabilities, but young people these days seem to be impressed with numbers," the older samurai said.

"You must think you are Musashi and Yagyū rolled into one," the tall thug said, stepping back into the small circle of people and drawing his sword. "No one kicks me and keeps his life. Do you know who we are?"

"I am quite sure you are some brothel guard with a fancy name like potato head gumi or something similar. You beat women and children and think you are tough because you wear a sword," the older samurai said.

"I'll give you potato gumi," the tall man said as he raised his sword to strike the older samurai from overhead.

The older samurai made three lightning quick strikes blend into one. Before the tall thug's strike had reached the apex of his swing downward, the older samurai had lunged forward with his left foot forward and right foot trailing, turning his scabbard one turn outward, allowing an earth-to-sky draw that started at the thug's ribs on the attackers right side and sliced muscle and bone to his left shoulder. The older samurai continued to the right and parried the next thug's downward strike by dropping the point of his sword while elevating the handle. The second attacking sword made contact and slid off the older samurai's sword to the left. Once the contact was made, the older samurai reversed his blade tip upward and sliced down, cutting deeply into the second thug's neck. The third thug on the left was so shocked to see his two friends killed that he froze. It cost him his life as the older samurai twisted the tip of his sword horizontally while still in the second thug's neck and swung the sword to the left and sliced into the head of the third thug just above the ear. It all happened in the blink of an eye.

The older samurai flicked the blood off his blade. "As you can see my one sword strike style means just that. Once you draw, you continue your motion until your opponents are dead."

"I think I understand now," the younger samurai said. He looked at the girl on the ground. "On your feet woman. Let us get a look at you."

The girl cocked her head to one side, not sure she was hearing correctly, but finally stood. She was bruised badly about the face with blood running from her nose.

"Well you are not much to look at," the younger samurai said.

The battered girl shrank from the two samurai. Their propensity for violence was evident on the ground at her feet. She turned and fled.

Before the girl got two steps the younger samurai drew his sword and cut her back from neck to hip. The girl screamed. The bone of her ribs lay white against the blood pouring from her body. She lay in the alley whimpering, her life's blood oozing into the dirt.

"I presume you wanted no witnesses," the younger man said as he wiped his sword clean and returned it to his scabbard.

"You presumed correctly lord. It is always best to play it safe," the older samurai said.

The two samurai moved northward toward Daito Kuji Temple. No shout rang out behind them. The alley was as silent as a grave.

"How does your style compare to Shinkage Ryu?" the younger samurai asked. "I've had some training with the Yagyū style. It is what we Tokugawa use."

"That is hard to say. The shogun's school does not allow its students to accept challenges. They protect their positions that way and they never have to prove themselves," the older samurai said.

"That will change when I am shogun," the younger samurai said.

"I would certainly hope so," the older samurai said.

VII

Family Dilemma

The Yoshinobu mansion in Edo was busy. The family, all retainers and trusted support personnel were gathered in the great room. No women were present except Yuki, Myo and Midori.

"It must be resolved tonight." Naga said.

"We can make a decision tonight Naga," Hideki said. "But I fear O'Fuku will resolve it. It is out of our control."

"Maybe she will have you boiled in oil and leave the rest of us alone," Naga said.

"Naga!" His wife Yuki chided from her position opposite her husband as she bounced their baby on her knee.

Hideki looked over the gathered assemblage of Yoshinobu retainers. This was just the eighty men of the Edo branch. There were twice as many samurai retainers back in Kii province. Hideki looked to the far wall where his friends Yoshi, Myo, Midori and Jubei sat.

"Yes, I probably should have killed her instead of crippling her two years ago when she attacked me in front of the Shogun Hidetada. But it didn't seem like a good idea at the time," Hideki said as he tried to make eye contact with Myo.

"Iemitsu has declared himself the new Shogun in his father's place. He is the rightful heir," Jii said.

Yagyū Munenori nodded his agreement as he stole a glance at his oldest son sitting at the far wall.

"Yes, he is the rightful heir, but he is a stutterer, has a blemish on his face and likes to bed young boys," Naga said.

"That is the argument made for a selection of the younger brother, Tadanaga," Hideki said.

"Lady Oyeo, the mother of both brothers, favors Tadanaga," Naga said.

"How could a mother do that?" Yuki asked.

"That is enough, you have all heard the comments and we have had endless discussion and allowed everyone to have their opinions. You must make a decision as to which brother the Yoshinobu clan will support," Jii said. "We have had overtures from Lady Oyeo to support Tadanaga. She has promised us more land and greater responsibility if Tadanaga is Shogun. Lady Oyeo also supported us against O'Fuku two years ago."

"That promise is baseless if Iemitsu becomes the Shogun," Hideki said. "We have enough land and all the responsibilities we need as it is."

"Well said," Yagyū Munenori said. "I will probably lose my position of chamberlain if Iemitsu becomes shogun. But it is the right thing to do. It is required by bushido."

"Jubei," Jii called out. "You are the only one here who has been around both heirs. What is your opinion of each?"

"Iemitsu is the rightful heir," Jubei said.

"We know that much, what else do you know?" Jii prompted.

Jubei rocked a little from side to side. Hideki knew this meant he felt uncomfortable.

"Iemitsu is thoughtful but arrogant," Jubei said.

Jii looked at Hideki to get some help. Hideki just shrugged his shoulders.

"Who is better with a sword?" Jii asked.

"Tadanaga," Jubei said.

Jii was really getting frustrated. Hideki asked the next question.

"Would not his sword skills qualify him to be the better shogun?"

Jubei's one good eye bored directly into Hideki.

"Never," Jubei said with conviction.

Jii looked to Hideki. Hideki continued.

"Why not?" Hideki asked.

"Iemitsu uses a sword as a tool. Tadanaga enjoys killing. He should never be shogun," Jubei said.

That comment caused much murmuring throughout the gathered samurai.

"You do not say much old friend," Hideki said to Jubei. "But what you do say is sage advice. Thank you."

Jubei returned to his stoic self, staring straight ahead at Jii.

Hideki turned to Jii. "I agree with both Yagyū. We have to support the rightful heir even if he comes with that demon woman O'Fuku."

"Yoshi you are our intelligence chief, what is your opinion?" Jii asked.

"Iemitsu," Yoshi said. "I hate his stepmother, the bird woman, but cannot stand a usurper, especially a crazy one."

"Myo you run our ninja and have become a loved member of the Yoshinobu. What is your opinion?" Jii asked.

"I agree with Yoshi. I hate the bird woman O'Fuku for torturing and almost killing Hideki, but Iemitsu is the rightful heir," Myo said.

"Midori, do you agree with your leader?" Jii asked Midori.

"Hai Jii sama," Midori said bowing from her sitting position.

The retainers were asked for their opinions and a poll taken. It was almost unanimous.

"The count places us behind Iemitsu," Jii said. "Do you four that dissented wish to continue as retainers with the Yoshinobu?"

The four that had sided with Tadanaga were not in a group. They were spread across the grand room. Jii pointed to each with his fan.

The senior of the four answered. "Jii sama, I am your retainer. You asked for my opinion. I gave mine. But I fight for the family. Wherever you lead I will follow."

"Good answer," Jii said. The other three answered in the same style. He then turned to Yagyū Munenori.

"We are honored to have the shogun's chamberlain with us this evening. Munenori let us hear from you," Jii said.

"Thank you old friend, it is an honor to be here. I do not

think it an exaggeration to say the future of the Tokugawa Shogunate rests in the hands of the people in this room," Yagyū Munenori said.

That statement caused a great deal of murmuring.

"It is true," Munenori said. "I will tell you why in a moment. But first I will tell the man you lovingly call Jii has been a breath of fresh air in the Roju. His time there has been eventful. He has made his presence felt which is what the late Shogun Hidetada intended. I will also commend Naga. His stint as the South Magistrate of Edo has been the talk of the country. His wisdom and fairness have the citizens at peace for the first time in many years."

"You are too kind," Jii said. "I would also like to recognize your son Jubei, whose friendship with my youngest grandson on his latest pilgrimage to Nagasaki gave me great comfort."

"I am not sure who protected whom on that journey. I have heard many strange rumors. I would like to get them confirmed sometime. It appears that Iemitsu is not the only one attempting to revamp the government," Munenori said.

Hideki visibly squirmed in his seat on the tatami. He did not know what to say so he said nothing.

"Shogun Hidetada is dead. His rightful heir is his oldest son Iemitsu. The second son with the support of their mother Oyeo is seeking to defeat Iemitsu. This action is a threat to the peace of the nation. Iemitsu has not remained idle. In two weeks' time Iemitsu will march to Kyoto for his investiture ceremony with the Emperor. Currently Kyoto is in an uproar. There are hooligans and bandits roaming the streets preying on the populace. Iemitsu will put a stop to it but he cannot be seen fighting his way into the capital," Munenori said.

The murmuring intensified. "Two weeks is very little time," Jii said.

"It is almost no time at all," Munenori said. "How long do you think it would take to muster the troops to escort Iemitsu to Kyoto?"

"It would depend on how large an entourage he was taking

and how eager the clans were to support him, but no less than two months," Jii said.

"You are an old campaigner, so you understand logistics for battle. But we do not have two months. That is why the Yoshinobu are so important to Iemitsu's plan," Munenori said.

"What does Iemitsu expect of us?" Hideki asked.

"First he has to know you are loyal to him. Some of the other inner families have not been. The defection of the Koga has made Iemitsu very wary. There is talk of the Satsuma Clan in the south supporting his brother Tadanaga," Munenori said.

"You have heard our decision to support Iemitsu. We will do as we are directed," Jii said.

"I knew we could count on the great Yoshinobu house," Munenori said. "I know you have had your differences with O'Fuku in the past. Please try to work with her. She is a master planner and has Iemitsu's ear."

"You may report we are loyal to Iemitsu," Jii said. "As far as getting along with O'Fuku, you might as well ask me to get along with a viper."

"You may do that yourselves. Iemitsu will soon call you all in for an audience," Munenori said.

"What is that concerning?" Jii asked.

"I can tell you no more except to remind you of what I hinted at earlier. The Yoshinobu are key in Iemitsu's plan to thwart Tadanaga and become the third Tokugawa shogun," Munenori said.

"We will be ready for whatever he has in mind," Jii said.

"I would not have expected anything less," Munenori said.

"I am hungry. I think it is time to eat," Jii said.

Yuki passed her baby to her husband and clapped her hands. Wives of the retainers and servants entered the great hall and set trays on small stands with food on them in front of everyone. They were followed by other women who placed sake cups and warm sake bottles beside the trays.

"Excuse me Jii," Hideki said, picking up his tray. "I think I will join my friends."

"You will probably join the young maiden with the jet-black hair," Naga teased.

"I am just following the fine example of my older brother," Hideki said.

Both Nagamasa and Yuki blushed. Yuki bowed to Jii and moved to her husband's side, retrieving baby Yoshitsune.

Hideki moved to the far wall and sat next to Jubei. Myo picked up her tray and moved across from Hideki. Midori did the same for Jubei. Yoshi moved to sit next to Myo facing Hideki and Jubei.

"Where is your wife Chiyo and mother-in-law Matsu?" Hideki asked.

"I have no idea," Yoshi said. "They have been quite secretive of late. I think Chiyo must be sick. She is avoiding me."

"I am sorry to hear that. I hope she is better soon," Hideki said.

"Me too," Yoshi said. "We've been making up for lost time since we returned from Nagasaki."

"You probably wore the poor girl out Monkey," Jubei said.

"That is not funny, sword master," Yoshi said. "We are still newlyweds."

Everyone smiled at Yoshi's discomfort.

"And so, it starts," Hideki said.

"It could not have gone any other way," Jubei said.

"Now you have five ninja women in your life," Myo said to Yoshi.

"How do you figure five?" Yoshi asked.

"You are married to one. Matsu is your mother-in-law and is the second. Then there is me and Midori and now O'Fuku," Myo said.

"I wonder which is the most dangerous." Jubei asked.

"That is easy," Yoshi said. "Myo is by far the most dangerous."

That earned him an elbow in the arm from Myo and a questioning look from the rest.

"Don't look at me with those questioning faces," Yoshi said. "Myo sleeps with our boss. Who knows what kind of bad things she says about us behind our backs?"

"For your information Yoshi, when I'm alone with your

boss we hardly speak at all," Myo said.

That brought catcalls from Yoshi and Midori. Jubei and Hideki stayed silent. Hideki turned red.

"O'Fuku bothers me," Hideki said.

"Well she should," Myo said. "She tried very hard to kill you."

"If it was not for Myo and Midori, I'd have a lot more of me charred than just my hand," Hideki said.

"How is your hand?" Midori asked.

"Thanks to Matsu and her ointments," Hideki said, "it is almost as good as new. I believe I am just as good with my right hand now as my left."

"Really?" Midori asked. "Does that mean you will go back to be a right-hander again?"

All eyes went to Jubei for confirmation.

"Hideki is correct. He could easily become a right-hander again," Jubei said.

"But I do not think I will," Hideki said.

"Why not?" Myo asked.

"Because being left-handed gives me options. In a sword fight it may be the difference between life and death," Hideki said.

"I guess this night marks the beginning of a new adventure," Midori said.

"It actually started last night," Hideki said.

"How," Midori asked.

"I was visited in my room by an unwelcome ninja calling herself The Mist," Hideki said.

"How did she get through our security?" Midori asked.

"She used paralyzing blow darts," Myo answered.

"Was there any permanent damage?" Yoshi asked.

"Just to my pride," Myo said. "She was very skilled. We will have to strengthen security around the compound and be very careful."

"What did she want?" Midori asked.

"She wanted the Yoshinobu to support Tadanaga," Hideki said. "But she knew a lot about we five sitting here. She knew the least about Yoshi and was especially curious about him."

"I knew you and your samurai ways would be the death of me some day Hideki," Yoshi said.

"How much did she know?" Midori asked.

"She knew about Jubei. And she knew about Myo and I being lovers. She knew about Nagasaki and called me Tengu killer. She hinted about me killing the governor. I believe we have all been under surveillance for some time," Hideki said.

"We must all be very cautious," Myo said. "She had superior skills. She admitted to being behind your welcome the other day by those assassins."

"Will your father need your sword Jubei?" Hideki asked.

"I have told him my sword belongs to the Yoshinobu," Jubei said. "My brothers and sister can protect him."

"What is our next move?" Yoshi asked Hideki.

"If I am not mistaken, we will all be asked to the castle by Iemitsu. You heard Munenori earlier. I expect we will all be baited and humiliated to see if we are in fact loyal," Hideki said. "What is said will determine our next move."

"I really do not trust O'Fuku," Myo said.

"Anyone who does is a fool," Hideki said. "All we can do is wait to be summoned."

"That doesn't sound like cherry blossoms," Yoshi said.

Hideki smiled at the reference they used to describe their current situation. A cherry blossom day meant all was good. A benjo day meant things were crappy. "No, my friend, it does not. It sounds like benjo," Hideki said.

VIII

Takechiyo

Iemitsu sat in his quarters cross legged tapping a very decorative sword with oil. There were many samurai and young apprentices at his beck and call who could have done this task, but it allowed him to think he was a real samurai. It also allowed him time to ponder and to plan.

"Where is he now?" Iemitsu asked.

"They have taken refuge in the Kyoto mansion on the grounds of Daito Kuji Temple Takechiyo," the woman said.

For the first time all morning Iemitsu smiled. "Only you are allowed to use my boyhood name."

O'Fuku smiled back. "That is as it should be Uesama."

"I am not the shogun yet," Iemitsu said. "Not as long as my loving brother remains a threat."

"The Koga ninja betraying us shocked the castle. I have reprimanded Hittori Honzo. But maybe we should fire him," O'Fuku said.

"No," Iemitsu said. "I know him to be loyal to the Tokugawa."

"But is he loyal to you? That is the question," O'Fuku said.

"Who does my loving brother have on his side?" Iemitsu asked.

"It is extremely hard to tell. Even the ones that claim allegiance to you could turn later," O'Fuku said rubbing her right elbow. "But if he's on the Daito Kuji Temple grounds you can bet that Bishop Inshin is involved somehow."

"Why should I worry about him? I thought you had

control of him," Iemitsu said.

"I did. But the Koga going over to his side so rapidly leaves us with more questions than answers. I no longer have my Fox Gang to carry messages back and forth. I am truly concerned about what that idiot Ugai may be planning," O'Fuku said.

"That is a little scary. But for Tadanaga to pull off my death he must have someone much smarter than Bishop Inshin pulling the strings. Is the Koga leader Ugai smart enough?" Iemitsu asked.

"He is vicious enough, but he is not smart enough to rally support among daimyo. He is a thug at best. If you want a throat slit, he is your man. If you want to plan a rebellion, you must look elsewhere," O'Fuku said. "I think we are safe for now."

"It looks like your plan may still be functioning. Is that elbow still hurting?" Iemitsu asked.

"It does, but what hurts most is the loss of my brother and sister ninja. Those damn Yoshinobu destroyed my entire network. I would have better information for you if my Foxes were still alive," O'Fuku said.

"They did slaughter hundreds of innocents and you did try to kill the Yoshinobu grandson twice once by burning him alive," Iemitsu reminded her.

"What of it? The Yoshinobu are trash. Hidetada was retiring and just like now your real mother was plotting to have Tadanaga follow him as shogun. You were going to lose your birthright. I could not let that happen," O'Fuku said.

"I know I owe you much. I probably owe you my life. Why did you stay loyal to me when everyone else abandoned me?" Iemitsu asked.

"Such an easy question," O'Fuku laughed. "I was a cast aside concubine to the great man himself, your grandfather, Ieyasu, the first Tokugawa. Alas he grew tired of me but enjoyed my wit and grasp of politics. He would talk to me long after I no longer warmed his bed. When you were born your mother refused to breast feed you. Ieyasu asked me to step in and help you survive. I have been doing it ever since. We are alike. We were both outcasts. I loved you then and I love you now. It was I who thought far enough ahead to get Ieyasu to commit to paper his desire that upon the death of your father that you would be considered for shogun."

"Yes, I know the story well. I just like to hear you tell it," Iemitsu said. "It reminds me how few people I can truly trust in this world."

"When you are shogun, we will rewrite the history books Takechiyo," O'Fuku said.

"We have to get there first," Iemitsu said. "And quit using my boyhood name. Others may find it disrespectful."

"Most of the Tozama daimyo support you lord and have declared their allegiance. We simply do not know about the Fudai. The outside lords are always plotting," O'Fuku said. "I will only use your boyhood name when we are alone."

"Even though the Tozama are called inside lords because they served with my grandfather at the great battle of Sekigahara, we should not take them for granted. They could easily rely on that argument to support Tadanaga," Iemitsu said.

"Then who can we trust?" O'Fuku asked.

"That is the great question. As you know, one of the most dangerous Fudai families is the Satsuma in the south. They hate the Tokugawa and would support my brother and then kill him if it means placing one of their own as shogun," Iemitsu said. "Unfortunately, my loving brother is too stupid to anticipate their duplicity. Just another reason he should not be the next shogun."

"With the Satsuma in the picture it means we may have to deal with the Fuma ninja," O'Fuku said.

"Yes, it is a bad time for the Koga to abandon us. But it cannot be helped. I am not sure if our remaining Iga ninja are strong enough to protect us and thwart both the Fuma and the Koga. We have to assume the Koga have gone over to Tadanaga," Iemitsu said.

"We can hire others," O'Fuku said.

"But will they sell us out for more money like the Koga did? The Satsuma have Nagasaki in their domain. It is a port large enough to support the entire country if managed properly. There is more money flowing through that port than in all of Edo. Remind me to do something about Nagasaki when I'm shogun," Iemitsu said.

"Yes lord," was all O'Fuku said.

"What is wrong? What are you thinking?" Iemitsu asked.

"Like I said previously, my Foxes were wiped out by the Yoshinobu," O'Fuku said.

"Are the Yoshinobu with us or against us?" Iemitsu asked.

"It is unknown at this time. I want them all dead, but your comment about ninja and loyalty made me think," O'Fuku said.

"Quit stalling. What are you thinking?" Iemitsu demanded.

"My Fox ninja were good at their craft. No ninja clan, to include the Iga, should have been able to destroy them," O'Fuku said.

"Yet the Yoshinobu did," Iemitsu said.

"They did with the help of their ninja," O'Fuku said.

"Do you know them?" Iemitsu asked.

"They are called the Five Families and run a courier service throughout the country," O'Fuku said.

"What a wonderful way to stay on top of everything throughout the land," Iemitsu said.

"I heard their leader recently died," O'Fuku said.

"Who runs them now?" Iemitsu asked.

"I do not know. It may be his daughter. She was in attendance when that slime Yoshinobu Hideki broke my elbow," O'Fuku said, raising her arm.

"You hate the Yoshinobu, but you would use them to your purpose," Iemitsu said.

O'Fuku smiled coyly. "Oh yes, Uesama."

"And after you get what you want?" Iemitsu asked.

"I will destroy them all," O'Fuku said.

"What of the Yagyū? Will you treat them the same?" Iemitsu asked.

"They cannot be trusted either. They are too close to the Yoshinobu," O'Fuku said.

"But the Yagyū have served the Tokugawa faithfully for

years. Munenori has been chamberlain for both Tokugawa shoguns," Iemitsu said.

"Yes, but both you and your brother are Tokugawa. Their past loyalty is no guarantee," O'Fuku said.

"You certainly give me much to ponder. But for the time being I think I must trust both families. Both Munenori and the old man of the Roju, the one they call Jii from the Yoshinobu wield much influence in the Taira and Roju. I must keep as many friends as I can. We are entering a dangerous period," Iemitsu said.

"I do not think you have anything to worry about with either family," O'Fuku said.

"You have just spent the morning condemning both and now you think I have nothing to worry about," Iemitsu said. "Please explain yourself."

"Both elders are old school samurai. Those old fools live and breathe loyalty. I've never understood it, but I've seen it," O'Fuku said.

"I hope you are correct in your reasoning. I need both families to make my plan work," Iemitsu said.

"You have a plan and you have not discussed it with me?" O'Fuku asked.

"I have many plans and some I do not discuss with you. I know your weak spot is the Yoshinobu. But I have learned well from you. I can plan and scheme and keep secrets. We will just have to mold both the Yoshinobu and the Yagyū to our wills," Iemitsu said.

"Oh Takechiyo, you are beginning to sound like me," O'Fuku praised.

"Yes, okasan and it is a little scary," Iemitsu said. "Now help me plan bringing the Yoshinobu and Yagyū together for an audience and ways to test their resolve."

IX

Ronin Rei

"Tsugi," the chief priest yelled. "Who is next?"

There were many applicants. The line of would-be samurai filled the courtyard in front of the wide-open great room of the temple that had been converted into an open-air three-sided dojo.

Like most of the applicants Matoumoto Rei had been waiting for two days to get this close. The worse part had been standing on the long flight of stone steps ascending the temple hill. Now he was in the front crush of men trying to impress the instructors inside the make shift dojo.

"What do you think the Ronin Army will be doing?" the young man behind Rei asked.

"I do not know," Rei said.

"Maybe we will be assigned to protect the capital and capture the Kyoto Street Killers," the young man said.

"I doubt they would need an army for that," Rei said.

"How long have you been waiting?" the young man asked.

"As long as you, I guess," Rei said.

"Have you been watching the matches?" the young man asked.

"Same as you," Rei said.

"The monks with the padded spears are the worse. They hit you with either end of the spear and inflict damage. They are so fast you do not have time to get inside with a bokken. We don't have enough reach with a wooden sword," the young man said.

Rei watched as shabbily clad ronin applicants were struck

by padded spears or knocked senseless by the non-sharp end and eliminated. The temple priests wielding the padded spears crushed whatever samurai pride the applicants had left. Rei had been in line two days eating prepared rice balls and drinking from his bamboo flask and had seen no ronin defeat a priest.

"If you cannot defeat a priest how are you going to protect the new Shogun Tadanaga?" the chief priest yelled. "The state of samurai swordsmanship is deplorable."

The priests wielding the long spears were very large men. The weapons appeared small in their capable hands. Their robes tucked into their obi and their shaved heads gave them an even more ominous appearance. Every time they stomped their bare feet on the polished hardwood floor of the temple the sound resonated throughout the hall.

The chief priest pointed to Rei. "Tsugi?"

Rei nodded and yelled, "Hai."

His new friend gave him a push to help him gain a foothold on the terrace that surrounded the great hall. He took off his sandals and live wakazashi and walked bare footed to the one permanent wall of the temple and selected a wooden wakazashi from the many bokken displayed.

The chief priest looked at him and laughed. "What do you expect to do with that?"

Rei looked down at his seemingly inadequate wooden sword. "I expect to defeat your best."

The rest of the priests laughed as did the first row of the applicants that could hear the exchange.

Rei's opponent did not appear to be a favorite of his fellow priests. One taunted him with, "If he beats you with that puny sword you will be laughed out of the temple."

This and other taunts infuriated Rei's opponent. He banged the butt of his spear on the wooden floor. "You are too thin and pretty to be a samurai. Are you sure you are not a girl?" he bellowed. "You can come warm my futon tonight for your rice."

"You are way too ugly to be a priest. Are you sure you are not a shaved bear?"

Everyone within earshot laughed at Rei's retort. The monk

opponent lost control and swung his spear around with one hand trying to take off Rei's head. Rei easily ducked the attack. The second time the spear came around in the same manner the priest dropped the arc slightly to strike Rei in the body. Rei leaned back so the spear head missed ever so slightly and as soon as it passed Rei shot toward the priest. With his waka-zashi in his right hand and his left hand behind the handle Rei pushed the point into the area above the priest's right hip, aiming for a spot beyond him. The huge priest crumbled and fell on his bottom. No one was more surprised than the priest when he found Rei's wooden wakazashi under his jaw.

There was instant applause from the several priests in the dojo and the first row of applicants who witnessed Rei's win.

"You are powerful and your yari is long, but angles of attack and speed will defeat you every time. I can show you how to counter that later if you would like," Rei said.

The priest's countenance went from embarrassment then to anger and finally he smiled. The priest got to his feet. "You will do. What is your name?"

"Matoumoto Rei," Rei said as he bowed, moving his wooden wakazashi behind his back.

"Well Matoumoto Rei, go see the abbot through those doors. Tell him you defeated Token. He will not believe you, but he will take you into the Ronin Army based on my word. We will meet again samurai."

"Domo Token, I look forward to it," Rei said.

Rei padded back to the edge of the dojo floor and retrieved his live wakazashi and straw sandals. The sword he tucked into his obi on the left side. The sandals he placed inside his black gi. He then turned and moved through the large doors.

The hallway he entered was short and austere. He heard voices on the other end before he saw anyone. There was another bozu (priest) in the same robes as his opponent Token. He seemed to be in charge. The three samurai lounging about took interest in Rei's arrival but said nothing.

"What have we here?" the bozu asked.

Rei stopped and bowed to the room.

"Well?" the priest demanded.

"Token told me to report here," Rei said.

The priest looked shocked. The three samurai took increased interest.

"Why?" the priest asked.

Rei was puzzled for a moment. "We fought. I won. Token said to report here."

"That is impossible. Some experienced samurai give Token a good fight and they get advanced here, but no one defeats him," the priest said.

Rei shrugged. "I guess I am the first then. What is next?"

Rei surveyed the room. The three samurai staring at him were dressed ruggedly with well-worn black kimonos with frayed lapels and patched hakamas. None wore the chomagae bald on top with a folded forward top knot fashionable in Edo with retainers of a lord. All had a full head of hair but two had their hair pulled back and tied at the crown with a flowing tail. The third had shoulder length hair that was combed but hanging free. Rei assumed he was the leader by his stance. None of the men wore any kind of identifying emblem or mon.

"How could you, a mere boy, with a short sword defeat the most feared warrior monk in the temple?" the long-haired samurai bellowed.

Rei looked the man in the eye unafraid. "If I did defeat the most feared fighter in the temple, that would make me the most feared now. Don't you think you might lower your voice when speaking to such a person?"

The other two samurai moved their hands to their swords. The leader with the long hair smiled and signaled for his companions to relax.

The priest took a step back when the threat of violence had appeared. "Name?" he asked.

"Matoumoto Rei," Rei said.

The priest wrote his name on a scroll and the leader of the samurai waved him away. The priest bowed and moved down the hallway toward the dojo.

"You talk very confidently for one so young," the leader said.

Rei waited.

The leader nodded. "You may call me Mondo. The one on

81

the left is named Abe and his companion is Watanabe. They are lieutenants in the Ronin Army. I am the captain. Our job is to defeat Iemitsu's forces and see Tadanaga made the third Tokugawa shogun."

Rei waited again.

"Look at him Mondo. He is too skinny and fair to be one of us," Abe said.

Watanabe and Abe both laughed. Mondo did not.

"I imagine that is what Token thought," Mondo said. "What questions do you have Matoumoto Rei?"

"How large is the Ronin Army?" Rei asked.

"We are now at fifty men. I want to grow it to 100 so that both Abe and Watanabe have a company of fifty men. I am looking for lieutenants," Mondo said.

"One hundred does not seem like much when you are going up against the established shogun," Rei said.

"He is not established yet. He still has to come to Kyoto for the investiture ceremony with the Emperor," Abe said.

Mondo ignored the interruption. "You are correct. But we are not trying to overthrow Iemitsu. All we must do is disrupt his arrival and do enough damage that the investiture is canceled or postponed. Both ways Iemitsu will lose face and Tadanaga will gain it. The more Tadanaga is seen to have power the more daimyo will flock to his banner."

"You can do that with 100 men?" Rei asked.

"Within the confines of Kyoto and its approaches, yes," Mondo said.

"If we survive, we will be given permanent retainer positions with a lord?" Rei asked.

"That is what Tadanaga and the Satsuma leaders have promised," Mondo said.

"And I can leave whenever I feel so inclined?" Rei asked.

"No," Mondo said. "Once you are with us, you stay with us. The only way out is death or Tadanaga victory. Think hard and think carefully."

Rei nodded. He had come to Kyoto from his father's farm for the announced benefits of joining the Ronin Army. His father was samurai who had lost his lord. Now a ronin taking care of a son and daughter he was reduced to farming and forging swords. Neither made much money. If the son had a chance to serve a lord, it would mean the difference between starvation and an easier life.

Rei nodded. "I am with you."

Mondo broke into a smile. "I had hoped so. I have no doubt your skills are excellent, but it is your youth and innocent look that will make you valuable. Welcome to the Ronin Army."

X

Whom Do You Serve?

The Yoshinobu sat on folded legs on the lower part of the tatami facing the place of honor on the raised portion of the floor. They had been waiting for quite some time. Old Jii was on the right. Nagamasa sat on Jii's left. Next to Nagamasa sat Hideki. To Hideki's left sat Yagyū Jubei and finally Yoshi.

O'Fuku entered and moved to the raised portion of the tatami and dropped to a folded leg position beside the main cushion. She faced the Yoshinobu and looked down on them from a slight height advantage. Somewhere behind the screens that hid the entrance directly from the castle chambers came the announcement that Tokugawa Iemitsu had arrived. The Yoshinobu bowed and remained that way until O'Fuku said everyone could raise their heads.

O'Fuku started the proceedings. "We have asked the Yoshinobu here to give us their decision on which they support the rightful heir or the usurper." she said.

Jii cleared his throat. "The Yoshinobu support the rightful heir Iemitsu and swear allegiance to him."

"The last time we met you opposed me in a gathering like this and your vicious whelp crippled my arm. Do you still claim allegiance to Iemitsu?" she asked.

Jii raised his head and met O'Fuku's gaze. "The last time we met you were leading a gang of murderous ninja across the land killing innocents and robbing merchants. Besides I believe Hideki crippled your arm after you tried to burn him at the stake and then tried to strike him with a katana in Shogun Hidetada's presence," Jii said.

"How dare you question me? You are nothing but country trash," O'Fuku blazed.

"Those were not intended as questions O'Fuku," Jii said. "My words were stated as facts."

O'Fuku stood. "I will have you and your whole family to include your new great grandchild boiled in oil."

All Yoshinobu eyes bored into O'Fuku's twisted face. It was Nagamasa who spoke.

"I am trying to decide if we made the right choice."

Iemitsu bellowed, "How dare you say that in my presence."

Nagamasa did not shout, but his voice was stern. "This viper has just threatened my family and my new born son. Who but a fool, when seeking support, would unleash this vile creature on us?"

"I'm a fool now? I will have her prediction made fact," Iemitsu said.

Then Hideki spoke. "I wondered how the rightful heir could have lost the loyalty of the Koga. Now I begin to see. You are just as twisted as this witch, but how could it be otherwise? She raised you."

"Hideki," Jii warned.

"No grandfather, our family has been threatened. Bushido demands we defend ourselves," Hideki said.

"You would all die before you reached us," O'Fuku warned. "Besides you only have your short swords."

"Maybe," Hideki said, "but if I slayed a Tengu with this short sword, I'm pretty sure I could take your heads before your guards arrived."

"Hideki, enough," Jii demanded. Then, turning back to Iemitsu, Jii said, "It is obvious that you do not want the Yoshinobu as allies. It was a mistake to come here." Jii bowed. "With your permission we will withdraw to our quarters and proceed to Kii Province."

"You will throw your support to the usurper?" O'Fuku accused.

"Never," Jii bellowed. "We will do nothing to harm the rightful heir. It is not our way."

"What is your way?" O'Fuku scoffed.

"No wrong too small to right, no right to small to defend," the three Yoshinobu answered in unison.

O'Fuku snorted her derision in response.

"What is that?" Iemitsu asked.

"It is our family motto, lord," Jii answered.

"You believe this?" Iemitsu asked.

"We live it lord. It is what we base our lives on," Hideki said.

Iemitsu tapped the side of his jaw. "I wonder if such is true."

"It is lord. This family lives their lives based on those principles," Jubei said.

"Yagyū Jubei, my old sword instructor. Why are you here? Do you serve the Yoshinobu?" Iemitsu asked.

"On occasion I serve them. But I am here because the Yoshinobu asked me to be. I am using my sword these days to conquer evil. If I'm with Hideki there is a very good chance I will be able to do so," Jubei said.

"Have you taught him all the secrets of Shinkage Ryu?" Iemitsu asked.

"I have taught him some over the last year lord. But he was also taught by Musashi," Jubei said.

"I have heard that," Iemitsu said. "So, what are the odds that Hideki could take our heads if he wanted to?"

Jubei measured the distance in his mind. "I would not bet against him lord."

"Very interesting," Iemitsu said. "I would have thought it impossible. But I still don't understand your allegiance to this clan?"

"Hideki and I are friends," Jubei said.

"Friends? I did not know samurai could afford friends. But your allegiance to a friend could get you killed today," Iemitsu stated.

"That is possible lord, but I owe Hideki my life several times over," Jubei said. "I think the likelihood of Hideki being successful in taking your heads today is fairly great. But if he was not successful, and you did kill all gathered here, the threat to your lives would not end today."

"What do you mean?" Iemitsu asked.

"I mean their retainers are fiercely loyal as are their ninja. It might take months or even years, but somewhere, some place when you least expect it, someone will take your heads," Jubei said.

"But I am the shogun," Iemitsu said.

"You are not yet the shogun. But you are dealing with a clan that has lived by bushido for at least three generations, probably more. Being shogun would not matter to them. If the clan was disbanded and dispersed, they would find a way to attain revenge," Jubei said.

"Are you threatening us?" O'Fuku demanded.

Iemitsu interrupted O'Fuku. "Jubei doesn't threaten. He is much like the wakazashi on his belt. He is either sheathed or slicing through air. There is no middle ground."

"You sound as if you respect these hooligans Iemitsu," O'Fuku said. "Are you afraid of these people?"

"No O'Fuku, I am not afraid of them. I am intrigued by them. In today's modern society they seem to be throwbacks to the age of the bushi warrior. They live their lives by bushido and engender a strong sense of loyalty in their followers," Iemitsu said.

"So what?" O'Fuku asked.

"So, we should be building on that kind of loyalty, not threatening it," Iemitsu said.

O'Fuku sat down.

"With your permission lord, the Yoshinobu will withdraw," Jii said.

"You do not have it," Iemitsu said. Then he turned again to Jubei. "Just how good are this man's skills with the sword? He appears to be deformed."

"In a very short time he will be teaching me lord," Jubei said. "Do not let the crippled hand fool you. It is an injury given by O'Fuku that he has overcome."

"Interesting," Iemitsu said. "This family really intrigues me. Everyone has heard of Nagamasa's wisdom as the South Magistrate. Your fame eclipses mine. The common people sing your praises."

"Thank you, lord, you are too kind." Nagamasa said but did not bow.

"And you, old man have a reputation for stirring up trouble in the Roju. They are not used to that," Iemitsu said.

"I believe that is why your father placed me there," Jii said.

"Jubei how do I get this family to pledge their support and their unusual loyalty to me?" Iemitsu asked.

"By getting rid of O'Fuku lord. You had the Yoshinobu support coming into this meeting. You destroyed it by letting O'Fuku threaten their family. Now you are going to have to earn their trust," Jubei said.

"Why should I have to earn their trust?" Iemitsu asked.

"Because all good leaders do," Jubei said. "Your threats today mean they will support you, but who among them would give their life for you when in the back of their mind they may think they would be better off without you."

"I see your point," Iemitsu said. "So how do I regain that loyalty?"

"I would begin my asking them to stay," Jubei said.

"That is all?" Iemitsu asked.

"It is a start," Jubei said. "If I understood my father's cryptic message a few days ago, you need the Yoshinobu to make your plan work prior to the investiture in Kyoto."

"I would not say I need them," Iemitsu said. "I would say things would go much smoother if I had their loyalty."

"Then I would bring them in close as part of your security and whatever else you want them to undertake. They work best when they understand the plan and believe it is right," Jubei said.

"You are talking the family moto again?" Iemitsu asked.

"Yes lord, the Yoshinobu will die for a just cause," Jubei said.

"Would you accompany them when I give the tasking?" Iemitsu asked.

"I often pledge my sword to Yoshinobu causes," Jubei said.

Iemitsu turned to Jii. "Would you consider the discussion today nothing more than me testing your loyalty by threatening what you hold dear and that you passed the test?"

"If you can guarantee all threats to my family are off the table and that neither I nor my family will ever have to be in O'Fuku's presence again, we will serve you lord," Jii said.

"Yes, yes all threats against the Yoshinobu are extinguished," Iemitsu said. "But I need O'Fuku's wisdom to help me change the country. I can guarantee if I am shogun and you remain loyal no harm will come to you or yours."

Jii closed his eyes and rocked back and forth slightly. He then opened his eyes and stared directly at Iemitsu. "Then it is enough. We await your orders lord," Jii said.

O'Fuku stared darts at Hideki.

XI

Daito Kuji Temple

It was unseasonably cold for October. A heavy frost changed the color of the meditation garden from green to a gray-white. Daito Kuji Temple now was famous for its garden and ornate statues of Buddha. The temple was initially constructed in 1319 as a simple Zen Buddhist building. Being in the northwest outskirts of the capital city of Kyoto, it had been destroyed by fire and war and rebuilt several times. The political importance of the now sprawling complex of twenty-two lesser temples and shrines got its start when the great warlord Hideyoshi Toyotomi held a funeral ceremony for his lord Nobunaga Oda. For the last fifteen years it was the home of Iemitsu's younger brother Tokugawa Tadanaga.

The great doors were shut, guards were posted at all entrances and ninja stationed in the high rafters. Privacy was paramount.

The Abbot of the temple, Inshin Suden, called the meeting to order. Tadanaga sat on the raised portion of the tatami. His mother Lady Oyeo was next to him. On the lower tatami in a semi-circle were men and women sitting on cushions in the Japanese folded leg fashion.

"Please raise your heads. I want to see all your faces," Tadanaga said with a beaming smile. "Please enjoy the hot sake on such a cold day as we talk."

The people waited until Lady Oyeo poured Tadanaga his wine and tasted it before they poured their own.

"I believe introductions are in order," Tadanaga said. "I will do the honors. On my far right is the host, the right honorable Abbot Inshin. This is his temple. Because my lands abut his, he has been my teacher since childhood. Thank you for allowing us to use your building Abbot."

"It is my great pleasure Uesama," Abbot Inshin said.

"I am not the shogun yet," Tadanaga protested. "My brother is claiming the same title. But I am confident that he is premature."

"We all hope that is the case," the man next to the Abbot said.

"Thank you, Yamada Arinaga," Tadanaga said. "For you that do not know of him, Yamada san is our representative from the Shimazu Clan of the Satsuma Han south in Kyushu. He has 2000 Satsuma soldiers standing by to aid us. You are a most welcome addition to our gathering."

"Thank you, lord, the Satsuma stands ready to aid you in your quest," Yamada said.

"When my brother marches you will reinforce us will you not?" Tadanaga asked.

"Most assuredly lord," Yamada said. "They are preparing now."

"Good, I am counting on you. The Satsuma will no longer be the poor cousins from the south when I am shogun," Tadanaga pledged.

"We are counting on that lord," Yamada said.

"Next to Yamada san is an old neighbor of mine. Murata Shingen is the leader of Kukuchinama castle here in Kyoto. If there is a need, we have castle walls to fight from. Thank you for your support Murata san," Tadanaga said.

Murata raised his sake cup to Tadanaga and drank.

"Next to Murata san is a newer member. She is called The Mist. She represents the Koga ninja clan that has thrown its support behind me in my bid for shogun," Tadanaga said. "She and her clan will provide badly needed intelligence and provide us with a stealthy direct-action element. Welcome Mist."

"It is my pleasure to be here Lord Tadanaga," The Mist said.

"We have another new member," Tadanaga said pointing to the next samurai in the semi-circle. He was no longer a young man. He wore the shaved pate and chomagae hair style of Edo. His clothing was silk, but his facial expression was a constant scowl. His aloof and distant attitude put off most.

"This is Itosai Ito. He is joining us as our strategist and fencing master. He is the master of Ito Ryu one strike school," Tadanaga said.

Everyone but the Abbot and the woman applauded.

"What brings you to our gathering?" Abbot Insin asked.

Ito knew a carefully baited trap when he heard it. He had been tutored well.

"Unlike you Abbot, I care little for the monetary gains participation will bring if Lord Tadanaga becomes shogun. My only desire is to advance my school and replace the Shinkage-ryu style with Itosai-ryu. The Yagyū have dominated the Tokugawa for too long. However, I will admit that being able to influence history is an opportunity not afforded many. I just have to determine if we have the right talent organized for the job," Ito said.

"Who do you suspect among us is not up to the task?" the Abbot asked.

"Several of you," Ito said. "Your promises of support sound hollow to me."

Everyone except The Mist moved uncomfortably.

"You are a thoroughly distasteful and disrespectful ruffian," Abbot Inshin said.

"Maybe so, but if Tadanaga-sama is to be shogun we must all be as ruthless as it takes to make good on our promises," Ito said.

"What are you talking about? Who has not lived up to their promises?" Yamada asked.

"You are the most blatant," Ito said.

Yamada's right hand grasped the katana at his side.

"That would be a grave error," Ito said. "I can draw and sever your head before your blade is drawn."

"Maybe you can and maybe you are all talk," Yamada said.

"I can back up my talk," Ito said. "I would not have been chosen as the man to bring down the great hereditary sword instructors to the Tokugawa. I can defeat the Yagyū."

Yamada let the sword return to the floor. But he was unable to let the comment go unchallenged.

"How have I not kept a promise," Yamada asked

"You pledged your troops would march when Iemitsu does," Ito said.

"So what?" Yamada demanded.

"So, if Iemitsu commences his march from Edo, how long will it take him to arrive in Kyoto?" Ito asked.

"With all his trappings it would take Iemitsu approximately fifteen days to arrive in Kyoto," Yamada said.

"And how long will it take your promised samurai to get here from southern Honshu and Kyushu?" Ito asked.

Yamada frowned. "Our troops would be here sooner if we have them staged closer."

"Yes, they would arrive if staged closer, but you do not have them staged closer. In fact, my information tells me there are no preparations being made to move anyone. So, your promise to Lord Tadanaga is a hollow one," Ito accused. "Your daimyo doesn't want to stage them closer because that would be an act of rebellion against Iemitsu and it costs money to move and quarter samurai. Your clan would rather take a wait and see attitude. If Lord Tadanaga is successful, then you'll move the troops north and attempt to curry favor after the fighting saving face and gold."

Yamada jumped to his feet sword in hand. "By the Buddha, I will not sit here and be ridiculed by a third-rate fencing instructor."

"Sit down Yamada," Lord Tadanaga said. "This is why Ito sensei is my chief strategist." Yamada sat back down. "I will expect a detailed plan from you and your clan to move troops in my support to Kyoto no later than two days from now. If I don't receive it, I will assume Ito san is correct and you have been lying to me. Do you understand?"

Yamada's head hung down. "Yes, Lord Tadanaga."

"Good. Ito who else has not lived up to their promises?" Tadanaga asked.

Ito turned his attention to The Mist.

"How did your talk with the young Yoshinobu go?" Ito asked.

The Mist smiled at Ito. It seemed to infuriate him more.

"I believe they will support Iemitsu," The Mist said.

"What?" Lady Oyeo gasped. "You failed?"

"I do not believe I did Lady Oyeo. There was no way to intimidate that man. He is the Tengu Killer," The Mist said.

"I don't believe that tall tale!" Ito scoffed.

"I always liked the Yoshinobu," Lady Oyeo said. "Their simple lifestyle and adherence to bushido inspires many. What was your impression of him?"

"You were correct Lady. He is young. But his skills are old," The Mist said.

"What does that mean?" Yamada asked, glad to have someone else being scrutinized.

"It means as soon as I dropped into his room, he was wide awake from a deep sleep with two swords in his hands," The Mist said.

"How do you know he was fast asleep?" Ito asked.

"Because I listened to his breathing before I entered," The Mist said.

"Maybe you made noises moving into his quarters," Ito said.

"You may know swords, but you do not know ninja. I do not make sounds when I move. It is why I am called The Mist," The Mist said.

"Any other impressions dear," Lady Oyeo asked.

"I rather liked him," The Mist said.

"There, you admit you did not kill him because you liked our enemy," Ito accused.

The Mist turned from Lady Oyeo to Ito. "I did not kill him because I do not think it could be done. Even after our conversation and he turned and went to his futon I would have had to cross the room and attack him. That would have meant death for me," The Mist said.

"You are a coward," Ito said.

"I have said you do not know ninja. Now I believe you do not know men," The Mist said.

"What do you mean you low life wench? If I had been

there, I would have killed him with one draw and slash," Ito said.

"I may be of low birth sir, but I have killed more men than you. I have only witnessed one other who gives off the aura of death as Yoshinobu Hideki and that is the one-eyed demon he travels with," The Mist said.

"That would be my old sword master Yagyū Jubei. You are right to fear him," Tadanaga said.

"I do not fear either of them lord. But I know unless I pick my circumstances very carefully, I could not survive an encounter with them," The Mist said. Then she turned to Ito. "And by the way, chief strategist Ito, if you face either of them you will certainly die."

"You are a fool. My sword style is the superior in all the land," Ito said.

"I do not know anything of you or your sword style," The Mist said. "But I know killers when I meet them. You are more a clown than a killer. You are not of their capability."

"Not only do you have no judgement, you are a coward afraid to engage if the slightest chance exists of you being hurt," Ito said.

"You listen but you do not hear," The Mist said. "He is a very hard man to kill."

"You are too shy. You did not complete your promise," Ito shouted. "It is unacceptable."

"My promise to Lady Oyeo was to meet with Hideki and convince him to come to Lord Tadanaga's side. I attempted to do so. I threatened him and his entire family. It meant nothing. He is a warrior. He does not respond to threats," The Mist said.

"But you failed to kill him," Ito bellowed.

"I never promised I would," The Mist said with a smile. "Lady Oyeo gave me the mission and it was carried out. No promise was broken."

"Do not smile at me bitch. Because of your inability I will now have to slay the traitor for you," Ito said.

"Good luck fencing master," The Mist said. "I look forward to seeing your blood in the street. You are not the one to best the Tengu Killer."

Ito reached for his sake cup and downed it in one gulp.

Lady Oyeo flinched at the bad manners.

Ito slammed the cup down on the hard wood floor and started to reach for his sword when he fell forward and started to shake and convulse.

"Has someone poisoned us?" Lady Oyeo shrieked.

A loud voice came from all over the temple yet emanated from no definite location. "Do not fear Lord Tadanaga. You are safe. I could not tolerate his arrogant ignorance any longer," the voice said.

"Is he dead?" Lord Tadanaga asked.

"He is not dead yet," the voice said. "But he will die if not given the antidote."

"He looks like he is in great pain," Lady Oyeo said.

"He is in great pain. I want him to reflect on his arrogance and on accusing my representative of promise breaking," the voice said.

"Oh," Lord Tadanaga said. "It is you Ugai, master of the Koga ninja."

"Yes, lord," the voice said. "It is I."

"It might be a good time to administer the antidote," Tadanaga said.

"Yes lord, I would prefer he die, and you find a real strategist, but I live to obey. Mist give the scum the antidote," the voice said.

The Mist nodded compliance, moved to the convulsing man and applied a drop of liquid from a glass vial she produced from her sleeve onto his lips.

Ito quit convulsing at once and lay still.

"Do not worry Lord Tadanaga. Your new strategist will live to boast falsely another day. But his consciousness has remained with him. This poison contracts and releases the muscles but you never really lose consciousness. I prefer this type when I have a childish person to correct," Ugai said.

The fencing master started to stir. He attempted to talk but made little sense.

"I cannot understand him Mist," Lady Oyeo complained.

"No Lady Oyeo, but he really didn't make much sense earlier either," The Mist said.

Lady Oyeo smiled at the comment.

"What is the purpose of this demonstration?" Tadanaga asked.

"The demonstration was to correct Ito's stupidity and to bring home the fact that we must get ruthless if you are to defeat your brother," Ugai said.

"Yes, civil wars are messy," Lord Tadanaga said.

"You were right to send The Mist to the Yoshinobu. They will indeed be an impediment to your plans. They are dangerous to us. Hideki is indeed the threat. If The Mist says he is dangerous, believe her," Ugai said.

"Do you have a plan to neutralize them?" Lord Tadanaga asked.

"I am working on one now lord. I have been told it will cut the heart out of the Yoshinobu. Do not be squeamish when you hear its execution," Ugai said.

"I will not be squeamish," Lord Tadanaga said. "But who told you this?"

"Someone you know well lord," Ugai said.

"Someone I know well? That is intriguing," Lord Tadanaga said. "Will you join us Ugai?"

"No lord, I will not join you. We work in the shadows and we die in the shadows. If you need to contact me do it through The Mist. She is an exception to our rule. We find it is useful to have a face to associate with our clan," Ugai said.

"Thank you," Lady Oyeo said. But Ugai did not reply.

XII

Missing Heir

The Yoshinobu, Jubei and Yoshi sat on their shins for a hastily called audience with Iemitsu.

"We have called you here because we have a tasking for the upcoming movement to Kyoto," O'Fuku said.

"We stand ready to comply," Jii said.

"What about you Hideki?" O'Fuku asked.

Hideki did not reply.

"Are you deaf? I know you are not dumb because I heard you during our last meeting," O'Fuku said.

"He is not responding because your question has already been answered," Iemitsu said.

"What does that mean?" O'Fuku asked.

"The elder Yoshinobu said they stand ready. He speaks for the family. Is that not so Hideki?" Iemitsu asked.

"You are correct Lord Iemitsu. Jii speaks for all," Hideki said.

Iemitsu smiled. "It is the samurai way," he said.

O'Fuku took control again as if no interruption had occurred.

"The Yoshinobu will form the advance party for my son's movement to Kyoto. You will scout out the route, planning with inn keepers and teamsters along the way and the persons in charge of the villages. You are responsible for our advance security as well." O'Fuku said. "What are your questions?"

"The route has not been chosen?" Jii asked.

"It has not," O'Fuku said.

Jii rubbed his grey head. "Do we know when we must arrive in Kyoto?"

"The Cloistered Court deems November 1st as an auspicious day for the investiture ceremony," O'Fuku said.

"That leaves us less than a month to travel the route, schedule sites and determine security," Jii said.

"Is this tasking above your capability?" O'Fuku asked.

"It may be, O'Fuku. How many will be in Iemitsu's procession?" Jii asked.

"We are planning on 300,000." O'Fuku said.

"That is ridiculous," Hideki said.

"You dare call Iemitsu ridiculous?" O'Fuku asked.

"I call whoever planned such a number ridiculous," Hideki said.

O'Fuku turned to Iemitsu. "You see Uesama? This is the type of insolence I expect from the Yoshinobu. Dismiss this rabble and destroy their house."

Everyone was starring directly at Iemitsu.

"Maybe we ought to hear their fears before we start burning houses O'Fuku," Iemitsu said. Then, turning his attention to Hideki, "What are they?"

Hideki looked at Jii.

"It is a little late to be looking at me for permission. You have already embarrassed me with your quick tongue. Answer your lord and please do it with intelligence," Jii said.

"Three hundred thousand is a wartime movement of troops. There are no facilities on the Tokaido to handle that many people much less feed them and their horses. You would have to call together your war council to arrange for transportation, shelter, water, grain and all manner of supplies. Such an undertaking would take 100 men 100 days, not thirty," Hideki said.

Iemitsu looked directly at Hideki.

"I know," Iemitsu said

That simplistic explanation did not satisfy Hideki. He was hoping for a few more details.

"If you know then why are you asking us to accomplish this undertaking in less than a month's time?" Hideki asked.

"I am starting a new administration," Iemitsu said.

"So, you are going to disrupt everyone's life and go on a war footing?" Hideki asked.

"Yes," Iemitsu said.

"Why?" Hideki asked.

Iemitsu smiled. "You see O'Fuku, this is what I miss, someone with the courage to ask questions."

"Sounds like insubordination to me," O'Fuku said.

"At a different time, you may be correct. But now I find it refreshing," Iemitsu said.

Iemitsu turned to address Jii. "Old man, as the head of your clan, what do you think I will find on the Tokaido and in Kyoto?"

Jii thought a moment. "I believe you are likely to find all the forces your younger brother can muster to include the trouble makers from the south lying in wait," Jii said.

"Ah yes, the Satsuma. They do pop up when not wanted," Iemitsu said. "Continuing to use your military expertise old man, if I am likely to meet such resistance but have to make the trip if I want to be shogun, what would you advise?" Iemitsu asked.

Jii did not hesitate. "I would advise an overwhelming show of force on a war footing Lord Iemitsu."

Iemitsu turned back to Hideki. "Does that answer your question Hideki?"

Hideki bowed low. "Yes Uesama, I should not have questioned you."

"On the contrary, I need those around me to question my decisions, but never my authority. Is that clear?" Iemitsu asked.

All the Yoshinobu bowed low. Jii answered for all. "Hai, wakarimasu, Uesama."

A messenger entered from the rear of the room, knelt, bowed. "Reporting," he said.

"Closer," O'Fuku motioned.

The messenger bowed low again, stood, and moved up onto the raised tatami and whispered in O'Fuku's ear.

O'Fuku looked surprised and then smiled and motioned the messenger to move further up the tatami to relay the message to Iemitsu. Iemitsu waved the messenger out of the room then turned to Jii. "There has been a fire at your Edo mansion. There are reports of fatalities and injuries. Go to your family."

All stood, bowed and backed out of the great room. In the changing room they shed the restrictive naga bakama with its extra-long pant legs for the traditional samurai garb of a kamishino consisting of upper haori and lower hakama over the kimono. No one spoke. Once changed they raced to the closest canal and boarded a shallow pole powered barge.

"The Yoshinobu mansion and hurry," Jii said.

Naga tossed the pole man a gold coin. The man caught the coin, nodded his head and began pushing off into the canal. A quarter of an hour later they had disembarked and raced to the mansion.

They were met with an organized pandemonium. A great deal of smoke hung over one of the wings of the mansion. No flames were visible. When Jii, Naga, Jubei, Hideki and Yoshi dashed into the compound samurai retainers were collecting empty wooden buckets to be returned to storage. Samurai with soot stained faces were being provided water by several women. Some were receiving ointment and bandages.

"Is anyone hurt badly?" Jii asked.

Yuki stopped her directing of the Yoshinobu resources and turned to answer Jii. "We have minor burns, smoke inhalation and one fire fighter fell off a ladder," Yuki said. "It is all I know about so far. The fire seems to be extinguished."

"Where is Yoshitsune?" Naga demanded.

Yuki smiled thru the sweat streaked soot on her face. "He is safe. As soon as the alarm was given, Hanaa and I got him out of the building. She took him to the retainer's quarters on the far side of the compound. I prepared to put the fire out," Yuki said wiping her face with her tied back kimono sleeve.

"Fine job Yuki," Jii said. "This could have been much worse without your fast thinking."

"I don't see Hanaa," Naga interrupted. "Where is our son?"

Jii turned to his eldest grandson. "Go find him Naga. I am

sure both he and Hanaa are fine. Hanaa was Yuki's wet nurse. She loves that child."

Naga took off at a trot toward the retainer's quarters.

Jii smiled at Yuki. "He does not mean to be short with you. He is just worried about your son."

"I know Jii. I would not leave Yoshitsune with anyone but Hanaa. I have known her all my life," Yuki said.

"The brigade captain said it started in the kitchen roof," Yuki said. "But I do not see how that is possible."

Hideki looked around. "Where is Yoshi?"

"He was with us a moment ago," Jii said.

"Myo has doubled the security on the compound since the visit from The Mist. Yoshi is probably off collecting information for us. He will have a report soon," Hideki said.

"Good thinking, Hideki," Jii said. "Let me know if you learn anything.

"Of course, Jii," Hideki said, then turned to Jubei. "What do you think?"

"I think what you are thinking. There was a fire where none should start. It happened while we were away. Something doesn't smell right," Jubei said.

Hideki turned to talk to Yuki and found Yoshi standing behind him. "By the Buddha Yoshi you scare me to death with that trick."

"No trick prince. Myo's ninja perimeter security is missing. I do not like it. The fire is beginning to look like a diversion. But what could the Koga be after?" Yoshi asked.

Yuki heard the conversation. Both she and Hideki answered together, "Yoshitsune," they exclaimed and took off running toward the retainer's quarters.

They found Naga bent over the body of Hanaa.

"Hanaa's dead. Yoshitsune has been taken," Naga screamed at Yuki. "Was the fire more important than our son?"

"Change your tone of voice," Hideki urged Naga. "She is in shock too."

"When did I ever need advice from you," Naga snapped.

"Since you became a frightened parent," Yoshi answered for Hideki.

Yuki staggered at her husband's public tongue lashing. Jubei caught her.

"Take her back to the mansion," Hideki said.

Jubei nodded and guided the crying mother back toward the main building.

"Naga, you have to pull yourself together. Yuki is going to need your strength," Hideki said.

Myo appeared out of the smoke.

"Yoshitsune has been stolen," Hideki said.

"It is as I feared," Myo said. "Three of my ninjas are dead on the perimeter.

"Anyone else missing that you know of?" Hideki asked.

Myo turned to Yoshi. "The only ones I am sure of are Chiyo and Matsu," Myo said.

"Are you talking about Yoshi's wife and mother-in-law?" Hideki asked.

A young boy Hideki had never seen ran up to Yoshi and whispered in his ear and departed. "It seems several of my pigeons are missing," Yoshi said. "But we cannot tell if they were stolen or released due to the fire."

Naga stood and wiped his eyes. "Who did this Yoshi?"

"It is a little early to speculate, but my guess would be that the Koga ninja stole your baby," Yoshi said. "This was a very sophisticated diversion. My guess is they are making good on the threats Hideki received from The Mist."

"That would be my guess as well," Myo said. "I was checking the perimeter when I found my first ninja dead. Before I found the second the fire broke out. They were watching Yuki's every move and reacted accordingly."

"They learned of the Yoshinobu support for Iemitsu and stole the heir," Yoshi ventured.

"Why steal the child? The Yoshinobu have already decided to support Iemitsu," Myo said. "Do they want a ransom?"

"It is possible," Naga said. "I deal with these types of cases all the time as magistrate."

"I do not think so," Hideki said.

"What do you mean?" Naga asked his brother.

"As Yoshi stated, they knew of our support for Iemitsu.

So, we are now the enemy," Hideki said.

"What does that mean?" Naga asked.

"It means they are punishing us. We will not be contacted by the Koga with a ransom demand. This is designed to get into our heads and demoralize us. It is classic Sun Tzu," Hideki said.

"What do we do Hideki? I have got to get my son back," Naga pleaded.

"I know brother. I will do everything I can to get him back. Myo will throw a cordon around for two ri in each direction. Check everything that could harbor a child," Hideki said.

"That would take twice as many men as I have," Myo said.

"That is why Naga you must get every police officer in Edo to officially establish this man hunt and assist with the cordon and offer a two hundred gold coin reward for the safe return of Yoshitsune," Hideki said.

"I hope the gods are with us," Naga said as he wandered off with his head down.

"I think we may have something better?" Hideki said.

"What would that be?" Yoshi asked. Myo turned to hear the reply.

"I think we have two ninja women with birds," Hideki said.

"Chiyo and Matsu?" Yoshi asked.

Yes. I think they saw through the diversion and took action," Hideki said.

"You have much faith in my relatives," Yoshi said.

"I do Yoshi. Because if I am wrong, we will never see my nephew again," Hideki said.

As Yoshi, Hideki and Myo returned to the mansion they heard a loud wail. They turned in time to see a woman collapse on the ground.

"That will be Naga delivering my sobering news to Yuki. I should learn to be more diplomatic," Hideki said.

"Your diplomacy comes at the end of a sword," Yoshi said.

"Yes, but she is my sister-in-law and I should have toned down my speculation to Naga," Hideki said.

"There is very little you can do to comfort a childless mother," Yoshi said.

"We could find her son," Hideki said.

"What is next?" Yoshi asked.

"Next we gather the key players in the Yoshinobu clan and Jubei. We need to figure out how we return my nephew to his mother and accomplish Iemitsu's bidding," Hideki said.

"What if it was O'Fuku who took the child?" Yoshi asked.

Hideki turned to Yoshi and smiled.

"Old friend you are a valued member of our family. Jubei calls you Monkey and Jii tried to skewer you with a wakazashi the first time he met you. But you have saved my life more times than I can count. But your true value to us is your ability to think where others don't," Hideki said. "If O'Fuku stole Yoshitsune it will be a good day for Tadanaga because I will kill Iemitsu and O'Fuku."

Yoshi didn't doubt him for a moment.

XIII

Council of War

When the Yoshinobu clan gathered in the great Hall it still smelled of smoke. Jii sat at the position of authority on the raised portion of the tatami. His immediate family sat just below him. Yuki sat across from her husband. Hideki noticed her red eyes. She had been crying again. Two days and still there were no leads on her missing child.

Hideki surveyed the room. The abduction of Yoshitsune cast a pall on the gathering. Sitting in the first row were Yoshi, Jubei, Myo and Midori. Next to them were faces he had not seen in over a year. Nichi led the police force under his brother's direction. He had been friends to the Yoshinobu from the beginning of their stay in Edo. Next to him was the leader of the Gumsumgumi Gang. Goro had never been friendly, but he still cast adoring eyes at Myo. Myo smiled back politely.

With Yoshitsune gone Yoshi had invited anyone that might be able to get the child back. With Jii's offering a two hundred gold coin return for the safe return of the child had he been taken by bandits the Yoshinobu would have heard something by now.

"Thank you all for coming." Jii said to the assemblage. "We are faced with a twofold dilemma. First is the tasking by the soon to be shogun to provide security and advance party efforts for his investiture ceremony in Kyoto. The ceremony takes place on the first day of November. His entourage will consist of 300,000. It is a tremendous task with little time to complete."

His words were met by a low murmur from the seated

retainers. One of the senior samurais spoke up. "Yoshinobu-sama, we are just eighty men. How can they expect us to do such a great task with so little time?"

Jii answered as if in a fog. "I am not so sure he wants us to succeed."

Hideki noticed the despair in his voice. He looked to Naga. No help there, he was staring vacantly at his wife Yuki. Yuki was fighting back tears. Hideki looked at Yoshi and glanced down at Myo and Jubei. Yoshi pointed to Hideki. Hideki stood up.

"Enough of this," he shouted.

All heads came up.

"The Yoshinobu are at a crossroads, we will either survive or we won't. We have been given a near impossible task to solve and the precious heir to the family has been taken," Hideki said. Then Hideki looked directly at Yuki. "All our hearts are breaking because some foul fiend has attempted to sway us from our duty by killing Myo's ninja and stealing your baby."

Yuki searched for hope in Hideki's eyes.

"I suggest we focus on both problems simultaneously," Hideki said.

"How is that possible?" Jii asked.

Hideki turned to his grandfather. "We have two jobs, but one priority. Our priority is to return Yoshitsune to Yuki and Naga safely."

A swell of approval swept through the room.

"Our secondary mission is one assigned us from Iemitsu. It consists of scouting the route for his investiture and assembling of the logistics and security needed to keep them safe," Hideki said.

"Jii, I think you should take personal charge of the secondary mission and use all of our retainers. Get a messenger to Kii Province and get all our home-based samurai marching now to join you in Kyoto."

The murmuring started again.

"Everyone in the Yoshinobu clan must be clear on our number one priority. If you are assigned to the Kyoto route your priority is to keep your eyes and ears open for a clue as to

Yoshitsune's whereabouts," Hideki said.

"Yes," Yuki said, hope on her face for the first time.

"What will I do?" Naga asked.

"You are the south magistrate of Edo. You must continue your post. We may need you to intercede on our behalf later. You and Yuki must remain here in case Yoshitsune is returned. You will have no retainers as Jii will have all able-bodied samurai. I suggest you get Nichi to post policemen inside and outside our mansion," Hideki said.

"What will you do?" Yuki asked.

"I and my friends will remain in Edo unless our search takes us towards Kyoto," Hideki said.

"What will you do here?" Jii asked.

"With the help of Myo and her five families, Yoshi, Jubei, Nichi and Goro, we will turn a city upside down to find Yoshitsune," Hideki said.

"I should be involved in that," Naga said.

"No, this is not the kind of job for you," Hideki said.

"I suppose it is a kind a job for you?" Naga asked with a sneer on his face.

"Brother, I know you to be good at what you do. I admire you for it. But what we must do will be outside the law. You cannot be involved," Hideki said. Then Hideki looked at his friends on the first row. "My friends and I have done this sort of thing before. This is what we do. And we are good at it."

"Poor Hideki," Yuki said. "What happened to the sweet innocent carefree boy of a few years ago?"

"You do not need him for this," Hideki said.

Yuki nodded her thanks and moved to sit beside her husband. "Can I not be of help to you?" Yuki asked as she sat down.

"You may be of assistance later. But right now, you are needed here," Hideki said. "Nichi, can you post six men here at the mansion?"

"I certainly can," Nichi said. "What is their function?"

"They will live here. They are the new bodyguards to protect my brother and his wife," Hideki said.

Nichi looked at Naga and then over to his wife. Then he

moved his gaze back to Hideki. "You are free to do your work without worry about them. The Yoshinobu Edo mansion will be as safe as my hotel in town," Nichi said.

"Thank you Nichi," Hideki said. "Goro?"

Goro's head came up.

"Can the Gumsumgumi turn over every rock in Edo and find us a lead that might help recover Yoshitsune?" Hideki asked.

Goro frowned at Hideki. "I have never liked you. But no one should steal babies. We will do as you ask," Goro said.

"Thank you Goro," Yuki said.

Goro blushed. "You are very welcome Lady Yoshinobu."

Hideki raised his voice again to get everyone's attention. "Jii-sama we must make use of every second. I suggest you stay with your retainers here in the great hall. Start your planning immediately. You must be able to start your march as soon as Iemitsu gives you the route."

Jii's attitude changed immediately. "Very good idea Hideki," Jii said.

"Everyone in the front row please follow me to the next room, you are all part of the family," Hideki said.

Goro pointed to his own nose. "Even me?"

"Of course, you, Goro," Yuki said. "You may be key to getting my child back."

Goro beamed as he made way for Yuki and Naga to follow Hideki's entourage.

Jii picked up his elbow rest and moved into the center of his samurai. Everyone made way. Rolled up maps were brought out. Serious planning began.

In the next room Hideki and friends formed a sitting circle.

"Please close the door Goro. The noise next door will intensify," Hideki said.

Once Goro sat and completed the circle Hideki looked at Jubei. "Jubei can we count on your sword to help us with this? I know your father is very busy."

Jubei looked at his ex-fiancé Yuki. "My sword is yours."

Yuki bowed her head in Jubei's direction. When her head came up, she said, "Domo Arigato."

Jubei returned the bow from his seated position.

Hideki looked at Yoshi, Myo and Midori. "Do you have any suggestions?"

"We think Yoshitsune is still in Edo," Yoshi said.

Yuki and Naga leaned in closer.

Yoshi addressed Yuki. "Myo's five families with the help of Nichi's police threw up a cordon around the entire neighborhood immediately after the abduction. Myo was moving as soon as we discovered the dead nanny. They have not seen any babies matching Yoshitsune's age and sex and they inspect everything."

"Are you sure Yoshi?" Yuki asked.

"You can never be sure about such things," Yoshi said. "But we have to assume ninja executed the abduction."

"Why?" Hideki asked.

"Ask Yuki, she and Jubei have both trained with the Iga ninja," Yoshi said.

Hideki looked to Yuki.

"He is right. First, they took out my eyes and ears with the killing of Myo's ninja. Then they set the fire to draw my attention away so they could set up the abduction. They knew I would send Yoshitsune as far away from danger as I could and still be on the compound. It was classic ninja misdirection," Yuki said.

"Now the question is which ninja clan did this?" Yoshi said.

"We know the Koga are attempting to sway our loyalty to Iemitsu. If you remember I was visited by The Mist two nights ago," Hideki said. "Who else could it be?"

"With a Satsuma supporting Tadanaga it could be the Fuma, a ninja clan from the south," Myo said. "But my spies on the southern island have seen no unusual activity."

"You have spies in Kyushu?" Naga asked.

"Quiet Naga, Myo has operatives all over the country," Yuki said.

"I do not believe any other ninja clans are active in Edo," Myo continued. "My money would be on the Koga clan. Their future depends on Tadanaga being successful."

"Do we know how to find The Mist?" Jubei asked.

"Excellent question Jubei," Hideki said.

"We can find her," Midori said.

Hideki looked to Myo. "Please find her as soon as possible. Then Jubei and I will call upon her."

Myo turned to Midori. "Arrange it," Myo said.

"Thank you Myo," Yuki said.

Myo bowed to Yuki. "Our only client is the Yoshinobu. To have the heir stolen is unforgivable. We will find your child and try to regain our honor."

"We all will," Hideki said.

"I have a question," Midori said.

"Please, ask away," Hideki said.

"I have not seen Yoshi's wife and mother-in-law since the incident happened. Where are they?" Midori asked.

"Very observant of you Midori," Yoshi said. "I do not know but since they disappeared at the time of the incident along with several birds, I am inclined to believe they were either captured by the perpetrators or …"

"Or what?" Yuki asked.

"Or they are already on the trail of the devils," Yoshi finished.

"Is that a possibility?" Yuki asked hopefully.

"Too early to tell Yuki, but those are my assumptions," Yoshi said.

"That is why you are the chief strategist for our clan Yoshi. Let us hope we hear from them soon. We cannot rely on this hope alone. We must find The Mist without delay," Hideki said.

"Who coordinates information we find?" Yuki asked.

"You will," Hideki said. "I will send a messenger to you each evening or immediately if we know something helpful."

"Good," Yuki said. "Then I'll know everything. And it will give me something to do. I will get Jii to give me maps of Edo and plot all the information on them."

"Nichi please place your guards on duty around and in the mansion as soon as possible and get the word to your policeman that we're looking for Yoshitsune. If your police find him the reward is theirs," Hideki said.

Nichi bowed to Hideki. "It will be done and this time the men will be glad to know they get to accept any reward," Nichi said looking to his boss Naga. Naga nodded his head affirming Hideki's statement.

Hideki turned to Myo. "Your ninja's efforts in this are paramount. If you must hurt people do it. I want my nephew back."

Yuki addressed everyone. "Mina san, domo arigato. You give me hope."

"As Yuki said, thank you all. Let's dismiss and find my nephew," Hideki said.

XIV

Pillow Talk

"Are you asleep?" Naga asked the darkness.

"No," Yuki answered from her side of the futon.

"I raised my voice to you and said some stupid things the day of the fire. I apologize. You did not deserve any of it. I was just so frightened," Naga said.

"You did not say anything that I had not said to myself," Yuki said. "I was a fool to not see the deception."

"Do not chastise yourself Yuki. Professionals took our son," Naga said.

"Yes, but I was once a professional too," Yuki said. "I should have sensed it."

"What? You mean like Yoshi and his haragai? I thought you told me that was a lost art. How could you be expected to sense this base a treachery?" Naga asked.

"I am Yoshitsune's mother, I should have felt something was wrong," she said, close to tears.

"I grew up without a mother," Naga said. "I have seen you with our son. No one could love him more. Now I truly know what a mother's love means. You cannot go on blaming yourself."

Now Yuki was crying and trying to speak at the same time. "But I do. I do not know if he's warm enough, or if he's been fed, or even if he's alive," she stammered through the tears.

Naga reached over and pulled his wife to him. She cried on his chest for a few more minutes and stopped.

"We have to put our trust in Yoshi, Myo, Jubei and that thug Goro. What a weird concoction," Naga said.

"If it was just them, I would really worry," Yuki said.

"What do you mean?"

"I mean Hideki is their leader," Yuki said. "They cannot function without him."

"Really, my little brother is a leader?" Naga asked.

"You did not see it tonight when he took the reins of a dejected Yoshinobu clan and gave us hope by the sheer force of his will?" Yuki asked.

"Yes, I was surprised by him. He really shocked me," Naga said. "He has always come through when needed. He is quite reliable."

"It is not just his character. There is something else about him that is different," Yuki said.

"What? He seems like my little brother of old," Naga said.

Yuki rose to her elbows and thumped on Naga's chest.

"Do not make that mistake my husband. Do you remember when I first met you?" she asked.

"Of course, I remember. We were in Kii Province and you came riding in with Yagyū Munenori and your entourage of Iga ninja," Naga said.

"Do you remember what I said when Yagyū Munenori asked me to look around the room to see if there were any samurai that I could not defeat with a sword?" Yuki asked.

"Yes, you stopped on Musashi and said he was formidable," Naga said.

"Why do you think I picked out Musashi? I had never seen him before," Yuki asked.

"I have no idea," Naga said.

"I could sense that he was dangerous. He carried the aura of death," Yuki said.

"Are you sure?" Naga asked.

"I have only felt it around three men," Yuki said.

"Jubei?" Naga guessed.

"That is correct. Jubei and my father Hittori Honzo both give off that smell of death," Yuki said.

"That is understandable," Naga said. "They have both killed many men."

"Yes, they have," Yuki agreed.

"Are you seriously telling me that my little brother is in-cluded in that group?" Naga asked.

"That is what I am telling you. Sweet innocent Hideki has become a killer of men," Yuki said.

"So that is what Jubei meant when I asked him about Hideki's sword skills. I was concerned because he is now left-handed," Naga said.

"What did Jubei say?" Yuki asked.

"He said Hideki was formidable and would surpass him in a few years. He said Hideki had a secret weapon, something called mushin," Naga said.

"Mushin? Are you certain, husband?" Yuki asked sitting up.

"Yes, very certain because Jubei sounded envious," Naga said.

"Then our little Hideki is not a good swordsman he is a great swordsman," Yuki said.

"That little left-handed clumsy fool, I used to beat him all the time in our family dojo." Naga said.

"Please do not try it now. I need my husband and Yoshit-sune needs a father," she said.

"You think he is that good?" Naga asked.

"I would say he is one in 10,000. Did you not see how he took over the meeting tonight? That kind of confidence comes from being secure in your capabilities," Yuki said.

"So how do you feel about Hideki now? You know he fell in love with you first. I'm a little jealous hearing you sing his praises," Naga said.

"He was just a young farm boy with a crush on the first female he was around," Yuki said. "I made the right choice."

"Good," Naga said. "I was beginning of think I was losing you to him."

"Do not pout, my husband. You are my only love. But I'm glad that Hideki is searching for our son. He and his friends are just as dangerous as the people who stole Yoshitsune. I feel positive about our child for the first time in two days," Yuki said.

"I agree, my love. Now that you mention it, I know Hideki

instills confidence in others. If anyone can find our son it will be my little brother and his nefarious cronies."

"And I will sleep for the first time since this nightmare began," Yuki said.

They both did.

XV

Thug Rei

Rei had received his white headband and white haori coat marking him one of the Ronin Army. He received a half a day's orientation by Mondo. The structure of the army was explained, and its mission discussed. Rei found the explanation a little vague. But he was smart enough to know to ask no questions. From what he had seen of the army thus far it was made up of some very rough men. His youthful appearance and lack of a katana made him a target of several bullying attempts. He decided to ignore them. That didn't work.

The last class of the morning consisted of each man getting his wages calculated and if anyone wanted a portion subtracted to be sent to another location the arrangements were made via a local courier service with national connections. Rei was thankful. His father and sister would get most of his pay. He could breathe easier now.

The noon meal was simple fare consisting of rice, sweet potato and radish. Rei did not complain. He'd eaten breakfast that day and now had a noon meal. That was two more meals than he was used to eating, plus he still had expectations of receiving a supper portion as well. Being able to send money home as well as a full belly bode well for this new job.

The last half of the day consisted of training. Mondo had Abe assemble the new men in the center of the training yard. Watanabe dropped an arm load of bokken at the head of the yard.

"You all have been introduced verbally," Mondo said.

"However, you do not know each other's skills. Today we will alleviate that problem. You cannot function as an army if you do not know the capability of your fellow soldiers."

Mondo nodded to Abe.

"There is one wakazashi in this pile. Rei, come up and take it."

Rei looked a little surprised but complied.

"There have been several of you that Mondo has noticed picking on our youngest member because he fights with only a wakazashi. Now is the time to step up and demonstrate your katana prowess against Rei's wakazashi. Who is first?" Abe asked.

Several ronin stepped up and selected a katana sized bokken. Smelling a beating in the offering a circle was soon formed of interested onlookers looking to win bets.

"Let's do this one at a time," Abe said. "Those that want to challenge the kid, form a line behind me."

The first ronin stepped to the center of the circle and extended his bokken toward Rei. Rei moved to the center and extended his wakazashi as well. They were interrupted by Watanabe.

"I'm giving three to one odds on Rei. Place your bets here," he said.

"That's crazy," many murmured. "That boy cannot stand up against a man with just that short sword. I'll take that bet."

Watanabe glanced to Mondo. Mondo nodded indicating that all bets should be covered. And they were.

"Too bad pretty boy. You won't be so pretty after this," were just some of the cat calls.

The older and more muscular opponent advanced on Rei. Rei had his wooden wakazashi in his right hand. His arm was extended with the point aimed at the man's nose. The man shuffled forward, dropping the bokken behind his head and let out a loud kiai. Rei did not flinch. The man moved back. Then he dropped his sword point toward Rei and lunged at Rei's head. Again, Rei did not flinch. Finally, the taunts from the crowd got to the man and he raised his bokken over his head and rushed at Rei. Rei didn't move until the last possible moment. Just as the hardwood sword was about to crush Rei's head, he shuffled slightly into the attack, raising his wakazashi to take the blow on its cutting edge. Rei's resistance was just enough to keep the attacker's momentum going and miss Rei altogether. Rei's angled shuffle brought him on the outside of the attacking arm. His blade left the attacking sword and traveled to the man's eyes. Rei's wakazashi struck the man solidly between the eyes. The forward momentum of the man's attack and Rei's strike brought the man's head up with a loud thwack. The man fell over backwards unconscious. Rei retreated several steps with is sword still pointed at the man. He then placed the wooden wakazashi behind him and bowed.

A hush fell over the gathered spectators.

Two men designated by Watanabe removed the injured man to the barracks.

"Any more takers?" Abe asked.

There were none.

Mondo stepped up. "That is the end of the demonstration. Never under estimate your opponent. Rei's father is a master of the wakazashi. Do you think him fool enough to challenge Monk Token if he didn't know what he is doing? Rei is dangerous. He defeated Monk Token. That is more than I can say for most of you. Rei is now a lieutenant in the Ronin Army. When he talks you listen," Mondo said.

Later assignments for the evening were being posted. Mondo cornered Rei.

"Nice job earlier," Mondo said.

"Is he conscious yet?" Rei asked.

"Yes," Mondo said. "He has a large bump on his brow, but his is smarter for the lesson."

"Am I really promoted to lieutenant?" Rei asked.

"Yes," Mondo said. "You are of equal rank with Abe and Watanabe. I needed a third lieutenant to handle patrols. That is your job. You set up patrols and keep the peace. Kyoto is getting very dangerous. I'll move you to business collections when I think you are ready."

"Business collections?" Rei asked. "What is that?"

"Businesses and merchants and other businessmen pay us

for protection. It is a vital source of revenue for Tadanaga," Mondo said.

"If Tadanaga is behind it I guess it is legitimate," Rei said.

"Of course it is legitimate," Mondo said. "We have to make money some way to ensure Tadanaga becomes the shogun. Besides, we have to be able to pay you so you can send that money home."

Rei was too busy the next few days to dwell on his misgivings. His squad of twenty-five men patrolled the city during the day and night. They stopped theft, broke up fights, settled arguments and tried to maintain the peace. Despite Rei's attempts he noticed that people shied away from those in the white headband and haori. He started seeing distrust and downright loathing in their countenances. He soon learned why.

"Rei the time has come for you to learn collections," Mondo said. "You will be accompanying Abe and Watanabe today. They will teach you the ropes."

The first establishment they entered was a dry goods store. Abe and Watanabe pushed past the clerks and entered the living quarters behind the store. Rei followed.

The owner was in discussion with a supplier when the trio crashed in.

"What is the meaning of this?" the gray-haired owner asked.

"The meaning is you are late on your taxes to Tadanaga. We are here to collect," Watanabe said, sitting down in front of the owner.

"I owe no money to Tadanaga," the gray-haired man said. "Leave my store at once."

Watanabe struck the man in the face with a fist. The man cried out in shock and rolled out of his sitting position on onto the tatami. Several clerks and family members rushed in.

"Otosan," a young daughter cried. She rushed to her injured father and applied a cloth to his crushed lips. "You are all ruffians and thieves."

Abe stood over her and drew his katana. Everyone froze in fear.

"Yes, little merchant wench," Abe said. "That is exactly

what we are. If you do not get six gold coins out here right now, I'm going to start cutting."

The gray-haired man sat back up. He reached into his kimono and extracted a leather purse. He counted out six gold coins and tossed them to Watanabe.

"There," he said. "You have your blood money. Now go."

Watanabe picked up each coin and examined them. "Pleasure doing business with you."

Abe kept his sword hovering over the daughter. "It would be a pleasure to get to know you better," he said.

"Come on, Abe," Watanabe said. "I do not think they like supporting Tadanaga."

Rei looked at the terrified face of the girl and the blood on the owner's lips. He could not meet their eyes. He felt sick. But he kept quiet.

"See, that is how it is done Rei," Abe said as they left the dry goods store. "The next one will be more fun."

Watanabe slapped Abe on the back as if congratulating him for a success. "Don't fall behind Rei. We have more stores to visit."

The next establishment was a candle shop. The scent of wax was strong as they entered. Here Abe pushed back into the heart of the building as well. He pushed the owner down and hit him in the head. His wife tried to intervene, but Watanabe held her back.

"This is the second time you have been late on your dues. Tadanaga wants his money. Where is the two gold coins you owe us?" Abe demanded.

"Oh please, do not hurt my husband. He is old. We do not have two gold coins to pay you. We barely make enough profit to eat ourselves," the wife pleaded.

"That is okay grandma," Abe said. "There is a cute little granddaughter around here someplace. I'll just take our pay our in trade."

The wife screamed. Watanabe hit her, knocking her unconscious. The old man tried to go to his wife's assistance and was beaten by Abe. He quit moving. Abe stood up and started a methodical search of each room.

"I knew you were here," Abe exclaimed. There was a series of screams from the room. Rei pushed past Watanabe and entered the room. Abe had the young girl on her back, he was on top of her fumbling with the belt of his kimono. He stopped his efforts when he realized a live blade was under his chin. He stood up carefully and tried to turn to see who was wielding the wakazashi.

"Mondo was right to suspect you," Abe said as Rei walked him to the sliding door.

Rei turned his head to the girl. "Go tend to your parents. I am sorry."

The girl rushed to return her clothing to a state of decency. Rei kicked Abe into Watanabe.

"Get out now," Rei said.

"You are going to pay for that," Abe said reaching for his sword.

"Go ahead you coward,' Rei said. "I am neither a young girl nor an old man. Draw that sword so I can cut your hand off."

"Come on," Watanabe said to his companion. "Let's get back to the barracks."

Rei returned his wakazashi to his scabbard and looked down to see the girl reviving her mother.

"This is not bushido," Rei said. "This is not even right."

XVI

Kitten

"Umi," the old woman said. "Put down that kitten and come eat."

"Yes grandmother," Umi said, placing the furry animal on the dirt floor. It immediately scampered off to explore more interesting parts of the smoky one room hut.

"What is for supper?" Umi asked.

The old woman looked at the little girl through squinted eyes narrowed by the smoke from a thousand wood fires. A black iron kettle hung above the fire in the irori in the center of the hut. The old woman scooped out the soup like substance into an ancient wooden bowl.

"You know what supper is. It is the same supper you have had for all the seven summers of your life. It is awa," Fugi said.

Umi took the bowl in her little hands and sat beside her grandmother.

"It is good if you're hungry enough," Umi said.

The old woman turned her head to the side and looked at the dirty face, ragged clothes and black hair.

"So, you are hungry enough?" Fugi asked.

"Oh yes Grandmother, kitten and I have played all day. We are both hungry," Umi said.

"Do not feed that cat. I do not cook for animals. Let it find a mouse or better yet a rat. We have enough of those around here," Fugi said. "It is all I can do to feed you."

"Do not be sad. We do not eat much," Umi said.

"It would be much more if your parents were alive."

Umi stared into the bowl. "I miss them Grandmother."

The old woman scooped out a bowl of the soup for herself. "It is your karma to be an orphan. It is mine to be an old woman raising a young child. I hope I live long enough to see you married. But that is probably pushing karma too far."

"I love you Grandmother," Umi said after eating several spoonfuls.

The old woman looked at the little girl. "You are seven years old. You love everything. You love me and you love the kitten," Fugi said. "If I can get you to love cleaning this hut and gathering firewood, I might love you."

The little girl smiled. "I know you love me Grandmother."

The old woman's eyes softened. "You are my only grandchild. Of course I love you." Fugi said.

Umi looked at the remaining soup in her bowl. "I'm going to feed kitten now."

"I told you not to give that kitten your food," Fugi said.

"It is not much Grandmother," Umi said. "Can I please give him the rest? Please?"

"Go ahead but don't wake me up tonight saying you are hungry," Fugi said.

"I will not Grandmother, I promise," Umi said.

Umi moved from her kneeling position and carefully held the bowl. "Here kitten, here kitten," Umi called on her little girl voice. "Come get food."

After a few moments of searching, Umi turned to her grandmother. "Grandmother, Kitten is gone," Umi said.

"He probably slipped out one of the holes in the thatch," Fugi said. "Buddha knows we have enough of those."

"But it is dangerous outside for kitten. Can I go look for him?" Umi asked.

"It is dark already. It is dangerous for us to be out after dark," Fugi said.

"But Grandmother kitten is my friend," Umi cried.

Fugi looked at Umi's little distraught face. It was true enough that the kitten was Umi's only possession. She did not even have a doll the play with.

"We have no idea where the cat went," Fugi said. "We

could be searching all night."

"Oh no Grandmother, I have seen it go to the old barn. It always goes there," Umi said.

"Well at least it has cat instincts. That old dilapidated abandoned barn would be were the most mice are," Fugi said.

"So, can we go see? It is just a short walk," Umi asked.

"Child you are more trouble than you are worth. These old bones can barely scratch a living out of this land, and you want me to go chasing your kitten," Fugi said.

"Oh, please Grandmother, I just know he is at the barn," Umi said.

"All right but don't use a candle. We have few enough as it is. Weave some straw around one of the sticks of firewood and put it in the fire until it flames. We will use a torch," Fugi said.

The little girl performed the task easily being careful to keep the flaming stick from igniting the walls of the hut. She waited outside the only door for the old woman to catch up. The old and bent woman was supported by her granddaughter's freehand as they trudged up the dirt path to the abandoned barn.

"Grandmother I think I see light in the barn," Umi said.

"It cannot be. No one uses this old building," Fugi said.

The old woman and the little girl slowed their pace and looked suspiciously at the decrepit ivy-covered walls of the barn.

As she was squinting at the walls and moving her head to get a better look, she let out a gasp as one of the many bushes growing near the building leapt up and punched her in the stomach. She collapsed immediately. The little girl was about to scream when a rough hand covered her mouth.

The little girl wanted to scream. Then she just wanted to breathe. The hand was covering both her mouth and nose. She saw her grandmother being lifted by the neck of her old thread bare kimono. Then the rough hand covered her eyes as well.

Eventually the old woman started to breathe. She had been moved into the barn. Her breaths were ragged. She was trying to be quiet. There were men in the old barn. That could only be dangerous for her and her granddaughter. She opened her eyes slowly trying not to disturb anyone.

"I will brook no arguments," the large man in black said. "I am Ugai. I am the leader of the Koga clan. The decision is made."

"How can you make a decision like this? This decision affects the whole clan. The whole clan should be heard," The Mist said.

The murmuring could be heard throughout the abandoned barn. The small lanterns in the center of the gathering gave each face in the first circle a demonic appearance. The seven men in his first circle wore black, were covered with black hoods and scarves around their heads. Only their eyes were visible; all save one. A woman of quality in a black winter kimono with red piping sat in the first circle. Even in the dim light her features were striking.

"If you want to keep your beauty, you will not argue with me Mist. I am the head of the Koga clan," Ugai said.

"As the head of the Koga Ninja Clan you are supposed to protect us. Instead you betrayed Iemitsu and put us in jeopardy. Do you think Hittori Honzo as director of both the Iga and the Koga is going to sit by and let this betrayal stand? If Iemitsu becomes shogun we will cease to exist. Hittori Honzo will have the Iga and the full force of the Tokugawa to destroy us," The Mist said.

"You fool, I have anticipated Honzo's reaction and taken steps to neutralize him," Ugai said. "I am more concerned about traitors in our midst."

The murmuring from those in the barn arose again.

"I am surrounded by fools. Not only am I faced with treacherous talk from The Mist, but now you have brought two witnesses into our midst. What kind of sentries are you?" Ugai asked.

"I found these two beside the barn. It looked like they intended to enter when they heard you yelling at The Mist. I think it is the old woman who owns this land and her grandchild," the sentry said.

"Once again I say I am surrounded by fools. Why do you

bother me with such trivia? I must oversee the development of a new nation. Why are they not dead?" Ugai asked.

"Ugai why kill an old woman and a child? The only face they have seen is mine," The Mist asked.

Ugai looked at The Mist. "I do not have time for your questions."

Ugai moved over to where the two captives lay in the dirt. With hands on his hips Ugai stood above the cowed and trembling relatives.

"Grandmother, do you know me?" Ugai demanded.

The trembling old woman looked at the black figure with leather covering his upper torso and left arm. She could not see his face but those piercing black eyes below the cowl and above the black scarf were enough to make her shrink.

"No lord," she mumbled.

"How about you little girl, do you know me?" Ugai demanded loudly.

The little girl dared not look up from her crouched position next to her grandmother.

"Look at me girl," Ugai demanded.

Fugi turned her face just inches above the dirt floor toward her precious granddaughter. "Do as he says child," she encouraged.

The little girl looked up at the black figure and caught sight of the black eyes and screamed and looked down again.

"Do you know me child?" Ugai demanded a third time.

"No lord," little girl whispered.

Fugi reached over and pulled the terrified girl to her.

"Please lord we have nothing. We worked the land as best we can, and we get enough only to feed ourselves. We do not know any of you. Please let us get back to our hut. It is way past our bedtime," Fugi said.

Ugai squatted down next to both of his captives. Then he pulled down his scarf revealing his face. "Look at me," he said.

Both the old woman and the little girl looked in Ugai's direction.

"Now you have seen me," Ugai said. While still squatting, Ugai extended his arms to the small of his back. When his arms moved up and outward each hand contained a kama. The curved blade attached to the head of the wooden handles gleamed in the lantern light. Both his hands slashed downward.

The point of the weapon in his left hand punctured the old woman's back just below the shoulder slicing through muscle and bone and pierced her lung. She groaned once and collapsed completely to the dirt. The right-hand weapon came down on the little skull. The little girl made no sound. The top half of her head with hair attached dropped to the dirt near the lanterns. Her little body collapsed in a heap. Ugai stood, bloody kamas still in his hands and stepped to The Mist.

The Mist did not flinch.

"Now they have seen my face and died for it," Ugai said. "Do you have any more stupid things to say Mist?"

The Mist looked at the lifeless bodies near the lanterns.

"No Ugai," The Mist said. "Your actions speak volumes."

Ugai spun to address the whole gathering. "We are on the path to change history," Ugai shouted. "Anyone not with me is against me. Who dares oppose me?"

There was no answer.

"Then we will proceed with the missions as I have out-lined. Mist, you leave first," Ugai said.

The Mist looked somewhat shocked.

"As you command Ugai," The Mist said getting her toes underneath her and rocking forward into a standing position. She bowed slightly to Ugai dusted off her kimono at her knees and walked carefully around the two bodies with their smell of blood and through the small door and out into the Japanese country night.

Once The Mist had walked a considerable distance, she gave voice to her thoughts.

"We are doomed," she said. "And there is nothing I can do about it."

XVII

Hunting The Mist

With the large outer doors folded back, Yuki and Naga
sat together looking out onto the courtyard of the Yoshinobu
mansion. Jubei and Hideki were in the center practicing with
bokken. The pace of the practice was furious. Jubei struck from
every angle possible as Hideki parried and attacked. The speed
of each was blinding. The early morning quiet was filled with the
loud thwack of a heavy wooden sword striking an equally heavy
wooden sword.

Jubei called a halt to the practice. "Drop the bokken and get
ready to learn something interesting," Jubei said. "Go to the far
side of the courtyard and prepare."

Jubei moved to the opposite end of the courtyard and
picked up a yumi and a quiver of arrows. Jubei placed one
arrow in the bow ready to draw and two arrows dangled from
his forward fingers in his left hand. The arrowheads had been
removed and fitted with weighted leather.

"If you can muster your mushin you might survive," Jubei
said.

"I have become accustomed to your daily attempts to
multiply my bruises, but this is something new," Hideki said.

"There is not much left for me to teach you. Yadome-jutsu
is one skill you lack. It worries me the most," Jubei said.

"What is the other?" Hideki asked.

"Shinkage ryu muto dori," Jubei said testing the draw of the
asymmetrical bow.

"Disarming techniques?" Hideki asked.

"Yes, they are important to know. So is learning to discern which arrows from a flight will take your life and then cutting or deflecting them with your sword," Jubei said.

"Sounds like magic to me," Hideki scoffed.

"Your mushin sounds like magic to others, but we both know it exists," Jubei said.

"So, you are going to fire three arrows at me and I'm going to pick the one that will do me the most damage and deflect it with the sword?" Hideki asked.

"Hai," Jubei said.

"What happens if all of the arrows will kill me?" Hideki asked.

"Then deflect or cut them all," Jubei said. "Or you may die."

"I do not like this," Hideki said. "Yadome-jutsu has not been practiced since ancient times and then at much greater distances."

"Stop the whining and get ready," Jubei said.

"You are always an empathetic one," Hideki said and squared his body with both hands on sword hilts.

Jubei raised the long bow, giving it a great pull as he brought it down on his target and released. He quickly and expertly brought the next arrow up by rotating his left-hand fingers to bring the feathered end of the arrow onto the string. He pulled back and fired. The third arrow was released the same way. All three were done in rapid fire.

Hideki did not have time to think. He drew his wakazashi with his right hand while dropping his body back into a low left foot forward stance. His mind went blank as the first arrow passed over his shoulder. The second arrow was met with the side of his short sword as he completed his draw deflecting the arrow harmlessly to the side. He brought the wakazashi back to his front in time to cut the next arrow in flight as he twisted to the left. However, the head of the arrow struck him in his left shoulder.

"Ouch," Hideki said rubbing his left shoulder.

"Not bad Tengu killer," Jubei said.

It took a moment for Hideki to rub the numbness out of his shoulder.

"You killed the Tengu as much as me," Hideki said.

"Nevertheless, you dodged one arrow, deflected another and cut a third. Were you in mushin?" Jubei asked.

"I guess I was. When those arrows were coming straight at me, I lost all thought," Hideki said.

"Good. That may well save your life one day," Jubei said. "Do it again."

Hideki got set as Jubei put three more arrows in place.

"I really do not like this," Hideki said under his breath.

From where the two warriors stood in the garden, they could not hear the conversation between husband and wife in the mansion.

"Hideki has really improved," Yuki said. "Mushin is evident."

"You mentioned mushin before. What is it?" Naga asked.

"It is the ability to react to an attack without thinking," Yuki said

"That tracks with what both you and Jubei were saying about Hideki having few equals in Japan," Naga replied.

"I am still lamenting the fact that the sweet boy I first met on the Tokaido is no more," she said.

Naga smiled. "I do not know if you can call a man who dodges arrows with a short sword and has the nickname of Tengu killer sweet anymore. What is this arrow cutting skill he is learning now?"

"It is an ancient art practiced by the bushi," Yuki said.

"They were the forerunners of the samurai, right?" Naga asked.

"Yes husband, they were the original warriors used by war lords. Their whole life was war. They took martial arts to its zenith," Yuki said.

"Samurai are elite martial artists," Naga said.

"I can see Jii did not pay much attention to your history lessons," Yuki said.

"Jii probably covered it. Hideki and I were good at not paying attention, especially Hideki," Naga said.

"Jii may not have known. As I said, it is an ancient art," Yuki said. "In the days of the bushi warriors from both sides would line up against each other. The entire army was made up of these elite warriors. The champion from each side would walk out in front of friendly lines and proudly sound off their warrior lineage. Then the champions would fight, and their fight might decide the outcome of the war."

"Certainly, an economical way to fight," Naga said.

"If the daimyo with the weaker champion didn't like the obvious outcome, he would line up archers behind his front lines. They would rain flights of arrows at the champion hoping to thwart the outcome of the battle," Yuki said.

"I get it. Yadome-jutsu was devised to help keep the champions alive," Naga said.

"See, I knew there was a brain in your head," Yuki said.

"So how did we arrive at samurai instead of bushi?" Naga asked.

"You answered your own question earlier. Economics put the bushi out of business. A daimyo could ill afford to feed two hundred elite warriors all the time. If he fired all but a few to train the farmers, then war was much more economical. The farmers were tied to the land. When war threatened, they were called to arms. The term ji-samurai made it into our vocabulary. Later it was reduced to just samurai," Yuki said.

"So, my ancestors were farmers?" Naga asked.

"Maybe they were farmers. Maybe they were descendants of the elite bushi that trained the farmers," Yuki said.

"Yes, the last story is easier on my ego," Naga said. "I don't think I would mention any of this history around Jii."

"I will not," Yuki said. Then she turned her attention back to Hideki. "Well he may be a Tengu killer, but some things have not changed. He is still humble and gentle. Did you see how he bounced our son on his lap two nights ago?" Yuki asked.

As soon as she said it Yuki wished she had not. It reminded her of her baby. She teared up.

Naga grabbed her by the shoulders. "Some things about Hideki have not changed. But some things have. He took charge of the entire Yoshinobu clan last night and organized a two-pronged approach to our dilemma. He placed the focus on finding our child. He is my younger brother, but he is very different now as you mentioned last night. I am thankful for the changes," Naga said.

"Yes, but it is sad to think that that sweet boy of a few years ago is now a master swordsman. He is also a killer. You can see it in his sad eyes," Yuki said.

"Let us let Myo worry about his sad eyes. I want our son back," he said.

"Yes husband, you are correct. I want him home safe. But secretly I want the ones that took him to die at my hands," Yuki said.

Naga was taken aback for a moment. "I keep forgetting my sweet wife and mother of our child is a swords woman herself. How did I get so lucky?"

Yuki smiled. "This is the first time I have smiled since Yoshitsune was taken. Hideki does that. He gives you hope."

"Yes," Naga said. "He does that. I am afraid today will get bloody in Edo."

The couple was interrupted by Yoshi who knelt at the sliding door at the threshold from inside the mansion. "Simasen, I must speak with Hideki."

"Is there any news?" Yuki asked hopefully.

"We have located The Mist," Yoshi said.

"Wonderful," Yuki said. "I will get ready."

"No, my dear, remember what Hideki said last night. This is his kind of fight."

Nagamasa motioned Yoshi to proceed through the room to the courtyard outside. Yoshi stood and moved silently through the room to the porch outside. He let out a loud whistle. The practice stopped immediately.

"Come children, we have work," Yoshi yelled.

Yuki smiled at her husband. "They are like brothers are they not?"

"Yes, just like brothers; brothers of the sword," Naga said.

After some travel by barge on the many canals of Edo's underbelly, Jubei, Hideki and Yoshi stood before a waterfront bar.

"I am sure they are aware of our presence," Hideki said.

"It is of no matter," Yoshi said. "Myo and her people have the exits covered. No one will escape unless you want them to."

"What about tunnels?" Jubei asked.

"Tunnels are possible, but not likely this close to the river," Yoshi said.

"Shall we?" Hideki asked.

The three moved through the flimsy tarp that sufficed for a door. All three moved through the threshold and stepped to the left and right to give their eyes a chance to adjust.

Hideki noticed the low wooden beams above. "Better use horizontal strikes," he said.

"You had better use your wakazashi," Jubei said.

"Monkey you use whatever you want," Jubei said to Yoshi.

"Worry about yourself sword master," Yoshi replied.

"How is the haragai Yoshi?" Hideki asked. "What kind of danger are we facing?"

"I feel no alarms. That is very strange," Yoshi said. "I would expect great alarm bells when wandering into a ninja lair."

The room was rectangular in shape. From the front entrance to about halfway back Hideki could see the rough wooden tables with benches on either side with a narrow aisle in the center. Where the tables stopped, a bar began on the left taking up half of the width of the room. There appeared to be a kitchen past the bar. Hideki could not see back into the kitchen due to the hanging beads covering the entrance.

There were four men of various occupations sitting at the last two tables. Two sat on the last table on the left and two occupied the last table on the right. On the left were a teamster and a merchant. On the right sat a priest and a traveler. No weapons were visible.

"No weapons showing," Jubei said.

"Doesn't mean much here," Yoshi said.

A muscular barman watched all three strangers as they entered and hung at the entrance.

Something was cooking in the kitchen, but Hideki could not see through the beads.

The barman stopped smearing whatever the dirty rag contained long enough to address the three strangers.

"You are in the wrong place samurai. We do not serve your kind here."

"Oh good, a welcoming committee," Hideki said moving down the aisle until level with the last tables.

Jubei moved to Hideki's right. As soon as the customer nearest Hideki reached inside his kimono Hideki moved his right foot forward, grabbed his short sword with his right hand, drew and sliced the man above his right ear. The cut was not deep enough to kill but it hurt and caused great pain. The man pulled his hand out of his kimono, grasped a dirty rag atop the table and pressed it to his head to staunch the blood flow. Hideki thought his use of curse words imaginative.

Hideki shifted to stand in front of the remaining man dressed as a merchant. Hideki dropped his center of gravity and pointed his wakazashi at the man. "If you value your life, do not move."

The man placed both hands on the table and froze.

On the right side of the aisle a man screamed. All heads turned to him. A dart was protruding from his right eye. He flopped around and dropped to the dirt floor dead.

Jubei never took his eye off the remaining man on the right. "Yoshi is not playing around," he said.

"Apparently not," Hideki agreed. "Watch them Jubei."

Hideki turned to the barman. "Tell The Mist to come out," Hideki said.

"Who?" The barman asked.

"If you keep that up every one of you will die this day," Hideki said.

"Relax samurai, I am coming out," The Mist said, emerging through the beads. "What is the purpose of your visit today?"

Hideki was loath to turn his back on the bartender. He returned his wakazashi to the short scabbard in front of his obi. Then with his right hand he rotated his katana scabbard ninety degrees inward. With a lightning draw he tapped the barman above his left ear with the back of the blade. The barman went down instantly in and unconscious heap. He dropped so fast Hideki wondered if he had killed him. Then he dismissed the thought. They had a job to do. They were going to do it.

"What right do you have coming in here and hurting my family?" The Mist asked.

"Your threat to kill my family a few nights ago provides me with reason enough," Hideki said. "But stealing my nephew, the heir to the Yoshinobu clan, gives me all the authority and anger I need."

The two remaining healthy men at the tables and The Mist said almost in unison, "What?"

"Two days ago, the Yoshinobu mansion was set ablaze and two of Yoshi's ninja guards were killed. As the mother evacuated her child, the Yoshinobu heir, a yet to be one-year-old baby, was stolen by ninja and the nanny killed," Hideki accused.

"We do not steal children," The Mist said.

"That is quite funny. You threatened to kill my nephew, myself and the rest of my relatives, but you have compunction against stealing children? I find that hard to believe," Hideki said.

"Believe what you like, but we do not steal children," The Mist said.

Hideki moved within striking distance of The Mist and returned his katana to its scabbard.

The Mist took a step back.

"If I have to kill everyone here and all the Koga in Edo I will do so," Hideki said.

"I guess you really are a Tengu killer," The Mist said. "I thought you to be more a gentleman."

"You base that on our meeting in the dark?" Hideki asked.

"That and information I gathered on you," she said.

The conversation was interrupted by the barman, who returned to consciousness and brought a large meat cleaver with him as he stood. He never got to deliver his throw at Hideki. Jubei flashed behind Hideki and thrust his blade into the bartender's shoulder. He screamed and dropped the cleaver and slipped below the bar, grasping his damaged shoulder.

"I will kill you for that," The Mist said.

"You will have to get out of here alive for that to happen," Hideki said.

The Mist moved her hand to her mouth and whistled. From behind the beaded curtain a man was violently thrown to the dirt at her feet. He was bleeding from a head wound. A black clad ninja followed him into the room. Hideki saw fear on the Koga lieutenant's face for the first time. The Mist reached inside her red piped kimono. The black clad ninja kicked her on the side of her right knee. The Mist screamed and dropped to the dirt floor clutching the wounded leg.

"Do that again and I will cut it off," the black clad ninja said in a feminine voice as she thrust her hand into The Mist's kimono and retrieved two shuriken.

"What now?" The Mist asked massaging her knee. "Are you going to kill me?"

"I should," Hideki said. "Then I would have one less Koga to worry about."

Hideki withdrew his katana with his left hand and placed the point of the blade at her throat.

"Where is the leader of your clan?" Hideki asked.

"I do not know. If I did, I would not tell you," she said.

"Give her to me. She will give up everything. I owe her for my dead comrades," the black clad ninja said.

"That might be the best solution," Hideki said. "Maybe there is another way."

"Do not listen to her, she lies for a living," black clad ninja said.

"Yes, I am aware of the ninja use of deception," Hideki said. "But we need to find a way to get Yoshitsune back to his mother."

The Mist gained some confidence. "So, the leader of the Five Families listens to her samurai lover?"

The black clad ninja removed the scarf covering her face. Hideki smiled. Myo smiled back.

"Sometimes," Hideki said. "Can you walk?" He asked The Mist.

The Mist tried to stand up. She was assisted by Myo grabbing her by the hair and pulling her up.

"You evil bitch," The Mist cried.

"Not so evil that I would steal a child," Myo responded.

"I told you crazy people that I have never stolen the child."

"Speaking of crazy, who in their right mind would steal

Hittori Honzo's only grandchild?" Myo asked.

The Mist turned toward Myo. "Hittori Honzo?"

"Yes, Hittori Honzo, the ninja killer. Yoshinobu Hideki is brother-in-law to Yuki, Honzo's only daughter," Myo said.

The Mist seemed to stagger with the news. Myo straightened her up by her hair.

"This is bad," The Mist said.

"I take it you know Honzo from your time with castle security," Myo said.

"Yes, he is like a god to both the Iga and Koga."

"Then why did you steal his grandson?" Myo asked.

"I did not. But if someone in the Koga did, Honzo will destroy everyone. His nickname is well-deserved," The Mist said.

"If that is the case, then the only way to save your clan is to tell us where the baby is so Honzo can be reunited with his grandson," Hideki said.

"I would if I could. Between you coming in here and wounding and killing my friends to the threat of Honzo, we will be lucky to survive," The Mist said.

"It is not only them you have to worry about," Jubei said.

"What do you mean?" The Mist asked.

"I mean your entire clan violated your contract with the Tokugawa. Iemitsu will come to power. Every Koga will be hunted down and exterminated with a huge bounty on their head," Jubei said.

"Ugai, you stupid bastard," The Mist cursed. "You have damned us all."

"Who is Ugai?" Hideki asked.

"He is our leader," The Mist said. "He said he was betting the future of the clan by backing Tadanaga. I had no idea how true that statement was."

"I say we turn her over to Honzo," Myo said.

Hideki looked at The Mist. "Look me in the eye and tell me you do not know anything about the disappearance of my nephew."

The Mist turned to Hideki. "I know nothing about the disappearance of your nephew."

"I believe her. You can let her go Myo, if she promises

to help us find Yoshitsune," Hideki said.

"Why should I help you after you come in here and killed and wounded my friends?" The Mist asked.

Hideki nodded towards Myo. "You already know Myo. Do you know this gentleman with the patch?"

"He is Yagyū Jubei, former sword instructor to shoguns and assassin for the Tokugawa," The Mist said.

Hideki turned to his right. "Do you know Yoshi?"

The Mist looked at the new man dressed as a merchant.

"Only by reputation; he is the one who sees through the darkness," she said.

"And I am the Tengu killer. Yoshi is employed by my family. Jubei is my sword instructor. Both are my friends. Myo is my lover. Which one of us do you think would hesitate to take your life given our current situation?" Hideki asked.

The Mist looked from one to another. "Fine, I will help. But I'm not going to help you kill more Koga," The Mist said.

"Where is Ugai?" Hideki asked.

"I do not know. The last I saw of him was in an old barn near Kyoto," The Mist said. "He all but cast me out of the clan over killing an innocent old grandmother and a young female child."

"Did he steal them too?" Hideki asked.

"No, he butchered them before our eyes. He has his own factions in the Koga. He wanted to impress upon the rest of us his willingness to do anything and to keep us in line," The Mist said.

"I do not believe my nephew has been moved out of Edo yet," Hideki said.

"What do you base that on?" The Mist asked.

"Myo?" Hideki asked.

"The Five Families established two cordons seconds after the disappearance," Myo said. "We have kept it up. No baby has escaped it."

"Tie her hands behind her Myo. We will return to the Yoshinobu compound," Hideki said.

Before he had finished the sentence, The Mist's arms were wrapped tightly behind her. Perhaps too tightly. Only The Mist seemed to mind.

XVIII

Honzo

Myo sat The Mist roughly on a woven mat in one of the rooms off the great hall of the Yoshinobu mansion.

"Ouch," The Mist said, landing on her bottom.

"You complain too much for a ninja," Myo said.

"I should have killed you the last time I was here," The Mist said.

"I was not here the last time you visited," Myo said.

"I got through your security easily enough," The Mist taunted.

"It is true you have skills," Myo conceded. "But why did you pick Hideki to confront. He is not the head of the family. He is only number three in line."

The Mist settled down and quit fighting the ropes around her upper torso, arms and wrists. "I wanted to see the Tengu killer."

"What did you find?" Myo asked.

The Mist smiled. "I found a boy."

"Yes, many people make that fatal mistake," Myo said.

"Is he a good lover?" The Mist asked with a smile.

Myo looked into her eyes. "The best," she said smiling back.

"So, tell me leader of the Five Families, how did a samurai and a ninja become lovers?"

"It is a long story," Myo said. "We did not know each other's identity when we first met."

The Mist nodded. "That answered one of my questions.

But how does a young samurai retain the loyalty of you, Yagyū Jubei and someone like Yoshi?" The Mist asked. "Yoshi is a ninja from the old school. I hear he is steeped in the black arts and his haragai is something out of legend."

Myo sat down next to The Mist.

"That question is easy to answer. If I were not his lover, I would be his friend. That is what Jubei and Yoshi are. They are his friends," Myo said.

"Friends? You must be joking. Family I understand, but friends?" The Mist asked.

"Okay, maybe family better describes it. Yoshi has the samurai title of chief strategist for the Yoshinobu. He, his wife and his mother-in-law all live in the Yoshinobu mansion here in Edo. The patriarch of the Yoshinobu, a member of the Roju, has us all call him Jii as if we were his real grandchildren. Yoshi's mother-in-law shares a pipe with Jii each night before bed," Myo said.

The Mist's eyebrows went up. "Do they sleep together?" The Mist asked.

"You will have to ask them," Myo said.

"You are asking me to believe that the samurai nobility treats you as part of the family?" The Mist asked.

"I do not really care what you believe," Myo said. "The Yoshinobu treat all as family. I would die to protect them."

"Does everyone here feel as you do?" The Mist asked.

"You will have to ask them," Myo said. "But if past experience is any indication, I would say the answer is yes."

"Do you think I stole the baby?" The Mist asked.

"What I think is immaterial. It is what Hideki thinks that will determine your fate," Myo said.

Hideki, Yoshi, Jubei, Nagamasa and Yuki filed into the room and took seats on the floor.

"Is this one of those that killed our nanny and stole my son?" Yuki asked.

"She was number two in the Koga ranks and she threatened our entire family with death if we supported Iemitsu," Hideki said. "But I can find no proof that she stole your son."

"If you know anything about my son please tell us."

141

The Mist bowed her head in Yuki's direction. "I know nothing about your stolen son," she said.

"I will be the judge of that," a voice boomed from the entrance. All heads turned to the samurai walking towards the group. He stopped a sword length from Jubei and bowed to Nagamasa.

Nagamasa returned the bow. "Welcome father-in-law."

Yuki bowed as well. "Welcome father."

Hittori Honzo wore leather armor over his torso and wrists. His katana was sheathed and in his left hand.

"Is this the trash that stole my grandson?" He asked pointing with the handle of the sheathed katana. He walked to The Mist who had her head down.

"Raise your face," he demanded.

The Mist complied.

"Mist," he said." It was not enough that Ugai broke all his oath's and contracts with the Tokugawa, now you steal my only grandchild?"

The Mist bowed her head again. "Master, I know nothing of this evil deed."

Hittori Honzo grasped his sword handle with his right hand.

In a dazzling display of speed, Hideki drew his sword with his left hand and placed the tip in the hollow of Honzo's throat.

"You would cross swords with me boy?" Honzo asked.

"If it meant sparing the life of the only lead we have in finding Yoshitsune, yes," Hideki said.

Honzo released his grip on the katana.

"I was not going to kill her, only cut her bonds. But you can release yourself now Mist. You have seen what you came to learn," Honzo said.

The Mist nodded to Honzo and wiggled in place for a few moments. The ropes sagged. She pulled them off and threw them behind her.

"The lady has skills," Yoshi said.

"She agreed to your capturing of her because she wanted to learn if the stolen baby story was true and who was running the Yoshinobu," Honzo said.

"You live dangerously," Myo said. "The stolen baby story is true."

"When Master Honzo spoke those words, I knew it was true," The Mist said.

"So now that you know the situation what are you going to do about my stolen grandson?" Honzo asked.

"Ugai has a group of Koga he is working with exclusively to cement Tadanaga's success and Iemitsu's failure," The Mist said.

"Ugai has already led the Koga down a dangerous path by backing Tadanaga. How do you see the stealing of my grandson?" Honzo asked.

"Stealing your grandson is disastrous to the Koga," The Mist said. "We are lost."

"What are you prepared to do about it?" Honzo asked.

The Mist looked at Hideki. "These three were crazy enough the barge into a Koga stronghold and start maiming people. I have no doubt they will continue to do so unless the baby is found. Master Honzo, if you start seeking us for the same purpose, we would be fighting the Iga as well as the Five Families. We would no longer exist," The Mist said. "I think I had better find the child."

"Ugai might not like that," Honzo said.

"I don't like it," The Mist said. "But it is better than the alternative."

"You will be going against your own clan," Honzo said.

"Yes, and I do not know if any of my clan will support me in this decision," The Mist said.

"I suggest you help the Yoshinobu and find my grandson soon," Honzo said.

Honzo looked to Hideki. "Has this been satisfactory for you?" Honzo asked.

"So far it has," Hideki said returning his sword to the scabbard on his right side.

Honzo nodded to his daughter and turned and walked out.

"That is a very scary man," Yoshi said.

"You do not really understand the reality of what you just said," The Mist said. Then The Mist turned to Hideki, "You put a sword tip to Hittori Honzo's throat. You are either really brave or really stupid."

Hideki turned to Yoshi. "Yoshi is our chief strategist.

Mist you will work for him. We will plan our movements as he dictates. What is first Yoshi?" Hideki asked.

"First, Myo and her lieutenants and I will meet to identify all Koga gathering places and prioritize them. We will need to visit them in sequence so we can recruit as many as possible to The Mist's side. Our priority is to find Yoshitsune. If we locate him, we can tighten a cordon and enter using our new Koga allies and the Five Families to rescue him," Yoshi said.

Hideki turned to The Mist. "Do you have any idea of the likelihood of success in this venture?"

"How would I know? The places we visit might be holding the child. No matter the outcome I'm dead either way," The Mist said.

"Maybe not, we will be with you," Hideki said.

"If they see you with me, they will flee and maybe kill the child," The Mist said.

"Not if you give the correct countersign," Yoshi said.

The Mist smiled. "I keep forgetting this is not a normal samurai household. We are among ninja."

"Yoshi," Hideki said. "Take The Mist, Myo and whoever else you need into the war room. Call us when you are ready."

Yoshi nodded and motioned for the others to follow him. When they were gone Yuki looked at Hideki. "Can we trust her brother-in-law?"

"We have no choice. She is our best option for returning your child," Hideki said.

"You almost crossed swords with Hittori Honzo brother," Naga said. "Do you have a death wish?"

Hideki failed to respond and moved out of the room.

"I believe you would be surprised at the outcome of such a match," Jubei said. "My money would be on your brother."

Jubei turned and followed Hideki out of the room.

"Is Hideki so good with the sword that he could defeat my father?" Yuki asked.

"Apparently so," Naga said. "I had better start being more polite to my little brother."

XIX

Pirate Rei

"Rei go with Abe to the teamster stables," Mondo said. "They are behind on their dues."

"Not another extortion?" Rei asked. "I told you I was not doing that anymore."

"Let me remind you Rei, you are in an army," Mondo said. "I am the captain. My word is law. If you defy me, I can have you killed."

Mondo, Abe and Watanabe all had their hands on their katanas.

"I signed on to get a chance at being a samurai with the Satsuma. I did not sign on to rob store owners," Rei said.

"By the Buddha Mondo, let me cut him down now. I've had enough of his insults," Abe said.

"If I thought you could do it, I would let you," Mondo said. "But I have a better idea for our righteous ronin."

"Like what?" Abe asked.

"Like Team Wang Zhi," Mondo said. "They are looking for a skilled swordsman to accompany them on their calls."

"That is a really good match, Mondo," Abe said. "He will not last a day there."

"Pack up your stuff Rei," Mondo said. "I'm transferring you to Wang Zhi."

"Anything will be better than robbing innocents," Rei said. "Just send me somewhere I can practice bushido."

"If you get on the road now you should be able to eat the noon meal with them in Shimabara," Mondo said.

145

"Shimabara?" Rei asked. "Isn't that the government sanctioned brothel?"

"That is the one and only here in Kyoto. Of course, there is Shinimichi in Osaka and the Yoshiwara in Edo," Watanabe said. "Most men would be happy to be sent there. Leave it to our whiner Rei to complain about this assignment as well."

"I'm not complaining," Rei said. "Any excuse to get away from this banditry is welcome on my part."

Rei collected his blanket roll and travelled south on the street that ended at Daito Kuji Temple. He walked for almost an hour when he came to Sixth Street. He turned east. After just a few more moments of walking he came to the large walled compound of Shimabara.

It was a city within a city. Shimabara was a small wooden castle. There were seven-foot-high wooden fences surrounding the two-acre compound designed as the pleasure quarters. There was one gate only and it opened onto Sixth Street. The gates opened at sunrise and closed at midnight. Anyone not in a hotel or sleeping in a brothel was arrested by the Shimabara police and fined. He approached the large open gates manned by samurai.

"What does the Ronin Army want in Shimabara?" one of the samurai guards asked.

"Same thing that everyone comes for you idiot," another chimed in.

"I am here on official duty from Bishop Inshin," Rei said. "I am to report to Team Wang Zhi."

"We don't care why you are here. Just keep the peace," the senior guard said. "Check your katana here."

"I do not have a katana," Rei said. "I only use a waka-zashi."

The senior guard had Rei raise his arms above his shoulders so the other two could search the folds in his kimono to ensure he was not smuggling in a long sword.

"You may keep the wakazashi," the lead guard said. "Never know when you may need to trim your nails."

The laughter didn't bother Rei.

Thirty paces inside the gate was a large inn. The name

on the front was the Blue Swan. He had found the lodging of Team Wang Zhi. He entered the establishment and found it was a hotel with a bar and noodle store in the front. The rooms ran back from the kitchen. A sign indicated the baths were in the rear. There was a second story of rooms up the stairs behind the bar.

Rei took a seat at the bar and inquired as to Team Wang Zhi from one of the hostesses.

"They are in the first two rooms samurai sama," she said. "But they do not get up until after noon."

"Why is that?" Rei asked.

"I have no idea," she said. "I just know they are very strange. I would be careful if I were you."

Rei decided to introduce himself when the Wang Zhi team left its rooms. He knew there were four of them on the team. He had bothered to ask the payroll cashier at the Ronin Army barracks before he left the Daito-kuji temple grounds. He knew Wang Zhi led the team. He was told to report to him. Rumors from some of the older members who would still talk to him indicated this team was not the normal configuration. In fact, several thought this team was not samurai at all. Some speculated they were bandits.

Rei decided to have his noon meal at the bar. A bowl of noodles and tea would tide him over until team Wang Zhi made its appearance. He took a seat at a wooden bench that allowed him good observation of the two rooms the inn hostess said were still occupied by the team.

Rei was eating his noodles and turning his head towards their rooms and did not notice the person that sat next to him on his left.

"Do you see something over there that interests you?" A feminine voice asked.

Rei turned to recognize a beautiful girl dressed in outlandish clothes about the same time he felt the point of a curved jeweled dagger in his side.

"Answer carefully samurai, we do not suffer spies lightly," she said.

Rei almost choked on his noodles and glanced down at the dagger.

"That is a very fine weapon you have there. I assume you know how to use it," Rei said.

"Even if I did not, at this range you'd be dead before you could move," the girl said. "Who are you and what do you want with those rooms?"

"My name is Matoumoto Rei and you can see from my haori and head band that I am part of the Ronin Army," Rei said.

"Is that supposed to impress me?" The girl asked.

"No, there is no reason it should," Rei said, "except I was ordered here to report to team leader Wang Zhi by Captain Mondo."

"Now why would Mondo send a pretty boy green pea like you to Team Wang Zhi?" the girl asked.

"I see you know Mondo," Rei said, attempting to turn toward her so he could bow. His attempted politeness was met with the point of the dagger moved more deeply into his side. Rei stopped turning.

"Sorry," Rei said. "I will just sit here and look at my noodles and answer your questions."

"Good choice," the girl said. "Maybe you are not as stupid as you look."

"Was that a question?" Rei asked.

The point dug deeper. Rei stopped talking.

"Now tell me," the girl said. "Why are you here?"

"I have already told you," Rei said. "I have been ordered here."

"I want to know why," the girl said.

"I do not think they like me much," Rei said.

The knife released some of its pressure.

"That is better," the girl said. "Why don't those morons like you?"

"I signed up for the Ronin Army to protect Tadanaga and get a position with the Lord of the Satsuma," Rei explained. "But all I have seen of Mondo and his crowd is thievery, thuggery and taking advantage of innocents."

"So, Mondo upsets your samurai sensibilities, is that it?" she asked. "Is the pretty boy afraid to dirty his hands?"

"I use my sword and my mind in rightful causes only," Rei said. "If your team expects me to kill innocents and rob merchants then you had better gut me now."

"Do you think I will not?" The girl asked.

"No, I think you are probably very skilled with that blade," Rei said.

"How did you ever get accepted by Mondo with that kind of an attitude?" The girl asked.

"The same way as the others I guess," Rei said. "I defeated Monk Token's naginata."

The girl really looked at Rei for the first time. "You must be very skilled with a katana for one so young."

"I do not own a katana," Rei said. "I fight with a wakazashi."

"You defeated Monk Token with a wakazashi?" The girl asked. "How?"

"Monk Token was overconfident. I took advantage of that," Rei said.

The girl returned the knife to her scabbard in her belt. "I do not know how we would use you Matoumoto Rei," the girl said. "It will be interesting to see if you fit in."

"So, you are part of Wang Zhi's team?" Rei asked.

"Yes, I am Aika," the girl said. "I joined just a few days ago."

Rei bowed his head. "Dozo yoroshuku."

Aika nodded back.

"Finish your noodles Rei," Aika said. "You never know when your next meal might be."

"My father used to say that," Rei said.

"Really?" Aika asked. "Then your father must have been a smart man."

"He still is," Rei said.

"Imoto, noodles and sake for me," Aika said to one of the young girls behind the counter.

"Hai," the girl shouted and scurried to the kitchen with the order.

"So, tell me about yourself Rei," Aika said.

"Not much to tell," Rei said. "I grew up on a farm. My father used to be a retainer, but the lord had to commit seppuku and we needed to eat. He became a farmer."

"Do not tell me you learned to defeat a naginata on the farm," Aika said.

"Yes, I guess I did," Rei said. "My father is the master of a wakazashi fighting system. He taught me."

"Now I understand," Aika said.

Aika's noodles arrived. She slurped the noodles and sipped her sake.

Rei kept stealing glances her way.

"Go ahead," Aika said. "Ask your questions."

"You look, dress and speak differently than any other woman I have ever seen," Rei said.

"I am a half breed," Aika said. "My mother was Japanese and my father Chinese. I am everything a samurai loathes. My dress is part Chinese and part Portuguese. I find the freedom of the Portuguese long sleeved shirt with a Chinese modified coat and peasant pants liberating. Because I like reliable foot-wear, I use the Portuguese leather boots. I also use the wide leather belt of the Portuguese. It allows me to carry my dagger, cutlass and a matchlock pistol. They all come in handy when boarding enemy ships."

"Who is the enemy?" Rei asked.

"Any other ship that I want to capture," Aika said.

"You sound like a pirate," Rei said.

"What do you know of pirates?" Aika said.

"Nothing," Rei said. "I have heard fanciful stories told by old seamen."

"Maybe not so fanciful," Aika said. "Most stories are probably true."

"What would a pirate want with the Ronin Army?" Rei asked

"You have too many questions," Aika said.

"The Ronin Army pay is good for me. It helps keep my father and young sister alive," Rei said. "But for someone used to capturing ships and looting cities, it is very small pay indeed. What are you really after?"

"You are very perceptive for one so young," Aika said.

"You keep calling me young. You cannot be much older than me," Rei said.

Aika laughed. "Farm boy, I am two lifetimes older than you."

"You do not look it," Rei said.

"Save your sweet compliments for Wang Zhi," Aika said. "You will need them."

Three of the most ill-kempt men emerged from the first room. They looked so unorthodox Rei was taken aback.

"What?" Aika asked. "You do not like the looks of your new companions?"

"They look like bandits, not ronin," Rei said.

The three passed by Rei and Aika without a word.

"They are on the move," Aika said. "Let us go."

Rei stood and left coins on the table for his noon meal. Aika did not.

"You must be running a tab," Rei suggested.

"Something like that farm boy," Aika said as she stood and moved behind the three Ronin Army members.

The three stopped at the gate to retrieve a collection of cutlasses and daggers.

The large leader noticed Rei with Aika. "Have you acquired a new toy?" Wang Zhi asked as he pushed his cutlass into his wide leather belt.

"He is a samurai Mondo has assigned to us," Aika said.

"What would we do with a samurai?" Wang Zhi asked.

"I have been wondering that myself," Aika said as she stuck a cutlass and a matchlock pistol in her wide leather belt.

As the five started for the gate Wang Zhi turned to Rei. "What is your name boy?"

"My name is Matoumoto Rei," Rei said bowing. "Dozo Yoroshuku."

"Never mind that," Wang Zhi said. "Where is your sword samurai?"

Rei patted the wakazashi in his obi. "It is here," Rei said.

"That is not a proper sword," Wang Zhi said. "That is an overgrown dagger."

All four of the Pirates laughed at Rei's discomfort.

"What can you do with that puny little thing?" Wang Zhi asked.

"I can keep or challenge the peace," Rei said.

"You are certainly full of yourself boy," Wang Zhi said.

"On the contrary team leader, I have much to learn," Rei said.

Wang Zhi looked to Aika. Aika shrugged her shoulders.

"Who claims your loyalty boy?" Wang Zhi asked.

Rei stopped to think.

"I will make it easier boy," Wang Zhi said. "Is your loyalty to Mondo?"

"Mondo is a petty thug," Rei said. "I have no loyalty to him."

"You do not get along with our leader?" Wang Zhi asked.

"They do not get along with me," Rei said.

"What did you do to provoke them boy?" Wang Zhi asked. "Did you threaten to carve them up with that child's toy?"

Rei patted his wakazashi. "It is no toy sir," Rei said.

"I think Mondo sent you here to spy on us," Wang Zhi accused.

"I think Mondo sent me here to die," Rei said.

All four of the Pirates stopped what they were doing and looked at Rei.

"Why would he do that?" Wang Zhi asked.

"Because I threatened his two lieutenants with my child's toy if I caught them robbing innocents again," Rei said.

Wang Zhi looked Rei over from head to toe. "I am Wang Zhi. I am the team leader. The bald one is Taka. The one with the scar is Saemon. You have already met Aika. Keep up and keep silent," Wang Zhi said.

Wang Zhi turned and started walking. Aika was beside him. Taka and Saemon walked together in the middle. Rei brought up the rear.

"What a braggart," Aika said.

"Something tells me the boy was not bragging," Wang Zhi said.

"Really?" Aika said turning to cast a glance back at Rei.

They walked eastward on Sixth Street until they reached

the Kamo River. There they turned south along the Riverwalk. The Riverwalk eventually left the water but paralleled the river. Multiple large trading companies had warehouses and offices opening on the road. They passed several and stopped at a large well-built building that Rei thought must open onto the river in the rear.

The entrance was a tall double door. One half of the door was open. As the five approached the entrance three large men barred their approach.

"State your business," their leader ordered.

"We have no business with you," Wang Zhi said. "Our business is with your boss. Please fetch him. Tell him Wang Zhi has arrived."

"One of the three men turned to the entrance and whistled. Soon five more men arrived holding hammers and bailing hooks.

"I did not come here to fight," Wang Zhi said. "But if you want to mix it with us, I will guarantee you will all be injured, and some will die."

"Big talk from a bandit," the leader said. "How do you think you will fare?"

Wang Zhi turned to look at his outnumbered team. "I think four of us will do quite well. I cannot speak for the boy. I have not seen him fight."

"We are aware of the Ronin Army. They are no better than you bandits," the leader said.

"We have no time for this," Aika said drawing her match lock. She sparked the fuse with a one-handed contraption and aimed it at the leader. "Either step aside or die."

The leader's eyes got wide, but he did not step aside.

Aika pulled the trigger and shot the leader in the body. He collapsed. Taka and Saemon raced around their companions and started hacking and slashing with their cutlasses. The waterfront toughs never had a chance. When their leader and the first two behind him fell to serious wounds the rest turned and fled.

Aika pinched off her fuse and reloaded her firearm. She looked up as she returned it to her belt.

"What?" she asked.

"Nothing," Rei said. "I have never seen a firearm used up close."

"What do you think?" she asked.

"I think both you and it are very dangerous," Rei said.

"Another astute observation farm boy," Aika said.

A middle-aged man in merchant clothing ran up to the pirates. "I am Yokan. This is my establishment. I am so sorry you were greeted this way," the man said bowing.

"What is with the welcoming party Yokan?" Wang Zhi asked.

"I am so sorry. I hired extra security and they did not hear of your arrival today," Yokan said. "It is a tragedy. This young man had a wife and a child."

"You are a liar merchant." All eyes went to Aika. "I would be surprised if you knew this fool's name. You hired him and the other river rats to test us to see if we were capable of protecting your cargo," Aika said. "This kind of treachery is common among merchants."

Rei was totally confused now.

Yokan smiled. "You would be the famous Aika. You are the right hand of the Osprey."

"I am," Aika said. "This is Wang Zhi whom I am sure you have heard of. The other two are Taka and Saemon. The farm boy is just tagging along."

"So nice to meet you Aika. You live up to your reputation," Yokan said.

"Stop the flattery and small talk. Show us the cargo so we can make arrangements for a barge," Aika said.

Yokan chuckled. "Certainly Aika, please step this way."

Rei kept quiet the whole time. The Pirates checked the cargo and wanted to know the draft of the barges and the depth of the Kamo River downstream. Wang Zhi, Aika and Yokan discussed availability of barges and cost. Rei was too far away to hear the arrangement, but it seemed that the two sides came to an agreement.

Everyone was silent on the way back to Shimabara. Everyone checked their cutlasses and pistol at the gate. The guards let Aika keep her curved dagger and Rei kept his wakazashi. When they entered the inn, Wang Zhi pulled Rei aside.

"You sleep in Aika's room. Stay alert. I suspect treachery from either Yokan or the Satsuma," Wang Zhi said.

"The Satsuma?" Rei asked. "What do they have to do with your business?"

"Do not ask questions boy," Wang Zhi said. "Stay sharp tonight and do not let anything happen to her."

Rei looked at Aika. She smiled and curled her fingers indicating he was to follow her. Aika stopped to talk to a hostess. "Make another futon for my room. My yojimbo will be staying with me," Aika said.

The hostess bowed and hurried off to accomplish the tasking.

"Follow me farm boy," Aika said.

Inside Aika's room Rei noticed her futon was already rolled out and under the far single window. It was a large room but with few furnishings. A wash stand with a bucket and a ladle was alongside one wall. Aika opened the wash stand cabinet to reveal towels and light cotton kimonos for bathing.

"Come on farm boy," Aika said. "Let us clean off the river mud."

Rei was more than a little shocked but caught the kimono and towel she threw him. He turned his back as Aika started to undress.

"Are you embarrassed farm boy?" Aika asked.

"Yes," Rei admitted.

"Have you never seen the naked female body?" Aika asked.

"Just my little sister when she was a baby," Rei said.

"What about your mother?" Aika asked. "Did she not bathe with you?"

"My mother died when I was young," Rei replied.

"So, the answer to my question is no," Aika said.

"The answer is no," Rei agreed.

"Well farm boy you may have a very educational night," Aika said, picking up the curved dagger and hiding it in her towel.

"Undress farm boy," Aika said. "You must be clean if

you are going to stay here tonight."

Rei gave up and changed with her watching. He wrapped his wakazashi in his towel.

"You are learning farm boy," Aika said and moved out the door.

Rei stayed a step behind her. Aika took the female entrance and Rei the male. He was the only one in the bathing area. It was still a little early for guests to bathe. Rei reminded himself that he was not in a traditional hotel. He was in a hotel catering to brothel visitors. Once clean Rei placed his lightweight kimono on a hook, his wakazashi on a rack, covered his private parts with his folded towel and entered the ofudo area. It was a large pool filled with heated water. He noticed Aika already sitting on the far side.

"Come join me farm boy," she teased.

Rei entered the hot water and left his towel just outside the water.

"You have many scars for one so young," Aika said.

"Farm work can be dangerous," Rei replied.

"Do not lie to me farm boy," Aika said. "Those scars are sword wounds."

"If you say so madam," Rei said.

"I am Aika," Aika said. "I am no madam."

"Yes Aika," Rei said, feeling more than a little embarrassed.

"You are blushing farm boy," Aika said. "It has been a long time since I saw a man blush."

Eager to change the subject, Rei ask a question. "What did you and Yokan talk about today?"

Aika placed her finger to her lips signaling silence. Then she rose up and moved to Rei. Rei averted his eyes but not before he noticed dark nipples on perfect breasts and a thatch of black hair between two tanned legs.

"You do not like what you see farm boy?" Aika asked as she sat beside Rei. She moved her mouth close to his ear. "Do not talk of our business aloud again if you value your life."

Rei nodded. Aika relaxed and let the heat of the water soak her naked body. Her legs touched his from knees to hips. He was anything but relaxed. Aika enjoyed the heat and chatted about things Rei could not remember. He was distracted by the heat in his loins. After what seemed like an eternity to Rei, Aika finally stood. He wanted to look the other way but could not and watched her leave the water, dry off and dress with the bath kimono before he rose and followed suit.

Inside her room she changed into the hotel-supplied sleeping kimono and sat down to eat the meal provided on two trays in the center of the room. Rei joined her. They both ate in silence. When she finished, she returned the bowls to her tray and placed the ohashi there as well.

"I cannot understand whether you are a toy or a weapon," Aika said.

"I can help you by telling you I am not a toy," Rei said.

"You do not care to sleep with me?" Aika asked. "Does my mixed blood and pirate background disgust your samurai sensibilities?"

Rei looked her in the eye. "You do not disgust me in any way," Rei said. "You are the most beautiful woman I have ever seen."

"Then why would you decline to sleep with me tonight?"

Rei thought about that a minute. "Because I value you."

"Value me?" Aika asked. "How do you value me?"

"You are beautiful," Rei said. "We have only just met. We are not in love. I think sleeping with a woman should be the culmination of love, or at least we should like each other."

"Are you crazy farm boy?" Aika asked. "We are in a hotel in the middle of a government sanctioned brothel area. Sleeping with females you do not love is what this place is all about."

"Be that as it may," Rei said. "If I was to sleep with you, I feel like I would be taking advantage of you. You are worth more than that."

"You are a virgin are you not?" Aika asked.

Rei surprised her with his answer. "Yes, and if I loved you and wanted to take care of you for the rest of my life and thought you felt the same way, I would sleep with you," Rei said.

Aika smiled. "You are a fool farm boy. You should take pleasure as you find it."

"Maybe so," Rei said. "But making love without any

thought beyond immediate release seems petty to me."

"I could make you sleep with me," Aika said. "I have done it before with others."

"Maybe so," Rei said. "But I would think less of you for it. I do not think you deserve that."

"I give up farm boy," Aika said. "You are too sweet for me."

"Before you go to sleep…," Rei said.

"Yes," Aika asked thinking he had changed his mind.

"Could you move your futon to the far wall? I will place the trays outside. I want to sleep in the center of the room," Rei said.

"Why?" Aika asked.

"Because when the lights are out it will be hard to see. We farm boys are familiar with the dark," Rei said.

Aika looked at Rei. "You keep surprising me farm boy. Go ahead and move my futon and then yours."

Rei rearranged the bedding. Aika placed her curved dagger under her covers. Rei placed his wakazashi in his left hand, blew out the candle and pulled the covers up to his chest.

They had been lying for some time when Aika asked, "Do you really think I'm beautiful?"

"As a summer morning on the farm," Rei said.

Aika chuckled. Then they slept.

Rei listen for Aika's breathing. It was even and deep. He moved his head slightly. Something had awakened him. He could feel a presence in the room. He assumed they had entered from the window. Then he heard the main door sliding back ever so quietly. It was dark outside and the celebration from the bar area and the brothels across the street had subsided.

Rei sat up and rolled to a kneeling position in front of Aika. His sword coming out of its scabbard awakened Aika. Rei sensed rather than saw a shuriken thrown at Aika. He deflected it with the wakazashi. Then they charged.

Rei fought from the kneeling position. He blocked the sword coming from the darkness on his right. He countered by slicing into the black clad knees of the attacker. The attacker fell onto Rei's bedding. Rei plunged the tip of his sword into the wounded man's back.

Immediately, Rei sensed a lunge from the left, parried down, and reversed the wakazashi to split the man's face open. He screamed and withdrew. The third attacker came from the wash stand area. This attacker dived over Rei to get to Aika. Rei sliced at the form but missed. Aika did not. Her curved dagger found flesh. Rei plunged his sword in the attackers back.

Wang Zhi, Taka and Saemon burst into the room with a lantern and daggers. The light showed three dead ninjas littering the room. Blood was seeping into Aika and Rei's bedding.

"Are you hurt Aika?" Wang Zhi asked.

"No," Aika said. "Thanks to my yojimbo, I am fine."

"I missed one Aika," Rei said. "My apologies."

"He leapt over you because he could not get through you," Aika said. "You have nothing to apologize for."

The commotion in the hallway culminated in three samurai police officers pushing the three pirates to one side to gain entry.

"What is going on here?" The leader asked, pointing a jutte at Rei.

"We were attacked by these three trying to take my life," Rei said.

"Who are they?" The leader asked.

"They are obviously ninjas," Rei said cleaning his wakazashi on the dead ninja on his bedding.

"Who are you?" The leader asked.

"He is with us," Wang Zhi said. "We came running when we heard the commotion."

"What are you doing in Shimabara?" The leader asked Rei.

"I am a lieutenant in the Ronin Army," Rei said. "My name is Matoumoto Rei. I was assigned to help these men in their business. I believe Bishop Inshin made the assignment."

The mention of the bishop's name changed the policeman's attitude. "The only weapon you used was a wakazashi?"

Rei snuck a peek downward to see if the curved dagger was hidden. It was.

"Yes officer," Rei said. "I only have the wakazashi your

guards allowed me to keep today. Thank you very much or we would've been defenseless."

"You do not know who these men are?" The officer asked.

"No," Rei said. "I can honestly say I do not."

"Saemon," Wang Zhi said. "Go retrieve that shuriken embedded in the wall."

Saemon did as instructed. Wang Zhi turned the multi bladed star in his hand, careful not to touch the tips. "This is a Fuma weapon," Wang Zhi said.

"The Satsuma ninjas?" The officer asked.

"The same," Wang Zhi said.

"Why did they attack you?" The officer asked looking at Rei.

"I think they got the wrong room," Rei volunteered.

"Yes, that must be it," Wang Zhi said.

"Well they won't get the wrong room again," the officer said. "Matoumoto Rei come to the bar area and make a statement. I'll have the owner move you to a different room and we will get rid of these vermin. Your wife can get dressed and move to the new room soon."

"Thank you," Rei said. "She has a very delicate constitution." Rei turned his head back toward Aika and winked.

Rei entered the new room and found Aika already in bed. But the candle was lighted and Aika was still awake. Rei pulled back the covers of his own futon which was now next to hers.

"That was quick thinking using the bishop's name," Aika said.

"We farm boys have to think on our feet," Rei said.

"I should thank you for saving my life tonight," Aika said.

"No thanks are necessary," Rei said. "It was my job as your yojimbo."

"What was that crack about my delicate constitution?" Aika asked.

"You seem delicate to me," Rei said.

Rei blew out the candle and got under the covers.

"Did Wang Zhi tell you anything?" Aika asked.

"He said you must depart in the morning for Osaka," Rei whispered. "I am to return to Mondo."

"There are still several hours before light," Aika said. "Are you sure you will not join me over here? I am delicate and need reassurance."

Rei thought for a minute. "Move over," Rei said. "I've decided I like you."

"Wise choice farm boy," Aika said. "You are really beginning to interest me."

XX

Baths

Hideki sat on a submerged rock bench. The hot water created a steam against the cooler air. He relaxed in the large ofudo of the Gumsumgumi run hotel. He was safe here in the huge bath. But the katana on the dry shelf behind his head within easy reach attested to his vigilance. It was night and half of the bath opened to the Sumida River below. It had been almost two years since he had visited the hotel. Much had happened since then. He let the almost unbearable hot water soak into his body and felt his tension evaporate with the steam.

"I must thank you Nichi for this," Hideki said aloud. There was no one to hear him as he had the large bath to himself. He thought about the last time he visited here. That night was full of wonder. He lost his virginity that night to Myo. He also lost his heart to her.

He moved the small cloth from the water to his head and covered his eyes.

"I could almost sleep here," he said to no one.

"That might be dangerous samurai-sama," a distinctly feminine voice said through the steam.

Hideki pulled the cloth from his eyes. He had not heard her enter. She had moved with ease across the cleaning area, entered the hot pool and moved to a bench across from him in total silence.

"You move like a ghost," Hideki said.

"Oh samurai-sama, you must be hard of hearing," she said.

"My hearing is fine. It is my heart that needs attention," Hideki said and quickly regretted his choice of words.

"You sound too young to have heart problems samurai-sama," the woman said.

Hideki strained his eyes trying to see through the steam. He could see her form now, at least from the shoulders up above the water, but her face was blurred. For a man who prided himself on discerning different dialects or bens he could not place her voice.

"Physically my heart is sound," Hideki said. "You just gave me a start appearing like you did."

"If your heart is physically fine," the voice said, "Are you are pining for your lady?"

Hideki could not place the dialect no matter how hard he tried.

"I cannot place your ben. It is not a southern dialect I recognize nor is it from Edo. Where is your home?" Hideki asked.

"Oh samurai-sama do you strike up conversations with lone women with that silly question?"

"Not usually," Hideki said.

"Samurai-sama are you interested in me or my voice?" she asked.

Hideki felt himself blush despite the hot water.

"I am sorry if my question sounded personal. It was your dialect that I had not heard before. It intrigued me," Hideki said.

Hideki strained once again to make out her face but the steam off the pool was too pervasive.

"The ben is Tsugaru," the woman said.

"Oh, you're from up north. No wonder I did not recognize it," Hideki said. "I have never traveled north."

"Do you travel often samurai-sama?"

"I travel sometimes," Hideki said.

"You look too young to travel much," she said.

"I am from Kii province. I have traveled from there to Edo via the Tokaido. Last year I went on a musha shugyo to Kyushu in the south with a friend," Hideki said.

"Was it a lady friend?" she asked.

"No, it was not," Hideki said.

"How sad, I think it would be romantic to take a trip with a lover," she said. "Maybe I can accompany you on your next journey?" she asked.

"I do not think so," Hideki said feeling flustered.

"Are you afraid your lady friend would find out?" she asked.

"Partly," Hideki said. "She seems to know everything."

"Then what is the other part?"

"She is my first real love. I do not want to do anything that would spoil our relationship," Hideki said.

"How romantic that sounds samurai-sama, but all men cheat. How long were you on your last travels?"

"I was gone one year," Hideki said.

"What? And you never slept with another woman? Are you a bozu?" she asked.

"No, I am not a priest," Hideki said.

"Then why did you not bed another?" she asked.

"I guess because I only want her," Hideki said.

"Oh samurai-sama you have not met me. I am trained in the art of pleasure. I bet I could make you forget your lover," she said.

"No thank you," Hideki said.

"But you do not know what you are missing samurai-sama," the woman said and then started to rise from her bench.

From across the pool Hideki could see her raven wing black hair and her alabaster white body. As she moved, he could discern her nude feminine form down to her hips where the water started.

"Do not come any closer," Hideki said nervously as he stood, grasped his katana and started towards the steps.

"Oh samurai-sama you do not have to run from me. I will not harm you," she said.

Hideki stopped in mid step and turned toward the woman careful to keep his sword out of the water. She had changed her speech pattern with those last words. She now spoke like a citizen of Edo in the Tohoku dialect. He would know that voice anywhere.

"Myo?" He asked as his lover appeared through the steam.

"Sit back down Hideki, I was just playing with you," Myo said.

"How did you disguise your voice like that?" Hideki asked as they sat beside each other in the water.

"Have you forgotten who I am?" Myo asked.

"That was incredible," Hideki said. "I did not know changing your dialect was possible."

"You are samurai Hideki. You think on one plane. I am shinobi no mono. Ninja exist on many planes," Myo said.

"I do not know what to say," Hideki said. "I feel really stupid not recognizing you."

"Do not feel stupid. Feel happy to see me," Myo said.

Hideki felt the hot water on his chest as he moved closer and placed his arm around Myo.

"I guess this was a test. Did I pass?" Hideki asked.

Myo turned her head to Hideki.

"You passed Hideki. But you know I would understand if you slept with other women," Myo said.

"But I would not understand," Hideki said. "How can you bed a woman you do not love?" Hideki asked.

"Men do it all the time. You are still a boy in many ways Hideki. I did not say I would like it, but I would understand," Myo said.

"I do not remember my parents. I was too young when they died. But I do remember my grandmother. Jii cherished her. She helped raise Naga and me. Jii would always tell us not to expect fidelity if we do not practice it ourselves," Hideki said.

"Jii is a man of character," Myo said. Then she changed the subject. "You know that I can never be your wife. I am not samurai."

"Then we will have to exist on our own plane because I cannot live without you," Hideki said.

Myo smiled. "Such pretty words to hear Hideki," Myo said. "You may expect fidelity because you give fidelity and I have never said that to another man."

Hideki looked deep into Myo's eyes. "Good, then I will

share you with no one. I will be selfish."

"I could sit here all night my love, but tomorrow will be a busy day. We must find your nephew so I can reclaim my honor," Myo said.

Hideki looked forward into the steam.

"We will find him," Hideki said.

"Yes," Myo said. "We will find him together. Come now I have a room for us."

"Well aren't you the efficient one?" Hideki said.

"Come samurai-sama I am trained in the art of pleasure," Myo said reverting to the Tsugaru dialect.

"Oh boy," Hideki said. He'd been thinking of sleep after the hot soak. Now he was wide awake.

Later while basking in the glow of post coital bliss, Hideki turned his head to a very naked Myo.

"I feel hypocritical to be feeling so good when my sister-in-law and brother suffer another night without their child."

"Do not think that way my love. Life is full of pain. Take pleasure when you find it. It will be short-lived anyway," Myo said.

"I suppose you are correct. You are my first love so I want to stay with you as long as I can," Hideki said.

"What about Yuki? Did you not fall in love with her first?" Myo asked.

"I was seventeen and fresh from the country. She turned my head, but she and Naga soon crushed my hopes," Hideki said.

"So, no lingering desires?" Myo asked.

"Of course not, she's a mother and married to my brother. Besides it's not every man who gets a girl trained in the art of pleasure," Hideki teased.

"You are teasing me now as I did you earlier tonight. But you forget I am ninja. We ninja know how to kill many ways and leave no trace," Myo warned.

"That is very true. I guess I better seek your forgiveness," Hideki said.

"That you should," Myo said. "But I would prefer we try the pleasure part again, if you are up to it samurai-sama."

"Before we reunite for pleasure, was there anything to report from the cordon today?" Hideki asked.

"There was one irregularity," Myo said. A palanquin with the hollyhock emblem with an escort of twenty guards left the city this evening."

"What?" Hideki asked sitting up.

Myo pulled him down again. "Relax, there was no way to inspect it, so I am having it followed. I will get word where it is going."

"I would bet that was Yoshitsune being escorted out of the city using the Shogun's emblem as camouflage," Hideki said.

"That would be my guess as well," Myo said. "But that leaves the question of whether we continue to raid the Koga strongholds with The Mist tomorrow?"

"We must, if for no other reason than cutting down on those loyal to Ugai and recruiting what we can to The Mist," Hideki said.

"You are very wise for one so young," Myo said.

"No, it is just common sense," Hideki said. "Do you have good people following the palanquin?"

"I have the best. Midori and her team are on it," Myo said.

"If Midori is on the trail, I have nothing to worry about," Hideki said.

"The only thing you have to worry about tonight samurai-sama is satisfying me," Myo said in a Tsugaru dialect.

"Yes ma'am," Hideki said.

XXI

Mother Grieving

"Haru, you must stop grieving. You are still young, and you have one of the most successful stores in Kyoto to run. I have been at your side all of your life and it pains me to see you spend your days cooped up in your quarters crying your eyes out," the old woman said.

The young woman in the expensive kimono and long black hair spread out over her shoulders raised her red eyes to her companion.

"Life is cruel Ume," she said sniffling. "I lost my mother early. Then my father arranged a marriage to a man I did not love. But I bore him a son. Then my husband and my father were cut down by Kyoto street killers on their way home. I hardly get them buried and my lovely almost a year-old son dies of a fever. My son is with Buddha and I am a widow with no family. I am cursed among women," she wailed.

"You are not cursed Haru. You are young. You are beautiful. You will find a new husband and have more children. But you must take control of your store or you will have no future. Many are relying on you," Ume said.

"Have you ever lost a child Ume?" Haru asked.

"You know I have never married," Ume said.

"Then you do not know the despair I feel. Leave me please," Haru said.

Ume departed from her mistress's presence and moved to the adjoining store in the front of the building. It was a large wooden building. The entrance from the street was double sliding doors. Bamboo poles on hooks announced the store's name in large vertical writing on large canvas banners. Yamakaya the banners proclaimed was the finest silk store in Kyoto. A much smaller hardwood plaque above the doors with a white chrysanthemum announced to the world that the store supplied the Emperor's household.

Ume moved through the wooden tables with clothing materials in many colors. Each table had a paper declaring the name of the material and the price per arm's-length. Many customers pawed through the inventory haggling with the store clerks who extolled the benefit of a purchase and downplayed complaints of price or selection.

Ume stopped at the chief clerk's area partitioned by a small wooden rail around a low hardwood desk. The chief clerk sat behind the desk with his legs crossed beneath him. As Ume approached the chief clerk was watching the exchanges between sales clerks and customers. His metal strongbox of money was positioned under his small desk. The soroban used to calculate numbers was in the center of his desk. Upon seeing Ume approach, he turned his attention to her.

"Any progress?"

"No," Ume said. "She is still pining for her son."

"If she does not snap out of it soon our competitors will band together to undercut our prices. You cannot be the largest clothing store in Kyoto and not show your face," the chief clerk said. "We are already finding it difficult to keep our suppliers."

"I know, I have a friend who may be able to help us," Ume said.

"Really?" The chief clerk asked. "Whoever it is have them make haste."

"It depends on many things. Most of all it depends on Haru being willing to accept a substitute," Ume said.

"You are going to find her a new son?"

"Why not? Her father adopted her husband into the family to provide him an heir to Yamakaya. Why not adopt a son?" she asked.

"Giving birth to your own child and adopting are two very

different things," the chief clerk said.

"Maybe so, but when the needle salesman comes in tomorrow ask him to see me," Ume said.

"Certainly," the chief clerk said.

The following day Ume rolled back the sliding doors of Haru's quarters a fraction. "Simasen Haru, the needle peddler is here to see you," Ume said.

Haru raised her head from the teacup. "Why would I be interested in seeing the needle peddler?"

"Because he has a situation that might benefit both him and you," Ume said.

"What could he have that would interest me?" Haru asked.

"With your permission I would rather he explain it to you," Ume said.

Haru sighed. "If you must, send him in."

Ume slid the door all the way back to reveal a needle peddler and a poor samurai woman in old clothing clutching a baby to her chest.

Haru did not wave the visitors into the room. Instead she rose and went to them.

"A baby," Haru said. "How old is it?"

The young mother bowed still clutching the infant. "He is almost a year," she said.

"Oh, that is the age when I lost my child. You must take extra care to protect him from illness," Haru said.

"Yes, I know," the mother said. "That is why we are here today."

"Oh?" Haru asked looking toward Ume.

The needle vendor bowed to Haru. "Honorable lady this woman is my niece. Our family was once samurai. But we fell on hard times. Our clan was abolished, so we had to learn new professions. I became a needle peddler and my niece married a poor samurai. He was recently killed by the shogun's guards and charged with treason even though he was innocent. She has another son four years old. He is waiting outside. I am helping her to get back to her father's lands in the south. The shogun's guards are looking for her. They are expecting to see a woman with an infant and a four-year-old," the needle vendor said.

"How dreadful for you," Haru said. "What can I do to help?"

"The risk of capture is too great if she continues her journey with both children. The risk for the baby is also too high to continue," the needle vendor said.

"What will happen if the shogun's men find you?" Haru asked.

"They will kill us all," the mother said.

"I am sorry, but I still do not see what I can do," Haru said.

"Please take my baby in and hide him for me. If I survive, I will retrieve him once I reach home. By then the shogun's guards will have forgotten about my dead husband," the woman pleaded.

Haru reached out and pulled the cloth from the baby's face.

"He is so cute. He reminds me of my own son. What is his name?" Haru asked.

"His name is Yoshi," the mother said. "He is a good boy."

Haru's eyes opened wide. "That was my son's name as well," she said.

"If you take the baby it would help ensure our survival. But I must warn you that it may take several months before we can get back and reclaim little Yoshi," the needle vendor said.

Ume noticed Haru smile for the first time in months.

"I will take the child," Haru said. "And I will protect him."

The mother bowed as low as she could with the baby in her arms. "Thank you, I will never forget this."

Haru reached across as the baby was placed in her arms and could not keep from smiling. She moved the cloth away from the baby's body and exposed his little hands, one of which grasped Haru's finger and would not let go.

"Oh my," Haru said. "I think he likes me."

The needle vendor turned to the mother who looked in anguish. "We must depart now if we are to live."

The mother nodded, stood, and took two steps to leave and look back. "Goodbye my son. I shall return," she said and clutched the cloth from her sleeve to dab her eyes. Then she turned and fled after the needle vendor.

Haru could not stop smiling. She looked to Ume. "Thank you, Ume. My life has meaning again."

"You are welcome Haru," Ume said.

A block from Yamakaya the needle vendor and the mother ducked into an alley.

"Do you think she suspects?" the mother asked.

"No, you did a superb acting job," the vendor said.

"Why does our leader want us to dump the kid here?" she asked.

"He did not tell us to dump the kid here. He just said to find a good home where the kid will be healthy and report back. You know Ugai, he never tells us anything except what to do," the needle vendor said.

The woman nodded and they departed into the maze of alleyways that constituted Kyoto.

XXII

Yojimbo Rei

"Abe take Rei and bruise the clerks. Watanabe and I will break some bones of the owner," Mondo said.

"This again?" Rei asked.

"What is wrong? Do you not like being a lieutenant in the Ronin Army?" Mondo asked.

"Not really. I joined to get a chance at having a samurai position with the Satsuma, but so far I have become a thug and a thief," Rei said.

"What you mean by that?" Watanabe asked, stepping close to Rei.

Rei didn't flinch. "I mean extorting shopkeepers to pay fees for Tadanaga and keeping the money yourselves is wrong. I am through threatening and beating up the innocent," Rei said. "This is not bushido."

"I told you boy, when you joined that once in the Ronin Army you could not leave," Mondo said placing his hand on his sword. "I even sent you to Wang Zhi to learn some manners. Why you returned will always be a mystery to me."

"You mean you are mystified why Wang Zhi didn't kill me?" Rei asked.

"Yes, I am curious why your holier than thou attitude was allowed among the Wang Zhi pirates," Mondo said.

"Maybe the reason I survived is they are a much more honorable bunch than you dung beetles," Rei said.

Mondo started to draw his katana.

"Go ahead and draw Mondo. All three of you step up at

once. You may get me, but I'm sure I'll take at least two of you with me," Rei said calmly.

All three stopped their draws. They wanted him dead but there was fear in their eyes. They knew him to be a fierce fighter with uncanny skills at entering an opponent's sword reach and slashing with that amazingly sharp single short sword of his.

Mondo relaxed. "No need for violence among ourselves."

"You are not going to let him get away with those words are you Mondo?" Abe asked.

"No need for confrontation," Mondo said. Then he turned to Rei. "I have a mission that might best suit your sensitivities."

"If it lets me practice bushido again, I will take it," Rei said.

Mondo extracted a paper from his sleeve. "You will be a yojimbo to a young mother."

"What is the rest of it?" Rei asked.

"There is no rest of it. She's a young widow and owner of Yamakaya in the old section of Kyoto," Mondo said.

"Yamakaya?" Watanabe said. "They are one of the largest stores in the city. Why haven't we collected dues from them?"

"I have no idea. They are not on the list," Mondo said.

"Why does the widow of Yamakaya need a bodyguard?" Rei asked.

"She is taking care of a young baby and Iemitsu's guards are trying to kill it. That is as much as I know," Mondo said.

"Does the widow know I'm coming?" Rei asked.

"That is your problem. This order came from Bishop Inshin of Tadanaga's staff. I'm glad to have you out of my hair," Mondo said.

The three turned from Rei and pushed customers and clerks aside as they entered the dry goods store.

Rei found himself alone on the street. He looked at the paper with Yamakaya's name and location. He tucked it into his ragged kimono.

"Well it is better than being a thug or a pirate," Rei said to himself.

A long walk across town to the old section of Kyoto

brought him to the front entrance of Yamakaya. The signs on
the banners across the entrance announced the store's name.
They also indicated they were the purveyors of fine silk and
clothing goods. As he approached the entrance, he noticed
a small plaque. The plaque was nothing more than a white
chrysanthemum, but it announced to all that the store was
worthy enough to provide goods to the Emperor's house.

Rei noticed women in fine silk kimonos entering and
leaving through the canvas flaps of the doorway. One young
woman in an expensive green silk kimono looked at Rei with
distaste. Rei looked down at his dirty and torn kimono and his
bloodstained haori of the Ronin Army and felt very much out
of place. But a job is a job, besides, as lieutenant in the Ronin
Army he was still able to send most of his pay home to his
father. He felt good about that. So, Rei puffed out his chest
and strode into the canvas flaps like he owned the place.

The chief clerk at his supervisory perch to the left of the
large entrance area signaled Rei over.

"This entrance is for customers only. Please go around to
the back," he said.

His tone was pleasant, but the delivery left no doubt in
Rei's mind that he was being dismissed.

"I am here on Bishop Inshin's order," Rei said just as
politely.

"We know Bishop Inshin. He is a very good customer. But
if you are here to pick up a delivery you must go to the back
like all servants," the clerk said with a smile.

"I have not come here to pick up a delivery," Rei said.

"I did not think so; I know all scheduled pickups. So why
are you standing before me?" The clerk asked.

"Do not let the lack of two swords fool you clerk. I am
samurai and here to protect the lady of Yamakaya," Rei said
with the same fake smile the clerk used.

"I know nothing of this," the clerk protested.

"There is no reason you should clerk. My business has
nothing to do with commerce," Rei said.

The clerk eyed the single short sword in Rae's obi. He
had never heard of a samurai with only one sword and a short

one at that. But the clerk profession required a sharp eye. He noticed the blood stains on the young man's Ronin Army outer coat. Then there was something about this young man's demeanor. It oozed confidence. So, the chief clerk bowed slightly, motioned for his assistant to take his place at the table and bowed again.

"You have my apologies samurai-sama. I shall go announce you to the lady of Yamakaya," the clerk said. "Please have a seat on the side." The chief clerk departed, and Rei moved to the wooden benches along the side of the entry room.

"Simasen," the chief clerk said announcing himself outside the sliding doors to the lady of Yamakaya's quarters.

"What is it?" Ume asked from inside the quarters.

"There is a young man at the entrance claiming that he has been sent by Bishop Inshin to protect our lady," the chief clerk said.

Ume slid back the door slightly. "Protect her from whom?" she asked.

"I do not know," the clerk said. "He seems very young for a yojimbo and he is only wearing one sword. But he is wearing the white Haori of the Ronin Army."

Umi turned to the smiling lady holding the baby in her arms. The lady did not take her eyes off the gurgling baby.

"I will see him. The mother said the baby was in danger from the shogun's guards. I must make every effort to protect beautiful Yoshi," the lady said.

"Yes, my lady," Ume said. Then she turned back to the kneeling clerk opposite her, "you heard the lady, send him back."

"Yes Ume," the chief clerk said and left.

The clerk returned to the front of the store and motioned Rei over.

"The lady will see you," he said. "But leave your filthy Haori here. We do not want to offend the lady."

"Oh my," Rei said. "I thought she was a merchant. I didn't realize she had been elevated to goddess status."

The chief clerk winced.

"Have it your way samurai. Follow me," the clerk said.

At the closed sliding doors, the chief clerk announced them. "Simasen, the yojimbo is here."

Ume ushered Rei into the large room that was the lady's quarters and closed the sliding doors. Rei noticed Ume and the lady and the baby. He swept the rest of the room noticing no other entrances.

The kneeling lady with the baby in her arms half turned on the tatami and bowed slightly to Rei.

"I am Haru," she said by way of introduction. "And this is Yoshi. Dozo yoroshiku onagai shimas."

Rei returned the bow. "I am Matoumoto Rei," he said. "It has been sometime since I have been addressed so formally."

Haru looked at the boy before her. He was dirty. That repulsed her. Yet there was a calmness about him that she found interesting. It was his eyes that disarmed her. When she looked directly in his eyes she shrank back involuntarily. Then she noticed the bloodstain on his haori.

"Thank the bishop for me Matoumoto Rei. But I think I will require someone with more experience," she said.

Rei smiled slightly. "I understand my lady. I am young. I fight with one sword and it is short. But I am confident in my abilities to protect you and the baby," Rei said.

"We cannot have a ruffian at Yamakaya," Ume said. "You would upset the clients. You would be bad for business."

"I am rough looking. That is because I have been working with rough men doing rough jobs," Rei said. "But I am honest or try to be and my sword is yours if you want it. If not, I will be going."

Rei stood, bowed to the room and moved to the sliding doors.

A commotion broke out in the front of the Yamakaya building. The yelling and destruction up front could be heard all the way in the back in the lady's quarters. The chief clerk ran back to the lady's quarters just as Rei was opening the doors.

The chief clerk pushed Rei out of the way and turned to the lady. "My lady, the shogun's men are here. They say they want to see Yamakaya's widow. They are wrecking the place and coming this way."

"How many of them are there?" Rei asked.

The clerk looked at Rei and said nothing.

"Tell him you fool," Ume said.

"There are four samurai. What are we going to do?" The clerk cried.

Rei grabbed the clerk by the front of his kimono and slapped him twice. The clerk's eyes got very wide.

"You will get another man and have a pushcart at the back of the building with straw covers," Rei said.

The clerk did not move. Rei raised his hand again. "Do you want to be struck again?" Rei asked.

"No samurai-sama," clerk said.

"Then move as if your life depends on it. It does. If the samurai coming this way don't kill you, I will," Rei said.

The clerk bolted down the corridor toward the back of the building. Rei looked at the opposite direction and saw the snooty girl with the green kimono being pushed down. Amazingly she turned just at the right time to miss the push. The pusher tumbled to the floor. Rei closed the door.

"Ume is it?" Rei asked searching for her name.

"Yes," Ume responded.

"Take this haori and my headband and hide it. Does the lady have any of her husband's old clothes?" Rei asked.

"Yes," Ume said.

"Bring the clothes to me as fast as you can," Rei said.

Ume raced to the chest on the far end of the room. She pulled out a silk kimono and obi and a pair of Chinese slippers placing the haori and the headband into the chest.

"Will these do?" Umi asked.

"They will have to. Go to the door and tell me when they are near," Rei said.

Umi complied.

"My lady you should turn away. I am going to change into these clothes," Rei suggested.

Haru smiled and did not move.

"Suit yourself," Rei said and started removing his clothes.

"You have many scars for someone so young," Haru said when he had finished dressing.

"A short but interesting life my lady," Rei said as he moved to the chest with his haori and headband and dropped his black kimono and hakama on top. When he returned to the sliding doors, he slipped his wakazashi inside the silk kimono and sat facing Haru with his back to the doors.

"They are coming," Ume said. "What should we do?"

"Join your mistress and do not venture toward the door again until I say it is safe," Rei said.

They could hear the samurai coming down the hall opening sliding doors and turning over furniture yelling and moving onto the next room. It was obvious they were looking for something or someone.

The sliding door was thrown back and an armor-clad samurai stepped in. This first samurai stopped when he came to Rei's back. His eyes got big when he saw Haru.

"Finally, we find the widow," he said and started toward Haru.

Rei rose and turned to block the man's movement forward.

"What business do you have with my lady?" he asked.

The samurai hesitated. "We are raising funds for Iemitsu's investiture."

"How much does Iemitsu need? Rei asked.

"We are on the shogun's business. We need one hundred ryu," the samurai said.

The two other samurai moved into the room. One remained in the hall. All of them still had their zori on their feet.

"I must protest samurai-sama. You burst into my lady's business. You harm her customers and destroy her property. Now you are in my lady's chambers with your straw shoes still on your feet and you have the temerity to want one hundred gold coins. Iemitsu must be in dire financial need to want so much money," Rei said.

"Stand aside merchant. If we do not get our gold coin, we will kill everyone in the building," the first man through the door commanded.

"Now I understand," Rei said.

"Now you understand what?" The second samurai demanded.

"Now I understand why the shogun's men are wearing no

hollyhock emblem and are equipped in ancient armor and still wearing shoes," Rei said.

"What are you trying to say?" The first samurai asked.

"I am saying that you are not Iemitsu's men as the chief clerk supposed. I do not think you are even samurai. I think you are bandits trying to extort money from a famous lady," Rei accused.

All four samurai went for their swords.

Rei put up his hand.

"Unfortunately for you, I am samurai and yojimbo to this lady. If you leave now we will not report you to the magistrate," Rei said.

"And if we do not?" The lead samurai asked.

Rei moved the silk kimono off his shoulder exposing the short sword at his waist. "Then there is a pushcart at the back of this building. I will kill you and your bodies will be dumped far from here and your families and friends can mourn your disappearance," Rei said.

"Let's get him and our money," the third samurai yelled.

The lead samurai started to draw his sword but froze when he looked into Rei's eyes. "Hold it," he shouted.

"Hold what?" the second samurai asked.

"This kid is a stone-cold killer," the first samurai said taking a step back.

"Get out of the way coward," the third samurai said pushing the first samurai out of the way and starting to draw his sword.

In a flash Rei drew his short sword and slashed along the throat of the closest man. He continued his movement to the right severing the artery in the second samurai's neck. The third man almost got his sword out when Rei leapt over the dying samurai at his feet and punctured the last samurai's right eye. Rei's third victim screamed and died instantly.

As soon as the three collapsed Rei turned around covering the first samurai. He was open mouthed and expecting death.

"Remove your sword with your left hand and place it behind you," Rei ordered.

The bandit complied.

"Drag each of your friends to the back and place their corpses into the cart. Take them to wherever you want, but I want our cart back tomorrow. Do you understand?" Rei asked.

"Yes samurai-sama," the bandit stammered.

"What is your name?" Rei asked.

"They call me Kudo," the bandit said.

"Kudo if I see you after you return the cart tomorrow you will be as dead as your friends. Now get them out. They are spoiling the tatami," Rei said.

Kudo reached down and carried the first corpse towards the back of the building. He made two more trips and did not return. The chief clerk showed up. He winced at the sight of so much blood on the tatami.

"That samurai took his three friends and one of our carts and said he'd return it tomorrow. What did you say to him samurai-sama? I did not think to shogun's guards could be so terrified," the chief clerk said.

"I think it was more of a demonstration," Haru said.

Rei moved the kimono back up onto his shoulder and placed the wakazashi inside. He looked at the lady. Ume was behind her with a shocked look on her face.

"It is safe to move again Ume," Rei said.

Ume tried to stand and eventually did.

"Please retrieve my clothes Ume," Rei said.

Umi turned and moved toward the chest.

"Just a moment Ume," Haru said.

Ume stopped and turned her head back toward Haru.

"Draw our new yojimbo a bath and get him clothes befitting a samurai in his new position," Haru said.

Ume smiled. "Yes, my lady, with pleasure."

Haru kept her gaze on Rei. "Yoshi and I feel safer already." Then she smiled.

XXIII

Departure

"Come in Yoshi," Myo said.

Yoshi slid back the door and entered the hotel room.

"How did you know it was me? I made no noise," Yoshi asked.

"It was because there was no noise. Besides, the crickets in the garden outside stopped singing,"

Myo said, pulling the kake buton back and rising naked to collect a hotel robe from the floor.

Yoshi averted his eyes. "Is the Prince of the Yoshinobu in any shape to join the living?" He asked.

Hideki stirred on the futon and pulled the kake buton to cover himself, but he did not wake.

"Let him sleep. I kept them very busy last night," she said putting on the robe. "Why, has something happened?"

"Today was to be our day to start the raids on the Koga," Yoshi said.

"Has the plan changed?" Myo asked.

"That is for Hideki to decide," Yoshi said. "I am just an advisor."

"You are just an advisor like Jubei is just a swordsman. You are like a brother to Hideki and old Jii elevated you to clan chief strategist," Myo said. "I am almost jealous. You live in the same mansion he does, and you accompany him on his little trips."

"Do not be jealous of me, leader of the Five Families. I do not sleep with him," Yoshi said. "And you are the only one he does sleep with."

"That is true. I guess I am blessed that way. It appears he

182

does stay loyal," Myo said. "What word of your mother-in-law and wife?"

"I now know where the missing pigeons went the day of the fire. I got a pigeon this morning. My wife thinks the baby is in Kyoto at a store called Yamakaya," Yoshi said.

"That means we need to move quickly. The Koga will realize immediately when Jii starts to march that the Yoshinobu are supporting Iemitsu. When they realize this, they will kill the baby," Myo said.

Hideki rose into a sitting position. "Killing Yoshitsune makes no sense. Why kill him?"

"Because they want to erase all evidence of their crime," Myo said.

"Yes, the Koga are betting their future on Tadanaga. If Tadanaga succeeds as the new shogun he cannot be seen as condoning the kidnapping of an innocent child. Exposing the Koga's evil deeds would mean exposing his complicity," Yoshi agreed.

"This information came from a good source?" Hideki asked.

"It came from my wife," Yoshi said.

"You cannot get any more reliable than that," Hideki agreed. "Get word to The Mist to accompany us to Kyoto. We will depart today."

Hideki reached for his clothes and Myo dropped the robe to put her clothes on.

"I can see why Hideki is fighting," Yoshi said, turned and left.

"What did he say?" Hideki asked.

"It was nothing important," Myo smiled. "He was only stating the obvious."

An hour later they reassembled in the Yoshinobu mansion. This time Jii joined them.

"What is the plan Hideki?" Jii asked.

"Grandfather, the plan remains the same. You must depart with all your retainers for the route survey," Hideki said.

"But what of Yoshitsune?" Jii asked.

"Yes, what about my son?" Yuki asked with Naga leaning forward.

"Yoshi, Jubei, The Mist, Myo, Midori and I will depart immediately to meet up with Chiyo and her mother. We will assess the situation and retrieve Yoshitsune," Hideki said.

"I am going with you," Yuki said.

Hideki looked at Yuki and the rest of his family and friends.

"Were it any other mother asking to go, I would be against it. But you are samurai and you trained as an Iga ninja. If you will promise to stay out of danger then your presence would be welcome," Hideki said. "Jii, we will keep you informed of all events. Myo's ninja will courier information wherever you are on the road."

"We will need horses," Yoshi said. "I hate the beasts."

"It will be a first; a monkey riding on a horse," Jubei said.

"We will see how good a horse man the rest of you are after bouncing up and down the Tokaido for several days," Yoshi said.

"Yes, we will. And I am glad that the first time I saw Yuki was after she made a mad dash on horseback from Edo to Kii province with Jubei's father to protect us. I know she's a good horse woman," Hideki said.

Naga started to open his mouth to protest but stopped when Yuki shot him a "don't you dare" look.

"Don't worry Nagamasa, we will not let anything happen to your wife or child," Jubei said.

"Any questions?" Jii asked the room.

No one had any.

"Let's leave at the same time Jii does with the Yoshinobu retainers to mask our movement," Hideki said. "Yoshi, get funds from the family storeroom for our trip. I have a feeling the good merchants along the way will be doubling and tripling rates."

"You do not think merchants have kind hearts?" Yoshi asked.

Hideki turned to Yoshi. "As you recall we worked for some

merchants in Nagasaki last year. I'm not sure if any of them have hearts at all."

"Let's get ready to move," Jii said.

Another council of war was taking place at Daito Kuji Temple in Kyoto.

"The advance guard of Iemitsu's forces has departed Edo," Yamada said.

"What? When? Who?" Abbott Inshin demanded, looking at each of Tadanaga's war council.

"How valid is your information?" Oyeo asked.

"My information is valid my lady," the Satsuma representative from the south said. "The Satsuma use very capable intelligence sources."

"That must be true. My intelligence sources seem to be sleeping," Tadanaga said, looking toward the far corner where the light from the evening fire could not reach.

Ugai's voice seemed unfazed. "Maybe you should answer the question," he said from the shadows.

"The Yoshinobu are the vanguard. They are about eighty retainers strong. They are led by the patriarch. They departed Edo at noon today," Yamada said.

"How could you know they departed today?" Oyeo asked.

"The Fuma ninja have carrier pigeon stations along the Tokaido. We have a lot invested in Lord Tadanaga. We do not want to be surprised," Yamada said.

"That is very disturbing news Ugai," Tadanaga said. "I thought you had some foolproof way of stopping the Yoshinobu."

"It appears to have failed," Ugai said.

"You stupid bastard," Tadanaga screamed. "There is too much riding on this for you to fail."

"Tadanaga-sama, please calm yourself," Oyeo said to her second son.

"Unfortunately, that is not the worst news," Yamada said.

All eyes turned to Yamada.

Yamada looked at the dark corner where everyone thought Ugai's voice emanated.

"You have gotten everyone's attention. You should deliver

your worst news," Ugai's voice came from the darkness.

"I have never liked the idea of dealing with rat scum ninja," Ito said.

"You are just unhappy because I exposed your weaknesses and pomposity before Tadanaga," the voice from the corner said.

"I am unhappy to be working with a spy that won't show his face, uses poisons on allies and has a history of treachery," Ito said.

"Ito's last remark has much to do with the worst news," Yamada said.

"Please tell us the worst news Yamada-san," Lady Oyeo said.

"The woman we met here at our last meeting who was supposed to be one of Ugai's Koga ninja is now with the Yoshinobu," Yamada said.

"The Mist is now working with the Yoshinobu?" Lady Oyeo asked. "How can that be?"

"I will boil you alive you villain," Tadanaga screamed. He grabbed his sword and raced to the corner where he swung in great arcs but hit nothing. His anger evaporated any control he might have had.

The voice of Ugai came from an opposite dark corner, or seemed to. "It is unfortunate if The Mist has become a traitor, but not as unfortunate as our potential new shogun losing all control in front of our Satsuma ally. He will now see an opportunity to exploit your weakness when you have had your investiture ceremony."

"Shut up. Shut up. I am surrounded by incompetents," Tadanaga screamed at the corners, still waving his sword.

"I recommend you adjourn the meeting Lady Oyeo. Try to get your son under control. I will control the Yoshinobu as I promised. Unlike Yamada, I know the real leader of the Yoshinobu is the second son," Ugai's voice said.

"Do you mean Hideki?" Lady Oyeo asked.

"Yes, he is the real leader. His title of Tengu killer is deserved. If I cut off the head, the rest will die. But first I will demoralize the entire clan," Ugai said.

"How do you plan on accomplishing all this ninja?" Ito demanded.

"It will not be by killing merchants and prostitutes in the

Shimabara like you do sword master," Ugai teased.

"How could you know…?" Ito asked.

"We will leave it all in your hands, Ugai," Lady Oyeo said.

"Is he still there?" Bishop Inshin asked in a whisper.

"I think we had all better act as if he is always there," Yamada said.

When his guards had escorted Tadanaga and Lady Oyeo back to their quarters, Ito, Bishop Inshin and Yamada stayed to drink sake.

"This gets less auspicious with each meeting," the bishop said.

"I had heard of the rumors of Tadanaga flying into rages and killing servants and retainers alike, but I had dismissed them," Yamada said.

"Really?" Bishop Inshin said. "I thought Ugai made a very cogent argument. I would have thought your Satsuma handlers would be making plans to move the capital to Nagasaki."

"Ugai is right about one thing," Ito said.

Both other men stopped lifting their cups.

"He must kill the Tengu killer and find some way to demoralize the Yoshinobu clan. The only way to stop the investiture ceremony now is to stop the advance party," Ito said.

"Can he do it?" Bishop Inshin asked.

"I do not know," Ito said. "You know as much about him as I do. The Mist's treachery has certainly dealt us all a blow. But that is what you can expect of ninja. They fight for money."

The other two men looked in each dark corner before raising the sake to their lips.

XXIV

Tokaido-Totsuka

It was several hours after sunset when Hideki and company entered the town of Totsuka. It was station number five of fifty-three on the famous Tokaido highway. There was very little movement on the street. They walked their horses to the largest inn and dismounted. Yoshi gathered up the reins of the five horses and started towards the stables normally in the rear.

"Make sure the baths are still open," Yoshi shouted over his shoulder. "Jubei smells worse than normal."

"Look who is talking," Jubei replied.

Jubei pounded on the closed doors.

"Hai," the feminine voice answered from within.

"Open up," Jubei demanded.

"I am sorry traveler, but our policy is not to open the doors once closed," the feminine voice said inside.

"I believe you are expecting the Yoshinobu here tomorrow are you not?" Jubei asked.

"I cannot give out information like that sir," the voice said.

"We are the advance party," Jubei continued.

Hideki looked at Myo. She nodded her head and disappeared down the adjoining alleyway.

"I have no word on any party after dark traveler. I am sorry," the feminine voice said.

"You are going to be a whole lot sorrier in a moment," Yuki whispered.

The next sound was a scream from a female inside. It was

cut short followed by the sound of a bar in the bottom track of the sliding door being removed and the door sliding back.

Jubei stepped into the large outer room scanned it and then looked up the stairs to the lodging rooms.

Yuki looked down to the young maid clutching her hand to her mouth.

"Is she okay?" Yuki asked.

"She is fine. I just scared her by appearing behind her out of the darkness," Myo said.

"Get on your feet," Yuki ordered.

The young maid obeyed.

"What is your name girl?" Yuki asked.

"I am called Hana," the girl said.

"Okay Hana, this is what you're going to do. First, you're going to wake the owners and all the staff," Yuki said.

"Oh, I have strict orders not to do that," Hana said.

Myo stepped near her. "Really?"

The Mist smiled.

Hana glanced at the strange woman who had appeared out of the shadows a moment ago and thrown her to the floor. Then she looked at the two samurai. One had a scarred hand. The other was missing an eye. Both look terrifying. But the woman samurai standing in front of her frightened her the most.

"Yes, my lady," Hana said and scurried off into the bowels of the large dark inn.

The four had managed to shake off the dust and hang their straw shoes on pegs in the receiving area. Each unslung their blanket rolls that hung across their backs and tied in front.

A large woman and a much smaller man moved toward the samurai. Hana trailed them holding a paper lantern.

"What is the meaning of barging your way into my inn at this time of night? You cannot get away with this," she said. The little man nodded his head in agreement.

Yuki stepped up to the main floor. "Sorry for the inconvenience, but we are on urgent business."

"I do not care. You cannot come in here and abuse my

staff just because you have an emergency," the large woman said.

Yuki looked at the large woman. Her entourage following behind the small man had grown by three more women.

"You're going to find us accommodation for the night to include a bath and supper and feed our horses. We can do this one of two ways. One way is we pay you handsomely for your trouble, you lose a little sleep and we are happy," Yuki said.

The large woman put her hands on her hips. "What is the other way?" she asked.

"The other way is I draw my sword and lop off your head. Then your staff will find us accommodation for the night to include a bath and supper and feed our horses. You will lose your life and your staff will be up all night trying to get your blood stains off the tatami and we will still leave tomorrow and be happy," Yuki said.

Hana made herself busy lighting several candles along the walls.

The large lady looked beyond Yuki. What she saw was indeed frightening. She was used to traveling samurai. What she was not used to were men who looked and carried themselves like killers. Her attitude changed.

"It seems you leave me little option. How many are in your party?" The large woman asked.

"We are six," Yuki said. "We have three men and three women."

"All we have available is the great room," the large woman said. "That will cost you a gold coin."

Yuki grabbed the handle of her sword. The innkeeper shrank back. "I'll pay thirty silver coins. If I like the service when we leave in the morning, I will pay your price," Yuki said.

The large woman nodded. Yuki took her hand off her sword.

Yoshi materialized behind Hideki making both him and Jubei jump.

"By the Buddha Yoshi, make a noise once in a while," Hideki said.

"You're going to get killed doing that Monkey," Jubei said.

"That is probably true, but not today and not by you sword master." Then in a whisper, "are you not both glad she married Naga?"

Yuki started up the stairs. Yoshi moved to the innkeeper, giving instructions to her staff. "Please bring extra kake butons and a rope to section off an area for the Lady and the two women," he said.

The innkeeper looked at Yuki ascending the stairs.

"That is no lady," she said so only Yoshi could hear.

"You could not be further from the truth. She is the lady of the great Yoshinobu clan. You will be hosting her father-in-law tomorrow. The Yoshinobu are cousins to the Tokugawa. Her father-in-law is on a mission from Iemitsu himself," Yoshi said. Then as an afterthought he added, "You will never know how close you came to losing your life tonight. If either of those two samurai heard you cast aspersions upon Lady Yoshinobu you would die on the spot."

The large woman and the staff close enough to hear all went pale.

Myo appeared at Yoshi's elbow. "We will depart early in the morning. Please have our horses ready at sun-up along with breakfast. I will pay now," Myo said.

Myo counted out 30 silver coins, then she gave the innkeeper 20 more.

"But we agreed on 30," the innkeeper said.

"The extra twenty is for your loss of sleep and for having breakfast and the horses ready early," Myo said. "What Yoshi just told you about your life is absolute fact. But Lady Yoshinobu keeps her word. If she is happy tomorrow morning, there will be another gold coin in it for you."

For the first time the large innkeeper smiled. She tucked the silver coins into her nightdress.

"She is the Lady Yoshinobu and those men are her bodyguards. Who are the rest of you?"

"We are whatever and whomever we choose to be." Myo said.

Myo nodded to Yoshi. "Good enough boss?"

Myo, Yoshi and The Mist climbed the stairs and

disappeared down the hall. When they entered the great room, Hana had already hung extra kake butons on a rope across half of the room. There were three sets of bedding on either side of the makeshift partition with the kake buton on top of each futon. When Hana returned she announced the baths were ready and gave direction for their use.

Yuki, Myo, and The Mist changed from riding clothes into hotel robes and walked to the baths in the back of the building with towels in hand. After cleaning themselves outside the ofudo area with buckets of hot water and soap they moved to the hot bath for a soak.

"We really cannot stay here too long," Yuki said. "The boys have to bathe as well."

"They can wait a little longer," Myo said.

"I am sorry, I really don't know either of you very well," Yuki said. "Of course, I know you Myo. I know you and Hideki are involved. And I know he thinks the world of you."

"You know that I was the reason Yoshitsune is missing," Myo said.

Yuki looked Myo in the eyes. "You cannot blame yourself for that."

"It was my people providing security. They failed so it is my responsibility," Myo said.

"Yes, and I am Yoshitsune's mother who fell for the fire diversion," Yuki said. "But you lost two members of the Five Families and I lost a child. So, let us stop blaming ourselves and get him back."

"Wise words Lady Yoshinobu," The Mist offered.

"Please, I am Yuki to my friends," Yuki said.

Myo smiled. "That seems to be a Yoshinobu trait. You call servants and retainers by their first name."

"Not all, just the ones I like," Yuki said.

"You just said you did not know me," Myo accused.

"I know you are a lover to my husband's brother. I know when he was captured and tortured cruelly by that bird woman you were the only one who rescued him," Yuki said. "I also know that all the Yoshinobu and Yoshi value you. That is all I need to know."

"Thank you, Yuki. That means a lot to me," Myo said.

"Please tell me about Hideki. He seems so different from the sweet boy I met on the Tokaido a few years ago," Yuki said.

"What would you like to know? Myo asked.

"Is he as good with the sword as I have heard?" Yuki asked.

"I do not know what you have heard, but Jubei respects him for his skill," Myo said.

"Yes, I have heard that from my husband," Yuki said. "But you saw him raise the hopes of the Yoshinobu clan and my own as a desperate mother by the sheer force of his personality the other night. The Hideki I knew could never do that."

Myo laughed. "Why do you think strong men like Jubei, Musashi and Yoshi follow him willingly?"

"I do not know but have often wondered," Yuki said.

"Hey, you are not thinking of trading brothers, are you?" Myo asked.

Yuki laughed. "That is one of the few times I've laughed since this nightmare started. Thank you Myo."

"It might be a good trade. Hideki is the second son and Naga already has a high position in the government," Myo said thoughtfully.

"You are right. It would be a bad swap on my part. But I happen to like my husband, so no deal," Yuki said.

"Good," Myo said. "I have got too much time and training invested to let Hideki go now."

"Ooh, that sounds deliciously erotic," Yuki said laughing.

"More than you can imagine Yuki," Myo said.

Yuki turned to The Mist. "We are both bearing our souls like sisters," Yuki said. "What should we know about you? Is your name really The Mist?"

"My real name is The Mist. I have always been Koga. I don't know when they started calling me The Mist. I think it was the old man's idea. He led us for many years before Ugai. He liked my ability to come and go like The Mist. He also wanted someone who could be the face of the Koga," The Mist said.

"So Ugai has not been the leader of the Koga long?" Myo asked.

"No, it was very recent that he took that title and no one

I know was involved in it. One day the old man was dead and the next Ugai was proclaiming himself leader and wanting no opposition," The Mist said.

"I do not know much about other ninja families, but the Five Families always held elections. Everyone had a say, and everyone voted," Myo said. "My father was thought to be the lifelong leader of the Five Families, but elections were held each year."

"We had always held elections each year as well," The Mist said. "Ugai assuming the role is very unusual."

"Is it okay if I just call you Mist?" Yuki asked.

"Certainly, you may call me Mist. May I call you Yuki? I know I am not a friend. In fact, you have every right to hate me," The Mist said.

"The only reason I did not kill you myself is I want my son back. Hideki thinks you can help. He is seldom wrong in his evaluation of people I am told," Yuki said.

Myo nodded in confirmation.

"The only other thing you need to know about me is I had no part in taking your child and I will help you anyway I can. I think Ugai siding with Tadanaga combined with taking your child have doomed my clan. I have nowhere else to be. I am an outcast now," The Mist said.

"She is a very skilled ninja Yuki," Myo said.

"You are the master's daughter. I saw you when you were a young girl in the castle," The Mist said.

"She means your father, Hittori Honzo," Myo said.

"I dropped into your lover's chamber one night," The Mist said changing the subject.

"I was curious about that. Why did you do it? The risk was great," Myo said.

"I was curious also. I wanted to see what the Tengu killer was like," The Mist said. "It was pitch black when I dropped silently into his room, he was up immediately with two swords in hand. I know he could not see me, but I felt he knew where I was."

"Yes, we discussed your entrance. I was a few moments behind you," Myo said.

"What is your opinion of Hideki?" Yuki asked.

"That was the very strange part," The Mist said. "It was pitch black in that room which should have given me an edge. But I felt that I was at a disadvantage somehow."

"What do you mean?" Yuki asked.

"I do not know how to describe it," The Mist said wringing hot water out of her small cloth. "I felt it I engaged him, I would lose. I had never felt that before."

"I have felt that," Yuki said.

"When?" Myo asked.

"When I met his first sword mentor Myamoto Musashi," Yuki said.

"You have met Myamoto Musashi?" The Mist asked.

"Yes, just briefly when I first joined Hideki and Naga," Yuki said.

"Wait, Musashi was Hideki's mentor and now he is instructed by Jubei?" The Mist asked.

"I am not sure who is teaching whom currently," Myo said. "But yes, Hideki has had the two-best swordsman of our era as teachers."

"Then I am very glad I did not engage him," The Mist said.

Myo smiled.

"My husband says Jubei believes Hideki uses mushin when he fights," Yuki said.

"Mushin? I thought that was a legend," The Mist said.

"It is not a legend. Musashi taught him," Myo said.

The Mist shook her head. "The more I am around the Yoshinobu the more I am amazed."

"Why?" Yuki asked.

"You have the Tengu killer in your midst who uses mushin. You have Yoshi who is supposedly adept in the black arts and sees through the darkness. Those are both thought to be lost capabilities," The Mist said.

"If Jubei attests to mushin then Hideki has the capability. Jubei does not exaggerate nor does he lie," Yuki said.

"That is my point exactly. You all have these extraordinary men revolving around the second son. Then you have ninja being treated as family. It is most unusual," The Mist said.

"I will ask Naga's grandfather and my father to get a pardon for you and any other Koga that forsakes Ugai and helps us with Iemitsu's investiture and returning my child to me," Yuki said.

"That is most generous. I do not look forward to being hunted down by this one," The Mist said pointing with her chin toward Myo.

Outside the baths on the walkway from the rooms a samurai stepped out of his room in his sleeping robe with a sword in one hand. He took a few steps towards the baths and stopped. A demon all in black with an eye patch stepped out from the shadows.

"What is the meaning of this?" the samurai demanded.

"The baths are occupied at the moment," Jubei said calmly.

"I know they are occupied. I cannot get any sleep because of all the noise," he said.

"I will ask them to be quiet in a few moments," Jubei said. "I would ask for your indulgence."

"I will ask them to shut up now," the samurai said.

"I would not advise that," Jubei said stepping to block the man's path.

"Who are you?" The man demanded.

"I am Yagyū Jubei guard to the women bathing."

"Yagyū Jubei? The Shogun's fencing instructor?" The samurai asked stepping back.

"The same," Jubei said. "I recommend you go back and bury your head in the kake buton. It is better than losing it here."

The man stepped back to his room and disappeared.

Yoshi stepped out of the shadows behind Jubei.

"I guess having a bad reputation has its uses," Yoshi said.

"Shut up Monkey. Are you here to relieve me?" Jubei asked.

"Yes, Hideki wants them to spend as much time as they want at the baths," Yoshi said.

"Works for me, we will take baths later," Jubei said and moved down the hallway past the samurai's room to the great room at the end of the hall.

"Is Yoshi on watch?" Hideki asked when Jubei entered.

"Yes," Jubei said.

"Anything unusual happen?" Hideki asked.

"We had one good citizen try to quiet the ladies," Jubei said.

"I wonder if he realizes you did him a favor." Hideki said.

"Probably not," Jubei said. "I would not want to tangle with those three."

The ladies finished their soak, dried off, put on robes, wrapped their hair with towels and exited the baths. They had taken just a few steps down the hallway when Myo halted them with her hand. All three stopped silently.

"Trying to get a peek, Yoshi?" Myo asked.

"That is not funny. Hideki set a watch so you can stay as long as you wanted in the baths," Yoshi said from the shadows.

Yuki moved past Myo. "It seems there is still some sweetness left in my brother-in-law."

XXV

Yamakaya

Haru was feeding the baby in her quarters. Rei was sitting near the door watching the maternal scene. In his new black silk kimono, he marveled at how his fortunes had changed so rapidly. He now felt clean in more ways than one after the bath.

Umi was sitting across from Haru ready with a soft white cloth. When the child was finished suckling Ume took him to her shoulder and patted him on the back.

"I can remember doing this for you Haru-san," Ume said.

"I hope I was as good a baby as Yoshi-chan," Haru said.

"Oh yes," Ume said. "You were like this precious one. You hardly ever cried."

Haru covered herself by pulling her pink silk kimono back on her shoulder. She then turned toward Rei. "Have you been around little ones Rei-san?"

Rei blushed and averted his gaze. When he looked up it was at Ume. "I have only been around my little sister," he said.

"Rei-san," Ume said. "You are blushing. Are you embarrassed to see a mother feeding?"

Rei shifted uncomfortably. "The feeding was beautiful," Rei said. "So was the mother."

"Oh Rei-san," Ume said. "Have you fallen in love with the Lady of Yamakaya?"

Rei blushed again.

"How old are you Rei?" Haru asked. The change in direction of the conversation gave Rei some reprieve.

"I am 18 years old," Rei said.

"Amida Buddha," Ume exclaimed. "You are almost the same age as the lady."

Haru looked at her attendant. "Ume are you matchmaking?"

Ume rocked the baby. "Yes, my lady. Being alone is not good for a rich woman, neither on a business level nor on a personal level."

"And you think Rei-san would be a good match for me?" Haru asked.

Rei rocked back and forth nervously. "Excuse me ladies, but I am still in the room and you are making me uncomfortable," Rei said.

Both women turned toward Rei. "I am sorry Rei-san," Haru said. "We are teasing you. We would not do that if we did not feel comfortable with you."

"That is right samurai-sama. It has been a long time since we have had a man around we could joke with," Ume said.

"I would say you are the first man I have ever been comfortable around," Haru said.

Rei blushed again. "What about your husband?"

"I did not love my husband and he did not love me. I was a toy they both used to get what they wanted. Although they both used me, they did not deserve to be cut down returning from one of their many pleasure district visits," Haru said.

Rei tried to keep the surprise off his face. "Then your husband was a fool," Rei said.

Rei had not meant to say that out loud. He had been thinking it. Why would any man with a beautiful and successful wife like Haru make trips to the pleasure districts? It was beyond belief to Rei.

"Oh Haru-san," Ume said. "I think you have a real admirer."

Haru looked closely at the young samurai before them. He was young, a little younger than herself. His ability to protect her had been ably demonstrated. The thought of his efficient killing of the bandits repulsed her and excited her at the same time. He was handsome enough. But he was a killer. He had sliced those bandits up as if they were nothing while keeping his wits about him. Could she ever love a man like him? More importantly, could she control such a man? Her instinct told her control would be based on his love. If he loved her she might be able to control him.

"Really?" Haru asked, looking intently at Rei.

Rei fidgeted. He wasn't used to talk about himself and certainly not to women about marriage. He was out of his element here. He would have to be careful.

"You ladies are not making me any more comfortable," Rei said.

"I am sorry Rei-san. I find your company comforting," Haru said.

Rei's thoughts raced in his head to find an appropriate response.

"I appreciate your comments ladies. But I am a poor country farm boy. I was hoping to get a samurai position through the Ronin Army. I know nothing about love or being a merchant," Rei said.

"Would you be willing to learn?" Ume asked smiling wickedly.

It was obvious to Rei that these ladies were enjoying his discomfort. But Ume's question surprised.

"I do not know," Rei said. "I have never thought of doing anything like this. I do not know if I can give up my samurai status."

Rei thought about his father and their pitiful farm. Would he allow Rei to trade his samurai status to be a merchant even if it meant a better life for his little sister? His father's samurai pride ran deep.

Haru placed her finger along her jaw. "You do not really have a samurai status now. You are a ronin. Why can you not be a ronin working with me as a merchant?" she pondered aloud.

"What would I be?" Rei asked. "I do not think I'd be a good salesclerk or a stocker? I do not have the skills nor the temperament."

"You are a farm boy. Farm boys know hard work," Ume said.

"You would not be a clerk. You would be Yoshi's and my

protector. I can always show you what you need to know about the business," Haru said.

"Toward what end?" Rei asked.

It was Haru's turn to blush. "You would be striving to be my new husband and eventually the head of Yamakaya."

"You know nothing of me lady," Rei protested.

"I know you are a skilled swordsman who thinks quickly during stressful situations and has no fear," Haru said.

"I am sorry to tell you that I am afraid. I just suppress it," Rei said, thinking that these ladies frightened him more than swords.

Haru spun toward Rei in her kneeling position. Her tone took on a serious note.

"You do not understand Rei-san. I lost my baby to fever. I lost my husband and my father to a madman all in the span of a week. I am a woman alone. I live in fear every night. Now that I have little Yoshi, I fear all the time. There is nothing stopping other crazy men entering in broad daylight and killing us," Haru said. "Since you arrived, I sleep well at night."

"We all do," Ume said. "Your quick work on those four bandits the other day has even the maids talking about the handsome samurai."

"Do you like it here?" Haru asked.

"Yes," Rei said, hesitating only slightly.

"Do you like me?" Haru asked.

Here was the real issue. He knew he liked Haru. She was beautiful and he liked the way she protected the baby. She was gentle but focused. She knew what she wanted, and he felt she would move heaven and earth to get it. Her fierceness appealed to his samurai spirit. Her offer could mean the difference between poverty and luxury. But did bushido allow such a thing? Would his father bless their union? All these questions and more made him hesitant.

"Very much," Rei said throwing caution to the wind.

"Then our proposition is possible?" Haru asked.

"Yes, my lady," Rei said looking into her dark brown eyes. He had never been in love before. He wasn't sure he was in love now. But these ladies needed protecting and had offered him more than he could ever hope for.

"Then you need to spend more time with me and decide whether you could love me or not," Haru said. "I will not marry another man I do not love."

"But this is so fast. How do you know you love me?" Rei asked.

"Please do not think me bold. This is a first for me as well. My life has been about being used as a pawn for my grandfather and father. I think I know the type of man I want as a husband this time." Haru said. "I am drawn to your strength and humility which I hope bleeds over into loyalty. I am also drawn to your good looks. I have never loved a man before. I am certainly interested in trying. So, use your quick-thinking skills and make up your mind."

Rei smiled. "It is a much better proposition than rejoining the thugs of the Ronin Army. But they have a strict policy of 'once in never out'."

"What does that mean?" Haru asked.

"It means if they find out I've stopped wearing my Ronin Army haori and headband, they will try to kill me," Rei said.

"That is very harsh," Ume said.

"It sounds like all the men of the Ronin Army are expendable," Haru said.

"Very well put my lady," Rei said. "So, you must really think hard about linking yourself to me."

Haru placed her finger along her jaw again.

"So, if you remain with the Ronin Army and stay here as my bodyguard I will sleep well, and you will eventually leave us for a samurai position elsewhere?" Haru asked.

"Only if Tadanaga is victorious," Rei said. "At least that was the plan."

"What if Tadanaga is not victorious?" Haru asked.

Rei watched that finger along her jaw. He was mesmerized by it. Rei shook his head to clear it. He had to think a moment to come up with the correct answer. "Then Iemitsu's forces will hunt down and kill the entire Ronin Army," Rei said.

"Let me summarize," Haru said. "If you leave the Ronin Army and remain here, I will still sleep sound at night and the

Ronin Army or Iemitsu's forces may or may not come here and kill you?"

"Yes," Rei replied.

Rei watched the finger move along the alabaster jaw. How could someone be so beautiful?

"Then your decision is easy. Stay with us. Protect me and Yoshi. We will pay you well. We will worry about the Ronin Army if they come. If we like each other, you may become the owner of Yamakaya through marriage. If we do not like each other, you will still have to confront the Ronin Army. I think the reasons for you to quit the Ronin Army and stay with me far outweigh any other arguments," Haru said.

Rei shook his head. This woman was beautiful and smart. He wished his mother had lived long enough to give him advice about a situation like this.

"I will try to protect you with my life. But I do not want to bring any extra danger to your home with my presence," Rei said.

"Ume do you feel more or less danger by Rei-san's presence?" Haru asked.

"Oh, that is easy. I and everyone in Yamakaya feel less danger with Rei-san under your roof," Ume said. "Even the stock boys, the sales clerks and the chief clerk like Rei living here."

Rei looked between the two women and let his gaze linger on Haru.

"Very well my lady, I will not put on the Ronin Army garb and instead embark on the most interesting journey of my life," Rei said.

"That was a very wise decision Rei-san," Haru said.

"I feel like a celebration is in order," Ume said. "My Lady has Yoshi to love and now has a protector and possible new husband."

"Ume, tomorrow we start by meeting with all the employees of Yamakaya and introduce my new betrothed. Our next stop will be to our suppliers to alert them Yamakaya now has teeth," Haru said.

The two women smiled at each other.

XXVI

Tokaido-Ishibe

For the six riders, each day was filled with the monotony of leaving early, arriving late, stopping for lunches of tea and rice at vendor stalls, resting horses and trading for new ones.

"We have slept in Totsuka, Hara, Shimada, Yoshida, Kuwana and now Ishibe. I have spent more time with a horse between my legs than I have with my wife. And my wife is much prettier," Yoshi said.

"If I was not so sore from the pounding, I would laugh at that Monkey," Jubei said. "How is Yuki holding up?"

"She is samurai," Hideki said. "She is putting a good face on this ride, but I know she is worn out."

"Yuki is one tough lady," Myo said. "I really under estimated her before this trip."

"I see you have become close friends. The three of you seem to enjoy the baths and chatting once we are off the horses," Jubei said.

"I like her," The Mist said. "She is not as pretentious or fragile as I had imagined."

"Join her in the women's room, I will get the baths started," Yoshi said to The Mist and Myo.

Hideki waited until the two women had moved off. "We are close to Kyoto. We should arrive by noon tomorrow."

"I have noticed a decided shift in the caliber of traveler we encounter as we get closer to the capital," Jubei said.

"Yes, some of the seediest ronin I have ever seen seem to be traveling there," Hideki said.

"We might want to set our watch on the women's room a little early tonight," Jubei suggested.

"Because of the seedy ronin and the fact that this is a one-story inn and the baths are separate from the main building?" Hideki asked.

"That is correct. The fact that the inn is full is also bothersome," Jubei said.

"Although we have been cramped with all six of us in one room several times this trip, it has been so much safer," Hideki said.

"With our room adjoining theirs, we will have to stand guard outside in the hall tonight," Jubei said.

"That is liable to make some travelers a little nervous," Yoshi said.

"That is too bad," Hideki said. "The two women who are the most precious to me are inside that room tonight. Nothing is going to happen to either one."

"How much do you trust The Mist?" Jubei asked.

"About as much as you do," Hideki said. "But Myo will sleep between them."

"That is good. Although Yuki is now married to your brother, I did love her once," Jubei said.

Hideki smiled. "That is just another plus for our side," he said as he signaled one of the hostesses.

"When you send up the food tonight for the ladies' room, include sake," he said.

"Hai," the hostess said and fled across the room to keep up with the orders of the filled bar and eatery.

"Let us eat here. We can keep an eye on the ladies' room while we eat," Hideki suggested. Yoshi disappeared.

Jubei and Hideki took a seat on the last bench before the rooms began behind a beaded curtain. They sat opposite each other out of habit. One watched the ladies' room and one watched the ronins and ruffians throughout the bar doing more drinking than eating.

Jubei's eyebrows went up when a boisterous group of samurai entered. They took the table next to Hideki's back and clamored for service. When the sake arrived, they slammed back the liquor.

"Women!" One of the six yelled. Jubei looked over his shoulder in time to see Yuki, The Mist and Myo exit their room in thin bath robes and towels headed toward the baths in the back.

The other five leaned over or stood to catch a glimpse of the female figures disappearing down the hall.

"By the gods, I will have one of them," one shouted.

"No, we will have all of them," another shouted gobbling his sake down.

All six wore white haori and headbands declaring them members of the Ronin Army.

"It is our duty to protect the innocents of Kyoto and its environs," another said.

"Let us join them," someone said, and everyone started to stand.

Jubei rose and blocked their path.

"Who are you?" The large leader with a scar down the left side of his face asked.

"I am the one giving you a chance to live," Jubei said.

The leader looked confused.

"I think what he is saying is if we do not sit down he is going to kill us all," the skinny one with the shaved pate said.

"Impossible," the leader with a scar said.

Then a voice from behind the six stated, "You are partly correct. With his skill it would be possible for him to kill you all. But with me behind you all your deaths are a certainty," Hideki said.

"Who the hell are you boy?" One of them asked.

"We are the yojimbo hired by those three ladies to keep from being disturbed by riff raff like you," Hideki said.

Everyone's hands went to their swords.

"You know who we are?" The scarred leader asked.

"I guess you fancy yourself the Ronin Army," Hideki said. "But I am not sure what that is."

The leader thumped his chest. "We are the army in Kyoto to support the rightful heir of the Tokugawa."

"Which Tokugawa are you talking about?" Hideki asked.

"Tadanaga is the rightful heir of course. No one in their right mind would support that twisted stutterer Iemitsu," the scarred leader said.

"Just how many are in the Ronin Army?" Hideki asked.

"We are about 100 now. But more are joining every day," the scarred leader said.

"I wish you luck," Hideki said.

"We will not need it, the scarred leader said. "Why did you say that?"

"Because Iemitsu will be moving soon with over 300,000 retainers," Hideki said.

"300,000 retainers?" The leader stammered. "We were told he could only muster 2000 at most."

"Well I salute your bravery. If 100 are going to stop 300,000, you must be very good and very brave," Hideki said.

The six Ronin Army members looked at each other and at the two bodyguards on each side of them and released the handles of their swords almost in unison. They murmured amongst themselves for a few moments. Then they turned and moved through the entrance and out into the street, all thoughts of the women gone.

Jubei moved to stand beside Hideki as they watched the last of the six file out.

"Do you think you divulged secret information?" Jubei asked.

"Maybe, but it is Iemitsu's problem. I do not want our women being bothered by them," Hideki said.

"It would not have been much bother to slay them all," Jubei said.

"The supreme art of war is to subdue the enemy without fighting," Hideki said.

"Okay, Sun Tzu," Jubei said. "Let us go make sure Yoshi has not fallen asleep."

In the baths the women enjoyed their normal time and joyously spoke of things dear to them.

"You have never loved a man?" Yuki asked.

"That is not what I said Yuki-san. I said I had never been in love. I have made love to many men. I am a ninja after all," The Mist said.

"You two truly amaze me," Yuki said.

"Why? Are you amazed because we have made love to many men?" Myo asked.

"It is a little shocking to me. I came to my marriage bed still a virgin," Yuki said.

"Really?" The Mist asked.

Yuki thought a moment. "Wait, that is not true. I used my position as bodyguard to Nagamasa to get him into my bed on our journey from Kyoto to Edo almost two years ago."

"Then you are just like us," The Mist said. "You used your assets to gain what you wanted."

Yuki laughed. "I guess so," she said. "You are in love now are you not Myo?"

"That is a very dangerous question Yuki-san. I am with Hideki. He does not cheat on me," Myo said.

"Verified?" The Mist interjected.

"Verified," Myo said. "I want to be with him, and he is the first man not of my clan that I trust with my life. But I can never be his wife. So, we must find our happiness with each other while we can."

"Sounds like love to me," The Mist said, and all laughed.

The three women eventually exited the soak, dried off, put on robes, and wrapped their hair to return to their room. Two men in hotel bathrobes and carrying towels stepped out of their room and moved towards the three women. They blocked the ladies' path.

"Why don't you ladies return to the bath with us?" One said. He slapped his hand to his neck then collapsed on the wooden floor. The second man scanned to the right into the shadows and slapped his throat and collapsed. Neither man moved.

"Is that you Yoshi? Yuki asked.

"Yes, my lady," Yoshi answered and stepped into the light clutching a blow pipe.

"Did you kill them?" The Mist asked.

"No," Yoshi answered. "They will probably miss breakfast, but the fugu poison my wife whips up doesn't kill unless I want it to."

"Your wife knows poisons?" The Mist asked.

"Ever hear a female ninja known as a goddess of poisons from the Dewa ninja clan?" Myo asked.

"All ninja have heard of her. I thought she was a myth," The Mist said.

"No, she is no myth. She is Yoshi's mother-in-law," Myo said.

"Is she the same one you said shares a pipe with the Yoshinobu patriarch?" The Mist asked.

"She is the same," Yuki said.

The Mist shook her head. "This is the strangest samurai family ever."

"True," Yoshi offered. "We will be standing guard throughout the night on your room. It is Hideki's idea, but I told him a room with two female ninja and a female samurai trained as a ninja does not require much guarding."

"That is okay Yoshi, I am sure it will make Jubei and Hideki feel useful," Yuki said as she winked at her two bathing companions.

XXVII

Kyoto

As predicted, noon the next day found the six riders dismounted and walking their horses across the great Sanjo Bridge. Kyoto lay on the other side of the river. The elevation of the bridge gave a great view of the old capital to the north. At the apex of the arched bridge a young woman in beggar's rags and straw in her hair approached Jubei.

"Samurai-sama I have walked far. I am tired. Let me ride your horse," she begged.

Yoshi walking beside Jubei responded. "Some other time girl, we are in a hurry."

"You will be dead where you stand if you don't put me on your horse you poor excuse for a husband," she said.

All three men asked in unison, "Chiyo?"

"That is correct gentlemen," Chiyo said smiling.

Yuki moved to the group. "Chiyo, what news is there of my baby?"

"He is fine my lady. He is being cared for by a recent widow. She lost her son about the same age as Yoshitsune," Chiyo said.

"Where is Yoshitsune?" Yuki almost pleaded.

"Do not worry my lady. My mother is watching the building. He is at Yamakaya. I will take you," Chiyo said.

Yuki grabbed Chiyo to her bosom with a great hug. "Thank you and Matsu for keeping him safe."

"We did little. We just tracked him. Mother suspected you and my worthless husband would arrive today," Chiyo said.

"Worthless?" Yoshi asked.

"Yes, you are worthless, how did you allow the Koga to steal little Yoshitsune?" Chiyo asked.

Yoshi hung his head down.

"As much as I find it distasteful to speak up for Yoshi," Jubei said. "It really was not his fault."

"That is true Chiyo." Myo said. "Security was my responsibility and I failed."

"Not true Myo. My husband is the chief strategist for the Yoshinobu. He should have anticipated such a tactic and set countermeasures," Chiyo said.

"Please, let us not worry about blame. I blame myself. But let us focus on getting him back," Yuki said.

"Put me on your horse worthless," Chiyo said to Yoshi.

"I guess I had better change your name from Monkey to Worthless," Jubei said.

That brought laughter to the group. They all moved slowly toward the capital and the home of the Emperor.

"We have rooms reserved for you across the street from Yamakaya," Chiyo said as they walked the horses.

"What is the status?" Hideki asked.

"Yamakaya is the largest clothing store in the city. Haru is the proprietress. Her grandfather founded the store. Her father adopted an heir into the family. It was a short marriage, but it resulted in a son a little less than a year ago. The son died recently of a fever. Haru's father and husband were cut down by a street killer who used the one-cut style. They were returning from the water world," Chiyo said.

"Two questions: what is the one-cut style and what is the water world?" Yuki asked.

"The one-cut style is a school headed by Ito Itosai. It focuses on killing with one stroke. The water world means prostitutes," Jubei said.

"The father took her husband to visit prostitutes?" Yuki asked.

"All men play," The Mist said. "Well most men anyway," she said looking at Hideki.

"Merchants are different than samurai," Hideki said.

"Deals are often consummated in such places."

"How would you know that?" Myo asked.

"I spent a lot of time as a yojimbo in such a place last year in Nagasaki," Hideki said.

"Is there security?" Jubei asked Chiyo.

"Normally the answer would be no. But it is rumored Bishop Inshin placed a yojimbo with the widow. He is a member of the Ronin Army. He wears only a short sword and is very young," Chiyo said.

"Bishop Inshin? He is tied to Tadanaga is he not?" Yuki asked.

"That is correct via the Daito Kuji Temple," Jubei said. "The temple is located on Tadanaga land."

"That means the Koga and at least Bishop Inshin are responsible for my baby's abduction," Yuki said.

"It also means Tadanaga's chief strategist is one of the Kyoto street killers," The Mist said.

"That also means your baby will soon be in danger," Chiyo said. "Did you not leave the day Jii departed?"

"Yes," Yuki said. "That is why we must move quickly."

"One boy with a short sword should offer little resistance," Yoshi said.

"That is what four bandits thought the day the boy took up his position. Now three of them are dead and the fourth has disappeared," Chiyo said.

"So, the youngster is formidable," Hideki said. "Let us go to the inn, stable the horses, clean up and call on the widow and her yojimbo."

Yoshi led the horses away and the remaining six entered the inn. Once they had stepped into the outer cloakroom Yuki stopped to turn and look at Yamakaya across the street.

"He is just across the street," Yuki said.

"You will see him soon enough Yuki. Let us get situated first," Hideki said.

"Welcome to my fine establishment," a man in an apron said. This was said as he slowly bowed scanning his potential clients with a practiced eye. His automatic smile froze when he spied Chiyo.

"I am sorry samurai-sama. We are completely full. I can try

to get you a room later but there are so many in the city waiting for the investiture that it might be difficult," the aproned man said.

Chiyo removed her wig. "I reserved two more rooms with you yesterday clerk. You took my money. If we do not have rooms these men will become very incensed. You do not want that," she said. "And do not act like you own this place, I have met the owners and we are on good terms."

The aproned man's countenance darkened. The one-eyed samurai in complete black clothing looked especially scary. Even the young man with the crippled hand seemed dangerous.

"I am sorry Miss. I did not recognize you, your disguise is superb," he said as he scurried behind the counter to retrieve two small wooden plaques with the unique names of two rooms on them and a hole drilled at the top. "Please place these plaques on the peg outside your rooms so the servant girls know which are occupied."

Chiyo took the plaques. "What servant girls? Mother and I have been here a week. You are the only servant girl we've seen," she said to the clerk's discomfort. Chiyo then gave one plaque to Yuki and one to Hideki. "Follow me please."

As the women moved up the narrow stairs Jubei whispered to Hideki. "Now I see why Yoshi spends so much time away from home. Chiyo is very pretty but very strong."

"It is a good thing for us that she is. We would not have a clue about Yoshitsune's location without Chiyo and Matsu," Hideki said.

"Good point. I was going to give the monkey a hard time about this, but think discretion is a better path," Jubei said.

"You are getting smarter as you age sensei," Hideki said.

"Who is the sensei now?" Jubei asked.

Thirty minutes later seven rough looking people exited the inn and walked across the hard-packed dirt road to Yamakaya. Both the clerk and the customers shrank away from the newcomers.

"We're here to see the owner of this establishment," Yuki said.

"Do you have an appointment?" The chief clerk asked.

"No, but she will see us," Yuki said.

"I do not mean to be rude, but not just anyone can gain an audience with the lady of Yamakaya," the chief clerk said.

Yoshi and Chiyo broke off from the group and disappeared among shoppers. Chiyo was dressed like a young wealthy merchant's wife and Yoshi looked every bit the partner to his wife.

"Wait here please. Whom shall I say is calling?" The chief clerk asked.

"Tell her I am the rightful mother of the baby she is holding," Yuki said.

The clerk's shocked expression was replaced by a look of dismay when a female shriek emanated from one of the rooms followed by the distinct clash of swords.

Yuki pushed past the clerk and headed down the passageway with Hideki, Jubei, Myo and The Mist hot on her tail.

Yuki drew her katana and threw back the sliding doors of the room with the commotion.

When she stepped in Hideki stepped to her right and Jubei to the left. Myo and The Mist moved to Jubei's left.

The young and well-dressed merchant lady was clutching a baby to her bosom with her back to the attackers to protect the child. The mother and child were hunched over the bleeding body of an older woman. There were two dead ninjas just beyond the mother and child. A young man in a merchant silk kimono was holding a wakazashi in his right hand. The blade was bloodied.

Seven live ninjas now turned towards the new threat behind them. Hideki noticed the ceiling tile missing on the far left of the room.

One of the ninjas reached into his gi top. A shuriken struck him between the eyes. He screamed and dropped. One of the ninja's eyebrows rose as he recognized the thrower.

The Mist motioned for Myo to give her a hand up into the rafters via the missing ceiling tile. Myo did so and turned back to the tense situation in the room.

"We will assist," Hideki said to the young yojimbo.

The ninja glanced at each other. They did not like the odds. Two moved slowly toward Yuki. Jubei and Hideki jumped in front to meet the attack.

The gray clad ninja directly in front of Hideki twirled the weighted end of a kusarigama in his right hand. His left hand held a kama, a sickle like weapon with a short handle and a razor-sharp curved blade attached perpendicular at the head of the wood. Also, in his left hand were several loops of chain connected to the base of the handle of the weapon. On the other end of the chain was a heavy lead weight tapered into a point. This was being twirled at ever increasing speed. The ninja launched the lethal pointed projectile with unerring accuracy at Hideki's chest.

"By the Buddha," Hideki thought. "To deflect to the left meant danger to Yuki."

Hideki drew his short sword with his right hand. In one motion the blade came out and connected with the projectile. Hideki's blade deflected the projectile minutely to the right. Hideki twisted his body to the right when contact was made. He felt the burn as the tip of the weight cut across his right arm. The deadly weighted end of the chain penetrated deeply into the wooden door frame with a loud noise.

The gray clad ninja tried to pull the weighted end using both hands on the chain. He was not quick enough. Just as he grasped the chain a dart entered his brain through his left eye. He fell with a partial scream on his lips.

The third ninja lunged at Jubei with his straight ninja sword. Jubei made a rapid iai draw, lunging forward and dropping to his right knee. Jubei's strike was below the ninja's sword. The tip of the ninja's sword passed just inches above Jubei's head. Jubei's longer katana slashed across the ninja opponent just above the hip. He dropped to the tatami mortally wounded trying to keep his intestines inside his body.

Now all four-remaining ninja charged Rei to complete the mission of killing the child. The young bodyguard parried the first two swords but was giving way under the pressure of multiple attackers. One sword point penetrated his thigh, but he continued to parry and strike back.

Haru's head came up when Rei dropped to the tatami on his wounded leg. She let out a cry when it became evident she and the baby were going to die.

Then two ninjas fell as Yuki slashed left to right into the rear of the attackers. The two screamed and dropped to the floor moaning. Yuki started to turn to the right to ward off one of the two remaining ninja as he spun toward her. Yuki was assisted by Rei as he lunged on his knee as his short sword plunged into the ninja's lower back. He screamed through his face wrapping. The scream was cut off by Hideki's diagonal slash across his head.

Yuki's turn to the right made her vulnerable as the last ninja lunged with his sword to her left side. The blade never made it. It was smashed down by Jubei's overhead cut. Jubei then rotated his wrists and brought the katana up to execute a right-to-left horizontal slash. The ninja was almost decapitated. He spiraled downward and collapsed onto the back of Lady Yamakaya.

The first to talk was Yuki. "Myo, can you send for a doctor?"

Rei dragged the dead ninja off the back of Lady Yamakaya.

"Are you hurt my lady?" Rei asked.

"No, little Yoshi and I are unharmed," Haru said. "We are just badly shaken."

Yuki sheathed her sword.

"I am Yoshinobu Yuki. I am the real mother of the baby you hold in your arms. He is Yoshinobu Yoshitsune and the heir to the Yoshinobu clan. Thank you for protecting him with your life." Yuki said.

Yuki bowed deeply to Haru.

Chiyo moved past Yuki to the bleeding Ume. "She is hurt badly. Hand me that towel," she told Yuki. Yuki was a little slow to move but Hideki grasped the towel and threw it to Chiyo. Chiyo opened Ume's kimono carefully and applied pressure to the wound with the towel. With the applied pressure came pain and Ume moaned.

"Please help her. She is like a mother to me," Haru said.

Myo arrived pushing a doctor into the room.

"Complain about my conduct later," Myo said. "Fix this woman's wounds first."

"I have never been treated like this in all my twenty years in practice. No one forces a doctor to leave his clinic to treat an unknown," the doctor said.

"Save the woman if you can doctor," Jubei said. "Your life depends on it."

The doctor glared at the black clad one-eyed samurai with the bloody sword. Then he pulled back as he noticed the six bodies strewn about. He stopped complaining and went to work.

"Check the young man's wounds too," Jubei told the doctor.

"No," Rei said clutching his thigh. "Ensure the lady and the baby are not harmed first."

Yuki looked down at the sitting yojimbo clutching his wounded thigh. "You are very young to be so skilled and compassionate. What is your name?"

"I am Matoumoto Rei," he said bowing his greeting. "Dozo yoroshiku."

The chief clerk and several employees of both genders started gathering in the hall. Haru turned to them. "Bring a tatami to carry Ume to her quarters. When the doctor is done ensure she is comfortable and have someone tend her. I will visit her later. Please bring bandages for our yojimbo," Haru said.

Swords were wiped clean and returned to scabbards. The dead bodies of the six ninjas were moved out of the room. Ume and the doctor were moved to Ume's room. Rei's wound was bandaged by Chiyo.

"Did anyone else sustain an injury?" Haru asked.

No one answered. "Hideki is bleeding from a wound to his right arm, but he is too proud to admit it," Yuki said.

Chiyo attended to Hideki's wound.

Rei spun in his sitting position toward Hideki. "How did you manage to deflect that projectile? I did not think that was possible. It was traveling so fast."

"It is called a kurisagama. It is a favored weapon of the Koga ninja," Chiyo said.

"Why would the Koga want the lady killed?" Rei asked.

"She was not the target. The baby was," The Mist said, dropping down from the hole left by the missing ceiling tile.

Yuki sat down next to Haru. "What is your name?"

"I am called Haru," Lady Yamakaya said.

"Haru-san, may I hold my child?" Yuki asked.

Haru turned the child away from Yuki. "I know this is rude, but I met a very convincing samurai woman just a few days ago who claimed to be his mother. How do I know you are his real mother?" Haru asked.

"I am glad you are so protective of him," Yuki said. "Let me hold him and I will prove it."

Haru looked at Rei for support. He nodded in the direction of Hideki and Jubei. "These are very skilled swordsmen. I mean they are very skilled. I do not think they would be involved in any nefarious plot to hurt the child. We just watched them risk their lives for him. Give Yuki-sama the child and let her prove she is the mother."

Haru reluctantly turned toward Yuki.

"I bet he has been a good boy and has not uttered a sound except for changing and feeding. Am I correct?" Yuki asked.

Haru smiled and nodded in the affirmative. She then passed the child to Yuki. "He hardly ever makes a sound. He is a very good baby."

Yuki broke out in a wide smile as she took the child in her arms. Pulling back the blanket to get a view of the baby's face her smile got even wider.

"There's my sweet baby boy. Mother has missed you, yes she has." Yuki said.

At the sound of Yuki's voice, the baby started cooing excitedly. In between excited waving of his arms he started uttering gibberish.

Haru looked at the child and Yuki in surprise. "It crushes my heart to admit it, but you are truly mother to this child."

"Yes, we are mother and child," Yuki said.

"I will miss him more than you will know. He gave me a reason for living again," Haru said.

"I understand your loss. I felt the same way when Yoshitsune was stolen," Yuki said. "I did not want to go on living. The entire clan fell into depression until Hideki set a plan in action to retrieve them." She looked up at Hideki. "I thank you brother-in-law."

"No thanks are necessary. The real credit goes to Matsu and Chiyo for following Yoshitsune without error," Hideki said.

"I still want to know why the Koga ninja want Yoshi or Yoshitsune dead. He is just a baby," Rei said.

All eyes went to Yuki.

"The Koga and the Iga ninja both used to work for the now dead shogun. When the younger brother Tadanaga decided to contest his older brother Iemitsu's claim for shogun, the Koga decided to support Tadanaga. The Koga stole the Yoshinobu heir, little Yoshi as you call him, to force us to switch sides to Tadanaga. Our patriarch held a vote with everyone giving input. Everyone agreed to support Iemitsu. So now that the threat of the death of the heir will not sway us, the Koga are punishing the Yoshinobu and attempting to erase all traces of their horrible crime," Yuki said.

"I am sorry for your pain. Only a mother who has lost a child can understand," Haru said. "What happens now?"

Hideki turned to Yoshi. "What do you think chief strategist?"

"Do not ask him. He is worthless," Chiyo said.

"That is enough of that. There is no one to blame for Yoshitsune's loss except the Koga and those supporting Tadanaga," Hideki said. "I asked you a question Yoshi."

Yoshi turned to Rei. "Who funds the Ronin Army?"

"The captain pays us. We were tested in the Daito Kuji Temple. We were promised positions in the Satsuma clan, but I never saw anyone from there. I assume the captain kept the loot they extorted out of the shopkeepers," Rei said.

"Were you extorted here in Yamakaya?" Yoshi asked.

"No, we never were," Haru said.

"There may be a reason for this," Rei said.

Yoshi nodded for him to proceed.

"We were selected by the chief priests at the Daito Kuji Temple. When I was placed here as a yojimbo the other two lieutenants wanted to know why the Ronin Army was not allowed to visit Yamakaya. The captain named Mondo could not answer. He said it was not on the list," Rei said.

"Interesting but what does that have to do with funding the Ronin Army?" Yoshi asked.

"The person who wanted a yojimbo here was Bishop Inshin," Rei said.

"Bishop Inshin could not afford to pay the Ronin Army," Haru said. "He is a very good customer here, but he pays on installment. He is wealthy but he is not rich. If anything, he is a whore monger who spends his money on little girls."

Yoshi walked around the small group rubbing his chin.

"Do not worry about my husband. He is thinking. I know I call him worthless, but he is anything but that," Chiyo said.

"Come on Monkey, out with it. What's the plan?" Jubei said.

"The money is being funneled through the Bishop. But the source is unknown. It might be Tadanaga, but he doesn't have access to the Tokugawa coffers. So, the money must be coming from a third party we haven't seen yet. The Satsuma has pledged money and troops, but it provided nothing," Yoshi said.

"That is pretty smart of the Satsuma," Yuki said.

"If the Satsuma were massing an army you would know about it would you not Myo?" Yoshi asked.

"You know I would," Myo said a little irked by the question.

"How many men are there in the Ronin Army?" Yoshi asked.

"They were hoping for a 1000, but I would say realistically they have no more than 150 fighting men. Most of those are second rate or just plain bandits," Rei said.

"What do you think Yoshi?" Hideki asked.

"I think we need to get Yuki and the baby out of here as

soon as possible and get a word of warning to Jii and Iemitsu," Yoshi said.

"By the Buddha you are correct Yoshi," Jubei said.

"Why is he correct?" Yuki asked.

"Because with the Koga failing to kill Yoshitsune they will now turn all their efforts toward killing Jii or Iemitsu," Hideki said. "If either of them dies the investiture ceremony is delayed or cancelled."

"Do they always finish each other's sentences?" Haru asked.

"Yes," Myo said. "They are that close."

"Yuki we must get back to the hotel and gather our horses. Can you travel with Yoshitsune on horseback?" Hideki asked.

Yuki clutched her son to her bosom. "He is samurai. We can make it," Yuki said.

"Will you be safe here?" Hideki asked Haru.

Haru smiled for the first time since ninja had descended upon her.

"I have nothing to fear. I am a merchant. I can make money whoever becomes Shogun," Haru said. "Besides I have a yojimbo now," she said smiling at Rei.

"Then you will protect her?" Yuki asked.

"With my life Yuki-sama," Rei said.

"Then we leave you in good hands, and you have my heartfelt thanks," Yuki said and stood with her child.

XXVIII

Preparations

Back in their rooms across from Yamakaya everyone was preparing for the rapid return to Jii and safety.

"We have to get word to my father," Yuki said. "Both Jii and Iemitsu are in danger."

"Midori is with Jii," Myo said.

"She loves the old gray one like a granddaughter," Yoshi said.

"Myo and Yoshi set up protection for Jii before we left," Hideki said.

"Ugai is very good. You should not underestimate him," The Mist said.

"Chiyo how do you and Matsu feel about racing on horseback to alert Jii and Hittori Honzo?" Hideki asked.

"But I have not slept with Worthless in a long time and I am trying for a child too," Chiyo said.

"If he does not get himself killed tagging along after Hideki and this handsome sword master, you will have plenty of time," Matsu said. "And if he does not come back you are young and pretty enough to find another."

"Mother!" Chiyo yelled.

Yoshi turned his head to the side looking at his mother-in-law.

"Do not worry Chiyo. We will bring the worthless monkey back to you," Jubei said.

Chiyo nodded to Jubei and smiled.

"Chiyo you and Matsu change your clothes for riding.

You will be going ahead of us at a much faster pace. We will be going a little slower as Yuki has Yoshitsune. Yoshi ensure they have enough money to change horses and find lodging," Hideki said.

Everyone started changing into traveling gear. A clamoring could be heard down below in the street. Yoshi disappeared. Yuki handed her baby to The Mist while she changed. The Mist rocked Yoshitsune and spoke in hushed tones.

"So, you are the little fellow who helped bring down the great Koga ninja. You do not seem big enough," The Mist said.

Yoshitsune did not like being held by The Mist. He started kicking and thrashing his little arms. But he made no sound.

"Yoshi," The Mist exclaimed. "You are a handful."

"You can let him play on the floor. Just keep an eye on him," Yuki said.

Yoshi returned. He looked to Hideki. Hideki nodded giving him permission to speak in front of everyone. "There are plenty of the Ronin Army assembling downstairs in the bar. More are amassing outside. I believe they plan to take Yamakaya," Yoshi said.

"How many are there?" Jubei asked.

"That is unknown. Approximately thirty downstairs and another thirty in the street," Yoshi said.

"I think they are waiting for a leader."

"How are they armed?" Hideki asked.

"Swords are all I have seen," Yoshi said.

Hideki turned to Yuki. "What are your orders?"

Yuki looked at Jubei, Hideki and Yoshi. "My maternal instincts tell me to gather all my forces and return with my child to Jii as quickly as possible," Yuki said. "Hideki you are the real leader of the Yoshinobu. What should we do?"

"I want to order Jubei and Yoshi to take everyone to Jii and I will return to Yamakaya. Bushido demands that I protect the woman who kept Yoshitsune alive," Hideki said. "But I know my friends well enough to realize they would not follow that order and I am fairly sure Myo would not as well. So, I will make a deal with everyone. Jubei and Yoshi and I will stay. Chiyo and Matsu will depart immediately to warn Jii and Iemitsu. Myo you and The Mist take Yuki and Yoshitsune to Jii."

"I do not like it," Myo said.

"What part do you not like?" Hideki asked.

"I do not like any of it," Myo said. "Three of you will be up against at least sixty men with more coming. The plan is crazy."

"It is not crazy. It is what we should do," Jubei said. "From what I know of Yuki herself and her two escorts you should all reach Jii within two days."

"Do you agree Yuki?" Hideki asked.

"I do. I feel responsible for Haru and Yamakaya," Yuki said.

"You samurai and your pride will get us all killed someday," Myo said.

Hideki smiled. "Do not worry Myo. I will return to you and Jubei has promised to return Yoshi to Chiyo. What could go wrong?"

"You are too dumb to argue with," Myo said. Then she switched to the erotic Tsugaru dialect.

"Please come back to me samurai-sama. I need someone to warm my bed at night."

All eyes went to Hideki. He blushed a bright red.

"Come on lover," Jubei said. "Let us go down and thin out the competition."

"Ladies you depart with us, you go to the rear of the inn to the stables and leave there. Stay on the Tokaido until you are with Jii. Sling Yoshitsune on your front as you ride. Myo and The Mist, I am entrusting the future of the Yoshinobu clan to you," Hideki said.

"It is your future I'm worried about," Myo said.

"Come with us Hideki," Yuki said.

"You know I cannot," Hideki said.

"The odds are too great," Myo said. "Come with us and live."

"Would you still love me if I did?" Hideki asked.

"Yes," Myo said.

"I would diminish in your eyes," Hideki said.

"No," Myo said. "Ninja are intelligent enough to know when to choose their battles."

"I would diminish in my own eyes," Hideki said. "Get Yuki and Yoshitsune safe to Jii."

"We will send back reinforcements as soon as possible," Yuki said.

"Do not waste time on that. Reinforce Chiyo and Matsu's report to Iemitsu by telling your father as soon as you see him. Ugai is a real threat to Iemitsu's life," Hideki said.

Chiyo and Matsu departed. The Mist helped Yuki sling Yoshitsune on her front.

"Where are the bags Matsu left? I know she did not take them with her on horseback," Yoshi asked.

All eyes went to Yoshi.

"Never mind, I found them," Yoshi said coming out of the corner.

"Chiyo and Matsu have already departed. Are we ready to go down?" Hideki asked.

Everyone nodded in the affirmative.

Yuki with her baby wrapped in a blanket roll cradled in her arms and tied in the back moved to Hideki and bowed. "You are really the leader of the Yoshinobu. Who would have thought the clumsy boy I met on the Tokaido two years ago would be saving my son's life?" Yuki asked.

Yuki bowed to Jubei and to Yoshi in the same manner. "Thank you all," she said.

When the group descended the stairs and moved to the stables in the rear the women received appreciative looks from the drinking Ronin Army at the bar but refrained from catcalls when they spied the two yojimbo accompanying them.

"Where did Yoshi get to?" Hideki asked.

"Who knows about the Monkey?" Jubei said. "One minute he is standing beside you and the next minute he's gone. I am sure he is up to no good with our opponents. Good luck Monkey."

Hideki and Jubei saw the three horse women off down the small alleyway that paralleled the main street in front of the inn. As they watched the three women disappear into the maze of buildings that made up Kyoto's merchant area, several Ronin Army members streaked past them for the toilets next to the stables. Then several more rushed past headed in the same direction as Hideki and Jubei entered the rear of the inn.

By the time Hideki and Jubei reached the bar area in the front of the building it was in pandemonium. Men were leaving the tables bent over with cramps, grasping their stomachs and trying to get to the toilet area in the rear.

When Hideki and Jubei exited the main entrance and stepped into the street across from Yamakaya they noticed more ronin army milling around in front of and on the side of Haru's building.

As the two samurai moved through the crowd, they heard a shout behind them. "Drinks are on the house from Bishop Inshin. Hurry or you will miss out," the voice said. A stampede back toward the inn's main entrance commenced.

Jubei looked at Hideki and smiled. "Now we know what the rush to the benjo was about. You must admire the Monkey. He just poisoned half of our enemy."

The two samurai were greeted by Rei as they entered Yamakaya.

"Hideki-sama, Jubei-sama, I thought you returned to Edo," Rei said.

"Where is Haru?" Hideki asked.

Rei bowed his head a little. "She is in her quarters. She is crying. I guess the loss of two sons was too much," Rei said.

"Rei get all the employees of Yamakaya out the back door," Hideki said. "Have them go home immediately and stay there until the investiture has ended."

"I have been watching my old comrades from the Ronin Army gather across the street," Rei said. "Do you think they will storm us?"

"I am sure of it," Hideki said.

Rei turned and gave the orders to evacuate to the chief clerk. "What about Ume?" The chief clerk asked.

"Place her gently on one of the handcarts. Take her to the nearest clinic," Rei said.

"If stopped tell them you suspect plague. Mix some rice powder with water and create splotches on her face," Hideki said.

"The chief clerk shouted orders and raced around to carry out Rei's commands.

"What if they have guards stationed in the rear?" Rei asked.

"Do not worry about them. Our colleague will take care of them," Jubei said.

"Is that the one you call Monkey?" Rei asked. "Who is he?"

"Yes, but I am the only one who can call him that," Jubei said. "And the answer to your question is simple. He is dangerous."

"Take us to Haru," Hideki said.

Haru was sitting in her quarters dabbing her eyes with her inner kimono sleeve.

"This is no time for tears Haru-san. We will be under attack in a few moments," Hideki said.

The lady looked from Rei to Hideki to Jubei. "Is Yoshi safe?" she asked.

Hideki saw the look of confusion on Jubei's face.

"He is fine. His mother just left with an escort," Hideki said.

Hideki then turned to Jubei. "She meant Yoshitsune," Jubei nodded his understanding.

"What do we do?" Haru asked Rei.

"I have already started an evacuation of all employees," Rei said. "We should go as well."

"What about Ume? She cannot travel," Haru said.

"She will have to," Hideki said. "Her only chance of survival is to get out of here and into a clinic."

"She is being moved as we speak," Rei said.

The discussion was interrupted by clamoring and shouting from the street.

"Sounds like Jubei and I had better go greet our new guests," Hideki said.

"I will accompany you," Rei said.

Haru clutched his arm. "Do not leave me alone Rei-san."

"Bushido requires I fight," Rei said.

The chief clerk appeared. "Everyone is out. Ume has been transferred as you requested Rei-san."

"Good job now get out yourself. We will be having unwanted guests in a few moments," Hideki said.

"My job is to stay with Lady Yamakaya," the chief clerk said.

"Suit yourself," Rei said. "I guess you will be her yojimbo now. We three will meet the crowd."

"We have another disciple of bushido. You are no longer alone Hideki," Jubei said.

"Haru, are there any weapons in the building?" Hideki asked.

"No, we are merchants not samurai," Haru said.

"What about escape routes, secret tunnels, false walls? Do you have anything like that?" Hideki asked.

Haru hesitated.

"Tell them Haru," Rei said. "He is thinking like the enemy. Even if we manage to hold off the first wave it will not take them long to decide to fire the building."

Both the clerk and Haru looked at Rei aghast.

"How horrible," Haru said. "A fire in Kyoto would spread for blocks and kill many people."

"I do not think they are too worried about lives and property," Rei said.

"Fire makes no sense. Everyone loses in a fire," Haru said.

"Remember Yuki-sama said her child was stolen to sway the Yoshinobu to Tadanaga's side. Those plans have been foiled. It appears they will take out their frustration on Yamakaya," Rei said.

"Tell me about escape routes. It will affect our tactics," Hideki said.

Haru nodded in understanding. "We have a tunnel. There is a trap door under the tatami in my room," she said.

"Where does it end?" Hideki asked.

"It terminates near the river at our warehouse," Haru said.

"How far is it from the Sanjo Bridge?" Hideki asked.

"It is just a block away on the near side of the river," Haru said.

"That is a very long tunnel and very good news," Hideki said. "We may get out of this alive. Much depends on Yoshi."

"Little Yoshi, how can that be?" Haru asked.

"He means big Yoshi, our friend," Jubei said.

"Yoshi?" Hideki called into the ceiling.

Yoshi appeared behind Jubei. Jubei jumped.

"Monkey stop that slithering," Jubei warned.

"You did call me," Yoshi said innocently.

"Are the guards in the rear dealt with?" Hideki asked.

Yoshi looked at Hideki. "What a hurtful thing to ask me," Yoshi said.

"Of course, I am sorry. I was not thinking. Were you listening when we learned of a tunnel in Haru's room that ends just short of the Sanjo Bridge?" Hideki asked.

"Yes, do you want me to go back to the stables across the street and have six horses ready to ride at the foot of the bridge?" Yoshi asked.

"As always, you have read my mind," Hideki said.

"Just a minute, there are many Ronin Army between here and there," Haru said. "How is he going to make it to the stables?"

"He will make it the same way he dropped in here undetected and frightened me a few moments ago. It is what he does," Jubei said.

Yoshi handed a cloth sack to Jubei. "I will not be here when these are most needed. So, I'm giving them to you. Keep them away from the fire."

"What is in it?" Jubei asked.

"Remember when we fought the Portuguese sailors that landed behind the Ryukyuan village?" Yoshi asked.

"Yes," Hideki answered.

"Remember the explosions?" Yoshi asked.

"Dear Buddha," Jubei said holding the bag at arm's length.

"How do you use them?" Hideki asked.

"Add flame to the fuse and throw," Yoshi said.

"Let me see," Rei said.

"This is way too dangerous for you Rei. I think I will keep them," Jubei said pulling the sack away.

When Hideki looked for Yoshi again he was gone.

"How does he do that?" Rei asked

"No one knows," Jubei answered. "But now I feel a little better about our chances."

XXIX

Conflagration

"Here they come," the chief clerk yelled.

Rei, Jubei and Hideki moved down the corridor to the front of the store. They spread out three abreast across the hardwood floor a step above the dirt entrance. The double sliding door at the street level was open. Approximately thirty ronin poured in. They filled up the entrance level. The front rank stopped at the step up onto the store floor when they spied the three samurai.

"Stay back if you want to live," Hideki said.

The ronin in the rear started to put pressure on those in the front who had stopped. The leader in the center of the ronin took a hard look at all three standing before him. The one black clad samurai on the right looked dangerous even with one eye. The samurai on the far left was very young and had a scarred right hand. He also appeared to be left-handed. He was an unknown. The one in the middle he recognized. He only carried a short sword. But the leader had seen him in action. He could be deadly. This was not shaping up to be the easy raid that Bishop Inshin had promised.

"We are the Ronin Army. We are here on official business. Where is the Lady Yamakaya?" The leader shouted.

"She is indisposed at the moment," Hideki said. "How can you be on official business? You are all ronin."

"Who are you?" The leader demanded.

"The dangerous man on my far right is Yagyū Jubei. Former fencing instructor to the now deceased Shogun Hidetada and to both his sons Iemitsu and Tadanaga," Hideki said.

Hideki saw fear in the leader's eyes.

"I am Yoshinobu Hideki. I am cousin to both Iemitsu and Tadanaga. My nickname is Tengu Killer," Hideki said.

Now the leader and the ten or so followers close enough to hear were confused. Should they bow?

"The young man in the center is yojimbo to the Lady Yamakaya. I believe you know him. He used to work for you, but Bishop Inshin placed him here. I think that will suffice for our introductions. Who are you to barge into this establishment frequented by the Imperial court?" Hideki asked.

"I am Mondo, captain in the Ronin Army. I have orders to secure Lady Yamakaya and her child," Mondo said.

"Who gave those orders?" Hideki asked.

"I do not answer to you," Mondo said.

"Maybe you will answer to my sword," Hideki said.

Mondo wasn't worried about a left-handed boy with a scarred hand. But his confidence in the face of both Rei and a fencing instructor was a little unsettling. Rei had beaten the best of the monks with that short sword of his. He had also seen Rei battle competent swordsmen wielding full-length katanas and defeat them.

The man on the right claiming to be Yagyū Jubei was a different matter entirely. He was dressed in total black. His kimono was black. His outer jacket was black. His hair was black. His eye patch was a black tsuba. His swords and scabbards were black. Even that one good eye looked black as death. Mondo had no illusions about him. He looked like he was ready to draw and start slashing given any provocation.

Mondo held his arms wide to keep from being pressured from the rear. His lieutenants on his right and left did the same thing. His mistake was now evident. He should have attacked from the back of the pack. Now he could be the first to die. Maybe he could reduce the odds against him a little.

"Rei you are a lieutenant in the Ronin Army. Come over here and assume your post," Mondo commanded.

"Sorry Mondo, Bishop Inshin himself sent me here to protect the lady of Yamakaya. I intend to do just that," Rei said.

This was not what Mondo was used to. Extorting merchants was one thing. Fighting samurai with the skill level of Yagyū Jubei was suicide.

Mondo turned his head to the side. "Abe, Watanabe get them to back up. We are in danger here."

The three began shouting at the pressing group behind them to back up. It had little effect as a group behind was trying to get in and plunder the store.

Jubei turned his head to Hideki. "I just saw horses exit the stables across the street. They were headed toward the river."

"Good, at least that part of the plan is holding," Hideki said. "Rei, move back to the lady's quarters. Without Yoshi back there we are vulnerable from the rear."

Rei nodded his head and departed across the wooden floor.

"When do we start thinning the ranks of this so-called army?" Jubei asked.

"Not until we must, remember Sun Tzu? Let us see how this develops," Hideki said.

Mondo, Abe and Watanabe yelled and screamed and banged heads and kicked and made the press of bodies reverse. When safely on the street, "do you think that was really Yagyū Jubei?" Watanabe asked.

"I do not know. I have never seen Jubei. But he looked like a demon to me," Mondo said.

"What are we going to do?" Abe asked.

"We are going back in but this time we are going to put a price of one gold coin to the man who slays either the one-eyed man or the left-handed cripple," Mondo said.

"That is a lot of money," Abe said.

"Yes, and they will earn it," Mondo said. "This time we will cheer from the rear. Go get your men whipped up again. They go back in once you get them organized. Let us see how good those three really are when faced with overwhelming odds."

"It looks like the time for Sun Tzu is over," Jubei said.

"Yes," Hideki said. "We have to keep them out of the store."

"There is some good news," Jubei said.

"Please tell me," Hideki said. "I could use some."

"We have more room to swing without Rei," Jubei said.

"You are not much in the way of good news," Hideki said.

"I am glad they are coming again," Jubei said. "I am tired of looking at them."

"We are in agreement there," Hideki said.

Thirty of the Ronin Army poured into the door of Yamakaya. They pushed forward and several tried to jump onto the wooden floor. Hideki met his first two with both swords. A wild slash aimed at his face was parried with the wakazashi in his right hand and the unfortunate ronin dispatched with a stab into the abdomen by the katana. The second man up was met with the same technique in reverse. He screamed as the short sword punctured his stomach.

The third man lunged directly at Hideki's center. Hideki deflected his sword with is katana and kicked him back onto the throng below. That stopped the pressure for a moment. Hideki stole a glance at Jubei. Six bodies littered the area around the deadly arc of his katana.

Hideki saw two of the three men who had been the leaders pushing from behind. They were shouting encouragement and screaming about one gold coin. The front row that had been catching its breath when the initial assault failed gathered their courage and made another run at the step up to Hideki's level.

Hideki slipped into mushin. He plunged his katana into one's eye. He cut off another's ear. A third lost a hand. A fourth was eviscerated. Hideki was conscious of nothing. He was reacting to every motion around him. Everything slowed for him. He was aware of his deep breathing and the sweat that poured into his eyes. He was acutely aware of every sword that neared him, and the counterattack needed to incapacitate the attacker. His mind was truly empty.

When the pressure from the crowd diminished, Hideki jumped off his platform and into the midst of the Ronin Army. His swords slashed up and down and horizontally. He gave no quarter and asked for none. He was a killing machine seeking more and more targets.

With no remaining opponents, Hideki dropped his swords

to his side. They dangled from useless arms. He could not move and his breathing was ragged. There was no more Ronin Army in the Yamakaya. Hideki's post combat trance was interrupted by Jubei's continual shouts. Hideki snapped out of his state and recognized the many bodies and blood littering Yamakaya's entrance.

Jubei took out folded paper from his black vest over his kimono and wiped his blade clean. He tossed the paper aside. It landed on several dead Ronin Army members.

"What happened?" Hideki asked.

"You just put on a very convincing demonstration of mushin fighting," Jubei said. "I was so impressed when you jumped into the middle of them that I had to do the same."

Hideki sat down on the step with both swords still in his hands.

"That was stupid," Hideki said.

"I will not disagree," Jubei said. "But it broke their back. No one that entered Yamakaya tonight lived unless they fled."

Jubei returned his now clean sword to its scabbard. Then he walked over bodies and grabbed Hideki under the arms from behind. He lifted Hideki to his feet.

"Can you stand?" Jubei asked.

Hideki nodded. "Yes, I am starting to feel my arms again."

"You need to regain your awareness if we are to live through the night," Jubei said. "We are still in danger."

Hideki stuck his katana into the dirt floor of the entrance. He pulled paper from his kimono and cleaned the wakazashi. He returned it to his saya. He then repeated the process for his katana.

"I'm back to normal," Hideki announced. "I have never had this happen before."

"I am assuming it is a result of fighting in mushin," Jubei said. "When you first started acting that way, I thought you had lost your mind. But then it became apparent you had turned into a demon of death."

"I am sorry," Hideki said.

"I am not," Jubei said. "There were too many of them. No one could stand up to that onslaught unless they wanted to die.

Neither of us wanted to die. So, your mushin saved us both."

"I am embarrassed," Hideki said.

"Why? You stopped them," Jubei said.

"I lost control," Hideki said.

"I like to think of it as finding control. You found a way to fight in mushin against huge odds. I do not think even Musashi could do that," Jubei said.

"How many did we lose?" Mondo asked.

"Over thirty," Abe answered.

"How is that possible?" Mondo asked. "Three cannot hold out against thirty."

"It was only two," Abe said. "Rei was not with them when the second wave launched."

"Two samurai defeated thirty men?" Mondo asked. "That does not make sense."

"You were not on that dirt floor. I was," Abe said. "The two of them were like farmers harvesting rice. They cut through our men like they were rice stalks."

"I believe you Abe," Mondo said. "I guess the dark one really is Yagyū Jubei."

"He was not the one killing the most men," Abe said. "That crippled left-handed boy killed twice as many as Yagyū. He jumped into the center of our men and chopped and slashed and punctured his way to the door. I barely escaped his wrath."

"Who could be a better killer than the legendary Yagyū Jubei? Mondo asked.

"I think they are both demons," Abe said. "They certainly kill like demons. Maybe the boy was correct. Maybe he is the Tengu Killer because he is a demon. How do we fight demons?"

"We don't fight them with swords. Abe, go get me a couple of barrels of whale oil. But do it quietly without alerting any attention. Watanabe get as much water in buckets as you can find. We will meet back here in the hour of the dog. Send runners to bring the rest of the Ronin Army. It will be dark by then," Mondo said.

"Arson is punishable by crucifixion," Watanabe said.

"Then get a few men you do not like and kill them afterwards. We testify they got carried away," Mondo said.

"You are the boss," Watanabe said as they departed.

"Damn right I am," Mondo said. "I'll get even with that little smart mouth Rei with his Yamakaya princess and the two big killer samurai."

When the hour of the dog arrived, it was dark.

"They are making preparations to burn us out," Jubei said looking out onto the street. "I don't think they want to meet your sword again."

"It is time," Hideki said. "Leave Yoshi's presents by the door."

Jubei placed Yoshi's grenades on either side of the door buried in the dirt. Only the fuse could be seen.

"I would like to think those three leaders will be close enough to feel Yoshi's sting. But that may be wishful thinking," Jubei said.

"Forget them. We have to get to Jii and then find Hittori Honzo," Hideki said.

"I thought that was Chiyo and Matsu's responsibility," Jubei said.

"It is," Hideki said. "Jii knows both Matsu and Chiyo. They will have no trouble there. But I anticipate all sorts of filters for them in getting to Hittori Honzo and Iemitsu."

Hideki and Jubei moved to Lady Yamakaya's quarters. "It is time to exit," Hideki said. "This place will be ablaze soon."

"What happened to you?" Rei asked looking at Hideki's attire. It was cut in several places.

"He got a little closer than normal to some swords," Jubei said.

"Is there no way to stop this?" Haru asked. "This is my home."

"We might be able to stop them, but the odds are very great. I do not want to risk everyone's life for a building," Hideki said.

"What will I do without a house and a business?" Haru asked.

"Lady, your foyer is littered with over thirty bodies. Two of us killed them all. You can see how it almost cost Hideki his life. You will be alive to decide what happens to your house and business," Jubei said. "If we stay here much longer we will all perish in flames."

"This city is going to continue to be lawless until my grandfather arrives," Hideki said. "Let us get into the tunnel and meet Yoshi with the horses. The Yoshinobu owe you a great debt. We will repay you."

"Come Haru-sama, let us leave," Rei said.

Haru snapped out of her depression. "Bring several lanterns with you Rei," she directed. "Jubei please raise these three tatamis."

Jubei complied. Removing the tatami exposed a large wooden trap door. Jubei raised it and saw a wooden ladder leading into darkness.

"Light one of the lanterns Rei and hand it down," Jubei said.

Once accomplished Jubei started down the shaft. At the bottom he looked as far as the light would allow.

"Come on down, we do not have to bend over. It is well dug," Jubei said.

Jubei led the five with the chief clerk, Haru and Rei in the center. Hideki brought up the rear. They traveled unheeded toward the unknown end.

Up above on the street Mondo gathered his two lieutenants.

"The men want to go in and gather the plunder they were promised," Abe said.

"Are your men in position?" Mondo asked Watanabe.

"Yes, they have burned buildings before. They know what to do," Watanabe said.

"Then start now," Mondo said. "We cannot afford to lose any more men to those sword demons."

Watanabe left to give the go-ahead signal. The Ronin Army was gathered outside Yamakaya. They were unsure why they could not enter.

"Fire," exclaimed one of the army.

"The Ronin Army started looking for buckets and water barrels. They found them and formed bucket brigades uninstructed. Soon the clanging of the firehouse bell could be heard. Firemen were soon on the scene in their thick weaved jackets and sloped helmets. They directed the bucket brigade and doused the buildings adjacent to Yamakaya.

The fire had started at the rear of the building and raced forward following the splashes of whale oil. When the fire reached the front of the building two huge explosions sent wooden projectiles screaming into the street, killing and wounding many.

"By all the gods, what was that?" The Fire Chief asked.

"I have no idea," Mondo said, looking at his ravaged army. "Did you lose any men?"

"I do not think so. My men were mainly on the adjoining buildings trying to get them wet."

"That was very lucky for you," Mondo said.

"What happened?" Watanabe asked.

"I do not know, and I do not care. Let us get back to our quarters, grab our loot and disappear," Mondo said.

"Why are you having this change of heart?" Abe asked. "Even if that samurai was Yagyū Jubei everyone in Yamakaya will be toasted by now,"

"You do not understand," Mondo said. "We have been getting our orders from Bishop Inshin. The Yoshinobu are reported on their way to Kyoto as Iemitsu's advance guard. Now a Yoshinobu and a Yagyū turn up at Yamakaya. Our end is getting near."

"What about our positions with the Satsuma?" Watanabe asked.

"That is what I am trying to tell you," Mondo said. "Have you seen any Satsuma troops?"

"No," Abe said.

"But we've seen a Yoshinobu and a Yagyū. That means the Yoshinobu forces are near. What happens if they get here before the Satsuma?" Mondo asked.

"I guess we fight," Watanabe said.

"What will the outcome be if the remnants of the Ronin

Army fight real samurai?" Mondo asked. "Do not forget what happened tonight when two of theirs killed thirty of ours."

"If they are like the two in the Yamakaya, we will perish." Abe said.

"We just killed two of them in a fire. Do you think they will think kindly of us?" Mondo asked.

"No," Watanabe said.

"Something has always been fishy about this whole deal. When we started extorting from shop owners, I knew this Ronin Army was fake. Tadanaga's whole grab for power is built on sand," Mondo said.

"What do we do Mondo?" Abe asked.

"We do not want to be associated with the Ronin Army when Iemitsu gets here. Take off your haori and your headbands. We have been defeated by a young boy and two demons. Let's gather up as much of our loot that we can and flee Kyoto," Mondo said.

The rest of the gullible Ronin Army worked well into the night to put out the fire their comrades had started.

Near the Sanjo Bridge Jubei emerged from a trap door into a large warehouse. The five exited into the night by unlocking the warehouse from the inside. Once through Rei closed the door and the lock was reset on the outside.

Yoshi saw the light from their lanterns and brought the horses to them.

"Did you have any problems?" Yoshi asked.

"None whatsoever," Jubei replied.

"If you call losing your home and business in one evening nothing, I guess I can concur," Haru said.

"You have lost nothing," Hideki said. "The Yoshinobu will help you rebuild. Let us mount and move."

"I do not know how," the chief clerk said embarrassed.

"Rei help him out once you have Haru mounted. We will be moving pretty fast for the first couple of hours," Hideki said.

"I do not know how to ride either," Haru said. "I am frightened."

"We forget only teamsters and samurai ride horses," Jubei said.

"You are correct Jubei," Hideki said. "Rei ride double with

Haru. Ride behind her and hold the reins. Clerk if you fall off, we are not stopping. Just give the horse his head and you hang onto the saddle as tightly as possible and keep your feet in the stirrups. He will keep up with the rest of the horses."

They rode into the night with Jubei in front and Hideki in the rear. Haru's fear of the animal diminished considerably with the systematic up and down motion and a pair of strong young arms around her torso.

XXX

Battle Plans

"Halt. Who goes there?" The sentry challenged, dropping the point of his yari into a ready position.

"Yoshinobu Hideki and five friends," Hideki said dismounting.

"I am sorry Yoshinobu-sama," the sentry said. "I did not recognize you. It was too dark."

"You would have been much sorrier if you had not challenged him," Jubei said.

"Where is my grandfather?" Hideki asked.

"The last I saw of him he was playing with his great grandson under heavy guard in the great room inside," the sentry said as he came to attention.

"Good work," Yoshi said as he trailed behind the rest into the inn. "How many other sentries are there?"

"I am sorry sir, you would have to ask the commander of the guard," the sentry said.

"That was the correct answer," Yoshi said. "Stay awake, you may have to use that spear."

The young sentry looked up at the tip of his yari. "Yes sir," he said, wondering if the strange little man was kidding.

It was easy to determine the great room. It was the one with four samurai stationed outside. The sentries bowed to Hideki and his entourage. Hideki opened the sliding door and stepped inside.

Jii sat in the middle of the room holding Yoshitsune in his lap. Yuki was watching next to Jii smiling as her baby tried to talk. Several wives of the Yoshinobu samurai acted as servants to the gathering.

"Sorry to interrupt your strategy session with Yoshitsune Jii but I thought you might like to meet the woman who kept your great-grandson alive and the man who protected them both," Hideki said.

"Hideki, Jubei, thank you for bringing them out alive," Yuki said. "Grandfather, this is Haru of Yamakaya and her chief clerk. The youngster behind her is Matoumoto Rei. He is cut from the same cloth as my brother-in-law and Jubei."

"Good cloth to be cut from, Jii said, eyeing each. "Welcome to my temporary home and sanctuary. Please come join us."

The chief clerk hung back and moved to the wall. Hideki, Jubei, Yoshi, Haru and Rei moved to sit in a semi-circle in front of Jii.

Haru and Rei bowed deeply.

Jii looked at the clerk. "Why do you stay back?"

The chief clerk bowed his head. "I am but a clerk samurai-sama."

"And I am but a very old man," Jii said and motioned the clerk over.

The chief clerk moved to the group and sat as formally as he knew how on the tatami and bowed again.

"My grandson and his friend Jubei are samurai. The man next to him is Yoshi. He is ninja and my chief strategist and counselor. Next to them is The Mist. She is ninja and new to our group. Next to her is Myo. She is ninja and the leader of our intelligence system. She is also the lover of my grandson although they don't think I know," Jii said.

Myo winked at Hideki. Hideki reddened.

"They don't think they can get married because they are of different class. I have never been much for ceremony. She has proven her love for my grandson many times over by risking her life for him. I would be proud to have her a part of the family," Jii said.

Both Hideki and Myo showed their surprise.

"Merit is what counts with me," Jii said still playing with

Yoshitsune. "If you helped the woman who fed and protected Yoshitsune, then you are welcome as one of my family."

Haru bowed her head. "Yuki told me the Yoshinobu were great. But I could not imagine how great until now."

"We are not great are we Hideki?" Jii asked.

"I would say we are just average grandfather," Hideki said. "What makes us unique is we are blessed with really good friends."

"Matoumoto? That is a very strange name," Jii said. "Is your father the master of Tamiya-ryu?"

"You have heard of my father Yoshinobu-sama?" Rei asked. "I am flattered."

"You will find that samurai who are serious about swordsmanship try to keep track of the real masters," Jii said.

Rei bowed acknowledging the compliment.

"Haru, how can I ever repay you for your protection of my great-grandson?" Jii asked.

Haru bowed. "I seek no reward Yoshinobu-sama," Haru said.

"She lost her store in Kyoto to the Ronin Army. It was also her family home for three generations. Her establishment was frequented by the Imperial court," Hideki said.

"Do you wish to build back in Kyoto?" Jii asked.

"I would like to. It was my home. I still have inventory in several warehouses. I still have my chief clerk. I still have my yojimbo who is very precious to me. We could build again with enough capital," Haru said.

"How big is the Ronin Army?" Jii asked changing the subject.

"Much smaller after Yoshi poisoned their sake and blew up the front to Yamakaya with them in it," Jubei said.

"They would be lucky to amass more than 40 men," Hideki said.

"They are more bandits than samurai. They do not understand bushido," Rei said.

"Haru, I will provide the money to get you started again in Kyoto if you wish. You will have to wait a month or two. I must clean out that Kyoto cesspool first. Please stay with us.

You, your clerk and Rei may consider yourselves my guests and you have my protection," Jii said.

The three new guests bowed their thanks.

"By the way Rei, will you stay and protect Haru when she returns to Kyoto?" Jii asked.

"Yes Lord," Rei said. "If that is what she desires."

"How long will you stay with her?" Jii asked.

"For as long as she wants or needs me," Rei replied.

"That was a good answer Rei," Jii said as he signaled one of the samurai guards. "You three please follow this young warrior. He will get you baths, food and lodging. We will depart for Kyoto tomorrow at noon."

Again, the three bowed their thanks and departed.

"Tomorrow and the next day should get interesting," Jii said.

"Have you given my grandfather the names of the Tadanaga supporters in Kyoto?" Hideki asked The Mist.

"Yes Hideki, Jii has been informed," The Mist said.

"Jii?" Hideki asked, wondering about her use of the informal pet name for his grandfather.

"Seems The Mist has been smitten by the Yoshinobu charm," Jii said.

"Did I overstep my bounds?" The Mist asked.

"Not at all young woman," Jii said. "I invited you to be a family member. My family calls me Jii."

Hideki, Jubei and Yoshi looked at Myo.

"Do not look at me like that. The Mist is one of us now," Myo said.

"Good enough for me," Yoshi said.

"I've learned not to argue with Myo," Hideki said.

Jubei nodded his approval.

"What about Iemitsu?" Hideki asked.

"Matsu and Chiyo have ridden to him with the full report. His entourage of 300,000 should arrive in Kyoto in three days," Jii said.

"Hittori Honzo should be well alerted," Myo said.

"Good," Hideki said. "I just did not like waiting for Ugai to strike."

"It is all we can do," The Mist said. "All his gathering

places will be changed now that he knows I am his enemy."

"I think we could hurt Ugai and Tadanaga if we went on the offensive," Hideki said.

"How?" Jii asked.

"We strike at his organization," Hideki said.

"Are you suggesting we eliminate the members of the cabal that The Mist identified?" Yoshi asked.

"That is exactly what I am recommending," Hideki said.

"We cannot touch Tadanaga or his mother," Jubei said.

"That leaves Yamada Arinaga the Satsuma representative, Itosai Ito the strategist, Lord Shingen Murada of Fukuchiyama Castle and Bishop Inshin of Daito Kuji Temple as targets," Myo said.

"Exactly," Hideki said. "We cripple his infrastructure."

"Be careful Hideki, you are plotting assassination," Jubei said. "You will turn into me."

"I know Jubei. I have thought about this long and hard. But if there is anything that I have learned in traveling with you it is that evil must be eradicated when found," Hideki said. "We are at war and we are trying to prevent a civil war. If killing these men saves the lives of thousands, then I will do it."

"What is your plan? Myo asked.

"Mist can you get Jubei and I onto the Daito Kuji Temple grounds without raising suspicion?" Hideki asked.

"It would be easier to get Myo, Yoshi and myself in. No offense gentlemen, but you are samurai. You tend to be noisy," The Mist said.

Myo and Yoshi snickered.

"They are clumsy, aren't they?" Yoshi said.

"They have their uses," Myo said eyeing Hideki.

"You can quit blushing Hideki and tell us the gist of your plan," Jii said.

"Jubei, Midori, Myo, Yoshi, The Mist and I depart earlier than your main body tomorrow. The Mist gets Myo and Yoshi inside the temple where Bishop Inshin, Yamada, and Murata are quartered," Hideki said.

"They may not be there lord," The Mist said.

"If they are not on the temple grounds then abort your

mission," Hideki said. "But the Koga spies have most likely told Tadanaga and followers that Jii will arrive tomorrow night. They will want to be on hand for our clash with the Ronin Army," Hideki said.

"What about Itosai Ito?" Jubei asked. "He is the most dangerous."

"Do you think his Ito-ryu style is that strong?" The Mist asked.

"I do not know," Hideki said. "But I believe him to be an evil man."

The looks on everyone's face pushed Hideki to explain.

"I do not think he is driven by greed. According to The Mist he wants his fencing style to be known as the best in the land," Hideki said.

"Then I should challenge him," Jubei said.

"That would be the logical choice," Hideki said. "You represent Shinkage-ryu, the shogun's fencing style. The Yagyū have been training the Tokugawa family in Shinkage-ryu for decades. You are well known. What would happen if Jubei's student challenged him?" Hideki asked.

"You are talking about yourself? You mean Ito might think you less skilled and perhaps be overconfident?" Yoshi asked.

"Perhaps," Hideki said.

"I am proud of you Hideki. You are starting to think like a ninja," Yoshi said.

"What if Ito kills you?" Myo asked.

"Then I expect Jubei to kill him and you to grieve," Hideki said.

"His style is lightning fast," Jubei said.

"Have you fought anyone from his style?" Yoshi asked.

"One of his students challenged me about two years ago," Jubei said.

"Obviously you were quicker," Myo said.

"Not by much. He struck like a mamushi viper. They try to kill on the first strike," Jubei said.

"They practice that first strike."

"So, it is an iai-jutsu strike?" Hideki asked. "They kill from the scabbard?"

"Yes, and they do it from a reverse foot forward stance. It

is hard to judge distance," Jubei said. "What is the real reason you want to challenge Ito personally?"

"He may very well be Kyoto's street killer. If so, he is beyond evil. Bushido demands that I protect the weak. I will bring justice for the woman who protected my nephew," Hideki said.

"I take it all back. You think like a samurai. You are a fool," Yoshi said.

"How do you plan to engage him?" The Mist asked.

"If he is the Kyoto street killer, he is obsessed with his skill. People have no meaning to him. His sick ego is what drives him," Hideki said.

"You plan to attack his ego?" Jubei said. "Will that work?"

"Tomorrow when Jii enters Kyoto, there will be blood in the streets as the Yoshinobu engage the Ronin Army," Hideki said. "I will wait at the gates of the temple. Myo, The Mist and Yoshi will enter the temple grounds and post my challenge to Ito throughout the temple grounds. Then they will strike Bishop Inshin, Yamada of Satsuma and Murata. That will cripple Tadanaga and leave him with no allies."

"What if Ito does not come out?" Myo asked.

"Then torch the buildings," Hideki said.

"Daito Kuji is a very holy site," Jii said. "There may be repercussions from Iemitsu."

"The Ronin Army are thugs," Hideki said. "They have no honor. When Jii arrives and starts slaying them they will try to escape with whatever loot they can carry. The most loot is in Daito Kuji Temple."

"Now you are thinking like a ninja again. The Ronin Army will be blamed for our fires," Yoshi said.

"Yes, and if Ito has not come out, the fires may drive him out," Hideki said.

"This sounds very risky. Why not ride in with me and we will force the traitors out?" Jii asked.

"Because they already have plans to fall back to Murata's Fukuchiyama Castle awaiting reinforcements from Satsuma," The Mist said. "The loss of life attacking a castle will be high."

The Mist turned to Hideki.

"You really think like a warlord," she said.

Jii nodded. "You are far thinking grandson. You are worthy of the Yoshinobu name."

"Not really Jii," Hideki said. "I have faithful friends who will risk their lives with my decision. My burden is to think far enough ahead that I do not endanger them needlessly."

"What would you have me do?" Jubei asked.

"I would like you to have a Yumi and a full quiver of arrows. I need you to keep the wolves off my back," Hideki said.

"That is not a one-man job. I will need Midori," Jubei said.

"It is nice to be wanted," Midori said making her entrance.

"You will have her," Myo said nodding to her lieutenant.

"Everyone should get some sleep," Jii said. "Tomorrow will be a very busy day."

"Wait," Yuki said. "Can Hideki defeat Ito? I do not want to lose my brother-in-law."

"That is an unknown," Jubei said. "Your brother-in-law is one of the three deadliest duelists in Japan."

"Who are the other two?" The Mist asked.

"That would be Jubei and Hideki's first instructor Myamoto Musashi," Yoshi answered.

"This is a great family," The Mist said. "But I do not understand why you take so many risks?"

"They are samurai Mist. They do not think like normal humans. But because the family is great, we ninja must keep them alive," Yoshi said.

"Well said Monkey," Jubei said.

All eyes turned to the old man holding his grandson as he surveyed the company with a confident eye: "Let's get some sleep."

As everyone moved to their respective rooms Hideki stopped and turned to Myo. "I guess there is no reason to sneak around anymore."

"You mean I can follow you to your room without having to drop from the ceiling?" Myo asked.

"That is exactly what I mean," Hideki said.

"Then let us bathe together as well samurai-sama," Myo said in the Tsugaru dialect. "I am skilled in the art of love."

Everyone turned to give catcalls to Hideki and cheer Myo. Hideki reddened again.

XXXI

Bad Koga

Iemitsu walked into the steaming room trailed by O'Fuku. Both were clad in shitagi and gettas. As soon as Iemitsu entered the wooden floored bath area he stepped out of his wooden shoes. He spread his arms out from his sides and two naked young female bath attendants moved to undress him.

O'Fuku watched each girl's movements with a sharp eye. One moved to unbutton the thin cloth undergarment at the throat while the other untied the thin cotton obi. Once the belt was removed so was the shitagi. Iemitsu remained standing as they unwound the only remaining piece of clothing, the fundoshi. Standing naked he dropped his arms to his side and sat on a small wooden stool.

Both girls bowed when O'Fuku nodded and commenced pouring hot water from the ofudo onto the next shogun. One worked soap into his hair and the other worked on his body. They were gentle yet thorough in their efforts. When his hair was lathered and soapy one girl bowed to Iemitsu and when he nodded, she placed a hand over his eyes and tilted his head back gently. Then she poured a small bucket of water over his head.

Once completed, Iemitsu's head was moved to the upright position. Her job completed, both women applied copious amounts of soap using sponges and commenced to lather his body.

With another signal from O'Fuku, the girls rinsed the prince. Now clean, Iemitsu stood and moved to the large above ground wooden bath. Using another stool, he climbed into the ofudo. With steam rising off the water Iemitsu was almost lost from sight. He moved to the far side, sat on a bench inside the bath and rested his head on the edge of the back wall.

"The soak is the best part of the day," Iemitsu said.

"Do not go to sleep in there," O'Fuku joked.

"Is there any reason I should not?" he asked.

O'Fuku dismissed the two girls with a clap of her hand. They scurried out.

"What is it okasan?" Iemitsu asked with his eyes closed.

O'Fuku smiled through the steam. "Yes, I am more a mother to you than the one that gave you birth," she said to herself. Then to Iemitsu, "We must discuss the daimyo that have not yet pledged support," she said.

"What do I care?" he complained. "You keep track of it."

"As you command," O'Fuku said. "It is a good thing I do so because your brother is gaining support."

"You will figure it out. You always do. I just want to relax," Iemitsu said. "I'm tired of trying to keep track of who is going to support me, which daimyo is trying to win favor this week with a gift I do not need and memorizing the boring and very stupid investiture ceremony for Kyoto."

"It is all important," O'Fuku said.

"If you say so," Iemitsu said. "What word from the Yoshinobu?"

"You heard the report from the mother and daughter they sent. We now know who the main players are in the traitorous group behind Tadanaga," she said.

"And we got that information from the one who changed sides. What was her name?" he asked.

"It was The Mist lord," she said.

"Do you know her?" he asked.

"Yes, I know her," she said.

"Are you not suspicious?" he asked.

"I am always suspicious," she said.

"Should we trust her?" he asked.

"Why not, if her information is planted by Ugai or if it is designed as an ambush all we lose is many Yoshinobu warriors. Maybe I'll get lucky and they will kill that brat Hideki," she said.

Iemitsu opened his eyes and looked at O'Fuku. "Your revenge is one thing, but do not lose sight of our goal. I am not shogun yet. The Yoshinobu have pledged their allegiance to me. So far, they have accomplished all the tasks I've assigned them. No, in truth they have exceeded my expectations. I will not have you repaying loyalty with treachery," he said. "Has Honzo increased security based on the mother and daughter's warning?"

As if on key, three gray figures crashed through the door and into the steamy room. O'Fuku watched from her vantage point in the near corner. The three did not see her. They were focused on the soaking body in the ofudo. O'Fuku silently drew her tanto from the sheath at her back. She took one step toward the nearest ninja and stabbed him in the kidney. His scream and her kiai were loud enough to alert any guards left alive and scared Iemitsu. He snapped out of his semi dream state and stared at the two-approaching ninja. "Who are you? What do you want? You know who I am?" The questions went unanswered.

As the two gray clad ninjas were about to jump into the Ofudo, a black clad figure fell from the ceiling into the water between the gray ninja and Iemitsu, startling everyone into a moment of inaction. The black ninja seized the opportunity and slashed the nearest gray ninja who had one leg in the Ofudo. His sword slashed back right eviscerating the last gray. He then climbed out of the Ofudo, pulled a whistle from a leather thong around his neck and gave it three blasts. He then turned towards Iemitsu and knelt, moving his sword behind his back.

"I am sorry my lord. I was careless. They should never have gotten this close."

O'Fuku recovered first. "Honzo?"

The black clad ninja revealed his face. "Yes ma'am; once again, my apologies."

"Koga?" she asked.

"Yes ma'am. There were three of them above in the rafters. They killed two of my Iga on watch there," Honzo said.

"What happened to them?" Iemitsu asked looking upward and shrinking below the water.

"I killed them," Honzo said.

Five men attired like Honzo burst into the bath. Honzo held up his hand to halt them. They complied and knelt behind their leader.

"Are the girls still alive?" O'Fuku asked.

The leader of the five nodded. "Yes ma'am, they were struck in the stomach. They should be fine."

"Send them in," O'Fuku ordered.

The naked Iemitsu was being dried. "Looks like the mother and daughter's warning was accurate," Iemitsu said.

"It would seem so, lord," Honzo said.

"Then the information provided by The Mist should be accurate as well," Iemitsu said.

"I believe so lord," Honzo said.

"You know her?" Iemitsu asked.

"I know her well lord," Honzo said.

"Then based on her information most likely being true, I would expect the Yoshinobu to take action on my behalf without having to be told," Iemitsu said.

"I do not think you have to worry about that lord," Honzo said. "I think such is a certainty."

Dried and clothed Iemitsu looked Honzo in the eye. "My mother here hates the Yoshinobu. Why do you think they will act on my behalf?"

"I expect them to act because they are samurai of the old school. My daughter married the older grandson. She would not have done so if the man was not exceptional. My only grandson and the heir to the Yoshinobu was kidnapped to get them to support Tadanaga. Still they pledged their allegiance to the rightful heir of the Tokugawa," Honzo said.

"Interesting," Iemitsu said. "Why have I not heard of this heinous crime?"

Honzo turned his head to look at O'Fuku.

"Honzo briefed me but I did not think it warranted bothering you," O'Fuku said.

"Was the baby recovered?" Iemitsu asked.

"Yes, the baby is back in the arms of my daughter," Honzo said.

"How is that accomplished?" Iemitsu asked.

"It seems the mother and daughter that briefed us followed the scum that stole the baby. The Koga made their escape from Edo in a Tokugawa palanquin," Honzo said.

Iemitsu looked at O'Fuku. "You are right, as usual," Iemitsu said. "We have traitors in the castle."

"Yes lord, and they are high placed," Honzo said.

"The only two people I trust are right here in this room. It appears that maybe I can trust the Yoshinobu as well. Is that your assessment?" Iemitsu asked.

"Yes lord," Honzo said.

"And you believe your son-in-law exceptional?" Iemitsu asked.

"I believe that is so lord. O'Fuku tasked him with being the south magistrate of Edo. At the time the police and courts were corrupt. Nagamasa held a public trial and resurrected the tarnished image of the government," Honzo said.

"Yes, all of Japan celebrates his fairness," Iemitsu said. "I am jealous."

"There is no need lord. You put him in his position. Any praise he receives reflects on you," Honzo said.

"I guess you are correct," Iemitsu said. "But one man could not have accomplished an overhaul of Edo's government."

"He was aided by his younger brother Hideki," Honzo said.

"Ah, the infamous Hideki. O'Fuku really hates him," Iemitsu said.

"For good reason, he and his friends ended the reign of terror O'Fuku and her Fox gang perpetrated on anyone remotely in competition with you to succeed your father," Honzo said.

"Yes, I know all about it. Who are Hideki's friends?" Iemitsu asked.

"He trained under Musashi Myamoto for a while," Honzo said. "His most close current friends are a funny little man I have heard strange rumors about and Yagyū Jubei."

"Jubei I know well. He is formidable and fiercely loyal. How did Hideki win his loyalty?" Iemitsu asked.

"That I do not know," Honzo said.

"What about the little man you mentioned?" Iemitsu asked.

"Very little is known about him. He is rumored to be a

ninja and steeped in the black arts," Honzo said.

"What are these black arts?" Iemitsu asked.

"It is the stuff of fairytales lord. It consists of clouding the enemy's mind, early warning of danger, conjuring assistance when needed and other nonsense," Honzo said.

"Do you believe in this stuff?" Iemitsu asked.

"I do not, but many of the old ones swear it's true," Honzo said. "All I know is Hideki has the nickname of Tengu Killer and a few days ago he braced me when he thought I was going to harm The Mist."

"Why did he want to protect The Mist?" Iemitsu asked.

"She was the best lead to my grandchild, Hideki's nephew," Honzo said.

"If you would cross swords how would it have ended?" Iemitsu asked.

"I thought he was crazy to challenge me but when I looked into his eyes, I was not so sure," Honzo said.

"What did you see?" O'Fuku asked.

"I saw a quiet confidence. That type of confidence is gained by many duels and killing many men," Honzo said.

"He is strong enough to make you concerned?" Iemitsu asked.

"I believe so lord," Honzo said.

Iemitsu looked past Honzo to the five-black clad Iga ninja kneeling just out of earshot.

"These Yoshinobu are beginning to really interest me," Iemitsu said.

"I believe they could be strong allies lord," Honzo said.

"I believe they are trouble and should be eradicated," O'Fuku said.

"I suggest these men of Iga, and I escort you to your sleeping quarter's lord, then we will double security until I am certain we have flushed all the rats out of the castle," Honzo said.

"As you wish," Iemitsu said. "Find out all you can about this Hideki and his friends. I have large plans for this country, and I need to know who I can trust."

"As you command lord," Honzo said. He turned and departed.

O'Fuku entered Iemitsu's bed chamber.

"That was a surprise," O'Fuku said.

"You have a flair for understatement," Iemitsu said. "What happened? I almost lost my life."

"I do not know, lord," O'Fuku said. "What could have made Ugai go down this path? Maybe I should set a meeting."

"That would be highly stupid," Iemitsu said. "Based on tonight's entertainment I think it is safe to say we are no longer on speaking terms with Ugai."

"What could have changed?" O'Fuku asked.

"There is only one thing that could have set Ugai off," Iemitsu said. "He has learned of your plan to use and then dispose of the Koga."

"How could he?" O'Fuku asked. "That is a very closely held secret."

"These are old castle walls. My grandfather built them to his specifications. I would imagine the Koga are privy to every nook and cranny," Iemitsu said. "They probably overheard one of our conversations. This changes everything."

"Yes, lord it does," O'Fuku said. "We are totally committed and so is Ugai. We must be very careful going forward."

"Now more than ever, I must rely on good men to support me. I hope the Yagyū and Yoshinobu are up to it," Iemitsu said.

"I believe they are lord," O'Fuku said. "We must watch Hideki though. He is wickedly smart."

"You are afraid he will figure it out on his own?" Iemitsu asked.

"Yes lord. I hate the little bastard, but have to admit he will help us immensely," O'Fuku said. "But we must keep our inner secrets from him. He will fight anything he sees as injustice."

"Good advice Mother," Iemitsu said. "Hideki is definitely a dual-edged sword."

XXXII

Killing the Killer

It was noon when Hideki and entourage stabled the horses at an inn across from Daito Kuji Temple. Most of the customers were worshipers or transient monks come to offer prayers for loved ones or participate in meditation, both aimed at bettering themselves in this life. They were lucky to get one large room on the second floor facing the main street. From their vantage point they had a good view of the road that dead-ended at the main gate of the temple grounds.

"We could not have asked for a better view," Yoshi said.

"See the service gate on the far left?" The Mist asked.

"Yes," Yoshi said. "Are we going in as merchants?"

"No, merchants are limited to the reception building. I want to go in as supplicants seeking spiritual advice and guidance," The Mist said. "We can adapt once we get in."

"Not bad," Yoshi said. "We can wander freely and blend in."

"Tell me why you have to fight Ito again," Jubei asked.

"Yes, I would like to hear that as well," Midori said.

"So, would I," Myo said. "Your last explanation made no sense."

"I am sorry if I have disappointed you," Hideki said. "Bushido requires I stamp out evil wherever I see it. Cutting down innocents in the streets in Kyoto is cowardly."

"Rudeness will not be tolerated?" Jubei asked.

"Something like that," Hideki said. "See, I have learned many things from you Jubei."

"But you are a prince of the Yoshinobu. If you die, we will all lose our jobs," Midori said.

"More importantly to the Yoshinobu, we will lose our leader," Myo said.

"No, we will lose our friend. I do not have many of them," Yoshi said.

"As your leader, I cannot ask you to do anything I would not do myself. As your friend, I do not intend to lose," Hideki said. "Besides, all of us are equal in worth."

"Nice speech Prince," Myo said. "If you get killed, I am out a future husband. They are hard to find in my profession."

"That is probably the best argument for letting the sword master handle Ito," Yoshi said.

"What? You would rather sacrifice me then Hideki?" Jubei asked, surprised.

Everyone responded in unison. "Yes!"

"I know you are all worried. I am not. I think any street killer is a basic coward with no regard for human life. I cannot kill Tadanaga. Only Iemitsu can do that. Ito is a different matter," Hideki said.

"Tadanaga?" Jubei asked. "Do you have reason to believe he is a street killer?"

"We all know his reputation for getting angry and killing servants and even retainers," Hideki said. "Haru said two people were suspected in the killing of her father and her husband. Who would Ito take on a street killing?"

"Either a protégé or someone he was trying to impress," Yoshi said.

"Exactly," Hideki said. "The Mist said he only cared about elevating his fencing style."

"Only Tadanaga could elevate his fencing style," Myo said.

"Smart woman," Hideki said.

"She is obviously much too good for you," Yoshi said.

"I agree," Midori said.

"So do I," The Mist added.

"You will get no argument from me," Hideki said.

"Before we ninja depart, I will place a hand cart out front of this inn. I will place your bow and quiver under several reed mats," Yoshi said.

"Where do you get mendicant monk garb?" Hideki asked.

"We already have it," The Mist said.

"Of course, you do," Hideki said. "I do not know why I always ask the obvious around ninja."

"Because you are only a samurai," Myo said. "You are a sweet one, but still a samurai."

"I would like you to post these ten notices on buildings inside the compound," Hideki said. "Do it as soon as you enter."

Jubei pulled one from the pile and handed the rest to Yoshi.

"Is this a challenge to Ito?" Jubei asked.

"Yes," Hideki said.

"But this calls him a coward and a murderer and a common street killer," Yoshi said. "Is your tactic to get him so mad he sees double?"

"No, I intend to wait outside the main temple gate as the notice says at noon today," Hideki said.

"It will certainly divert everyone's attention away from our attempts," Yoshi said.

"I like it," The Mist said. "It is simple."

"So, what can go wrong?" Hideki asked.

"We will have to place these notices without drawing too much attention to ourselves and then execute our real missions," Yoshi said.

"Yes, timing is critical," Hideki said.

"Ugai could be in the temple," The Mist said.

"That is possible," Hideki said. "But I think he is busy planning Iemitsu's execution just before or during the investiture."

"What if he's here instead?" The Mist asked.

"Kill him if you can but only if it does not place your life at risk," Hideki said.

"What if the Ronin Army storms the temple during your duel with Ito?" Myo asked.

"It is Midori's and my job to keep them off his back," Jubei said winking his good eye at Midori.

Midori smiled her understanding.

Yoshi changed into his mendicant monk garb. Myo and The Mist changed into supplicant white travelers' clothes.

Hideki watched with interest as Yoshi and Myo placed shurikens, tetsu-bishi, darts, and then glass vials of different dimensions inside secret pockets of their clothing.

"If you are searched you will be discovered," Hideki said.

"You samurai only think of the obvious," Yoshi said. "We will not be discovered."

"Why not?" Hideki asked. "There must be 100 samurai standing guard."

"Yoshi is reprimanding you my love for thinking on just one plane, like a samurai," Myo said.

"How else am I to think?" Hideki asked.

"Think distraction and misdirection lord," Midori said.

"What do you mean?" Hideki asked.

"If a guard stops us, what would happen if Myo drops something expensive and fails to pick it up?" The Mist asked.

"The guard would either pick it up for her or wave you through hurriedly in an attempt to steal it," Hideki answered.

"Exactly," Yoshi said. "Either way the guard will be distracted long enough for the rest of us to kill them or enter unnoticed."

"I stand chastised," Hideki said.

"It is not your fault my soon to be husband. You are only samurai," Myo said.

"Wait just a minute," Hideki said. "If we do wed you will be a samurai as well."

"I know my love. I will either have to increase your education as quickly as possible or pretend to be very stupid," Myo said.

Hideki smiled at Myo. "Please come back to me unharmed." Then looking around the room Hideki said, "That includes all of you."

The ninja departed except for Midori. Hideki retreated to the opposite side of the room and started to oil his sword.

Midori moved to Jubei's side and spoke in hushed whispers.

"Can he defeat Ito?" she asked.

"That is unknown. Victory does not always go to the best. Sometimes it goes to the luckiest," Jubei said.

"I really do not like him taking such risk. What is he trying to prove?" she asked.

"Hideki does not strive to prove anything. He strives only to improve his skill," Jubei said. "He adheres to bushido more than most."

"You samurai look at life very strangely," she said. "Do you think Hideki and my leader will wed?"

"That is also unknown," Jubei said. "Jii's comment caught all of us off guard."

"It caught Hideki and Myo off guard more than the rest of us," Midori said.

"The whole family is different. They seem to place value on action over lineage," Jubei said. "It is the old way."

"Yes, the grandfather lets me call him Jii," Midori said. "But I am worried. Can Hideki survive this duel?"

"I have told you that this is unknown. If he can avoid the initial draw he will have a chance. My only concern is this type of thing is not in character for Hideki," Jubei said.

"What do you mean?" Midori asked.

"Hideki is making a strategic offensive attack. He is attempting to eliminate Ito to strike at Tadanaga," Jubei said.

"Why is that a problem?" Midori asked.

"Because he has only done that one other time since I have known him," Jubei said.

"You are talking about bad Heizo in Nagasaki," Midori said.

"Yes, but then he used you as a weapon. It was you that killed the governor of Nagasaki," Jubei said.

"So, what is different now?" Midori asked.

"Now Hideki will wield the sword himself that results in the death of a man he has targeted," Jubei said.

"That is new for Hideki? I thought he had slain several men and one Tengu," Midori said.

"Yes, but all those men and the Tengu were in self-defense. If Hideki is successful today, he will feel that he has become what he detests," Jubei said.

"You are worried that he will feel he has become a street killer?" Midori asked. "That is ridiculous."

"That is ridiculous for us," Jubei said. "But Hideki has a conscience and a driving will to live up to his family's motto."

"Do you mean 'no wrong too small to right and no right to small to defend'?" Midori asked.

"Exactly, it is his belief in that motto and his living by bushido that attracts men like me and Yoshi to his banner," Jubei said. "I know what he does today will haunt him."

"You are worried he will hesitate and be slain?" Midori asked.

"Yes," Jubei said. "Without the guilt he is a match for anyone. Besides he has a secret weapon," Jubei said.

"He has a secret weapon?" Midori asked.

"Yes, he can fight using mushin," Jubei said.

"Mushin? I thought fighting with no mind was a myth," Midori said.

"It is not a myth. Musashi taught him. If he uses it, he will be victorious," Jubei said.

"Can you use mushin?" Midori asked.

"I cannot. That is why Hideki is one of the deadliest swordsmen in the country," Jubei said.

Midori looked up from their hushed discussion to glance at the young man across the room tapping the length of his sword with an uchiko ball. He started at the base and worked his way to the tip.

"He looks so innocent and peaceful," Midori said.

"Most of the time he is," Jubei said. "But if the innocent are being preyed upon that peacefulness turns into a smoldering rage against the perpetrators."

"I have heard the story of him crippling O'Fuku in front of the now dead Shogun," Midori said.

"That is a good example. Bushido demands that the innocent are protected and the guilty punished. He punished the one responsible for the deaths of many innocents," Jubei said.

"Did you see it?" Midori asked.

"Yes, I was very proud of my friend that day," Jubei said.

"He is exceptional is he not?" Midori asked.

"Yes, he is exceptional," Jubei said.

Midori looked up into Jubei's good eye. "You are pretty exceptional as well," she said.

Jubei turned to smile. It did not quite work. "I am his friend and mentor. Following him is redemptive for me. Do you understand?"

"I think so. We have both done bad things. By helping Hideki, we come close to balancing the scale," Midori said.

"You do understand," Jubei said.

"Yes, because Hideki's decisions are steeped in bushido. He will always try to decide what is right," Midori said.

Jubei looked at the woman next to him and pulled her close to his side. It was the closest thing to affection he was capable of. It was enough for Midori. She smiled. "I am surrounded by good men who are supremely dangerous. I love being ninja," she said.

Hideki finished cleaning his sword and stood up.

"It is time," Hideki said.

"I believe so," Jubei replied.

Midori changed into a black hakama with a white gi top with duel swords in her belt and her hair tied back. She looked like a female samurai.

"Nice look," Hideki said.

"Do not worry about interference Hideki. We will keep them from you no matter which direction a threat comes from. Just kill this man and return to us," Midori said.

"I will do my best," Hideki said moving down the stairs.

Midori took a position next to the inn's entrance. Jubei stepped outside and stood next to the handcart. He moved the straw mats aside to inspect the Yumi and quiver of arrows. The bow was unstrung. The arrows were tipped with iron heads. He knew they would be accurate up to 150 paces. That would be more than enough to reach the temple main gate. He strung the bow and positioned his arrows.

Hideki nodded to both and moved to the center of the hard-packed dirt street before the temple gate. He waited.

"We have visitors coming from the south," Midori said.

"Are there any long-range weapons?" Jubei asked.

"None that I see," Midori said.

"How many individuals?" Jubei asked.

"Five," Midori said.

"Do you require my help?" Jubei asked.

"Unknown," Midori said. "But do not let Hideki become injured."

"You mean I am not to abandon Hideki to save you?" Jubei asked.

"That is exactly what I mean," Midori said.

"What if I do not see things that way?" Jubei asked.

"Look, if things get too intense for me, I will just run and let them attack you from the rear."

"Somehow I doubt that," Jubei said.

"I would do it tearfully," Midori said.

"You are a funny little thing," Jubei said as he turned and drew his bow in the direction of the approaching man from the South.

"That slowed them down," Midori said.

"Who are they?" Jubei asked.

"They are wearing the same white headband and haori that we have seen before," Midori said. "I think they are the Ronin Army."

"Make yourself useful," Jubei said. "Kill them all."

Midori smiled. "Very well sword master. I shall try," Midori said moving to the center of the road placing herself between Jubei's back and the approaching men.

When they got within hailing distance the leader called to Midori. "Who are you and what are you doing here?"

"Good questions," Midori shouted. "Who are you and what are you doing here?"

The men moved closer cautiously.

"We are the Ronin Army. It is our job to keep the streets safe," the leader said.

"Then go about your business," Midori said. "This street is safe."

"We cannot allow a man with a bow to stand in front of the Daito-kuji temple. Bishop Inshin lives there. We report to him," the leader said.

"After today reporting to him may be difficult," Midori said.

"What do you mean?" The leader asked.

"I mean the Yoshinobu are advancing on Kyoto. They are Iemitsu's advanced force. Iemitsu is coming with 300,000 retainers. The Yoshinobu will be here tomorrow. Anyone supporting Tadanaga might not survive," Midori said.

The Ronin Army men stopped their advance and looked at each other. The leader shouted down their objections and turned toward Midori. "That is tomorrow, we have to do our duty today," he said.

"You should be fleeing Kyoto if you want to live," Midori said.

"We have had no word on Iemitsu's forces coming here," the leader said.

"Of course not," Midori said. "Your leaders want you to fight and die while they escape."

That caused the men to begin to argue again in hot discussion. They arrived at a decision and started walking quickly toward Midori.

Midori had no sword drawn. She placed her right hand inside her gi top and extracted two shuriken. She placed one in each hand. The right hand she brought up and threw the multi-bladed star overhand toward the leader. The weapon struck him in the forehead. He dropped dead. The second was thrown reverse side arm at the man on the end. The weapon struck him in the eye. He screamed and fell clutching his ruined orb.

The remaining men drew their swords and charged Midori. She drew both of her swords.

"Fighting Musashi style, are we?" Jubei's voice came from behind her.

"There are three coming at me," Midori said.

"You do not count well," Jubei said as he turned toward her and released an arrow and loaded a second and fired again.

Two of the charging men were halted in their tracks by arrows hitting them so hard in the chest that it moved them back a step. They both fell.

The third continued to charge from an overhead strike position and brought down his katana hard. The deadly attack almost reached Midori's head, then she disappeared.

The attacker realized the miss when the expected contact did not materialize. For a split second he panicked, not knowing where the wraith had moved. Then he spun on his forward right foot, raising his sword to the right for a horizontal slash to the left. An awful pain shot through his body as his arms turned limp. The girl was now in front of him and would have been cleaved in two if his sword would respond. Looking down toward the pain he found her katana lodged deeply in his stomach. He collapsed to his knees attempting to utter something, but the pain was too intense.

Midori ended his pain by thrusting her wakazashi deeply into his left eye. She extracted both swords and he pitched to the left, dead before he struck the dirt.

Midori wiped both blades on the dead army member's white tunic and returned her swords to their proper scabbard.

"Why do you persist in stopping my fun?" Midori asked.

Jubei kept his good eye on Hideki's back. "I worry about such a fragile girl in the evil world of the ronin," Jubei said.

Midori smiled. "Does this mean you care for me?"

"Maybe a little," Jubei said.

"More than your katana?" Midori asked playfully.

"Absolutely not," Jubei said.

"More than your wakazashi?" Midori continued.

"No," Jubei said.

"As much as your yumi?" Midori asked.

"Yes," Jubei said.

Midori giggled as she took her place back on the inn's small porch. "Jubei likes me as much as his yumi," she sang.

"Quiet woman," Jubei said. "I may have to do more shooting soon."

Midori lowered her voice but continued to chant.

Jubei placed an arrow in the yumi in firing position and dangled two more from his front right hand.

"Crazy woman," he muttered under his breath, then tried to smile.

It was past noon when the gates parted. The man who emerged had to be Ito. He walked with a swagger of total confidence. The second man that walked behind Ito was younger.

He moved to a position to Ito's right and one pace behind.

"Are you the upstart who has challenged the head of the Itosai style?" Ito asked.

"Are you the cowardly dog that kills innocents on the streets of Kyoto?" Hideki asked.

"You are a mere boy with a crippled hand, and you dare to say such words to an accomplished martial artist as myself? Do you wish to die?" Ito asked.

"I do not want to die. But bushido demands I eliminate street killers," Hideki replied.

"What proof do you have that I am a street killer?" Ito asked.

"None save you do not deny it and you curry favor with the usurper Tadanaga," Hideki said.

"Why you little guttersnipe, I'll see you gutted for that," this from the man standing behind and to the right of Ito.

The man took one step forward and froze as an arrow dug into the dirt at his feet.

"I would not get involved in this prince," Hideki said. "My friends are here to see this is a fair fight."

The man flew into a rage. "You know who I am, and you threaten me?" He screamed.

"I know who you want to be, and it will never happen," Hideki said.

"I will kill you and your whole family," the man screamed as he took another step towards Hideki. He was stopped by another arrow dropping with great velocity at his feet.

"No lord," Hideki said. "Your brother is on his way with 300,000 retainers. As soon as I kill this street killer, you will have only Ugai to rely on and his days are numbered. When your brother arrives two days from now and is granted the title of shogun, you will have to commit seppuku and your mother will spend the rest of her days in a nunnery," Hideki said.

"You know nothing, peasant. I have more than enough troops waiting to move," the man screamed.

"No, you do not lord. The Satsuma have not begun to move. They are cleverly waiting to see how you and your Ronin Army fare before committing," Hideki said.

"The Ronin Army is waiting for my orders," the man screamed.

"No lord, their leaders have fled. They are now busy looting Kyoto. It will not be long until they move north and ransack Daito-kuji Temple," Hideki said.

Tadanaga fell silent. "Kill this piece of excrement for me Ito, and then we will deal with the rest."

"With pleasure lord," Ito said as he moved closer to Hideki.

As soon as Ito started moving forward Hideki drew both swords and placed the tips almost together in front of him. His katana was in his left hand and a shorter wakazashi in his right.

"Musashi style?" Ito said still moving forward.

"Musashi was my teacher," Hideki said.

Ito stopped his forward movement. He had not planned on his opponent being skillful.

"Such a lie, Musashi does not teach," Ito said.

"Keep coming and find out," Hideki said.

"This was not in the plan," Ito said aloud. "She said to join Tadanaga and report."

"Kill him Ito," Tadanaga screamed and turned to wave his hand at the gate.

Three archers appeared on the walls of the gate. They released their arrows. As soon as they released each one was struck with an arrow and fell back off the wall.

"Bless you Jubei," Hideki thought then stepped back with his right foot and deflected an arrow to the right with the katana in his left hand. The second and third arrows arrived at almost the same time. Hideki did not think to twist his body; he did it unconsciously and cut one of the arrows with his wakazashi. The third arrow impaled itself into Hideki's left shoulder. The pain was immense. He could still hold his katana, but he doubted he could swing his arm. Now he was in trouble.

Ito smiled.

Ito moved within striking distance and dropped his center, grasped his saya with his left hand and twisted it in a 45° angle outward. His right hand grasped the katana sharkskin handle.

Hideki subconsciously registered the twist. He did not know if he could get into mushin with the pain in his shoulder. Ito was going to make a one-handed horizontal draw coming from left to right. If the first cut did not draw blood, he would rotate the sword up into a two-hand grasp and most likely bring it down diagonally from right to left striking Hideki somewhere between his left ear and left shoulder.

When the draw came it was so fast Hideki had no time to think. He didn't need it. He slipped into mushin automatically. Hideki ducked the incredibly fast razor-sharp sword coming at his right side and elevated his short sword in his right hand to ensure the attacking blade was deflected slightly upward.

When Ito registered the fact that his first lightning fast draw had missed, he stopped the trajectory going right and brought the sword high and grasped it with both hands to bring it down into Hideki's head and shoulder area.

Hideki felt the clash of Ito's sword off his wakazashi and slipped forward with his left foot bringing the tip of his katana toward the midsection of Ito. Hideki could not slash with his wounded shoulder, but he could thrust. Hideki thrust his katana before Ito had a chance to make his second attack.

Ito let out a scream, dropped his sword and fell to his knees. Hideki pulled his katana free as Ito grasped his punctured stomach.

"She said all I had to do was report back. This is not the way," he stammered between painful breaths.

"Who is she? Hideki asked.

"Damn Musashi and his two swords and damn her for putting me in this position," Ito said as he collapsed and died.

Tadanaga stepped forward next to Ito's dead body.

"I guess he was not as good as he thought," Tadanaga said.

"Oh, he was good," Hideki said.

"Then you must be the best. How would you like a job?" Tadanaga asked.

"I am not the best. My sensei is better and the man who fired the arrows is better," Hideki said.

"Then how would all three of you like a job?" Tadanaga asked.

Guards came streaming out of the main temple gate.

"Thank the Buddha that you are not harmed," the leader said. "Bishop Inshin, Yamada and Shingen have all been killed. We do not know how it was done," he reported.

"You had better return to the temple lord," Hideki said. "You seem to have run out of allies."

"Who are you?" Tadanaga asked.

"I am Yoshinobu Hideki," Hideki said.

Tadanaga turned to his group leader. "Kill this man."

Two of Tadanaga's guards moved their hands to their swords. Both were struck in the chest with arrows.

"Go back inside lord and await word from your brother. Your days of killing innocents are over," Hideki said.

Tadanaga seemed to be trying to control his rage. While he was so disposed two more of the samurai were struck with arrows, one in the head and another in the arm. His remaining retainers surrounded Tadanaga to protect him from the arrows and hurried him behind the temple gates. The gates closed behind Tadanaga and his guards.

"Pretty good swordsmanship," Jubei said as he approached Hideki.

Hideki wiped the blood off his wakazashi on the clothing of Ito. He returned the short sword to its scabbard in his Obi. Jubei helped him with his katana as his left arm would no longer work.

"Midori, help him back to the inn," Jubei said, moving to grasp Hideki's belt from behind. "Get on his right side."

"Does this make you the best in the land?" Midori asked.

"No Midori, there are plenty better," Hideki gasped through the pain.

"Did you use your secret weapon?" Midori asked. "I forgot what it's called."

"Yes, Midori I did," Hideki said.

"What is it called again?" Midori asked.

"Friends," Hideki said. "It is called friends."

Jubei looked at his girlfriend's questioning face and tried to smile. It did not work this time either. Once back in the inn, Hideki was laid on a futon and given sake.

"Send the owner for a doctor," Jubei ordered.

"Hai," Midori said bolting for the door.

"Tell the owner if the doctor has not arrived at the time this half empty bottle of sake is finished, I will kill him slowly," Jubei said.

"There is no need for that. I will kill him myself," Midori said, flying through the door.

"I take it back," Hideki said.

"What?" Jubei asked, bringing Hideki's head up for another sip of sake.

"Yadome-jutsu is not an archaic art form," Hideki said.

"You are learning," Jubei said.

"I just wish I did not have to always learn the hard way," Hideki said.

XXXIII

Inshin, Murata & Yamada

Yoshi approached the gates of Daito Kuji Temple alone. He was dressed as a mendicant monk. He wore the white kimono with a black long sleeved pleated outer garment. Around his neck was a bright yellow scarf thrown over his left shoulder. The scarf was the hardest thing for The Mist to acquire. She had to go through six drying racks before she found one close to the color the Fuke Zen priests wore. As a komuso priest he was sworn to poverty and chastity and relied on the largess of others by begging, offering blessings and playing the shaku hachi flute. One flute he brought with him. It was special. Yoshi's purchased flute was in his right hand. The special one was strapped to his back.

The Mist had obtained his clothes from a local secondhand shop for two brass coins. Yoshi purchased a second flute there and a very used tengai. The tengai was a large woven reed basket covering his head except for the slit for his eyes. It was supposed to cut him off from the natural world and alleviate ego. Yoshi donned it because no one could see his face. Besides Fuke monks come and go. They were never inspected at government checkpoints and rarely by local daimyo.

"State your business," the guard at the gate said.

"I am seeking enlightenment through suizen," Yoshi said.

"You carry a shaku hachi," the guard said.

"You are very observant," Yoshi said.

"Let us hear you play," the guard said.

Yoshi started the long flute to his lips.

"Not just any tune, I want to hear Shike no tone," the guard said smiling. The other two guards placed their hands on their swords.

"As you wish," Yoshi said. He then started the difficult tune and played so well many of those walking by the gate stopped to listen. The guard noticed the large number gathering to hear the melodic tune usually played by monks to help them march forward in their travels. The guard became concerned.

"All right, all right you can stop now. Nobody but a monk who has trained for years would know that piece. You may pass," the lead guard said.

Yoshi marched forward continuing to play the tune as he moved into one of the many great courtyards of the sprawling grounds. His thanks were not to Buddha but to his mother-in-law who had made him practice until his fingers were tired. When he finally stopped playing, he halted and raised his reed hat high enough to recognize the meditation hall.

Yoshi entered the hall, found an open spot, knelt and meditated for an hour with his eyes almost closed. Occasionally a senior monk would walk behind him and slap him on the shoulder with a long stick.

The pain meant nothing. It was supposed to aid his concentration. What it did was make him lose track of the comings and goings outside. The meditation hall was on a small mound. It was rectangular in shape with the two long side walls retractable. During the day the side walls were folded back despite the season. The elevation and the open side walls gave Yoshi a great observation post.

When it was time for noon meal Yoshi moved to the dining building. Here he acquired an austere meal of millet, stewed daikon radish and halved sweet potatoes. The drink was hot green tea.

Like the rest of the monks Yoshi produced his begging bowl. Once his bowl was filled Yoshi sat on the wooden benches with the other monks. Yoshi placed his reed basket hat behind him and thrust his flute in his obi. Many of the other monks looked at Yoshi's eye patch and his scar that started at his forehead, disappeared under the eye patch, reappeared below it and travelled down his cheek. One summoned the nerve to talk to the dangerous looking little monk.

"Are you a Fuke priest?" The brave new monk across the table asked.

Before Yoshi could respond the monk eating at his left asked, "Do you truly take a vow of poverty?"

Then a cascade of questions began.

"Do you have vows of celibacy?" Another asked.

"You did not take vows of silence, did you?" Asked another.

Yoshi looked around at all who had asked questions. "We take our vows seriously," Yoshi answered.

"You are truly amazing," the monk across the table said. "But why did you come here to meditate?"

"Am I not welcome in Daito kuji?" Yoshi asked.

"Bishop Inshin takes anyone," one said.

"Only if you have the money," another laughed.

"Or women, he will take you if you have a little sister," several laughed.

"I'm sorry to hear he does not adhere to the principles of Buddha," Yoshi said. "I had hoped to see him again."

"You have met him previously?" The curious monk across the table asked.

"Yes, he complemented me on the shaku hachi and invited me to visit when in Kyoto," Yoshi lied.

"This is a bad time to visit him," the man across the table said. "He has been in a foul mood since the Ronin Army disintegrated into common thieves."

"Maybe my flutes will calm his spirit," Yoshi said. "Where is he?"

"You will find him in private prayer in his quarters," another snickered.

"I do not think you can calm his spirit like the two women he took into his quarters before noon meal," another laughed.

"I will wait until the needs of the flesh are met," Yoshi said. "Can you tell me where his quarters are located? This is a very large compound."

Yoshi was given direction. When he arrived at the building his Fuke disguise was once again intact to include his reed basket hat.

Yoshi moved to the modest looking building made of wood with the clay tile roof. The roof appeared to be the only extravagance visible. No guards were present, so he entered. It was a typical Japanese building made on a square with the garden in the center of the square surrounded by a wooden walkway. Each side opened onto large ten tatami rooms with sliding doors for entrance. There appeared to be no one in attendance except in the far room where the doors were ajar and sounds of the samisen and female voices emanated.

Yoshi checked each room to ensure there were no others about. There was a break in the walkway to the left side of the noisy room. It had a three-step stair leading downward to what Yoshi assumed to be the kitchen and servant's quarters. Yoshi ignored it and moved to the slightly open doors and the sound of music.

Through the slit in his reed basket hat he saw the bishop in fine silk being entertained by two young girls. The fronts of their kimonos were open, and their female bodies covered only by the white linen wrap women used to support their breasts and cover their private parts.

Yoshi left his tengai on the wooden walkway. He replaced the musical shaku hachi in his right hand with the instrument sheathed on his back. He then eased open the sliding door and took two silent steps into the room.

The bishop was reclining on an armrest with his back to Yoshi. One girl was playing the samisen with her head down concentrating on the strings and masking Yoshi's movements. The other girl was engaging in a game of hanafuda with the Bishop. Her eyes were on the cards before them.

Yoshi swung his flute of hardwood and struck the female card player high on the neck. He twisted the flute and instantly and had a long thin sword in his right hand and a cudgel in his left. He placed the blade under the bishop's chin. With his left hand he struck the surprised samisen player on the head. She pitched backwards striking a sour note on the instrument.

"If I yell you will die," the bishop said.

"It will be the last sound you make," Yoshi said.

"Do you know who I am?" The bishop asked.

"Please tell me who you are," Yoshi said.

"I am Bishop Inshin," a man said. "Daito Kuji Temple is mine. How dare you threaten me?"

"Thank you very much Bishop. I do not want to kill the wrong man," Yoshi said.

Yoshi rotated the blade from under the Bishop's chin around his neck. The point now rested between the neck and the shoulder. Yoshi plunged the tip straight down with his right hand, dropped the cudgel in his left and covered the Bishop's mouth to stifle the scream. The bishop thrashed for a moment and lay still.

Yoshi tied and gagged the two girls and moved out of the room and down the three steps to the kitchen area and servant's quarters. When he came upon an older woman squatting and washing vegetables, he made the sign of the Buddha with his right hand extended, fingertips up in the center of his body. The old woman grinned at the blessing and at the priest with the tengai on his head and continued washing.

Yoshi almost made it to the compound exit when voices hailed him.

"Hey, Fuke did you find the bishop?"

Yoshi turned to see three of his lunch companions.

"No, he was heavily engaged in good works," Yoshi said.

"No doubt," one of the monks said.

The last member of the group teased Yoshi. "See I told you to join our sect. We have much more fun."

"I am almost convinced," Yoshi said and turned and walked through the guarded gates out into the streets of Kyoto.

When Yoshi came to the first alleyway, he turned into it, found a dark area and shed his priestly clothing. He then removed the eye patch and peeled off the scar Myo had made from flour paste and a rouge and charcoal mix.

The disguise he deposited in several bins. When he emerged from the alley, he was a common laborer carrying a box of tools someone would be missing. He headed for the inn and his friends.

Myo and The Mist entered Daito Kuji by the smaller gate. They were clad in white garb. They had a white cloth wrapped around their hair, white kimonos and hakama and white leggings. Around their necks they wore prayer beads. Their travel items were rolled in white blankets draped over their backs and tied in the front.

Both women carried walking sticks. Their first stop was the dining building, but unlike the men they entered via the servant's quarters in the back. They washed their hands and feet and left their zori on the steps. Once in, both women helped the servants and the cooks by loading trays and filling bowls with miso soup. They also engaged the women in conversation.

"Nice of them to tell us where Yamada and Murata are located," The Mist whispered to Myo.

"They were very accommodating," Myo said.

"How do you want to handle it?" The Mist asked.

"Do you have any poison?" Myo asked.

"Koga carry a derivative from a purple flower, we call it monk's hood," The Mist said.

"Do you have any cuts on your fingers?" Myo asked.

"No, I do not," The Mist said. "I checked in the hotel room."

"Dilute a few drops into tea. Switch disguises to one of the servers in the grand hall and place a few drops in Yamada's and Murata's tea. I will become an Eta and a benjo attendant. I do not want you to kill them instantly," Myo said.

"I get it. You want them running to the benjo where you will finish them off," The Mist said.

"If they drop dead in front of you it will make it difficult to flee," Myo said.

"I will place it in their tea and stick around long enough to ensure they drink it," The Mist said. "Then I will excuse myself and meet you by the benjo."

When The Mist came to the benjo she was met by a young woman with straw like hair, dirt under her fingernails with several black teeth. She wore a torn and dirty burlap bag. She was ugly with no shoes. The Mist ignored the dirty Eta girl and opened the door to the odious female toilet.

Murata came holding his stomach. He bolted past the Eta girl who held the door open.

"Hurry up you bitch," Murata said.

Myo grunted at Murata because Etas were not supposed to speak. She started to assist him with removing his clothes. Murata stopped what he was doing as Myo plunged the tanto into his kidney and clapped her hand over his mouth. The large man fell back into Myo's arms.

"Get over here but check first. This one is one heavy bastard," Myo whispered.

The Mist dressed as a serving girl stepped out of the female benjo and looked back up the dark alleyway.

"No one is coming," she said and opened the male benjo door to help Myo carry Murata's corpse into the female benjo room. Once in, Myo lifted three of the floor boards and dropped the heavy corpse into the waste below.

"What about Yamada?" Myo asked.

"I timed it so he would be running next door anytime now," The Mist said.

The Mist remained in the female benjo and Myo took up her Eta post.

Almost immediately the same process was repeated with Yamada.

When finished Myo stole back into the kitchen store room where her acolyte clothes were stored, washed her hands, legs and face with a pan of water used for vegetables. The Mist stood guard and then helped Myo comb her hair and tie it back. The Mist then changed to her acolyte clothing. Both women put on their zori, grasped their walking sticks and prayer beads and headed for the small gate through which they had come.

Myo and The Mist entered the inn through the back and proceeded to their room.

Their first site was a doctor and nurse leaning over a wounded Hideki. Neither said a word. Myo looked into Yoshi's eyes for reassurance. He motioned with his head toward the second room. All stepped carefully around the prostrate and unconscious warrior. Jubei kneeled at Hideki's head holding down his arms while Midori held his legs. The windows on the alley were the only light allowing the doctor to extract the arrow from Hideki's shoulder. A nurse held a cloth in one hand and a small bamboo tray in the other.

Myo, The Mist and Yoshi moved to the next room. Yoshi closed the door behind them.

"Did you have any problems?" Yoshi asked.

"Forget about the mission, what is wrong with Hideki?" Myo demanded.

"Keep your voice down. The doctor is cutting out an iron arrowhead," Yoshi said.

"An arrowhead, what in Buddha's name happened?" The Mist asked.

"Apparently Ito was not as confident as we thought. Three archers appeared on the wall and fired three arrows at Hideki just as the duel with Ito was about to begin," Yoshi said.

"Digging out three arrowheads means he will die," The Mist said.

"You do not know my Hideki," Myo snapped.

"Jubei said Hideki deflected and cut two of the arrows that would cause him harm and took only the one in the shoulder," Yoshi said.

"What do you mean? Is that possible?" The Mist asked.

"Yadome-jutsu," Myo whispered. "But I did not know his skills were that advanced."

"Midori said Jubei had taught him just three days ago," Yoshi said.

"Bless you Jubei. You saved my man," Myo said. "He can survive a shoulder wound."

"What happened to Ito? The Mist asked.

"Hideki slew him even with an arrow sticking out of his left shoulder," Yoshi said.

"I am finally working with warriors who have both honor and skills," The Mist said.

"Now you understand," Yoshi said.

"You mean why ninja exist alongside samurai and think of them as family?" The Mist asked.

"That is what he means," Myo said.

"Then yes, I understand," The Mist said. "What happened to the archers?"

"According to Midori, Jubei fired off three lethal arrows into them before their bowstrings could be drawn again. He also fired warning arrows at Tadanaga and killed several of his guards that attempted to kill a victorious but wounded Hideki," Yoshi said.

"What an excellent story. The Yagyū and Yoshinobu deeds could fill ballads," The Mist said.

"Maybe, but we are writing history here not creating music. What happened to Yamada and Murata?" Yoshi asked.

"They will trouble us no more," Myo said. "What about Bishop Inshin?"

"He is playing with young maidens in hell," Yoshi said.

"So, with the exception of my clumsy lover who cannot keep from getting hurt, everything went as he planned?" Myo asked.

"That was a little cruel," The Mist said. "He was hurt because of the evil of Ito and Tadanaga. They had no honor," The Mist said.

"Hideki is full of honor and belief in bushido. But that does not keep him from getting hurt. What is the first thing you learn as a ninja?" Myo asked.

"Live at all costs," The Mist said.

"It is the same with all ninja. The mission can be accomplished another day if it means your life. But my pigheaded lover has never learned that lesson," Myo said.

"Maybe it is time for you to teach him. We all depend on his leadership for our existence," Yoshi said.

A tear ran down Myo's cheek. "I will try Yoshi. But everyone must help me."

The Mist patted Myo on the shoulder. "We will all help. He is too valuable to lose," she said.

When Myo was in control again they all moved back into Hideki's operating room.

"The arrowhead is out. We have bandaged the wound after putting healing powder in it. We must worry about fever now.

The nurse will stay here tonight and place wet towels on his forehead and try to get him to drink cold tea. We should know more by morning," the doctor said.

"Thank you, doctor," Jubei said.

Midori moved to the doctor's side and placed a large gold coin in his hand.

"This is way too much for my services," he complained.

"You do not understand his importance," Jubei said.

The doctor looked into Jubei's cold eye and decided to change his plans.

"I will be back in a few hours to check on him," the doctor said.

Jubei nodded.

The doctor almost fled out of the room.

"Oh my," the nurse said. "I wonder what got into him."

"He probably realized that if this patient dies, he dies as does all of his family and everyone involved," Midori said.

The nurse's blood ran cold. Hideki became her most important patient ever.

XXXIV

Investiture

Iemitsu's headquarters was on the southern outskirts of Kyoto. Three hundred thousand men created a small city just south of the Sanjo Bridge. Hittori Hanzo got them the audience. Security was equivalent to Iemitsu's paranoia.

"Why do you bring such creatures before us?" O'Fuku demanded.

"They have knowledge that can help us," Honzo said.

"I will not have Iemitsu defiled by their presence. Get them out. Get them all out before I have them killed," O'Fuku cried.

"Too late," Iemitsu said as he entered the great room of the inn.

O'Fuku removed herself from the seat of importance and took a position lower and to the right of Iemitsu.

Honzo, Hideki, Jubei, Myo, Midori and The Mist bowed.

"Raise your heads. I have heard what you have done for me here in Kyoto," Iemitsu said. Then, turning to Honzo, he said, "That is what I was talking about with you earlier."

"Yes Uesama," Honzo said. "I told you they would not let you down."

"Was Ito strong Jubei?" Iemitsu asked.

"I believe he was lord, but I did not fight him. Hideki slew the man," Jubei said.

Iemitsu looked first at Hideki with his left arm encased in a sling. Then he looked at Jubei.

"Then what did you do during the fight?" Iemitsu asked.

"He kept your brother and his retainers off my back Lord," Hideki said.

"You could've ended this whole threat with a bow and did not take the shot? Whose side are the Yagyū on?" O'Fuku asked.

"It was not his place to slay Tadanaga. Your brother is Tokugawa. Only one man can order his death," Hideki said, not addressing O'Fuku.

"How dare you speak you cripple. No one asked to hear from you," O'Fuku shrieked.

"Watch your temper okasan. I am conducting the session," Iemitsu said.

"Yes lord," O'Fuku said, her hatred for Hideki showing in her eyes.

"That was well spoken Hideki. Only I can take my brother's life," Iemitsu said. "I understand the Yoshinobu are related to the Tokugawa."

"Only distantly lord," Hideki said. "We are cousins."

"Am I going to have to worry about you once I have disposed of Tadanaga?" Iemitsu asked.

"Now you are thinking lord. Cut him down before he is a problem," O'Fuku interrupted.

"If you want to stay here, remain quiet," Iemitsu commanded.

"You have nothing to fear from us lord, we live to serve the rightful heir," Hideki said.

"Talk is cheap Hideki. You are the Tengu Killer of lore and your brother is loved by all Edo. Prove your loyalty," Iemitsu said.

"That is what I thought I have been doing," Hideki said.

"I will concede you have done me a great service, but why are you here?" Iemitsu asked.

"Do not listen to anything he says Uesama," O'Fuku demanded. "The Yoshinobu only know lies."

"Leave us woman," Iemitsu commanded.

O'Fuku looked shocked. Then she bowed to Iemitsu and moved out of the room.

"She does not like you Hideki," Iemitsu said. "Crushing

her elbow was not a good idea. Is your wound bad?"

"No lord my wound is healing thanks to a good doctor and fast thinking friends. Regarding O'Fuku, it was she who tried to burn me alive and killed scores of innocents throughout the land," Hideki said.

"Yes, I know. To her credit she did all that for me," Iemitsu said. "She loved and protected me when no one else would."

"I have no doubt of her love for you Lord. I will not use the opportunity to tell you of the heinous tasks she has attempted. She is your stepmother. The Yoshinobu will try to stay out of her way," Hideki said.

"Thank you. Now why are you here?" Iemitsu asked.

"The day after tomorrow is the investiture in the Imperial compound," Hideki said. "You will be most vulnerable then."

"It cannot be helped. Samurai are not allowed into the Emperor's presence," Iemitsu said. "I can only be accompanied by three maidens to help with my clothing."

"We will have the compound surrounded by my men and I will accompany Uesama to the Emperor's building," Honzo said.

"It is too early to call him Uesama. There is still one very dangerous villain at large with considerable skills and only one aim in life, to kill Iemitsu," Hideki said.

"What are you proposing Hideki?" Iemitsu asked.

"I propose the three maidens that accompany you be these three women here," Hideki said.

All three women looked at Hideki in surprise.

"I do not know these women," Iemitsu said.

"The one next to Jubei is Myo. She is the head of the Five Families ninja. Next to her is her lieutenant Midori. Both are well-trained and have saved my life more than once. Myo is my lover. Midori is Jubei's lover. We would not offer their services if we did not fully trust them," Hideki said.

"Who is the third on the end?" Iemitsu asked.

"She is called The Mist," Hideki said. "She was the second in command of the Koga ninja."

"I have heard of you," Iemitsu said. "Why did you change sides?"

The Mist bowed her head. "Lord, Ugai was crazy to risk

the Koga as he has done. His treachery has placed the Koga
at grave risk. I want to survive. I want my friends who are not
loyal to Ugai to survive as well. I want to take what's left of the
loyal Koga with me when this is over. Ugai has abandoned all
reason. He is totally out of control."

"How can I trust you?" Iemitsu asked.

"Myo and Midori will be with her lord," Hideki said. They
will not let you be harmed. On top of that I trust her and so
does my grandfather."

Now it was time for The Mist to be surprised. She looked
from Iemitsu to Hideki.

"What about you Jubei? Do you agree with this?" Iemitsu
asked.

"In truth this is the first I'm hearing of it. But like most
plans Hideki comes up with it makes sense. You will be without protection in the Emperor's chambers. I would feel much
better with these three by your side," Jubei said.

"Are they good enough for the task?" Iemitsu asked.

"I used Midori to protect my back when I was aiming
arrows near your brother. Myo's skills are legendary. I have no
way of gauging The Mist's motives, but I have watched her
in two life-threatening situations, and she has handled herself
well," Jubei said.

"Let me accompany you lord. Let me prove that not all
Koga broke their vows," The Mist pleaded.

"How do you rate Ugai, Jubei?" Iemitsu asked.

"Ruthless," Jubei said. "He stole the heir to the Yoshinobu,
a baby, and convinced most of the Koga to break their vows to
you. He is formidable and desperate. He must be eradicated at
all costs."

"Do you concur in this plan Honzo?" Iemitsu asked.

"Yes lord, I was going to use three Iga women. However,
none of them are as adept as Myo and Midori. I've been keeping my eye on them for several years now," Honzo said.

Myo and Midori looked at each other.

"Do you believe The Mist?" Iemitsu asked.

"I do lord," Honzo said. "I had an opportunity to talk with
her at the Yoshinobu mansion when my grandson was stolen.

She helped to get him back. But I have been working with her for many years in the castle. There is none more committed."

"Very well, we will go with Hideki's plan. Will you women be armed?" Iemitsu asked.

"Yes Lord," Myo said. "It would be stupid to go against Ugai unarmed."

"But the weapons will be concealed?" Iemitsu asked.

"Do not worry about us being searched Lord," The Mist said. "No one will find them."

"Jubei, you taught me swordsmanship. Hideki, despite my stepmother hating you, you have proved to be an asset to me. Honzo, I want them there by my side when we move into the Emperor's chambers," Iemitsu said. "I'm beginning to think the Yoshinobu are my good luck charm."

"As you command lord," Honzo said.

"By the way Hideki, how was Ito able to cut you?" Iemitsu asked.

"Ito did not cut me lord. Your brother tried to augment Ito's sword skill with three archers," Hideki said.

"Interesting," Iemitsu said. "I want to find out more details later."

Two days hence Hideki and Jubei were part of Iemitsu's guard outside the Emperor's compound.

"This is as far as we go," Honzo said. He then nodded to Myo, Midori and The Mist. The women were dressed in white silk from head to foot. They gave the illusion of shrine maidens.

Iemitsu was clothed in fine blue silks and had a huge blue gold trim cloak. Myo and Midori held two wings of the cloak off the ground and The Mist held the rear. All four people moved to the center of the room and prostrated themselves.

Two high ranking courtiers welcomed Iemitsu on behalf of the divine majesty. Iemitsu and the women raised their heads.

For what seemed like an eternity the two courtiers sang the praises of the Emperor and extolled Iemitsu's virtues. The courtiers solicited gifts using veiled diplomatic doublespeak.

Myo and The Mist took turns carrying precious boxes filled with gems and pearls. The Mist was saved from such duties being behind Iemitsu. She was the only one who knew what Ugai looked like. Hideki had always suggested she keep her hands free.

For the next two hours the investiture ceremony was conducted. The Emperor sat in a chair behind finely woven silk screen. A person sitting in a chair could be seen, but no details could be discerned.

The courtiers would utter a proclamation from the Emperor and Iemitsu would bow and spout platitudes. All the time the three women scanned the surroundings looking for threats. None appeared. They communicated via nods and imperceptible hand signals. No threat was detected.

One of the last acts of the ceremony involved the Emperor giving Iemitsu a celestial sword with which to protect the realm and a proclamation scroll announcing he was shogun. One courtier uttered the Emperor's blessing, reached through the screens to receive both items. Once received, the first courtier passed both items to the second courtier.

Both courtiers were dressed in flowing gowns with piqued black hats. Their faces were powdered, and their eyebrows shaved and replaced by dark coal smudges. Their mouths were painted in the center of their lips with a red pigment. The second courtier held the celestial sword and proclamation scroll out in front and bowed his head as he walked on his knees to present the gifts to Iemitsu.

At the last moment the courtier unsheathed the celestial sword and attempted to thrust it into Iemitsu's heart. Myo was on Iemitsu's right and deflected the sword downward with her iron ribbed fan held in her left hand. She followed it with a fist strike to the courtier's left ear with a dart protruding past her fingers.

The courtier screamed and dropped the sword and smashed Midori in the face with a backhand. She dropped motionless. He then reached inside his flowing gown and pulled out two kama. He raised his arms to plunge the razor-sharp blades downward into Iemitsu.

As soon as Midori saw his arm raise up, she launched her attack. She plunged her tanto into his right armpit. The sharp tip penetrated a lung and pierced his heart. He opened his mouth to scream but died before it escaped his lips. His forward momentum carried the blades downward toward Iemitsu.

Iemitsu screamed and dropped into a ball. The blades were coming for the middle of his back when The Mist threw herself on top of the Shogun. She screamed as the blades entered her back.

Myo was up and grabbed the dead courtier's sword and spun toward the first courtier. Midori moved the bloody Mist off Iemitsu.

"Are you injured Uesama?" Myo asked.

"That is correct. I am shogun now," Iemitsu beamed. "Myo bring that noble over here."

Myo looked at the shrouded area that housed the Emperor. He was no longer there. She put the point of the celestial sword to the nobleman's neck.

"You heard the Shogun. Crawl to him," Myo ordered.

Iemitsu screamed for his guards. Honzo bolted in with his men.

"Myo tend to The Mist's wounds. Honzo surround this building. No one gets out. I want another audience with the Emperor," Iemitsu said. "And gather all the courtiers and nobles in this room."

"As you command Uesama," Honzo said.

The nobles were rounded up and herded around the shrouded Emperor's place of honor. Several of the nobles began objecting to this type of treatment in the Emperor's compound.

"Honzo, find the noisiest and shut him up permanently," Iemitsu said.

Honzo moved to the oldest, fattest noble leading the chorus of complaints, drew his sword and lopped off the nobleman's head. There was a great intake of breath and all went quiet. The only noise was the spurting of the blood onto the hardwood floor. Honzo flicked the blood from his sword and returned it to his scabbard. He returned to the Shogun's side.

A shadowy figure appeared behind the thin silk.

"I know it is a breach of etiquette for a samurai to directly address the Emperor, but I believe an assassination attempt on me in this chamber is also a breach of etiquette," Iemitsu said.

"You cannot accuse the Emperor of wrongdoing and your barbaric acts will not be tolerated," another nobleman said.

"Myo please give me my celestial sword," Iemitsu said.

Myo moved before Iemitsu and complied.

"You are correct nobleman. I cannot accuse Emperor. But you will all pay for the attempt on my life. As I depart here, I will burn every building in this compound except the Emperor's. The gold and silver and other gifts are forfeit. I will also cut your rice ration in half for the rest of the year," Iemitsu said.

"You would not dare. The people of this nation will revolt against you," the loud nobleman argued.

"I have 300,000 samurai in this city. I can do what I want. If I hear of you trying to raise rebellion again, I will burn this building as well and cut all your rations. So now starve in silence and ponder your poor choices," Iemitsu said. "And because I know this nobleman was in on my assassination, I will deal with him myself."

Iemitsu plunged the celestial sword into the throat of the first courtier. He flopped about trying to breathe blood.

Iemitsu stormed out of the chambers and watched as samurai put the buildings to the torch. "Two questions Honzo. How is The Mist and did Myo and Midori kill Ugai?" he asked.

Honzo went back into the chambers and returned dragging the corpse of the courtier who had tried to assassinate Iemitsu. He dropped the body at Iemitsu's feet.

"This is Ugai. And he is very dead," Honzo said.

Midori and Myo had The Mist's kimono off and were applying cloth bandages to her wounds in her back. Iemitsu saw this and walked over to them.

"She is in shock now. But she will survive Uesama," Myo said.

"Thank the Buddha you three were with me," Iemitsu said. "I told you the Yoshinobu were my good luck charm."

"It appears so," Honzo said winking at Myo.

"Let us get back to Edo. Let the Yoshinobu cleanup this cesspool. I am tired of the stench of this place," Iemitsu said.

As the new shogun strode into the sunlight, he spotted Hideki and Jubei.

"Hideki," Iemitsu said.

Hideki knelt and bowed. "Yes Uesama," Hideki said.

"Get word to your grandfather to surround Daito Kuji Temple. I am going to put an end to my brother before I depart," Iemitsu said.

"That was accomplished yesterday Uesama," Hideki said.

"Then tell your grandfather I want this Ronin Army rabble eradicated," Iemitsu said.

"Yes Uesama, he is in the midst of taking action on that very subject," Hideki said.

Iemitsu was getting a little agitated.

"Is there anything that has escaped your imagination?" Iemitsu asked.

"Yes Uesama," Hideki said. "What you want to do about your brother?"

"You Yoshinobu do think quickly. I like that. Take a note to my brother under my chop that he is to commit seppuku before nightfall," Iemitsu ordered.

"What about your mother?" Hideki asked.

"Treat her with kindness and respect but put her in a nunnery of her choice," Iemitsu said.

"As you command Uesama," Hideki said.

XXXV

Lovers

Iemitsu had returned immediately to Edo triumphant and the new shogun. It took the Yoshinobu a month to institute the change in Kyoto directed by Iemitsu and another fourteen days of leisurely travel to arrive in Edo from Kyoto.

Life returned to normal for the Yoshinobu. The bulk of their forces from Kii returned to the home province. The remaining eighty samurai settled into routine life at the Yoshinobu compound. On the far side of the Yoshinobu mansion in Hideki's room the lights were out. Only the moonlight provided luminescence.

"Why do you think he wants to see us?" Myo asked.

"I do not know. It has been two months since the investiture. Maybe he is getting around to taking care of loose ends," Hideki said tracing the curve of her naked breasts with his left hand.

"What does that mean?" Myo asked.

"He was worried about the Yoshinobu being a threat to his shogunate. Besides, O'Fuku has had plenty of time to completely poison his mind against us," Hideki said.

"But Jii is a member of the Roju," Myo said.

"Iemitsu is making radical changes. It is rumored that he will change the Tairo and the Roju," Hideki said.

"But if it was not for the Yoshinobu he might still be fighting Tadanaga," Myo said.

"That is true. But samurai life is not always fair," Hideki said, moving his finger down her smooth stomach.

"Tadanaga's dead. He slit his belly as ordered by Iemitsu," Myo said.

"So maybe he is now looking for new threats," Hideki said moving his hand lower.

"If you keep that up you will not get any sleep tonight," Myo said.

"Sleep is highly overrated," Hideki said.

"What do you think about letting The Mist join the Five Families?" Myo asked.

"I think that is entirely up to you. You are the leader of our ninja. I would just be sure she does not bring any Ugai supporters with her. That would give Iemitsu more than enough ammunition to harm the Yoshinobu," Hideki said. "How are her wounds?"

"She is healing nicely. Midori has been working with her," Myo said.

"Is she adapting to life inside the Yoshinobu compound?" Hideki asked with his hand transitioning from smooth skin to course hair.

"You must be kidding. Like the rest of us, she is living better than ever here. She and Midori are like sisters," Myo said.

"Jii treats everyone fairly," Hideki said. "I would die for that old man."

"We all would," Myo said. "But I have a special appreciation for one of his grandsons."

"Why don't you roll on top of me and I'll show you my appreciation," Hideki said.

"Samurai-sama, I do not think you can keep up with me. I am trained in the art of giving pleasure," Myo said in the Tsugaru dialect.

"Buddha be praised," Hideki said.

In another room on the other the end of the Yoshinobu mansion Midori rose and dressed.

"It is a little late to go calling. Are you going to go visit your man?" The Mist asked.

"Hey, you are my roommate not my mother," Midori said.

"But the answer to your question is yes."

"You are getting very close to Jubei. I would not have thought it possible," The Mist said.

"What do you mean?" Midori asked.

"Well, he is so fierce looking, and I have not heard him speak more than two sentences," The Mist said.

"Tonight, he will not have to do much talking," Midori said.

"So, you are serious about him?" The Mist asked.

"I am as serious as you can get as a ninja," Midori said. "You know how it is. We live day by day. I take pleasure where I can find it."

"You do not plan to marry then?" The Mist asked.

"My boss has been Hideki's lover for two years now. But despite Jii's words the gap between ninja and samurai is vast. I will believe in their marriage when I see it," Midori said.

"I guess I will just have to find me a samurai lover," The Mist said.

"I find them much more attentive than ninja lovers," Midori said.

"Why is that?" The Mist asked.

"It probably has something to do with that crazy bushido code, I guess. Look at Hideki. He shuns all offers of a pairing to stay with Myo," Midori said.

"If I am going to be joining the Five Families, I guess I had better get used to samurai," The Mist said.

"Throwing yourself in front of Ugai's kama to protect the Shogun was a damn good start," Midori said.

"I suppose so. Do not let me do that again," The Mist said. "So why are we being called for an audience with Iemitsu?"

"I have no idea," Midori said. "You must sacrifice some freedom when working with samurai. We could get congratulated or we could be killed. You just never know."

"Well if you had not jammed that tanto into Ugai's armpit I would be dead now. Just a little more momentum and those blades would have punctured both lungs," The Mist said.

"You are the one who saved the shogun. Usually kunoichi have better sense," Midori said.

"I do not know what came over me. I did not have a weapon to counter Ugai's kama. I do not know what kind of shogun Iemitsu will be but Tadanaga would have been horrible," The Mist said.

"That is right. You were once in his inner circle," Midori said. "What made you switch sides?"

"Two things made me run from Tadanaga. First, Ugai condemned the Koga to death by his treachery. Iemitsu would have to be assassinated for Tadanaga and Ugai to win. I suspected Tadanaga and Ito were street killers. There was no way the country could be ruled by someone who places no value in human life," The Mist said.

"Sounds like sensible reasoning to me," Midori said.

"Secondly, something always bothered me about Ito," The Mist said.

"Hideki took care of him. He will not trouble anyone anymore," Midori said.

"True, but I never thought Ito was very smart," The Mist said. "Yet he rose from almost obscurity to chief strategist for Tadanaga overnight. How did that happen?"

"Are you saying there was an outsider influencing Ito's climb?" Midori asked.

"I believe so," The Mist said.

"Who do you suspect?" Midori asked.

"I have no suspects at this time. Who would have a working knowledge of Tadanaga's mind as well as his mother's?" The Mist asked. "No one in Tadanaga's inner circle was that shrewd."

"You had better talk to Myo and Hideki tomorrow before we go in to see Iemitsu. They like to think things through," Midori said and put the final touches on her black ninja garb.

"Have fun tonight," The Mist said.

"I intend to," Midori said and left through the window.

XXXVI

Merchant Rei

"Why do you think the Yoshinobu have to see the shogun?" Haru asked.

"I have no idea," Rei said.

"Do you think they are in trouble?" Haru asked.

"Again, I have no idea," Rei said.

"You are samurai," Haru said with a little more tension in her voice than she intended. "You should know these things."

Rei returned his wakazashi he had been oiling to its scabbard.

"I am from a samurai family. I have never held a samurai position working for a lord. The Yoshinobu appear to be a great family from what I have seen. They are cousin to the Tokugawa. They even saved the current shogun's life. But any answer I would give you about their current situation would be speculation on my part. I would prefer not to guess," Rei said.

"How can you be so calm?" Haru demanded. "I have lost my home and my business and the closest thing to a mother I have ever had. She is lying gravely wounded far away in Kyoto. I do not know if she is alive."

"That is true," Rei said. "But you are alive and the Yoshinobu are indebted to you."

"What is that supposed to mean?" Haru asked.

Rei looked around the six-tatami room with this beautiful scroll of Chinese design hanging on a wall and closet space on one side of the room.

"I know you are used to luxury, but I am not. To me this is

the best I have ever lived. I think you need to relax and wait for Jii and Hideki to make good on their promises to help you."

"You do not understand," Haru said.

"That is correct. I do not understand your turmoil," Rei said.

Haru started crying.

"Haru please stop that. I do not know how to help you when you cry," Rei pleaded.

Haru calmed herself. Between sniffles she looked up at Rei.

"I have never been in charge of my own destiny," Haru said. "My father married me to a man I did not love for his own personal gain. I had a beautiful baby and it was taken from me. Then both my father and husband died at the hands of Kyoto street killers. Then I got a reprieve when little Yoshitsune was dropped in my lap. Then he was taken from me. Then my life was threatened, my business and my home were burned. Ume was gravely wounded. Now I am stuck in Edo with nothing."

"I see," Rei said.

"What do you mean you see? How could you possibly know how I feel?" Haru asked.

"I guess I cannot," Rei said.

"That is correct. You are neither a woman nor a widow nor a two-time mother," Haru said.

"I am none of those things," Rei said. "I am samurai. If I am alive, I have a chance."

Haru set straight up and looked Rei in the eye.

"What does that mean?" Haru asked.

"It means you should focus on the positive things in your life. You are alive. You are beautiful. You are young. You are smart. A very powerful family loves you and wants to help you. I want to help you," Rei said. "You have more things going for you than going against."

"So that is the way samurai look at life?" Haru asked.

"I can only speak for this samurai," Rei said. "We live or die day by day based on the situation and our skills. There is no use crying. If we lose and are still alive then opportunity lives."

Haru used the white inner kimono sleeve to dry her eyes.

"So, you really think everything will be fine?" Haru asked.

"I do not know if it will be fine. Life is tricky for the best of us. You are worrying about your future. I used to worry about my next meal," Rei said. "Each new day will bring new challenges and new opportunities. Just make the best of what you have."

Haru breathed deeply. "I feel better now. You have that effect on me."

"Do not worry about what you cannot control Haru. I will help you face your challenges," Rei said.

Haru smiled for the first time since breakfast.

"You really think I'm smart?" Haru asked.

"You are much smarter than I," Rei said.

"Do you really see me as young?" Haru asked.

"You cannot be much older than me," Rei said.

"Do you really think I am beautiful?" Haru asked.

"A blind man could see that," Rei said. "I'm attracted to your beauty; there is no question of that. But I am also attracted to your inner beauty."

"What you mean by inner beauty?" Haru asked.

"Your loyalty to Ume displays inner beauty. Your chief clerk's loyalty to you shows your goodness. That is inner beauty. You cannot buy that type of loyalty. It is earned. Your willingness to give up Yoshitsune to his rightful mother although it made you miserable is inner beauty. All of these things shine brightest to me," Rei said.

"You make me blush Rei-san," Haru said.

"You should not flinch from such praise. It is your due," Rei said. "Most of the calamity in your life you had no part in. Your husband cheated on you and your father chose your husband. Both were foolish. Your husband for not seeing your worth and cherishing it and your father for not letting you marry the man of your choosing. If he had, you and your chosen husband could have formed a dynamic team and worked together to build your father's legacy. You have nothing to be ashamed of."

"Rei-san you sound like a love letter," Haru said.

"I am a plain man. I speak what's in my heart," Rei said. "I will admit I am in love with you Haru. But I have had little experience with women. I have had much life experience since leaving my father's farm. I believe if you see something you admire you should try to be part of it on any level you can. It is the reason I accept the yojimbo assignment."

"Do you still want to stay with me?" Haru asked. "I do not have a store any longer."

"I have never been interested in your store," Rei said.

"What if the Yoshinobu offer you a position here?" Haru asked.

"Accepting such an offer would depend on whether I could stay by your side or not," Rei said.

Haru clapped her hands together in joy.

"Oh Rei-san, could that be true?" Haru asked.

"If I say it lady, you can be sure it is true," Rei said.

"Can you give up the samurai way of life and become a merchant?" Haru asked.

"If it means being by your side then yes," Rei said.

"Come sit closer to me Rei," Haru said.

Rei rose carrying his wakazashi in his left hand. He sat close to Haru.

"Would you marry an old widow merchant woman Rei?" Haru asked.

Rei put his hand to his chin in contemplation.

"My only concern would be if I could support her. I do not have a job yet," Rei said.

Haru laughed. "Rei-san do not worry. I have enough money for both of us."

"But your store burned down," Rei said.

"Yes, but I have goods warehoused all over Japan," Haru said. "I also have gold held in several enterprises in Nagasaki and Kyoto. We have enough money for several generations."

"I do not know Haru-san. I would like to earn my keep. I do not want to live off you," Rei said.

"Do not worry silly. I have plans to make more and more money and you will be a key part of that plan," Haru said.

"Do you think I can do it?" Rei asked.

"What you do not know I can teach you Rei. But I cannot teach loyalty as you say. You were willing to stay with me in any capacity before you knew I was rich. I cannot teach that," Haru said.

"Then I will answer your original question now Haru. I will marry you whenever or wherever you ask," Rei said. "My father has taught me that if I meet a woman I love I should marry her and cherish her forever."

Haru threw her arms around Rei's neck.

"Oh Rei-san we will be so happy," Haru said.

"Well, I know of a little girl who will be happy," Rei said.

"Do you mean your little sister?" Haru asked.

"Yes, she has never been off the farm. But she is a sweet and inquisitive young thing," Rei remembered fondly.

"How old is she?" Haru asked.

"She is ten years old," Rei said.

"Rei, I would love to have a little sister for a companion. I could teach her so much and we could be best of friends," Haru said.

"That would depend greatly on my father," Rei said. "He might not want her to become a merchant lady."

"Do not be silly, Rei," Haru said. "We can set your father up with his own forge and black smith shop if he wants. Both of their lives will be easier as merchants."

"I am willing because of you," Rei said. "But samurai pride can be pretty strong. My father is old school."

"Well, we will leave it up to him," Haru said. "But we can make the offer."

"Thank you Haru," Rei said. "That is a great load off my mind."

"I would like to bring Ume here to Edo." Haru said.

"I think you should," Rei said. "I will go get her if she is up to the journey."

"Will the Yoshinobu help us?" Haru asked.

"I would bet they would," Rei said. "They owe you much."

"Then please talk to that Yoshi person and get him to send pigeons or whatever they use and find out about moving Ume," Haru said.

"I shall do so tomorrow," Rei said.

"Rei will you visit my room tonight?" Haru asked hesitantly.

"You mean as in sleep with you?" Rei asked.

"Yes," Haru said casting her pride to the wind.

"Shouldn't we get married first?" Rei asked.

"I've been married," Haru said. "It means little to some. I believe partly in what your father told you. I think if you love someone you should not let him go."

"I would love to Haru, but I do not want to cheapen you in the eyes of the Yoshinobu," Rei said.

"Let me worry about my reputation Rei," Haru said. "By the way Rei-san, have you ever been with a woman before?"

"Just one," Rei said. "She was a pirate."

"What, a pirate?" Haru exclaimed. "Oh Rei, you have to come tonight. I want to hear that story."

"I slept with her because I liked her," Rei said. "I will sleep with you because I love you. I think we will make a better story."

XXXVII

Audience

All the Yoshinobu and friends were present. Hideki could not decide who was more uncomfortable. Was it Jii with the ridiculous kamishino clothing that he wore every day as part of the Roju or Yoshi? Yoshi could take on the persona of anyone but still looked out of place and clownish in the castle formalwear. The exaggerated shoulder wing points and extended pants not only looked ridiculous; it made any movement except baby steps with a sliding shuffle impossible. Both men appeared entirely uncomfortable.

Jii was on the far right in the first row facing the raised tatami stage where he assumed Iemitsu and O'Fuku would be looking down upon them. Naga was on Jii's left and Hideki beyond that. To Hideki's left sat Jubei and then Yoshi. Behind Jii in the second row sat Yuki. To her left sat Myo, Midori and The Mist.

Off to the side between the Yoshinobu audience and Iemitsu stage sat Honzo. A wooden chest was next to him. Opposite Honzo on the other side sat an important man. He was Yagyū Munenori, Jubei's father and the chamberlain for the old shogun Hidetada and Iemitsu's father.

An older woman with an obviously crippled right arm did her best to make a grand entrance from behind one of the many standalone shoji screens at the back wall of the raised tatami. She wore expensive flowing robes and sat on her shins and scanned the Yoshinobu before her. The Yoshinobu nodded slightly.

"I do not know why it is my misfortune to be plagued by the Yoshinobu. You are always underfoot. If I had my way every one of you would be boiled in oil," O'Fuku said.

"Then it is good fortune for both the Yoshinobu and the country that you are not shogun," Jii said.

O'Fuku's face contorted showing the inner rage she felt for those in front of her.

"Save your venom okasan," Iemitsu said, entering from behind one of the many screens.

Everyone bowed low and stayed low.

"Raise your heads everyone. I want to see your faces," Iemitsu commanded.

When all eyes were on him, "Mist, how are your wounds?"

The Mist bowed her head and said, "Almost healed Uesama. Thank you for your concern."

Shogun Iemitsu continued. "I will admit I had planned to extinguish every Koga from the face of the earth until you took those blades intended for me."

"Thank you for letting me keep my life Uesama. But my sisters from the Five Families saved your life. Both Myo and Midori acting as a team killed Ugai," The Mist said.

"Yes, I am not forgetting their actions. I'm not forgetting Hideki's part in coming up with a plan to protect me either," Iemitsu said.

"It was all good luck on their part. The Yoshinobu always have good luck on their side. But the Yoshinobu are plotting your demise even now," O'Fuku said.

Iemitsu smiled. "Calm down mother, we know what you think of the Yoshinobu. Do you want to defend yourself Hideki?"

"I do not know if I can Uesama. O'Fuku's hate is based on me eradicating her pet ninja who roamed the land killing innocents and robbing merchants. But I do have a question for my accuser," Hideki said.

"Then pose it. We'll see if it has merit," Iemitsu said.

"I already know the answer to this question, but I would like to ask O'Fuku, who has your best interest at heart. Why did she prop up Tadanaga's rebellion with money and plant a strategist like Ito on their staff?" Hideki asked.

Mouths opened and all eyes went to O'Fuku.

"How dare you accuse me of such a thing? Where is your proof? You have already crippled me and now you want to smear my good name in front of the shogun?" O'Fuku asked.

"I am not sure you have ever had a good name O'Fuku. The proof of my allegation is Ito's dying declaration to me and common sense." Hideki said.

"Then you have no proof. Anyone near you when Ito died has perished. There is no one to confirm your filthy allegation," O'Fuku said. "What common sense are you claiming? The Yoshinobu have no sense at all."

"The common sense is that Ito was a nobody one day and is Tadanaga's chief strategist the next. He came from nothing to prominence almost overnight. He did that because someone of influence and power engineered the introduction and exploited Tadanaga's basest desires, the willingness to kill innocents. Ito led Tadanaga to become a Kyoto street killer," Hideki said.

"What has all this fantasy to do with me?" O'Fuku asked. "You have no proof at all."

"I have Tadanaga's own admission when I accused him of it just before he had his archers loose arrows at me," Hideki said. "I always knew Ito was not smart enough to impress Tadanaga with wisdom. But he was vicious enough to find a like-minded villain in Tadanaga. Who was politically savvy enough to plant a spy into Tadanaga's staff? Who was familiar with Tadanaga's character to exploit his weaknesses? Who had access to enough money to funnel funds needed to back a rebellion? It was you O'Fuku."

O'Fuku stood and screamed. "You think you are so smart. You know nothing."

"I had a hard time understanding why you went to all the trouble," Hideki said. "Iemitsu could have killed Tadanaga at any time. But then I realized Tadanaga was not the real target. You fermented rebellion to draw out the Satsuma and other daimyo so you could crush them in a civil war. You were willing to have thousands of innocents perish to ensure you would not be met with resistance later. I must admire your viciousness as well. But then you are The Bird Woman. You have a snake for a heart."

There was total silence in the room.

"Those were very interesting deductions Hideki. It confirms my assumption that you are wickedly intelligent. But as you have no proof, your allegations are groundless," Iemitsu said. "Or do you think I was part of this wicked scheme as well?"

"I will think not unless you tell me different Uesama," Hideki said bowing.

"That is treason," O'Fuku screamed. "He condemns the Yoshinobu by his foul mouth. Kill them all Takechiyo."

Iemitsu's ice cold gaze moved O'Fuku to sit. O'Fuku stopped fidgeting after a while and fanned herself even though the temperature was almost cold in the castle.

"I see you are still in a sling. Hideki how is your wound? You sustained that during your duel with Ito. I believe you told me you were struck by arrows?" Iemitsu asked.

"Yes, you are correct lord. Your brother had three archers on the wall at Daito Kuji," Hideki said.

Iemitsu leaned forward.

"Three archers? How many wounds did you receive?" Iemitsu asked.

"I was only struck once, lord," Hideki replied.

"What happened to my brother's archers?" Iemitsu asked.

"As I mentioned previously, Jubei's yumi eliminated them as threats," Hideki said.

"Were they bad archers Jubei?" Iemitsu asked.

"On the contrary," Jubei said. "They were good archers."

"Then was Hideki just lucky as my mother states?" Iemitsu asked.

"Luck played no part," Jubei said.

"Then how is it that Hideki is before me with minor injury? Three archers at close range should have killed him," Iemitsu said.

"Do you remember the lesson I taught you and your brother as young men concerning Yadomae-jutsu?" Jubei asked.

"Yes, but we both thought that was so much nonsense," Iemitsu said.

"Hideki is a better student," Jubei said.

"You deflected or cut two of the three arrows?" Iemitsu asked.

"Yes lord," Hideki said.

Iemitsu looked at Jubei then at Hideki.

"Now I have four master swordsmen in my employee," Iemitsu said. "Two Yagyū's, Honzo and now Hideki make up the four. Who is the strongest?"

"Hideki," Jubei said without hesitation.

All eyes went to Jubei. "Explain that remark," Iemitsu said.

"Hideki has been trained by both me and Musashi. But most importantly he can fight in mushin," Jubei said.

Now all eyes went to Hideki.

"Indeed? I thought that was a myth also," Iemitsu said.

"As I said lord, Hideki is a better student," Jubei said.

Iemitsu pondered these remarks a moment then turned his attention to Jii.

"Jii, may I call you by your nickname?" Iemitsu asked.

Jii bowed his silver hair low. "Please do Uesama. It is what I answer to most often."

"Good. Jii you have heard that I am revamping my own government as well as the country?" Iemitsu asked.

"Yes Uesama, I have heard the rumors," Jii answered.

"How would you like to be part of it?" Iemitsu asked.

O'Fuku spun on her knees. "Why involve that old goat? He is in league with the devil," O'Fuku said.

"I need him because he lives his life based on bushido. He cannot be bought or threatened into doing anything his principles do not allow. His loyalties to the old ways appear inviolate. He has trained both his grandsons this way. That is why they stand out against those that call themselves samurai today. I need such men around me," Iemitsu said.

When it was certain O'Fuku would not continue Jii bowed his head. "I would be honored Uesama, but I am getting old. I would like nothing better than to end my days at home playing with my great-grandchild," Jii said.

Iemitsu nodded. "You have certainly earned your rest. You defeated the Ronin Army and your quick thinking to surround the Daito Kuji Temple caught our enemies off guard," Iemitsu said.

"Your acknowledgement is our reward Uesama," Jii said.

"Alas there will be little rest for you. I am placing you in charge of planning and executing the reforms I want. You are elevated to the position of chamberlain," Iemitsu commanded.

There was a moment of dumbstruck silence. Then everyone looked at Jii.

"I will have two chamberlains. You will be one working on the future and Yagyū Munenori will be the other maintaining order for the present," Iemitsu said. "You both report directly to me and coordinate with each other. Only I give you orders. Do you understand?"

"Yes Uesama," Jii said.

"As you command Uesama," Munenori said.

"Good, that is taken care of," Iemitsu said. Then looking down at O'Fuku, "Mother please depart."

"What?" O'Fuku asked.

"You heard me. Leave us now," Iemitsu repeated.

"You would have secrets from me and embarrass me in front of the likes of them?" O'Fuku asked.

"Please leave and do not linger by the entrance," Iemitsu said.

O'Fuku rose with some difficulty and exited as she had entered.

"I left orders with the guards that she is not to eavesdrop," Iemitsu said, rising and moving forward and stepping down onto the level of the Yoshinobu.

All bowed low as he rose.

"Raise your heads. My mother will try to interfere with what I'm about to say anyway but I want to postpone that as long as possible. When it comes to the Yoshinobu she loses all rationality," Iemitsu said.

All heads rose.

"I am changing this country. I'm going to require the Tozama to have homes in Edo and visit here for four months each year. Their wives and children must remain in Edo. I am going to stamp out all sense of rebellion. I am going to demand they have increased military arms and troops at my disposal under my command. That is what a shogun does. He is the military commander of the country," Iemitsu said.

Iemitsu paused to see if anyone had any objections. There were none.

"Then I am going to close all ports to foreign trade except Nagasaki. I plan to run the Portuguese from our shores," Iemitsu said.

"You are going to bring down the Dutch from Hirano," Hideki said.

"Hideki you always see into the future. You are correct. The Dutch do not spread their religion and culture to our people," Iemitsu said. "I'm going to shut Japan off from any other contact. No Japanese man or woman may travel outside the country without my permission."

"You will make a lot of enemies. Several daimyo have ports and earn money with them," Hideki said.

"Yes, I expect to make enemies. I am going to banish the Kirishitan religion," Iemitsu said.

"Uesama many good Japanese are also Kirishitans," Hideki said.

"I do not care. They cannot have allegiance to a great father in Rome and to me," Iemitsu said.

"You know they will revolt," Hideki said. "Most of the population of Kyushu is Kirishitan."

"I will prepare for their revolt. What do you think the current governor of Nagasaki will do when I ban Kirishitans?" Iemitsu asked.

"He is not a Kirishitan. His wife is but has no great ties to the church," Hideki said.

Iemitsu stepped back to look at everyone. "You are probably wondering why I am asking Hideki all these questions concerning global politics. It is because he is intelligent and has had a hand in restructuring them already," Iemitsu said.

All eyes went to Hideki.

"I will not lie to you Uesama. I did kill the old

governor and install the new one," Hideki said.

Jii's jaw dropped.

"You do not think that was greatly overstepping your bounds?" Iemitsu asked.

"I know it was Uesama, just as I knew it then. But something had to be done. They did not call him Bad Heizo for nothing," Hideki said.

"Hideki shut your mouth," Jii said. "I apologize for my grandson's loose mouth Uesama."

Iemitsu smiled. "On the contrary, it is his adherence to the Yoshinobu motto of 'no wrong too small to right and no right to small to defend' that has me talking to everyone today."

All eyes went back to Iemitsu.

"Jubei you are friendly with Hideki and accompany him on his travels I hear?" Iemitsu asked.

"Yes, that is true Uesama," Jubei said.

"And what do you have planned for the immediate future?" Iemitsu asked.

"I was going to talk with my father first," Jubei responded.

"That is always a good idea," Iemitsu said. Then Iemitsu spun to his left and addressed Munenori.

"Munenori do you need your son for anything?" Iemitsu asked.

"Both I and my son are yours to command Uesama," Munenori said.

Iemitsu turned back to Jubei. "That makes you mine does it not?"

"As always Uesama," Jubei said.

"Good," Iemitsu said. He then turned and looked down at Nagamasa. "I want you Nagamasa to continue in your current post as South Magistrate but with your own stipend of 10,000 koku. That will establish your personal authority within the new government and make you appear free from Yoshinobu entanglements. You can remain at the Yoshinobu mansion if that is what everyone desires. I do not want you to cut all ties with your family in the name of appearing independent, but I want to be able to depict your independence when your detractors appear. Believe me, they will appear."

Iemitsu then addressed Jii. "Jii, if Nagamasa continues to reside under your roof you can continue to play with your grandson and Honzo can visit both his daughter and grandson."

Jii bowed low and expressed his thanks. So did Honzo.

"Hideki, I want to take advantage of your wanderlust, your sword skills and your unbridled righteousness," Iemitsu said. "I want you to continue your travels. Overtly you will be a swordsman in training visiting dojos around the country traveling with whomever you wish. Covertly I want you to check on the worthiness of the local governments. When you find something wrong, as you did in Nagasaki, I want you to fix it anyway you see fit. You will carry my seal but use it sparingly. Do you have any questions?"

"You tasking is a huge responsibility, Uesama. I am not sure I am worthy of such authority," Hideki said.

"Do you see yourself staying in Edo always under the shadow of your grandfather and older brother?" Iemitsu asked.

"No Uesama," Hideki answered.

"You are going to continue to travel anyway, always testing your skill and learning new things and purging evil. Why not do it with official sanction, get paid for it and help strengthen my government at the same time?"

"As you command Uesama," Hideki said.

"Besides if you are out of the capital, I don't have to worry about you coming after my job," Iemitsu said without a smile.

"I know my limitations Uesama. I do not envy your crushing load," Hideki said.

"Jubei you will assist him. Do you have any problem with that assignment?" Iemitsu asked.

"No Uesama," Jubei said. "Hideki is my friend and student."

"Excellent, both of you will be listed on the roles of the government as Councilors to the Shogun. You will each have a stipend of 5,000 koku," Iemitsu said looking at the second row.

"For the rest of you, I expect you to continue to support the Yoshinobu."

The second row bowed and uttered something like, "yes Uesama."

"Honzo bring the gifts forward," Iemitsu said.

Honzo bowed, opened the chest and brought forth four tantos in lacquerware scabbards with mother-of-pearl inlaid. The most striking thing about these knives was a gold seal of the Tokugawa on each side.

Iemitsu handed one to Myo, one to Midori, and one to The Mist.

"I thought a significant tanto might commemorate your courage in killing Ugai as well as my appreciation for protecting my life. Each of you now has the approved capability to display the sacred golden Hollyhock when needed and invoke my protection. I thought it might come in handy in your line of work. If you are working for the Yoshinobu, you are working for me," Iemitsu said. "Honzo, the proclamations if you please."

Honzo reached into the chest and extracted four paper scrolls.

"These scrolls make The Mist, Myo and Midori samurai. This has not been done since Hideyoshi's time. If you remember he was once a farmer and rose to prominence as first Nobunaga's sandal warmer and later one of his greatest generals. He did not want anyone repeating his rise to fame so he declared everyone had to remain in their caste. You three have saved your shogun and continue to impress me with your talent. By elevating you to samurai status I can make better use of your skills in the future," Iemitsu said.

The three ninjas were too shocked to speak. They each took their scrolls and bowed.

Iemitsu looked behind Jii. "Your name is Yuki?"

"Yes Uesama," Yuki said.

"You are daughter to Hittori Honzo and wife of Nagamasa?" Iemitsu asked.

"Yes Uesama," Yuki said and bowed again.

"You have trained as an Iga ninja as well?" Iemitsu asked.

"Yes Uesama," Yuki said.

"The three women beside you who are now samurai were helpful in returning your stolen baby?" Iemitsu asked.

"Yes Uesama," Yuki said.

"Then I would like you to help them in all they need to know in their new lives as samurai. I would not be surprised if they already knew most as they have probably impersonated samurai in their ninja lives," Iemitsu said. "They will be better able to serve me if they can freely move between their ninja and samurai existences. Do you understand?"

"I understand," Uesama. "They are like sisters to me and I will help them all I can."

When Iemitsu got to Yoshi he handed him a tanto and a scroll. "I do not know you, but my mother hates you almost as much as Hideki. Normally that would make you my enemy. But I have heard you are smarter than Hideki and are the chief strategist for the Yoshinobu. I also heard you have been instrumental in all of Hideki's significant actions. I admire that and offer you the same appreciation now that the Yoshinobu will be on the leading edge of my steering of the country," Iemitsu said.

Yoshi bowed. "Thank you Uesama."

Iemitsu stood and stepped back so all eyes were on him. "Honzo please provide me with the last two gifts."

Honzo brought two urushi nuri inro cases to Iemitsu. One was a beautiful deep black texture with gold inlay of the Tokugawa symbol, the golden hollyhock. The other was also an inro case that dangled from the obi by a silk knotted cord when men travelled. This one was a deep red with the same golden hollyhock. The red one he presented to Hideki. The black one went to Jubei.

"I like the black one better," Iemitsu said. "I would have given it to you Hideki, but Jubei's favorite color seems to be black."

"Thank you for the gift Uesama. I think I can tell from the deep texture and the beautiful workmanship the artisan who made both items," Hideki said.

"By the Buddha, you are correct Hideki," Jubei said looking at his gift.

"You know this artisan that has become the talk of all the merchants in Edo?" Iemitsu asked.

"Yes lord, her name is Mei. Jubei acted as her protector from Bad Heizo," Hideki said.

"Use these inro in your travels as a badge of my authority. Use them sparingly, but if you need power to reinforce the Yoshinobu family motto, then use them," Iemitsu said. "I trust both of you implicitly."

Both Hideki and Jubei bowed low.

"As you command Uesama," Hideki said.

"Hideki you and Jubei get together with Munenori and Jii. Your jobs in the new era will be important in determining how my reign will be seen by history. More importantly it is significant in how I am judged by the people," Iemitsu said.

Iemitsu turned, stepped up onto the raised portion of the tatami and walked behind one of the screens and disappeared.

There was an immediate period of silence.

"Let us go home," Jii said. "I am speechless now. But I want to talk to everyone."

XXXVIII

New Directions

The Yoshinobu hierarchy gathered in the Yoshinobu mansion over the noon meal. Everyone that had been in the meeting with the shogun was present. Jii added Yoshi's wife and mother-in-law (Chiyo and Matsu) and Haru and Rei to the gathering.

"I am to become co-chamberlain with Yagyū Munenori. He is focusing on the present and I am focusing on restructuring the government the way the shogun wants. Hideki is to travel with Jubei throughout Japan to report on changes he's made and how they are implemented. More importantly Hideki is to correct any wrongs on the spot. Hideki and Jubei will carry the golden hollyhock symbol and can use it as he sees fit. Naga has been given a 10,000 koku position in his own name. Yoshi, Myo, Midori and The Mist have been elevated to samurai status. Does that pretty much sum up our meeting?" Jii asked.

"That summarizes it pretty well Jii," Hideki said. "The only thing you missed was running out the Portuguese and installing the Dutch in Nagasaki. Additionally, you missed the part about closing every other port to foreign trade except Nagasaki. Then there was the part about banning the Kirishitan religion. Other than that, I think you portrayed the gist," Hideki said.

"So, what are your thoughts?" Jii asked.

"I guess my question is do we want to do all this?" Hideki said.

"I think we have to," Jubei answered.

"Yes, I agree," Jii said.

"Does everybody trust Iemitsu?" Yoshi asked.

"Trust is not an issue with the shogun. He commands and we obey," The Mist said. "Isn't that right? I am new at this samurai stuff."

"That's a good way to get us all killed if O'Fuku gets her way and changes the shogun's mind," Yoshi said.

"I think all people in power must strive primarily to stay in power," Nagamasa said. "I was taken by surprise by Hideki's allegations of O'Fuku's involvement with Tadanaga. I do not believe that Iemitsu was not aware of what she was doing. If Hideki and friends had not stepped in, we would be in the midst of a civil war. The fact that Iemitsu might be willing to plunge us into civil war to further his own end is frightening."

"So, what are you saying Nagamasa?" Hideki asked.

"I am saying that I agree with Yoshi," Nagamasa said. "We obey as long as we think it is right."

"You could not have said it any better Nagamasa. I am proud of you brother," Hideki said. "None of us must violate our conscience just to please the shogun. Ostensively, that is why he is placing such unusual trust in us. He wants us to be his conscience. That may change and we may die as a result. But we follow the family motto. No wrong too small to right, no right to small to defend."

"I am wondering how Iemitsu knew about our actions in Nagasaki," Hideki said.

"I think he was just repeating the stories he had heard, and you opened your big mouth and fell into his trap," Myo said.

That brought laughter from everyone.

"You are right Myo I feel stupid," Hideki said. "I am not good at political games."

"If you were good at political games, I would not love you," Myo said.

"Where do we start Jii?" Midori asked.

"I guess the first target would be the Satsuma clan. They promised to help Tadanaga and have always been a threat to the Tokugawa," Jii said.

"I disagree on this issue Jii. The Satsuma were wily enough

to not leave a trail back to their doorstep in the Tadanaga matter. They are shrewd. To go journeying there this soon would be to invite trouble. We will get there eventually, but we should not start there," Nagamasa said.

"Then where will you begin Hideki?" Jii asked.

"I think we will start along the Tokaido and into Kyoto. That snake pit is going to be a nightmare for the Magistrates. I think we can lend a hand there," Hideki said.

"I guess we are going to smell your foul birds again Monkey," Jubei said.

"That is very likely sword master," Yoshi replied. "Mist are you completely healed?"

"Hai, I will be ready in about a week," The Mist said.

"Haru are you still determined to reopen Yamakaya in Kyoto?" Jii asked.

"No Jii. Since I have been living in Edo, I think opportunity lives here as well. If you do not mind, I would like to reestablish my store here," Haru said.

"That is an excellent idea," Jii said. "We will help you relocate any staff you want to bring with you."

"Rei you wanted to be a retainer of a samurai family and then thought about being a merchant. How would you like to be both?" Hideki asked.

"How is that possible?" Rei asked.

"We will make you a Yoshinobu retainer. You then marry the Lady of Yamakaya. This way you will be involved with Yamakaya in Edo. That will give you reason to travel to buy goods and look to expand the store. You will also be able to observe and report to Yoshi on things that do not seem right to you. You are already a samurai. You will have to learn to be a merchant," Hideki said. "I hope that arrangement is agreeable with both yourself and Haru."

"That arrangement sounds excellent to me," Haru said.

Rei looked at Haru lovingly. "That is very fine with me Hideki."

"We can always use another sword in our travels," Yoshi said.

"I take it we will have the help of the Five Families on

these travels Myo," Hideki asked.

Yoshi turned to Myo. "What say you leader of the Five Families?"

"I will do whatever Jii wishes. We will support Hideki only on the condition he agrees to marry me, and I can continue being a kunoichi," Myo said.

That brought a shocked silence to the group.

"But I may have to bed some sweet young girl to gather information," Hideki said, winking to Jubei on the side.

"You may die in your sleep also," Myo said.

"I cannot marry you under these conditions," Hideki said.

There was a shocked look on Myo's face.

"I believe it should be the man asking the woman to marry," Hideki said. "So Myo, newly made samurai, will you marry me?"

Myo nodded yes. That nod was followed by cheers, laughter and slaps on Hideki's back.

"When will you depart Hideki?" Yuki asked.

"I think we will give The Mist the week she needs and add one more for planning and preparation. That will give her enough time to integrate those Koga she trusts under her new banner. Having a sixth family of ninja working with us may be unwieldy at first but it could give us an advantage in keeping our adversaries at bay," Hideki said. "I do not trust O'Fuku in this. I think she was pulling the strings on her Bunraku puppets Ito, Ugai and maybe Bishop Inshin. She will rear her ugly head if given the chance."

"You think she had a hand in Ugai's defection to Tadanaga?" The Mist asked.

"It is very possible, but we will never know for sure," Yoshi said. "Your instincts and mine are the same on this matter. None of those men had the sophistication to pull in the Satsuma. Someone else was the mastermind."

"Iemitsu had the sense to run O'Fuku out of our meeting but she has spies throughout the castle. She will know our mission by now. I have no doubt she will try to eradicate us," Hideki said. "Jii you and Nagamasa are going to have to be on alert at all times here in Edo by yourselves."

"That is good advice," Yoshi said.

"Who will travel with you?" The Mist asked.

"I will start with Jubei, Myo and Midori. We will travel as husband and wives looking for work. We will stop as we travel and challenge dojos," Hideki said.

"Oh, I like that part," Midori said winking at Jubei.

"Challenging dojos? Isn't that dangerous?" Yuki asked.

"It is not dangerous the way we do it," Hideki said. "Yoshi I will need you here to coordinate our needs and keep an eye on the Yoshinobu, especially my nephew. I do not know if O'Fuku engineered stealing him, but I would not put it past her."

"Oh, that is good news," Chiyo said. "My husband is going to be a father."

"What?" Yoshi asked.

"That calls for some sake. There will be another little monkey on the way. Let's hope he or she takes after Chiyo," Jubei said.

"I do not care whether it is a boy or girl, as long as it is healthy," Jii said, moving to pour Yoshi some sake.

Yoshi kept looking from his wife to his mother-in-law in shock.

"What a momentous day for the Yoshinobu," Jii said.

"Yes, Grandfather, the clan is growing," Yuki said rocking Yoshitsune in her arms.

"Myo can you alert your network along our path of our coming in case we need support?" Hideki asked.

"They have already been alerted," Myo said." You are a little slow, but then you are samurai."

"You can no longer use that insult on me," Hideki said." You are now samurai also."

"It looks like we will be traveling again," Jubei said.

"Yes, but it will be different this time," Hideki said.

"How will it be different?" Jubei asked.

"We will have a mission and the Shogun's authority. And this time our companions will be prettier," Hideki said.

Jubei raised his cup to Midori.

"I will drink to that," Jubei said.

Glossary

Ben: Dialect.

Benjo: Ancient sewer system used to move human waste to farm lands for fertilizer.

Bokken: An often-lethal Japanese wooden sword used for training.

Bunraku: Famous Japanese puppet theatre.

Bushi: Fore runners of the samurai; Elite and skilled warriors in many forms of combat.

Bushido: The way of the warrior; a code of ethics for the bushi class and later samurai.

Diamyo: Powerful overseers of vast domains; warlords; ostensibly subservient to shogun.

Dojo: Martial arts training hall.

Domo: Thank you.

Fugu: Japanese puffer fish with a toxic poison in its inner organs.

Geta: Formal Japanese wooden foot ware that elevated the wearer out of the mud.

Gomen: Sorry.

Hachi Maki: Headband.

Hai: Yes.

Hakama: A pant like outer garment with pleats worn usually by males.

Haori: Traditional hip to thigh length outer jacket wore over a kimono usually by males.

Haragai: A sixth sense allowing the user to "see through the darkness."

Hato: Homing pigeons.

Jii: Japanese slang for grandfather.

Jiyu Waza: A free form of martial arts sparring.

Kamae: A Japanese martial art term for posture that implies correct distance from an opponent.

Kama: A very sharp cutting weapon derived from a farm implement used for cutting rice stalks.

Kamishino: Ancient Japanese clothing worn by Edo period samurai in the shogun's presence; consisting of the kataginu (sleeveless top) and a lengthened hakama that made walking difficult.

Katana: Main sword carried by samurai in Edo period; approximately 28 inches long blade and razor sharp.

Kirishitan: Christian.

Kuji Kuri: Nine symbols cutting; finger weaves used with mudras or chants to open energy centers for the ninja; considered part of the black arts by some.

Master: One of a higher station; in martial arts master could be a Soke or head of the system (ryuha).

Matte: Japanese word used in martial arts to signal a halt or to wait.

Metsuke: Edo era government spies; secret police.

Mon: A family or clan crest or emblem often worn on the chest of haori or kimono for men.

Musha Shugyo: A warrior's pilgrimage by budding swordsmen travelling the country side looking for challenges and improvement to their skills with a sword or other samurai weapon.

Mushin: A mental state (no mind) into which elite martial artists attain when fighting; thought is not required once in mushin; the practitioner's subconscious takes over and he reacts automatically.

Nagasaki: A seaport city in southern Kyushu, Japan; established by the Portuguese.

Obasan: Honorific title for an older woman.

Ofudo: Japanese hot bath where washing is done outside the tub and soaking in hot water is done inside the tub.

Oishi: Japanese word for food that tastes good.

Okasan: Mother.

Otosan: Father.

Roju: Lower house of Edo government consisting of six to seven men responsible for keeping the country running.

Ronin: A samurai who has no master; literally "wave man," noting no ties to a lord.

Samisen: Three-stringed musical instrument.

Seppuku: Samurai ceremonial suicide using the wakazashi slicing into the belly, going across and up.

Shinkage-ryu: A school of sword fighting founded by the Yagyū family and favored by the Tokugawa shoguns.

Sumi Masen: Excuse me.

Tabi: Japanese socks with a separate area for the big toe.

Taira: Upper house of the Edo government consisting of two men responsible for advising the shogun.

Tanto: Knife

Tengu: A mythical Japanese creature found in folk tales; considered a type of Shinto god.

Tozama: Outside Lords, those that did not side with the Tokugawa during the battle of Sekigahara in 1600 and therefore deemed less trustworthy.

Tsuba: Hand protector on a Japanese katana and wakazashi.

Udon: Thick noodle dish; often served hot in soup.

Urusai: Noisy

Urushi: A Japanese tree whose sap provides the base for urushi nuri lacquer ware.

Wakazashi: The shorter sword worn by Edo period samurai.

Yari: Japanese spear.

Yojimbo: Bodyguard.

Yumi: Traditional asymmetrical Japanese bow for shooting arrows.

Zori: Outdoor straw sandals.

About the Author

William Marcus Charles II (Marc) is the author of *Simplified Self-defense for Women,* published by the Marine Corps Association. He has been published in the *Marine Corps Gazette* and in *Ensign,* a global monthly of the LDS Church.

Born in Murfreesboro, Tennessee, Marc spent his formative years in Warren, Michigan. He graduated from boot camp in San Diego at nineteen and for the next twenty-four years wore the Eagle, Globe, and Anchor proudly until retirement as a Lieutenant Colonel of Marines.

He spent much of his military career in Asia where he studied martial arts. He is a Roku-dan (sixth degree black belt) in Okinawan Kenpo Karate and a Roku-dan in Kobudo (the weapons of Okinawa). He has trained in Aikido, Jujitsu, American Kenpo, Shorinryu, Judo and other lesser known styles. He has founded three martial arts schools in the United States.

Marc graduated with honors from Park College with a BS in Management and Finance and has an MBA from National University.

He and his wife Sako currently reside in Encinitas, California.